K.E. MCKENZIE

Someone Should Write A Book About My Life

Although this book originally sprang from true anecdotes, it is a work of fiction. Any resemblance to actual persons and events is purely coincidental.

First published in February, 2020
This edition published January, 2021
ISBN 9780648978602
© Kristy McKenzie 2019

—For Neeny. I love you, friend wife. X

September

CHAPTER ONE

I couldn't stop running and turn around now. So I kept going, despite the fact that I was finding it hard to breathe and my low-budget sports bra wasn't really keeping up its end of the bounce-preventing bargain. Running always seemed like a good idea at the time. Past Justine, when she'd set her alarm, had visions of herself flying down the Yarra River Trail—hair swinging to the beat of her pumping feet, face set in a confident "This-is-what-I-do-I-run" expression. The reality of the situation for Present Justine set in after I'd taken my first fast-walking steps and broken into what could only be described as an enthusiastic hobble.

When did I last run anywhere? Maybe down the fifty-million Parliament Station escalator steps when I was late for a train and even then they were powering me forward at peak-hour speed. So, just that time and now. That was it. Probably for the last ten years.

Not great.

The high spirits I'd been in when I began my attempt at a morning run about three minutes earlier started to droop along with my high ponytail. I was vaguely aware that my mouth was hanging open with the effort of forcing my feet forward. Not just that, but somehow drool had been jolted from my mouth and was sliding down my chin towards my jawline. At that moment, Running Man materialised, merging onto the track directly in front of me.

My eyes slid from his tight Lycra singlet to his rippling calves that flexed with each effortless bound he took. Although I was behind him, there was no doubt in my mind that he was wearing a seasoned "This-is-what-I-do-I-run" expression.

If I could just run a little faster, I'd have a better view of his biceps, I encouraged my legs. They acquiesced with some resistance and as the gap between us narrowed, Running Man slowed down to adjust his earphones.

Suddenly, I was running far too close to him and as he slowed even more, I realised with cold horror that I would have to overtake him to avoid a collision. I was also panting audibly, which caused Running Man to turn around to investigate his energetic stalker. As he did, I burst forward in a surge of adrenaline.

As I passed him, I wiped my forehead with the back of my hand as if I was mopping up sweat but then dragged it down my face in an attempt to wipe away the drool. Unfortunately, the offending saliva smear was sticky and a long line of elastic spit now ran from my mouth to my hand. I shook my hand vigorously, then decided to shake the other one as though I was trying to stimulate my circulation.

I realised that I hadn't increased my speed enough to overtake Running Man and we were running side by side. Also, he had witnessed the entire drool-face debacle. I definitely couldn't stop running now. My chest burned as I sped up.

What now? What now?!

STOP RUNNING! My brain screamed in response to its own question, *YOU'RE GOING TO DIE!!*

I noticed a "No Dogs Off Leashes" signpost ahead and decided I could make it look as though that was the point where I usually turned around. Running Man wasn't to know that I'd only run about 200 metres. I staggered to the post and for some reason tapped it purposefully before completing a U-turn and heading back the way I'd come. As I pushed my furious body further, I heard heavy footsteps behind me. Running Man had turned around at the stupid dog post too!

What are the bloody chances?! I wonder if he tapped it as well?

My brain was dangerously close to exploding.

A drinking fountain! My saviour!

The fountain was just ahead and a legitimate, non-weirdo reason to stop running. All I had to do was get there with no more bodily-fluid-related incidents. I began to veer left when Running Man came flying past me and headed straight for the fountain.

NO! I SAW IT FIRST!

My mouth felt desperately arid and there was no way I was going to be able to continue this running farce. So I stopped, about a metre behind Running Man. Even his side-on drinking profile was lovely. He must be gorgeous. Unless the other side of his face was incredibly asymmetrical to this side. That was possible. Maybe he didn't look like a bronzed God after all.

Oh geez, I am just staring at this poor innocent man who is trying to partake in some cool refreshment on his morning run. DO SOMETHING ELSE!

I started jogging on the spot like one of those running people who can't get enough of running so even when they stop running they wish they were running so they just keep running even though they're not running anywhere. I was immediately infuriated with myself. You can't stop running on the spot once you've started. You have to keep doing it.

Do I have to keep running while I'm standing at the drinking fountain with the water bubbling up and down in my face?

Any minute now Running Man was going to stop drinking, turn around and see me jogging on the spot.

Quick, I told myself, *Adopt a "This-is-what-I-do-I-run… on-the-spot" expression!*

He rose like Poseidon from the fountain, face completely symmetrical and equally pleasing on both sides. Not even a drip of water on his face.

How did he do that?

Then he smiled and said, "How's it going?"

I accidentally answered "Running!" and jogged the very small distance to the fountain. For some reason, Running Man didn't choose to speed away as fast as his glorious calves would take him.

This is my chance to say something incredibly witty and redeem myself for the ridiculousness of the last ten minutes.

6

I smiled, probably charmingly, and quipped, "Run here often?" as I bent over the fountain. Unfortunately, just as the words came out of my mouth, I automatically turned the knob and a spurt of water emerged, shooting right into my open throat and causing a coughing fit of epic proportions.

Somewhere in the middle of this near-drowning experience, Running Man attempted to smile, but it was definitely more of a wince. Then he replaced his earphones and disappeared into the distance, leaving me with water dripping steadily from my nose and chin.

I flopped onto my couch and unlocked my phone. I was keen to message my bestie Steph so I could transform my running failure into a hilarious anecdote that we'd retell regularly, enough to feel as though we were discussing our favourite scene from a movie. But my news feed popped up automatically and there he was. Ben, smiling his awkward photo smile right at me. He was so familiar that even after two years, I still felt a little comforted to see him. But then, something so unfamiliar: a tiny squish-faced newborn—with Ben's thick lips and dark hair—lying in his arms.

For a minute, I felt like I was sitting in empty space, completely suspended by the devastating image of the man I had loved holding his firstborn. But not born to me. It was supposed to be me. Of course, due to an impressive depth of internet stalking, I'd known this was coming. That they—it should have been *we*—were expecting and

7

that soon their love for each other would take solid form in the world. But, in that moment, it still destroyed me. I sat there on the couch Ben and I had bought together and cried.

CHAPTER TWO

"It's funny enough that you went for a run!"

Steph, sitting across from me at brunch the next day at our favourite cafe, Mouth Feels, was clutching her stomach and laughing very hard.

Plump clouds dragged lazily through the spring sky above us, as though being ushered along by an overzealous personal trainer. That reminded me of the three free personal training sessions I'd been "gifted" by my gym but had yet to redeem. And by "my" gym, I obviously meant the gym that I charitably sponsored with my monthly direct debit but had actually only stepped foot in twice. And one of those was to sign up.

"I run!" I objected, my mouth full of red velvet pancake.

"You do *not* run. And apparently when you do, you end up waterboarding yourself!"

"Don't forget the drool," I offered.

"I will *never* forget the drool! That was the best bit."

Steph sipped her milkshake through a candy-striped paper straw and didn't look up as she said, "So, have you been on social media lately?"

"Of course I have. Unfortunately."

I took another bite of cushiony pancake. I didn't know why neither of us had unfriended Ben. Weird, inappropriate curiosity, I guess.

"Well, yay for no stretch marks!" exclaimed Steph. "And yay for hot nights with strange men!"

We toasted and the chocolate-filled doughnuts perched on top of our milkshakes

9

wobbled precariously. It was a token toast to make me feel better. Steph hadn't had a hot night with a strange man since our last year of uni when she'd hooked up with her now-fiancé, Charlie.

"It wasn't even cute," she mumbled around a mouthful of doughnut.

She was lying. It was damn cute and I knew it. Newborns tended to look like bits of weirdly mushed play dough to me, but not this one. She took another sip through her soggy straw.

"So, how are you?"

The truth was that I was mostly over Ben. I had deleted all the photos of us together, cried uncontrollably during sad movies while eating a tin of condensed milk with a spoon, dyed my hair twice and travelled through Europe for six months. I no longer dreamed about him all the time, I didn't miss him when I went to bed anymore and I'd stopped dropping his name into conversations just to remind myself he existed once. But I still felt like the life we'd planned together had been stolen from me, given to someone else while I was busy picking up his dishes and remembering to call his Mum for her birthday. I'd expected to be engaged or married by now like most of my friends. I thought my only concerns would be about which blood-soaked TV series Ben and I would binge together or where we'd spend our dirty weekends away. Or even... with our own little play dough mush—gazing at it lovingly while it slept in our arms or fighting about who had to clean the vomit off the carpet. Instead I was single at thirty-one, feeling adrift in a life I hadn't expected to be living.

"I'm OK," I simplified and then changed the subject. "I've got a date tonight."

"Ooh!" Steph exclaimed, leaning forward with her chin on her fists. "Is it the cop?"

"No, that turned out to be nothing."

"Nothing?" She indicated a small measurement with her thumb and forefinger.

I laughed and shook my head.

"No, *that* was actually something, but the rest was… meh."

"Oh, OK. The dreadlocks guy then?"

"No. A dreadlock repeatedly smacking me in the face during sex was not quite the turn on you'd imagine. Plus, apparently you *can* receive too many gym selfies in a day."

"Who would have thought?"

"I know! It's actually a new guy. He was riding an elephant in his profile pic. We haven't texted that much, so it's hard to get a sense of him. He was really keen to catch up in person. Maybe too keen."

Finished with my pancakes, I pulled my feet up onto the seat of the patio chair I was sitting on and leaned against the white picket fence that ran alongside the outdoor tables. From experience, I knew it would hold my weight and not collapse embarrassingly onto busy Burwood Road beside us. We frequented Mouth Feels so often, and it was so close to my apartment building, that it felt like an extension of home.

"Well, let me know if you need the old emergency call."

11

I nodded and ran a finger through a smear of cream on my plate, bringing it to my lips as Steph slurped down the rest of her milkshake and sat back with her hands on her belly.

"If it's possible to get diabetes from just one brunch, we're screwed," she said.

I picked up the doughnut from my own milkshake and bit into it, closing my eyes for a minute to enjoy the blissful sensation of liquid chocolate coating my tongue.

"At least we'd die happy," I sighed.

"Don't you get gangrene from diabetes?"

"Ew, really? We should have got the muesli."

We laughed heartily. We would never get the muesli.

I dressed quickly. I'd developed a dating uniform: tight-fitting skinny jeans and a nice top with enticing but still seemly amount of cleavage. It was appropriate to almost every dating occasion and it limited the knee-deep pile of tops, skirts and pants I used to wade through before going out.

I looked at my date's profile picture again. He sat on top of an elephant wearing a little beaded doily on its head. Why was it wearing that? It looked like a weird belly-dancing elephant that might break into a shimmy at any moment. I imagined it heading home after a long day of heaving sweaty tourists around and hanging its doily on an elephant-sized hat stand. Elephants don't have hat stands, I knew that, but it didn't stop the image flashing into my brain.

Do not mention the elephant hat stand on the date.

I looked at his face. Not the elephant's face, its face was pretty indistinguishable from other elephants as far as I could tell. Was the fact that I'd become obsessed with elephants in the last five minutes indicative of how this date was going to go?

No. Stop analysing the whole thing before you've even met the guy.

Aidan, his name was Aidan. His face was nice. He had a cheeky smile and blonde hair, which was a bit on the fluffy side. I might be tempted to give him a noogie on his fluffy head when we met. But no, I wouldn't do that. I probably wouldn't. If I did, I could pretend there had been a moth on his head.

Oh no, I'm already coming up with excuses for noogieing my date.

With this thought, I checked my hair and face quickly in the bathroom mirror. Acceptable. I grabbed my keys from the kitchen table and opened the door. I was determined not to think it this time, but the thought popped into my head anyway:

This could be The One.

I got to the cinema about five minutes early. It was one of those artsy cinemas where they don't try to upsell you an esky full of popcorn for an extra couple of dollars. I was sitting opposite the Candy Bar and I squinted to look at the prices. They had called their biggest popcorn "Massive". What kind of marketing was that? I was not looking forward to *that* conversation with the Candy Bar attendant.

"Hi, I'll just have the small popcorn, thanks... Er... Don't you want to offer me the Massive for just two dollars extra? No? Oh... OK, I'll just have the Massive. Yes, the Massive. It's ten dollars extra? Right. Thanks."

I sighed and checked my phone. Five minutes past when we were meant to meet and no messages. I was really hungry. I hadn't eaten much dinner in case my skinny jeans felt too tight during the movie. Maybe I could get the Massive now and have it finished by the time Fluffy Aidan arrived. I imagined him walking in, spotting me with my mouth full of popcorn and just carefully turning around and walking back out. Maybe he'd already seen me and walked out. I searched the growing crowd for fluffy heads. He might be really tiny and hard to spot. It was possible he was tiny because he was on an elephant in the photo so it would be hard to tell.

I looked at his first picture again, but it was tricky to figure out the perspective. Fluffy Aidan seemed to be normal height from his other photos. I checked the time again. Twenty-five minutes late; the previews would start soon. I had texted him to let him know where I was waiting, but he could have gone to the wrong spot. In the wrong cinema. In the wrong suburb. At the wrong time. I double checked the name of the cinema he'd suggested. It was definitely this one, definitely at this time.

My phone suddenly lit up in my hand. I'd already silenced it for the movie that I wasn't sure if I was still seeing. Fluffy Aidan was calling me.

"Hey, it's Aidan."

"Hey, Aidan. How's it going?"

Where are you? What are you doing? Fluffing your hair to perfection before you leave the house?

"Yeah, I'm good, thanks. Um, I'm stuck in traffic. It's shocking down Punt Road."

"Oh, sorry to hear it. That really sucks."

I felt relieved that I wasn't being stood up, regardless of the fact that anyone who lived in Melbourne knew that Punt Road was ridiculous at this time of night. I'd deliberately avoided it and I didn't even drive very often. I'd borrowed my brother Riley's car due to the lack of public transport to the cinema.

"Yeah, so I've parked my car and I'm getting my housemate to pick me up. He's going to drop me off on his way to footy training. I guess I'll be there soon."

"OK, great. See you then."

Great? Not great.

The logic of how getting his housemate to pick him up from Punt Road was going to somehow defy traffic was utterly baffling. What did this footy-playing housemate drive? A monster truck? I imagined Aidan's fluff being buffeted by the wind as he thrust his head out of the monster truck window and yelled, "Don't worry, I'm coming Justine! Get the Massive!" Well, if it was really what imaginary Aidan wanted, I'd better oblige. I bought a Massive and sat back down.

The crowds cleared as people trickled into the cinema. I was about a quarter of the way through the Massive when Aidan arrived. He burst through the glass double doors and walked hastily up to me. His hair was at maximum fluff levels (which made the monster truck theory more credible) as he gave me a quick, awkward hug and apologised.

"So, I'll get the tickets if you want to buy the snacks?" he said as we walked towards the ticket machine.

I looked at the Massive tucked conspicuously under my arm.

Have I not already bought the snacks?

Aidan paid for the tickets and I followed him to the Candy Bar. The bored-looking attendant eyed me judgmentally as though she was thinking, "You've had the Massive and now you're back for more? You probably don't run either, do you?"

To stop myself from screaming "I RAN ONCE!" at her, I turned to my date.

"What do you feel like?"

"How about a champers?" he said, smiling.

He does have a nice face.

"Sure! Why not?" I replied.

Turning back to the attendant, I ordered two champagnes.

"And four of those beers," Aidan said, pointing at the drinks fridge and I could have sworn he winked at her.

Four beers?! WHY?

Were two of them for me? I didn't like beer. Even fancy beer tasted like fermented dishwater to me. But I had said I'd get the snacks, and it would be too uncomfortable to say "Oh no, you don't!" now, so I nodded to the attendant and paid for the drinks, which cost well over what the tickets had.

"Would you mind?" asked my gallant date, nodding at the champagne glasses. He expertly grabbed two beers in each of his hands.

I juggled the Massive and the glasses into the darkened cinema. We took our assigned seats, much to the annoyance of the people whose faces we had to brush with our bums to get there. At first Aidan attempted to fit all four beer bottles into the drink holders on either side of him. Then he looked at me, shrugged, and nestled two of them between his legs. I hoped that settled the question as to whether any of them were meant for me.

I looked up at the screen, where the movie had already started, and sipped champagne to calm myself. There was an audible gulping sound beside me and I looked over to see Aidan had skulled his champagne and cracked open a bottle. He smiled out of the corner of his mouth at me without staunching the flow of beer into his throat. Well, maybe he was nervous too.

I turned back to the movie but couldn't concentrate on the unfolding rom-com due to the continuous *glug-glugging* from my right. In my peripheral vision, I could see Aidan setting down the first empty bottle and starting on the second.

What is going on here? Is my date an alcoholic? Is he hoping to meet up with his mates after footy training and doesn't want to play catch-up when he gets there?

Aidan gave an audible burp as he set down the second beer, then loudly whispered, "Excuse me." There was a clinking sound from his crotch that indicated he'd retrieved the third bottle. I had the horrifying thought that he might be underage and this was his elaborate (yet entirely successful) attempt at having alcohol bought for him. I turned to look at him again and studied his face. No signs of acne. There were lines across his forehead and a slight recede to his fluffy mop. No, he had to be at least mid-twenties.

Well, whatever weirdness was going on, I did not want to be on this date anymore. I wanted to be off it. I wanted to get into my pyjamas and read my book, snuggled up in bed. But I couldn't use any of the usual tricks (emergency phone call from Steph, sudden onset of illness, remembering something urgent like, "Oh shit, I left my cat in the oven.") because we were in the cinema. I resolved to just try to enjoy the movie and make a quick exit afterwards.

I started to become interested in the establishing of the relationship between the two main characters and was only faintly aware of the fourth beer being gulped down beside me. The main couple had moved into the guy's parents' place, unaware that the parents were swingers, and hilarity was just about to ensue when I felt Aidan's hot breath on my ear. I also *smelt* Aidan's breath.

"Pssst!" he hissed.

No one actually says that out loud in real life, do they?

"Pssst!" Aidan tried again and I was forced to face him, which was like turning my face towards a beer-breath tsunami.

"Yes?" I whispered.

"Hello there."

What?!

"Hi."

"So… I'm hungry. You?"

No. I've eaten half a Massive and have since been entirely put off my appetite. Maybe forever.

"Not really," I hissed back.

People were starting to look at us with irritated glares.

"OK, well, I'm going to get some food. Shouldn't drink on an empty stomach, y'know? I'll just squeeze past you here."

He deliberately brushed his hand along my knee as he edged off down the row of furious cinema patrons. I didn't blame them. I sort of hoped someone might have the presence of mind to trip him up, but he made it safely to the end of the aisle and headed to the nearest exit. I looked at my phone. At least another hour until the movie ended. What if he tried to kiss me when he returned?

NO!

What if I just left?

YES!

I'd be gone when he returned to his seat, like a shadow in the night, a whisper on the wind.

Pyjamas and book, here I come.

But I couldn't do it. Regardless of how he'd behaved, I just couldn't bring myself to leave him here alone.

I sunk back again into my seat and became interested in the movie again. For a long time. A really long time. In fact, the distraught couple in the movie were finally confronting the swinger parents—made difficult by the fact that the parents were completely naked—when I realised that no Candy Bar line would take this long, and maybe Aidan wasn't coming back. He must have been gone for over forty minutes. Right, that was it, definitely a good excuse to leave now and not feel bad about it. But as I gathered my bag onto my lap to leave, I heard an obnoxious rustling of plastic and turned my head towards the aisle to see Aidan shoving his way back down the row with a shopping bag in each hand. I felt my mouth fall open in shock as he flopped into his seat beside me and rummaged loudly through one of the bags.

"Pssst!"

Oh good. Here we go again.

"Yes?" I hissed back and people shushed me angrily.

"I got heaps of good stuff. Chips, chocolate, some of that whipped cream in a can. Want some?"

I must have become slightly hysterical with the bizarreness of the moment, because I almost giggled at the thought of him sensually squirting whipped cream into my mouth in the middle of the cinema.

"Ah, no."

"Suit yourself."

He settled for one of those packets of chips that boast an extra 25% content that you can definitely only get from a large supermarket. I could also see a box of washing powder through the side of one of the shopping bags.

He's bloody gone and done his weekly shop.

Aidan crunched away through the rest of the film, which ended disappointingly with the swinger parents conceding that all they really needed was each other. As soon as the first of the credits rolled into sight, I was up and ready to escape. Aidan collected his shopping bags and stood, stretching.

"Well, wanna find a bar somewhere for a drink?" he asked.

I glanced meaningfully at the empty beer bottles left leaning like old mates against each other in his seat. He didn't seem to pick up on it though, and continued to look at me expectantly.

"Um, no, I'd better not. I've got an early morning tomorrow."

Aidan followed me down the aisle and we both turned towards the exit.

"Oh yeah? On a Sunday! What've you got on?"

"Just, ah, going for a run."

I almost gave up the game by laughing as I said it.

"Oh, OK. Well, will we catch up again soon then?"

His giant chip packet scrunched into the bin as we passed.

Should I just be polite and say "Yes", but then never message him again? Or do I tell the truth and risk a certain amount of awkwardness?

I thought about all the times I'd wished that guys had just been honest with me.

"Oh, I don't think so, I'm sorry…"

I teetered on whether to give an explanation or not. It could save other women from suffering similar horrible dates with him in the future. But then again… the awkwardness.

"…Yeah. No. Sorry."

He turned his head to one side like a confused cocker spaniel, the illusion completed by the soft flops of hair on either side of his ears.

"We haven't even had a chance to talk yet."

For a minute I wavered. Maybe I had written him off too quickly. Was I being too picky, or unfair? Then my gaze fell on a corner of the washing powder box poking through a shopping bag. No, I was not.

"I know… I just don't think we're suited."

"That seems a bit judgemental. But whatever."

Champagne and fury bubbled together in my stomach.

"Judgemental? You were late, you skulled over five standard drinks, expensive drinks which *I* paid for, then you left the cinema for *forty-five* minutes to do your weekly shopping—"

"I went for snacks! They're a rip off at the Candy Bar!" He glanced down. "I only got washing powder because it was on special!"

22

"Fine, that's fine. But this was not a good date and I just really want to go home now."

Mercifully we'd reached the door and I could see Riley's car where I'd parked it across the street.

So, so close to freedom.

"Yeah... yeah. Probably for the best," Aidan said, running a hand through his fluff.

"Well, bye then."

I turned to walk out the door, feeling elated at not being forced into an uncomfortable goodbye hug.

"Ah—wait!"

Oh no. Oh no, no, no. Do not try again. Let it go, my fluffy friend, just let it go.

I turned around with a completely irrepressible grimace on my face. Aidan looked sheepish.

"Can I get a lift to Punt Road?"

My mother had once spent a whole night making a papier-machè donkey piñata for a church picnic, only to have the priest decide at the last minute that it would be disrespectful to hit it with a stick, considering that one of its kin had carried a very preggy Mary all the way to Bethlehem. Throughout my childhood, I'd regularly observed Mum's people-pleasing efforts end in disappointment after they went ignored or unappreciated. But somehow, I'd still become her.

All my friends knew I was a people-pleaser, which made me their first point of call for help with moving, pet-sitting, child-minding, event organising and any other general favours. In their defence, they weren't really taking advantage of me. They had no idea how many of their requests I'd accepted while lamenting my own inability to simply say "No."

And that was exactly how I came to be sitting in Riley's car on the way to Punt Road with Aidan in the passenger seat. He spent most of the ride sulking out the window while I made the odd redundant comment about traffic or the week's weather. Finally, I stopped behind his illegally parked car and flinched as his grunt and slam of the car door signalled the end of our "date".

I parked on the street outside my apartment. As I rummaged around in my bag for my house keys, I pretended I was a sweetly-singing cartoon princess who, upon entering her apartment, would summon all her animal friends to dress her in her pyjamas so that she could fall into bed and read about another world that didn't involve disappointing dates or exes with infants.

I opened the door to my building and was humming a tune to myself as an impossibly attractive woman emerged from one of the ground floor apartments.

"See you soon," she breathed, her voice as smooth and rich as liquid chocolate.

My equally attractive neighbour, Dan, was leaning against his door frame. He waved in reply and she floated past me, smiling euphorically. At least someone had enjoyed their date tonight. I was unsure of whether to keep walking up the stairs or to stop at Dan's door and say hello, so I weirdly wobbled back and forth at him in complete indecision.

"Oh hey, Justine."

He didn't look embarrassed at all about his departing guest. Well, you wouldn't. She looked like one of those social media models who gets all her clothes for free just so she'll be seen in public wearing them.

"Hi, Dan. Had a good night?"

Oh God, does that sound like I'm implying he just had sex?!

I'd seen a beautiful woman leaving his house and then asked if he'd "had a good night". How was he going to interpret that? He smiled, showing a row of white teeth, all sitting straight and in their correct places. Braces? Or was he just born that way, with great teeth genes? Should I ask him?

Oh geez, please don't ask him about his teeth genes.

"Yeah, certainly can't complain. You?"

"Oh yes, you know, just… had a date."

Why did I tell him that?

Maybe because then he would think I was desirable to men. He didn't have to know what calibre of man. What if he asked for details? Then I'd lie. *Lie, lie, lie.*

"How did it go?"

Lie!

"Terrible."

Nice one.

"Ah, that's shit. You want me to say some generic crap about fish in the sea?"

Oh God, he's being beautiful AND funny at me.

"Ha ha, no, that's OK…"

I was so in awe of his attractiveness, I just trailed off. He was still standing there as if he was willing to continue chatting, but I had no idea what to say.

Make a joke! No, don't make a joke! It's too risky after yesterday's water fountain scenario.

"Well, I'd better head to bed. I'm going for a run in the morning," I blurted out.

Really, with the running again?!

Presumably the intelligent, rational part of my brain had suffered a small burnout from lust and excitement.

"You run? That's great! We should go running sometime. Night then."

He disappeared behind his door before I had time to respond to his suggestion. Which was lucky, because I probably would have responded with something like, "Sure! How about now?"

A combination of this interaction and the drawn-out catastrophe before it had completely exhausted me. As I headed up the stairs, I felt glad of two things: that tomorrow was a Sunday, and that I'd had the presence of mind to bring the half-empty Massive home with me.

CHAPTER THREE

Sleeping was my superpower. I could sleep anywhere, at any time, through anything, on anything, in anything. I slept so well that night that my "Soothing Beach Sounds" alarm had escalated to roaring waves and furiously berating seagulls before I regained consciousness. It took me some time to realise why I'd actually set an alarm—my first, confused thought being: "That's right, I'm going running." After stretching and rolling onto my bedroom floor, still embedded in my doona cocoon, I remembered that it was Roast with Pops Day. I loved Roast with Pops Day. My grandfather was brilliant company and an even better cook.

I wriggled along the floor, still ensconced in my doona—partially to amuse myself and partially because I was not quite ready to extract myself from its warmth. Finally, I reached my door and broke free from my doonary refuge. A glance in my full-length mirror confirmed that I was not quite the fresh, beautiful butterfly I'd hoped to emerge as. My mascara had somehow smudged across my jawline, not to mention the fact that all my hair had migrated to one side of my head and formed something of a nest there. Not particularly glamorous. Not that Pops would mind; he always told me I looked lovely, regardless of what I actually looked like.

I hastily tied my hair into what I fancied to be a stylish messy bun, but was probably akin to a small scruffy dog curled atop my scalp. I sniffed at my armpits and deemed them tolerable, spritzing them with my favourite (cheap) perfume to tide me over until a shower later. Finally, I threw on some clothes—jeans, a t-shirt, a long-sleeve top, a woollen jumper, a jacket and heeled boots—and grabbed an umbrella. The forecast said 20 degrees and cloudy, but no true Melbournian would take their chances with the weather.

I checked my phone while hurrying down the stairs. I could make the next train if I set a brisk pace. I was nearly at the building door when I brisked straight into Dan on his way in.

"Hey!" he said in a friendly tone as I steadied myself with a hand on his arm.

Wow. Nice arm. And he has two of those things.

He surveyed my outfit.

"You went out for your run earlier, hey?"

I smiled and jiggled my head somewhere in between a nod and a shake, satisfying myself that I wasn't directly lying. If he wanted to believe that I was a motivated sunrise runner then I wouldn't stand in his way.

"How'd *you* go?" I asked, not being able to think of any other topic to discuss with him. As far as he knew, I was a passionate runner who just loved chatting about running.

"Nah, not great today. I only managed about twenty laps of the oval. Had a niggle in my hammy. Or else that's my excuse. I think I just needed this so badly." He held up a drink bottle full of murky liquid. "Anyway, maybe I'll have you there to keep me going next time?"

"If you can keep up!"

I had no idea why I'd said that. It seemed cheeky and fun. I was sure he was flirting with me. It seemed unlikely, but nonetheless true. Maybe he was just one of those guys that flirted with every girl, regardless of his interest in them. Or maybe he was just really, really nice and my radar was totally off. Anyway, I didn't have time to consider it further; I was going to be late.

Time for a smooth exit.

"Anyway, I'd better let you get into that."

I motioned in the general direction of his right hip, where he'd previously been holding his drink bottle, but during my musings he'd put the bottle to his mouth and I'd accidentally gestured to his groin instead. He looked down his body to where I was still pointing and I couldn't help but stare at the same spot in shock at what I'd implied. He looked at me again with raised eyebrows.

"By *that*... I meant... your drink. Not your crotch," I stuttered. "But you can get into that too, if you want. Not that you'd need to because... you're so... well, women must find you very... Oh... I'm late and have to go, sorry. Bye!"

"Right. Cool. See ya."

I had no idea what his facial expression meant as I caught a quick glimpse of it while fleeing out the door, but it made me wonder if some days I should just stick to what I'm good at and stay asleep.

I turned the handle to Pops's door and sure enough it was unlocked. Although Pops had moved to a small unit in the outer suburb of Belgrave to be closer to Riley and I, he was born and bred a country boy and I doubted he'd ever locked his door in his life. Pops's face brightened when he came out of his kitchen and saw me. After a strong hug, he held me at arm's length and said, "You look lovely!"

I smiled, feeling safe and happy while blanketed in Pops's warm scent of wool and Imperial Leather soap. His fine white hair was carefully combed to one side and he wore a woollen vest and painstakingly pleated pants. His days of wearing mud-spattered oilskin coats and waterproof pants on the farm were forever behind him.

"I'm so glad to see you!" he exclaimed. "Here, would you mind putting these on my iPod for me?"

He handed me a list of songs he'd written down on a notepad he kept next to his digital radio, or "computer wireless" as he called it. Although he had a surprising grasp of technology for someone of his age—he sent texts, internet searched new recipes and played word puzzles against my Mum on an app—he hadn't quite worked out the logistics of transferring music onto the iPod he listened to on his daily walk.

I skimmed down the list of popular songs he'd written down and stopped at one of them.

"Pops, do you know what this song is about?"

I pointed and he looked over the top of his glasses at it.

"Oh yes, that's a beautiful one. About a young fella who wants to have a dance with his lady friend."

"Yes, um, but in this song 'dancing' is a euphemism for…" I grappled with the right words to explain the explicit meaning of the song as Pops looked at me, confused. "No, you're right, it is a beautiful one, Pops. I'll make sure it's on there."

His face broke into a pleased smile and he hugged me again.

"What would I do without my little Juzzy?" he asked.

You probably wouldn't have access to music's answer to soft-core porn, I thought as I plugged the iPod into his computer and began downloading songs.

"Well, you know the story of how I met your Gran," Pops said over my shoulder.

I turned around from the computer screen to look at him. Pops would tell that story every day as long as there was someone willing to hear it. Yes, I knew the story very well, but I hadn't yet heard it too many times and suspected I never would.

"I can't quite remember all the details Pops, maybe you could tell me again?"

He smiled at my answer and I thought I saw his eyes shine with tears for a moment before he began.

"Well, your Gran, when she was young, had brilliant red hair. You wouldn't believe the colour. These days you see young ladies trying to dye their hair the colour of hers, but it never looks real. We don't have any coloured photos from then, so you'll

31

just have to take my word for it, Juzzy, she was…
Well, she was a looker alright. Anyway, where was
I? Oh yes, I was at a dance with some other young
fellas. We'd just finished the milking and I suspect
we still had a whiff of the night's work about us, if
you know what I mean. Well, be it that reason or
another, none of the sheilas had come near us all
night, so we're just talking rubbish amongst
ourselves.

"Then I see Ellen, your Gran, with *that* hair,
and she's wearing a brilliant green dress—very
stylish at the time. Well, I was full of a young lad's
bravado back then, so I say to my mate, Jez, that I
reckon the colour's got to be fake because no one's
hair could really be that vibrant. Now, Jez isn't the
most tactful fella, and he's had a few nips, so he
marches over to her and I see him pointing at mc
and then at Ellen's head! I'm burning, Juzzy, just
burning with embarrassment. I see her look at me
with disgust and then, can you believe it, she
marches over with Jez in tow."

"Did you tell your friend here that my hair
colour is fake?" I mouthed along with his words.

It was my favourite part of the story. My
Gran sounded brilliant.

"Well, then I have to own up to it," Pops
went on. "So I stammer, 'Yes, I did' and she
narrows her round eyes at me—almost to slits,
Juzzy! She says, 'Well, you're wrong and you can
just see for yourself.' I don't know what else to do
other than peer really closely at her scalp and she
looks up at me, eyes as big as saucers again, and
says, 'If you're going to stand that close, we might

32

as well be dancing.' I take her in my arms and we dance. We dance until the song is over. And then we sit and have a yarn for the rest of the night. And if we hadn't, love, you probably wouldn't be sitting here now."

His face was a complicated mixture of nostalgia and pain.

"You look a bit like her. Your eyes are like hers... but not the hair. I've never seen hair like it on anyone else."

I always felt sad after hearing stories about Gran that I didn't have any memories of her. I was three when she died of cancer. Mum told me that after Gran's death, Pops had visited every professional he could find—doctors, naturopaths, psychologists and even a psychic—as though he was looking for someone who could either give her back to him or take the pain away. But no one had managed either and it was like he carried a little suitcase of sadness with him everywhere—dragging it alongside him on his walks and setting it down beside himself at dinner.

"How old were you, Pops?"

It was the first time it had occurred to me to ask.

"A young fella of 20. Couldn't even grow a beard!" he chuckled.

"20?! But you married only a year after you met. Didn't you ever wonder whether... How did you know you'd made the right decision?"

He looked at me as if he didn't understand the question.

"What do you mean, Juzzy? I met her. I learnt her. I loved her," he said simply. "Of course it was the right decision."

The timer on Pops's oven went off and I followed him to the kitchen. After serving up the food together, we sat across from each other to eat. The roast was amazing, as always, and we barely spoke for our enjoyment of the food.

"Great lunch, Pops," I said, wiping my mouth and feeling thankful for the considerable stretchiness of my jeans. "You've outdone yourself again. That seasoning was a triumph!"

"It was, wasn't it? I used the recipe of that young cockney bloke, the one who doesn't wear any clothes. I'm not sure about his life choices, but his recipes ain't half bad."

"Pops, he doesn't really cook naked. He's called the Naked Chef because of his raw passion for cooking," I said, hiding a smile behind my napkin.

"Well, it's a strange thing to call yourself then. It's hard not to imagine his bits going to and fro while he's bustling about in the kitchen, dangling into the sauces and glazes and what not."

Now I was openly laughing, which, I realised, was exactly what Pops had intended. He looked at me with a straight face, but there was a twitch to his eye that told me he had been messing with me and I'd fallen for it.

"Your brother said he might pop by with the kids later, if you want to stick around."

I loved my niece and nephew. They were delightful balls of energy and fun who adored me, but just the thought of entertaining them for the afternoon after my late night thoroughly exhausted me.

"I'll catch him later when he picks up his car. I'd better get home. I've got to do my planning."

This was very true; I had no idea what I was going to teach my class this week.

"No worries love, I've wrapped up some lamb for your lunches."

"You're my hero."

We both rose from the table and Pops gave me a big hug.

"You didn't tell me how the fellas are treating you?"

I thought about last night.

"Not as well as I'd like, to be honest."

Pops looked me right in the eye.

"Juzzy, a good man—or woman, if that's what you'd prefer, if you're one of those TGIF people—will come along. And whoever he or she is, they will love you as much as I do."

Now it was my turn to tear up.

"Thanks, Pops," I hugged him again. "But I don't think they make 'em like you anymore. Ah, also, I'm not LGBTQ or I. Just for the record."

After cobbling together a plan for the school week and handing Riley back the keys to his car, I sat on my couch with a reality TV show about renovating on to stop me from feeling lonely. My housemate, Ellie, was a doctor and was already in bed to compensate for the early shifts she was doing. I looked at my silent phone and felt deflated. On a whim, I uninstalled my dating app. I lamented for the millionth time that I was single in the age of app dating. Although it should have made life much easier—hundreds of single guys available at the swipe of a fingertip—the unwritten rules of app etiquette were completely overwhelming.

I thought of Pops and Gran, and the simplicity of asking someone to dance. Of sitting down to talk and not ever having to have "The Talk". They hadn't had the "Are we in a relationship, or aren't we?" awkwardness; they were both content in one single person's company and that was enough. I flicked off the TV and sighed, maybe just to hear the sound of a voice in the quiet apartment.

Sleep, I told myself. *Everything will feel better in the morning.*

CHAPTER FOUR

The first part of the week dragged slowly along like a sulking child scuffing its shoes as it refused to pick up the pace. I caught myself looking at the clock repeatedly on Monday afternoon, while singing and dancing to the Hokey Pokey in an attempt to teach my clueless Prep students their left from right. I spent Monday night making little dare cards for Steph's Hen's Night, which was organised for the upcoming Saturday.

Steph had swiftly dismissed suggestions of winery bus tours through the Yarra Valley or high teas in Melbourne's more elegant suburbs for her Hen's, saying, "Nope, it shouldn't be a classy affair. Everyone knows I'm not a classy gal. Just a good old piss up in the city, thanks."

I had figured out with the other bridesmaids that we would do an evening pole dancing class and the theme would be "Emergency Services", due to the fact that Steph had been dressed as a firefighter when she met Charlie at a uni party. After the pole dancing, we would head to a rooftop bar where Steph could enjoy a decent "piss up" before going to a pub later for a dance.

I tried not to think too much about Steph getting married. We'd been wildly single together all the way through uni until the end of our last year when she'd met Charlie. Since then Charlie had been a permanent fixture in my life, just an extension of Steph. I assumed he knew everything I told her and I didn't mind, because I loved and trusted him too. But, not counting the first few months after they got together when they'd spent all their time tangled up in each other, Charlie had never really affected my relationship with Steph. Marriage seemed different. I couldn't quite explain why to myself, but I deeply feared it would cause a change in what we'd had for over ten years. Marriage was for adults, for people who were doing things like acquiring mortgages, having babies and writing wills. None of these things were in my near future.

What if we have nothing in common anymore? What if the easy, fun-filled banter changes into serious conversations about interest rates and breastfeeding?

I felt sick just thinking about it. So I was trying not to think about it, while still being a superb maid of honour and friend. It was a tricky balancing act.

Tuesday was another painfully slow day. The most exciting event of the day occurred when a child discreetly pressed his tooth into my hand and whispered, "Can you please give this to the tooth fairy? I'll collect the cash from you tomorrow morning."

Hi, I'm Justine Hertz, Minion to Mystical Creatures. Pleased to meet you.

On Tuesday night, I reinstalled the dating app out of boredom and lined up a date for Thursday. The guy seemed nice and normal... but didn't they all? I rang Steph to distract myself from over-stalking his profile.

"Howdy lady, how are the covert preparations going for my final night of being an unmarried, unboring chick?"

She sounded chipper and her enthusiastic greeting cheered me immediately.

"Great! Just trying to figure out how we're going to get from the dirty chicken shop to the underground S&M dungeon. Any ideas?"

"Hmmm… We could ride a stripper?"

"That sounds both enjoyable *and* economical. I'll look into it."

"Excellent. Have you recovered from last Saturday night?"

After I'd dropped Aidan off, I'd sent her a selfie of me with the Massive and a brief summation of the date.

"More or less. I've got another date on Thursday now so I guess that's the definition of getting back on the horse… man… Getting back on the man?"

"Yeah, you get back on that man! Hang on a minute… Charlie is saying something… He wants an update on Hot Neighbour. Is he single? Remember when we ran into him last time we were there and he was all sweaty from footy training? Mmmm… Even Charlie came home with a man crush."

"Dan. Yeah, I remember. I have no idea about his relationship status. We're not friends on social media." I took a breath. "But he did kind of casually put it out there that he'd like to hang out… You know, somewhere out of the building."

"Really?! Where?"

"Oh, just, you know…" Damn, I was going to have to say it. "He said we could go running together."

I didn't think it quite warranted the volume of laughter that blasted into my ear. Even Charlie was cackling away in the background.

"Running hasn't been entirely successful for you in the recent past."

"I remember," I grumbled, losing my enthusiasm for the conversation.

The problem with couples was that they wanted to live vicariously through your single life experiences, but they didn't really understand the harsh reality of it all.

Yes, they're funny stories. But they also really happened to me. I actually had to live through them.

"Anyway, have you got your outfit for Saturday?" I changed the subject.

"Yep," Steph replied, "I just picked it up today. I was trying to think of Emergency Services that wear a white outfit. Y'know, cos I'm a virginal bride."

I snorted before offering, "Ghostbuster?"

"Sperm?" I heard Charlie suggest in the background. "They're like an emergency service. They come quickly when you need them."

"That one needs work, Charlie," Steph critiqued before returning her attention to me. "I went with nurse."

"Hot."

"I will be."

"Do it, then."

"Oh, I'll be doing it. See you Saturday. Good luck on your date!"

"Cheers, it can't be worse than the last one."

I hung up with the ill feeling that I had just jinxed myself.

Wednesday and Thursday seemed to go quite quickly, possibly because I was dreading the impending date. In the two years that had passed since Ben had broken up with me, I'd had a handful of what could only be described as short flings, along with an innumerable number of one-off dates and one-night stands. I was exhausted with dating and finding it hard to remain positive. I didn't *need* a man. I had several groups of friends, I was financially sound, I had a loving family and I usually had veggies with dinner. But I did, deep down, desperately *want* a man. I wanted what all my friends had, regardless of how their partners pissed them off or held them back at times. I saw their complete, genuine happiness in being with the other person, the kind of happiness I thought I'd felt with Ben. I yearned to feel that way again.

I peered into the bathroom mirror on Thursday afternoon, having made the mistake that day of giving my Preps glitter with the instruction "Go nuts!" Just as I'd suspected, I looked like a tired, overworked fairy who desperately needed a double shot of magic potion. I left my laptop and book-filled bags where I stood and hastily showered, donning my dating uniform in record time. I made an unsuccessful attempt to remove the green glitter that still clung to my face, hair and hands with a makeup wipe and did a defeated shrug as I grabbed my keys.

Don't think it, don't think it, don't think it.
...This could be The One.

I passed Dan on the stairs on my way out, and he flashed me his perfect smile, but he was on the phone and we continued in opposite directions. He always wore gym clothes, always. He must work at a gym. Or an active wear shop. I was surprised to realise that although we'd lived in the same building for over two years, I didn't know anything about what Dan did, or where he came from. Conversation was always easy, he seemed to know something about all our neighbours, but rarely spoke about himself when we ran into each other. Saturday night was the first time he'd ever suggested catching up on purpose. I was trying not to get too excited about it. As far as I knew, he was just being conversational. Also, I'd recently seen a very satisfied-looking supermodel leave his apartment.

I stepped outside. The air was warmer than it had been in months and there was a honeyed perfume to the breeze. Spring had deigned to descend on Melbourne, at least for this evening.

My thoughts began to wander as I jumped on a tram heading to the city. I hadn't been expecting it—the break up with Ben. I wasn't completely oblivious, I knew we had issues. He wouldn't talk about his feelings and would walk out of the apartment every time we argued, and I made passive aggressive comments that came out nastier than I'd intended. But every couple I'd ever come into contact with had issues. It was my limited understanding that you worked through them to become a stronger unit.

I'd come home from work one day with takeaway, imagining a relaxing night with no cooking or dishes, of sitting side by side and laughing about our old favourite jokes or even making new ones. Instead I saw him sitting there, on *our* couch, his elbows resting on his knees and his hands clasped tightly together. I wasn't sure but he looked like he'd been crying. His olive skin was blotchy and creased at his temples and across his forehead.

Don't ask him anything, I'd advised myself. *Be light, funny. Then nothing bad will happen.*

I'd set down the takeaway and started with "So… guess what happened to me at the Chinese shop?"

It was a funny story and Ben loved the way I retold stories. I knew that in a few minutes, I'd have him in stitches.

"It's over," he had half-whispered, just audibly enough for his words to stab me in the ears. "I still love you. But we both know it's over."

That was basically as far as he went in terms of an explanation and he was wrong, I hadn't known it was over. So I held onto the "I still love you" part, believing we'd get back together. That was until I found out—from social media—that he'd been seeing someone else for a month before the break up. Even now, when I could think about that "It's over" moment with little more than a stinging sensation, I didn't really understand what had gone so terribly wrong. It was a frightening thought, because how would I stop the same thing from going wrong next time? If there ever was a next time.

I physically shook my head to clear the pointless reminiscing. It wasn't a great way to psych myself up for my date. The worse problem was, as a woman looking for love in my thirties, I accidentally went into every date thinking: *This could be The One.* I tried not to think it. I told myself *STOP THAT!* every time I did. But without fail, just before each date, there it was, that tiny hopeful voice inside my head saying:

Pssst! This could be The One.

I realised suddenly that the tram was about to continue past my stop. I stood up and frantically tugged the chord. The driver glared at me in his mirror as the tram squealed to a halt. I jumped from the steps and walked the half a block to the bar where my date had suggested we meet.

John, I thought, *His name's John. Don't forget his name is John.*

At least I didn't have to worry about him being late; I noticed him sitting at a booth as soon as I walked in. He stood up and shook my hand as though we were in a business meeting.

"John," he said.

"I know!" I replied, distracted by the fact that he only came up to my shoulder. "Sorry... I'm Justine."

"Hi," he said.

"Hi John."

Well, at least the conversation is flowing.

"Have you been here before?" asked Little John.

Don't call him that, not even in your mind!

"No," I responded, confused by the booth situation.

What is the deal here? Do I sit next to him or across from him?

I took in the tables, which were heavy wood and oddly wide, and the loud music pumping from a nearby speaker. I decided to sit next to him, knowing there was a good chance I wouldn't hear much of what he said if I sat opposite. That would be a benefit on some dates, but I couldn't judge this one yet.

"How was work?" I asked, sliding into the booth beside Little John. I'd remembered from his profile that he was a solicitor in the city.

"It was work," he replied, studying the menu.

"Yep, I know what you mean. I apologise in advance if I get glitter in our food. Glitter is like herpes—easy to contract, hard to get rid of."

I was doing the thing that I did in awkward situations, which was desperately try to fill silences with jokes that inevitably ended up making the situation more awkward. Little John was silent beside me.

DON'T CALL HIM THAT!

"Not that I know about herpes personally. I've just heard... It was a bad joke really."

He blinked at me briefly and then went back to his menu analysis.

"Do you like cheese?" he asked.

45

"More than chocolate, which is a pretty big deal!" I replied, sounding desperately enthusiastic as though I was trying to cheerlead the date into being enjoyable.

"Great, we'll get the cheese platter to share. Do you want a cocktail?" Little John handed me the drinks menu.

"Umm... OK, sure."

"OK, I'll have the Long Island Iced Tea. It's not table service so... If you want to go and order for us?"

I decided he'd suggested this based on the fact that he was sitting next to a wall and I was blocking him into the booth. I went and ordered the cheese, Iced Tea and an Espresso Martini for myself. The bartender, a hipster-looking woman with a sleeve tattoo and thick-rimmed glasses, asked where I was sitting.

"Oh, over there next to the little... the man. That man, there." I pointed in Little John's... *stop that*... direction and she nodded.

"Oh yep, I gotchya. Table 10," she said.

Why didn't I just check the table number?

I carried the drinks back to the booth, taking my time in a show of not spilling them, but really not looking forward to investigating what hadn't proved to be a stimulating connection so far. When I finally arrived, Little John was staring at a couple sitting at another table. I felt uncomfortable, so I busied myself arranging our drinks until he remembered he had a date too.

"Thanks," Little John said and sipped his Iced Tea through a straw in an off-putting way, although I couldn't quite figure out why. Something about the way he tightly pursed his lips together.

"So, do you work near here or—" I began.

"That couple are having a fight," Little John interjected, gesturing towards the table he'd been intrigued with.

"Are they?"

"Yes. She thinks he works too much and he said they need the money. I can lip read."

How am I supposed to react to that? Impressed? Aroused?

"That's impressive."

Well, I certainly wasn't going to say "That's arousing."

"Yeah."

"So, well, I saw this movie recently and it was about this couple who move in with…"

I couldn't believe I was so desperate to make conversation that I'd brought up the movie from my last horrendous date.

Little John wasn't listening anyway. He was still engrossed with the arguing couple. The hipster bartender appeared and set down our cheese platter. Little John turned his attention to her as she talked about the cheese, but I couldn't take it in. I wanted to get out of there, only twenty minutes in. As Hipster Girl walked away, I resolved to stay for the cheese and then make a polite excuse to leave.

I reached for the cheese knife at the same time as Little John put his hand out. I quickly pulled mine away to avoid an accidental hand-touching incident over the knife, but I needn't have worried as he proceeded to twist off a piece of blue cheese with his fingers. I stared as he pursed his lips tightly and pressed the cheese into them. His tongue poked out slightly and dragged the cheese lump back into its dank lair. Then Little John returned his fingers to the board, continuing to molest more cheese into his mouth.

I felt sick, even more so when I realised I was going to have to eat at least some of the cheese that he was pulling apart with his saliva-slick fingers. It was the worst thing I had ever seen. I wasn't a germaphobe, but this far exceeded my limits of bad public hygiene. And it was weird. It was so, so weird. I made a show of taking the knife and delicately cutting a piece of vintage cheddar from a corner he had yet to violate. I bit into it and politely shielded my mouth as I chewed. I became aware that we'd been eating cheese in silence for at least ten minutes.

"So, do you live near the city?" I tried again to make conversation, hoping nothing better was going on at a nearby table.

"Yes, about ten minutes away. Easy transport."

Grab, pucker and push. Grab, pucker and push. I wanted to look away in disgust. I had given up the façade of eating any cheese myself. On the upside, he'd nearly finished the whole platter and I'd had time to rehearse my leaving excuse in my head.

"Do you like wagyu?" Little John finally asked me a question.

"Wagyu? Like the beef?"

I was a bit confused about where this might be going.

"Yeah, it's amazing here."

"Oh, OK, great. Um, but…"

"I'm going to order us some."

He started to stand up, forcing me to stand as well to let him past.

NO! I wanted to scream at him, *Don't do it! I have to leave immediately! DON'T DO IT!!*

In my desperation, I even contemplated diving at his feet and holding onto them to stop him from ordering. I continued to feel sick as I watched him approach Hipster Girl. She glanced at me with a look of disbelief, as if she'd witnessed the whole cheese debacle and couldn't believe I was still there. Little John came back and waited for me to move over for him. Great, now I was physically trapped.

"You're going to love it," he told me, sitting down way too close.

I tried to move over further but found a stone wall in my way.

"So," Little John said.

He attempted to look into my eyes but was forced to lift his head up, even though he was sitting down. It seemed I suddenly had his full attention, even though I didn't want it. I was aware of his hand inappropriately close to my leg on the vinyl seat. I had the urge to burst into an operatic Christmas carol, just to distract him from the fact that he'd obviously decided to try some of his "moves" on me.

"What is the most awkward date you've ever been on?" he continued.

THIS ONE! my mind screamed at him. *AND THAT IS NOT AN EASY FEAT!*

"Oh, well, I've been on a few," I answered vaguely.

"Well, describe them."

"I can't think of specifics... What about you?"

"I don't date much."

I doubt I achieved a surprised face. I was saved from this conversation, if you could call it that, by the wagyu arriving. To my extreme relief, Little John deemed it worthy of cutlery. I hastily forked beef into my mouth, not really tasting it, trying to come up with a way to get the hell out of there. It was probably a huge waste; the one thing I knew about wagyu was that it was expensive. Little John put his knife and fork down, still chewing.

"So," he said with a mostly empty mouth, fumbling his hand onto my knee. "How many dates exactly have you been on?"

My head was awash with nauseating waves of surprise and disgust. His hand was shaking slightly on my knee, presumably from nerves. He started to rub it up and down my leg, reaching the middle of my thigh. I stared straight ahead and tried to move further over, but bumped my shoulder against the wall again.

Why isn't he getting the hint?

"I've... I'm... Oh God, I feel really sick."

I wasn't strictly lying. Little John reluctantly pulled his hand away.

"Are you going to vomit?" he asked, sounding mildly disgusted himself.

"I… I might. I think I have to go."

I pulled cash from my wallet that would cover well over half of the bill and the relief of my imminent escape flooded through me. I stood up and began to leave, forcing Little John to stand to let me past.

"Are you sure you—" Little John sounded disappointed but even my people-pleasing instincts would not deter me.

"Sorry, Little… I mean, John. Sorry, John. Bye."

He looked shocked, but also like he might be inclined to hug me, so I turned around and walked out the door.

On the tram home, I rested my forehead on my knees. There were only a few other people scattered around me and they were engrossed in their phones. The sick feeling started to subside, replaced by anger and revulsion over what had just occurred. At least I could see the humour after my date with Fluffy Aidan. After this one I couldn't think of anything but how much I wanted a shower. Or three. I slowly raised my head and leaned it against the cold window, probably creating a glitter-encrusted smudge to join all the other head-smudges visible on the glass.

What did I do, I thought sadly, *to deserve this?*

CHAPTER FIVE

I surveyed my police uniform in the full-length mirror.

Ha ha! Uniform!

It was a tight, low-cut singlet top of faux leather pinned with a plastic silver badge that said "Officer Sexy". The skirt was a stretchy Lycra that in its unstretched state had looked like it might belong to a toddler. Even with a full Spanx leotard underneath, I'd barely managed to get it on. The outfit was completed by a pair of black underwear I'd found on sale at a lingerie store, with the words "Punish Me" written in hot pink italics across the bottom.

I took a shallow breath—the only kind I'd be capable of taking that night—and felt the pure satisfaction that comes from squeezing into an outfit like the one I was wearing without a team of people to help. I slid into my shiny black heels and walked, with some difficulty, from my bedroom to the bathroom. I looked at myself in the mirror. I'd accentuated my round eyes with smoky shadows and plumped my lips into a bright red pout.

Not bad at all.

As I stepped out into the evening, I shook my shoulders in an attempt to shrug off the icky feeling I'd had all day resulting from last night's date. Three showers hadn't even erased the memory of the trembling, unwelcome hand rubbing my leg.

I looked towards the city. The evening was another warm one, and the sky was a cocktail of bright pinks and reds, with a thin ring of clouds circling the tops of the tallest skyscrapers. It would probably be another nice day tomorrow. Not that I was likely to see a lot of tomorrow. I suspected I'd be safely tucked up in the smothering embrace of a hangover. My only physical movements would be opening my laptop to binge-watch trashy shows or opening my door to receive bags full of trashy food.

A car parked nearby beeped to indicate that it was the ride I'd booked and I began to feel nervous excitement about the night out that stretched enticingly before me.

"Hi there," said my driver as I opened his passenger door.

I smiled at him. He was a mid-forties guy in a suit. He had gone to a lot of effort just to drive around, picking up strangers.

I must remember to give him a good rating.

"Hi, had a busy day?" I asked, climbing into the car and shutting the door. He looked a bit confused but shrugged. He pulled at his collar, as though it was too tight.

"So, how does this work?" he asked.

I realised this must have been his first time driving for the app I'd booked him through. I'd done it heaps of times, so I felt pretty confident explaining it.

"Oh, you're new to this. That's fine, I don't mind, as long as you know how to get there! Payment goes through the app."

I held up my phone. He nodded slowly.

"There's an app? Oh… that's easy. Well, in that case, I guess I'd like the works. How much for everything?"

I stared at him for a minute, trying to figure out what he meant.

"Uh… What are you talking about?" I asked, starting to feel like something was very wrong.

He pulled at his collar again.

"Well, the… uh… service. I'd like you to…"

As I stared at him, he seemed to suddenly get the "Something is very wrong" memo. His eyes widened in horror.

"You… You're… You're a hooker, right?"

Oh God, oh no.

"No! I'm dressed up for a Hen's Night! I thought you were the ride I'd booked!"

I opened the door, jumping back onto the footpath and flailing my arms to keep my balance.

"Oh dear, sorry for the mix up," he rushed as I shut the door. The car pulled onto the road and sped away. A minute later, another car pulled in and the driver wound down the passenger window.

"Hello, are you Justine? I'm Fred, your driver."

After exchanging pleasantries, Fred and I rode in silence, save for the 90s pop bouncing from his speakers. I wasn't really up for conversation after my previous interaction. Dropping me at the corner of Latrobe and Elizabeth Streets, Fred wished me a very enjoyable evening. Steph was already there, looking outstanding in white latex with a giant red cross printed on her chest.

"You look amazing!" she yelled and embraced me.

"Give thanks to Spanx," I replied and we Japanese bowed to each other.

As we clicked along the footpath in our heels and I filled her in on the car misunderstanding, we received more than a few appreciative honks and whistles from passing drivers. Steph laughed and laughed and then, when she stopped to breathe, she said, "I know I've said it before, but someone needs to write a book about your life."

I stopped outside the pole dancing studio and Steph nodded approvingly.

"Oh yes, I am so into this!"

There were about twenty of us—dressed as doctors, nurses, paramedics, police officers and firefighters—groping hopelessly at poles. The moves weren't complicated per say, but several of the girls had indulged in too many pre-drinks and others were more concerned with retaining a hint of mystery in their skant outfits than with perfecting the routine. Charlie's mum's pole happened to be located directly behind mine, and I was rather conscious of her receiving the command to "Punish Me" each time I dropped to the floor.

We all whooped loudly as Steph was brought to the front of the class to perform the routine on her own for the conclusion of the lesson. She made the most of her big moment in the tacky, school-disco-style lighting with some improvised twerking and a rather inspired pelvic thrust at her pole as the finale. I almost teared up with pride.

As we walked to the rooftop bar, we all laughed giddily, re-watching videos from the pole dancing class and exchanging solemn promises that they would never see the light of social media. My underwear made several appearances on the videos, and I was actually glad I hadn't opted for a more spacious beige pair.

We blew onto the rooftop in a flurry of perfume, sweat and feminine joy. Steph threw her hands in the air and yelled, "I'm getting married, buy me a drink!" which received a scattering of applause, as well as a few smirks and eye rolls. I linked arms with her and we headed to the bar.

"I'll buy you a drink, Stephie. At least then you know for sure that it's been spiked."

"Hooray!" Steph cried as we joined the sizeable queue. "When are you going to do your dare?"

I shifted my weight between my already-aching feet as we edged forward in the line. I'd given out the dare cards outside the pole dancing studio, deliberately choosing a pretty tame one for myself and saving the more risqué challenges for the most adventurous guests.

"Give a stranger a massage?" I asked. "Probably after I've quenched my thirst more sufficiently. What about yours?"

"Find someone with the same name as the groom and give them a kiss," Steph recited. "It sounds like one of those corporate ice-breaker games."

"Well, that would be an HR nightmare but I get your point."

She shrugged and tapped the stripy-shirted shoulder in front of her. Its owner turned around.

"Is your name Charlie?" she asked.

The man attached to the shoulder looked her up and down, which I had always thought was just a phrase until I grew breasts and found out that it was a real thing that actually happened. It also seemed to me that the more drunk a man was, the less of an attempt at subtlety was made. Why didn't women do it? Was it because men's clothing was too loose-fitting? I could honestly say I'd never checked out a guy's crotch on a first meeting, although I probably would have if they were wearing tights.

From the way Striped Shoulder's neck actually bent down and up again as he checked out Steph, I estimated his drunkenness at about five beers. He ended in a lingering gaze at her cleavage. Maybe seven beers.

"I could be Charlie," he said.

Steph attempted to raise one eyebrow at him, but, not being in possession of that particular skill, she looked more like an overzealous mime excited about the prospect of engulfing an invisible banana. "Charlie" looked somewhat discouraged.

"You don't look like a Charlie," she told him. "You look like a Gaz or a Smithy or something."

However drunk, he looked offended.

"It's Miles, actually."

"HA!" she exploded and turned to me. "Have you met *Miles* here? He said he was a Charlie but nope, he's actually a *Miles*."

"OK, hi Miles," I said, steering Steph by the shoulders. "Come on, it's our turn to order."

"Buy you a drink?" Miles tried, but his heart wasn't in it. I just slightly shook my head, continuing to guide Steph towards the waiting bartender. He was one of those guys who for some reason had grown a full lumberjack beard, hiding what was clearly a very attractive face behind a massive clump of wiry curls.

"What can I get for you ladies?" He had a deep, rasping voice with a strong ocker accent.

"What is your funniest named shot... um..." Steph leaned across the bar, attempting to read his name tag.

He leaned closer to her to give her a better look and tattoos appeared from under his short-sleeve shirt.

"It's Charlie," he said. "And I can give you a Blow Job."

"You've got to be kidding me," I heard Miles mumble under his breath behind us.

"If you give me a Blow Job, can I give you a kiss?"

Steph smiled sweetly at Charlie the Bartender. He winked back in a way that only sexy bartenders can manage without seeming creepy.

"You're on," he said.

In mere seconds, he had produced a shot glass, filled it with at least two different kinds of alcohol, and squirted cream on top.

"Now," he said, sliding it across the bar. "You've gotta pick it up with your mouth."

A couple of people who were waiting for drinks cheered as Steph made a show of putting her hands behind her back and slowly bending over to close her lips around the glass. There was actual applause as she tilted her head back and downed the shot. She opened her mouth to drop the glass back onto the bar—her nose, cheeks and chin now smeared with whipped cream—and beckoned with a finger to Charlie the Bartender. He grinned, leaned all the way across the bar and presented his cheek. Steph planted a big, creamy kiss on him, painting the top of his beard white with her lips.

"Thank you Charlie," she said. "You've been most helpful."

It reminded me of her wild and flirtatious ways when we used to go out together, and how she'd intoxicated men with her outrageous confidence. That was before she had settled down with Charlie. I felt that sad pang again; we'd never have another night like that. In a month she'd be a married woman, and I would still be swiping away on my phone, trying to find something real amongst the filtered photos and loaded messages.

I shook off the melancholy feeling as I ordered a drink from Charlie the Bartender, who poured with one hand and wiped a tea towel across his soiled beard-cheek with the other. Tonight wasn't for sadness, tonight was only for silliness and fun.

We all stood on the platform at Melbourne Central Station, feeling in jolly good spirits and making a ruckus, as we believed to be our right and responsibility as a Hen's Party. Some of the girls had fashioned paper hats from a newspaper they'd found on a bench and were in the process of rolling the Entertainment section into a telescope.

I'd stayed relatively sober for most of the evening to ensure that everything ran smoothly, but in the last hour at the bar I'd enjoyed a few drinks, as the only items left on the itinerary involved catching a train to Flinders Street and then walking to our favourite pub from our uni days. It was probably those few extra beverages that inspired my excellent idea. I walked to the escalator that led to the Melbourne Central shops. I sat down on the silver aluminium platform that ran alongside the escalator and used both my hands to grab onto the moving rubber handrail. I shouted to the girls as I began to glide up the side of the escalator, "Look, everyone! I'm Mary Poppins!"

They clapped and cheered uproariously but I'd barely had time to bask in the applause when I heard a harsh ripping sound. I instinctively let go of the handrail in shock and quickly slid down the aluminium, shooting back onto the platform. I landed on my feet, attempted to regain my balance—which was a losing battle in heels—and fell to my knees in front of the whole Hen's Party. Shaken, I stood up with the help of Steph and her sister, Lily, and then put my hand to the back of my skirt to see what had happened.

The damage was serious. I realised my skirt must have caught on a sharp part of the aluminium, because it was torn from just below the waistband all the way to the hemline. It was only about 20 centimetres, but it was still an important 20 centimetres.

"We'll form a semi-circle to cover you," said Meghan, a friend from uni. "Turn around and show us how bad it is."

I turned around as they shuffled into a tight group around me. My backside was received with further cheers and laughter.

"There are other ways to attract guys! You don't have to rip your whole skirt off!" someone screeched, to loud cackles.

Why do women become so squealy and high-pitched when they're drinking?

I made a mental note to speak more deeply than usual for the rest of the night in order to compensate for this irritating phenomenon.

"Look!" someone else squealed. "I can see a tuft of it still stuck up there!"

I followed where she was pointing to and there was a lonely swatch of my skirt, caught on a screw in between two sheets of aluminium, flapping slightly in the wind from the approaching train.

Steph—best friend in the universe despite her inebriation—looked at the oncoming train and quickly assessed the situation. She whipped off her novelty veil and tucked it into the waistband of my mangled skirt so that my "Punish Me" underwear was concealed by generous layers of tulle. I craned my neck to peer down at my own bottom. It wasn't a bad fix. I just looked a bit like I was wearing a bustle and my tipsy mind fancied it as an old-world touch to an otherwise daringly modern costume.

We rushed to board the train and squeezed on as one stumbling, squealing mass. I steadied myself against a green pole and wiggled my hips at Steph. The veil swished against the back of the head of the woman sitting behind me. She turned around and shot me an annoyed look. I mouthed "Sorry," and she turned back around.

"I would do the same at my real wedding, with my real veil, if you needed it," Steph said.

I doubted there would be any escalators at her real wedding, but I still appreciated the sentiment.

"You're the best, Stephie," I said, remembering my earlier promise to myself to lower the pitch of my voice when I was drunk.

"What are you doing there?" Steph said. "Are you doing your Barry White impression? Are you trying to seduce me?"

"I'm trying not to be annoyingly high-pitched."

"Well, you're being annoyingly low-pitched instead."

"Fine," I said in my normal voice. "Want to know where we're going?"

"Oh, I know where we're going."

She swung around a pole next to the doors, replicating some of the choreography we'd learnt earlier.

"We're going to The Famous Cock. Where else would we be going on my Hen's Night? We pretty much had shares in that place once upon a time."

She was right, of course, that was exactly where we were going. It had been a long time, but back in our uni days we had ended every big night at The Famous Cock. It was a seedy, English-style pub with cheap drinks and a perpetually sticky dancefloor that very few actual Melbournians ever frequented. We had always loved it though, because we always got in regardless of our drunken state. Also, the DJ played every song we requested, which sometimes amounted to an entire playlist. It was only right that Steph's send-off to unmarried life ended there.

We got in without even a second glance from the bouncer and headed straight for the dancefloor. We rolled, swayed, shimmied and shook until our sides hurt and we couldn't feel our feet anymore. Then Steph and I collapsed into a booth for a rest while the other girls danced on. There was soccer on a big screen TV above our heads. A few lounging patrons kept cheering and then groaning as if something had almost happened in the game but then didn't. Steph grabbed my hands across the table and stared at me with red, glassy eyes.

"You're not going to try to make out with me, are you?" I asked her, dropping my heels from my feet and wriggling my numb toes.

"Would it cheer you up?" she asked with only a slight slur.

"I'm not sad."

"Yes you are. I can tell. I can always tell. But Juz, I promise, marrying Charlie will never ever change my love for you."

"I know that. It's just… You are still the person I turn to and rely on for everything. But for you, now that person is Charlie. He's your special one. I'm just an extra person now."

"Juz, you are not just an extra person. You are everything. If there was such a thing as a friend marriage where you could legally commit as a best friend to the other person forever, I would do that. I would friend-marry you."

I felt a bit teary.

"Oh, Steph! I would friend-marry you too."

"Also, Charlie's really average at painting my nails, I'll still need you for that. And going shopping. And eating food that will probably kill me. I'll need you for that. And buying a house and deciding which health insurance to get and all my other life decisions. I'll never stop needing you."

This time I actually had to wipe away a rogue tear.

"I love you, friend wife," I said.

"And I love *you*, friend wife. Now, don't think I am too drunk to notice, that you, Giver-of-Dares, have yet to complete your own. So, off you go."

She stretched out her arm and made a sweeping gesture that encompassed the soccer watchers.

"I don't know, they're watching the game. I don't know why, it's nearly over and no one has scored yet, but they still seem interested. I'd better not."

But I was putting my shoes back on because I knew how this conversation was going to go.

"Oh no, I kissed a random after a Blow Job. You are not getting out of this."

Steph was up and surveying the prospects. She lurched at the closest unsuspecting potential massagee.

"Hello sir, how are you this fine night?" For some reason she was affecting a posh English accent. "I just noticed you are looking rather tense. It's my Hen's Night. I wonder if you might allow my Maid of Honour, Justine, to assist you with a relaxation massage?"

The Soccer Fan looked unsure but shrugged and nodded. I sighed and plodded over to them.

"Any problem areas?" I joked while placing my hands on his shoulders, hoping to make this awkward situation more bearable.

"A few," he replied, turning to look up at me for the first time.

He was quite nice looking, although a little on the young side. He smiled up at me and my tummy turned a bit. I started massaging and he let out a long "Mmmm, that's great," as the other guys around him jumped up and yelled at the TV. I couldn't even tell if they were happy or sad about what had happened. I had definitely fulfilled the requirements of the dare; I could go now. Steph had wandered off to re-join the party, so I could easily make my excuses to leave and find her. But I was reluctant to walk away. Previous one-night stands had never proved to be ultra-fulfilling but when I was out, I often found myself back in this situation: tipsy, horny, lonely, and thinking to myself *Why not?* Most of the girls would be going home to their loving partners. I would be going home to my indifferent vibrator.

Soccer Fan turned around to look at me again. I leaned down and kissed him. He kissed me back, and I couldn't figure out whether I should keep going with the massage or stop and concentrate on the kissing. It was tricky because I was still standing behind him and he was craning his neck to make out with me. Soccer Fan solved the problem by pulling me down onto his lap. He had one hand on my bare knee and it was making its way higher and higher as his tongue danced around in my mouth. I wasn't crazy keen on the idea of the other soccer fans being treated to some surprise half-time entertainment so I whispered to him, "Want to get out of here?" It wasn't my most inspired pick-up line, but I figured he wouldn't complain.

"Sure!" he said, rather eagerly and with a jump that almost knocked me out of his lap.

I detangled myself from him.

"Your place or mine?" Soccer Fan asked, slightly more subduedly.

"Yours, if that's ok? My housemate is on weird shifts and will be pissed off if we wake her."

"Sure," he said again.

"I just need to tell my friends. I'll meet you at the door."

"No worries," he said. "I'll sort out a ride back to my place."

Soccer Fan pulled me in for another quick kiss before I went to find Steph. The whole group were back on the dancefloor, performing Steph's favourite dance move: "The Shower". I mimed turning on the taps along with them and we did the jazz fingers running down our bodies to symbolise running water. As Steph was performing the grand finale—pretending to towel herself off—I pantomimed making out with someone and driving away at her. It was a testament to our friendship that she nodded understandingly and waved goodbye before returning to her imaginary towel.

Soccer Fan was just finishing on the phone as I met him at the exit. We pushed through the heavy wooden door together and emerged onto the buzzing corner of Flinders and Swanston Streets, nodding to the negligent bouncer as we exited. I guessed it was about 2am. People were scooping handfuls of hot chips out of brown paper bags while talking and laughing loudly as they stumbled past in varied stages of inebriation. The smell of fried food was more intoxicating than the several shots I'd had.

"Mmmm, let's get food!" I said to Soccer Fan, and then, as an afterthought, "Hey, what's your name?"

He smiled and put his arm around me.

"Luc," he said. "Nice to meet you... Uh, I know it was a 'J' name."

"It's Justine. When is your ride coming? Do we have time to get chips? Please, please, please say 'Yes'!"

He laughed but then looked uncomfortable.

"Actually, it'll be here any moment but I just need to let you know... before she..."

There was an elongated beep as an expensive car rolled into the taxi parking spot opposite us. The passenger window lowered and the driver, an attractive woman in her mid-fifties, leaned towards us.

"Taxi for Twoooo!" she sung out, then laughed and raised the window again.

My worst suspicions were confirmed when Luc dropped his arm from around me and went to the car. As he opened the front passenger door, he said, "Mum, no one takes taxis anymore." He climbed into the front, leaving me to open the back door.

What did this mean? Was Luc's mother a hardcore helicopter parent who hovered around on a Saturday night, waiting to drive her grown-up son back to his place? No... Even my drunken brain could figure this one out. Over the back of the driver's seat, I could see a slippered foot resting on the brake. She'd come from home to bring him home. To her home. Because it was also still his home.

Oh geez. He lives at home. And we're going there to hook up. This is the worst possible situat—

"We just have to swing by another pub to pick up your Dad. He's out with Kev."

"Uh, sure."

68

OK, now it's the worst possible situation.

"Well, aren't you going to introduce me to your lovely friend here? Must have been an eventful soccer game."

Luc's mother winked at me in the rear-view mirror as she pulled out of the parking spot to much fist-waving and angry beeping from waiting taxis.

"Looks like people *do* still take taxis, Lucas."

I suddenly remembered what I was wearing. Cleavagey top, fake police hat and torn skirt with veil bustle attached.

Oh no.

"Mum, this is… uh, Jessica. She was out for a Hen's Night."

"Oh fun! Did you see any strippers, Jessica? Oh, I loved the strippers! Back when I was younger, of course. And they were often just very nice men trying to make a few bucks. They were certainly quite pleasant to—"

"Mum!"

"Oh, come on Lucas. We're all adults here. Speaking of…"

She pulled into a bus zone without indicating, coming to a halt in front of two middle-aged men in suits who were leaning against each other. They were laughing or crying, it was almost impossible to tell which. Once again, Mrs. Luc's Mum lowered the passenger window, this time hollering, "Hey, no dirty old man loiterers allowed in this area!"

One of them gave her the finger but the other staggered up to the window and—no joke—

ruffled Luc's hair before leaning across to kiss his presumed wife. I shuffled across the backseat to allow Mr. Luc's Dad and Kev to crowd in beside me. It took them about ten minutes and many repeated comments of "Nope, that one's my hole" (followed by snorts and chuckles) to buckle themselves in. When the two men were finally safely secured, we set off again. Mr. Luc's Dad turned to me.

"Hello there, love. What's your name?"

Before I could answer, Mrs. Luc's Mum chimed in with, "This is Jessica. She's been to the strippers."

"Good for you, love," said Mr. Luc's Dad. "I could have been a stripper."

This time the whole car (except me) burst into laughter.

OK, it's contingency plan time. Make an excuse and get out of here. Nothing good can come from this night.

"I'm starving. Let's go through the drive through," said Kev before emitting an impossibly loud burp.

OK, fine. Chips first. Escape plan later.

By the time we'd finished the food, I'd learnt that Luc's Dad and Kev worked together in Construction Management while Luc's Mum was an architect, and they all holidayed together on the Gold Coast. I knew absolutely nothing about Luc himself, but his parents were actually very funny and they made me feel like part of the family. Well, they made Jessica feel like part of the family.

Before I knew it, we'd delivered Kev safely to his door and arrived at the door of Luc's family home. It was stunning, even in the dim security light. Mrs. Luc's Mum (who insisted I call her Lyssa) told me she'd designed the whole thing herself and her husband and Kev had built it.

"Well, young lovebirds," said Mr. Luc's Dad ("Call me Eric or Mr. Powell—but don't call me late for lunch! Ha ha ha ha ha!") as he clapped his hands together. "Us oldies better get to bed. At our age we need our beauty sleep. Lovely to have met you, Jessica."

He gave me a friendly hug and ruffled Luc's hair again before they both disappeared upstairs, but not without one more wink from Lyssa. I'd been so absorbed in the whole surreal situation, I'd forgotten why I was there in the first place. Luc was looking at me apologetically.

"Sorry Jessica, I meant to warn you before… that happened."

He stepped towards me, but looked unsure of how to progress, as it had been at least an hour since we'd first kissed.

"It's OK. Your parents are great. Particularly with the excellent tips about landscaping… if I should ever be in possession of a garden." I took both his hands. "Um, if you don't mind me asking, how old are you?"

"Twenty-two."

I breathed out. It was actually better than I'd expected, if he was telling the truth. At least I hadn't inadvertently groomed a teenager.

"Is that OK?" he asked hopefully.

I looked at him. I had a flash of myself at twenty-two. I'd just begun to feel like an adult but still had much more fun than responsibilities. I was hopeful then too. I shrugged. It wasn't like I had anywhere better to be.

CHAPTER SIX

Luc was still asleep when I woke the next morning.

Excellent, all the easier to sneak out the front door of his family home.

I crept out of his room, which still held his childhood trophies for Little Athletics, carrying my heels and police hat in one hand. I had to walk through the family room to get to the front door and Lyssa was already at the stove, frying something delicious-smelling in a pan.

"Morning, Jessica!" She smiled at me, despite the likely mascara rings around my eyes and the scrunched lycra and tulle mess that I'd just shoved myself into.

"I made pancakes for breakfast, if you'd like some?"

I did want some, as it happened, and the hunger was much stronger than the urge to avoid the awkward morning-after-a-hook-up moments with Luc.

"I'd love some, Lyssa," I said, dropping my heels and hat and sliding onto a stool at the breakfast bar.

"I hope you two had a nice night," she said, flipping a pancake expertly. "I always tried to bring Lucas up to be considerate of women. I hope... that he... was?"

Oh geez, what do I answer to that?

Apparently the most awkward moments after the hook-up were going to be between Lyssa and I.

"You raised him well."

I was worried that she might press for further details, but she busied herself with arranging jams and sauces in front of me. I ate three amazing pancakes and thankfully Luc still hadn't come out of his room. It was time to make a getaway.

"Thank you so much for breakfast, Lyssa, it was lovely. But… I'd better head off now."

"You won't wait for Lucas to get up? He's a deep sleeper, but I could wake him with a bit of water."

"I don't think I will. Sorry."

She looked disappointed, but nodded her head.

"I understand. I wish we could see you again. You seem like such a lovely girl and you'd be so good for him."

I felt sad. I would have loved to see her again too. Luc, not so much.

"Well," Lyssa said, perking up. "Before you go, let me at least fix up your skirt for you. Just a quick run on the sewing machine and it'll be good as new. And then I'll take you home."

Shit. I rifled around again inside my bra, where I usually kept my house keys in the absence of pockets. I realised they hadn't fallen out when I took it off last night, just my phone, ID and lip gloss. *Shit, shit, shit.* Where were they? With some effort from my hungover brain, I did a quick mental backtrack to before I'd left the house the night before. It felt like three weeks ago. I'd gone to collect my keys from the kitchen table but then texted Steph to see if she was bringing a bag. After that, I'd gotten distracted wiping smudged eyeliner away in my compact mirror and then Fred the driver had messaged to say he was a few minutes away. *Shit.* I hadn't thought about them again. I'd done this before, but I'd just called Ben and he'd been able to let me in. Ellie would be at the hospital and uncontactable.

Determined not to let the lack of sleep, the weird sad goodbye with Lyssa, the loneliness of coming home to an empty house and the frustration of finding I couldn't even get in cause a complete breakdown, I decided to problem-solve. I was resourceful and creative. I could figure this out.

Rocket ship? Grappling hook?

No, I couldn't fit my keys into my outfit; I certainly couldn't have fit a rocket ship or a grappling hook, even if I had owned either.

I should get a grappling hook, though.

This wasn't going so well. I wondered if I was still a bit drunk. Suddenly my desperate gaze fell on a cluster of wheelie bins. The apartment building's gardener had dumped the grass catcher from his mower next to them and then had obviously forgotten to collect it. How could he remember his mower but forget the catcher?

Well, how could I remember my lip gloss but forget my house keys and my non-existent grappling hook?

I decided to make the forgetful gardener's loss my gain. In my mind I'd become half sad-girl-without-house-keys and half suave-superhero, and I swept up the mower catcher with gusto. I wheeled a bin around to just below my apartment and positioned the catcher on its lid. With me on top of it, I might just be able to reach my bathroom window, which I could pull open from the outside.

Huzzah and whoop!

I felt excited as I clambered unathletically onto the bin and then stepped up delicately onto the catcher. I had grossly overestimated my own height. I couldn't even reach the bottom of the window sill.

I heard a noise behind me and turned around, causing the catcher to wobble dangerously. Dan had just pulled into the communal car park and was gathering several reusable shopping bags from his backseat.

Quick! Act natural.

I tried to sit down so that I'd at least be able to cross my legs as he passed, but I slipped and ended up in a sprawling straddle. I was acting so natural that Dan almost didn't notice me as he passed, his biceps flexing with the weight of the shopping bags. God, he was gorgeous and from this height I couldn't help but notice his dark, thick hair. He had excellent coverage for a man in his thirties. Just as I was contemplating if he'd visited one of those places advertised on TV that looks like an expensive private hospital except they just grow your hair there (I was sketchy on the details of how, maybe in a petri dish and then implanted it, like hair IVF?), when he looked up.

"Justine? Is that you?"

He was clearly taking in my uniform, and at a very dodgy angle at that.

"Go about your business, citizen. Nothing to see here," I joked with a friendly wave, keeping one hand on the precarious structure to steady myself.

It was probably not charming, but it was the best I could do given the circumstances. Dan actually laughed (*YAY!*) and responded, "There's actually plenty to see from where I'm standing."

"I'm maybe having a little trouble getting into my apartment."

He stepped closer, though still standing clear of the bin/catcher apparatus, which was advisable.

"And the outfit…?"

"My sexy WorkSafe inspector one was in the wash."

"Fair enough, although I think even Sexy WorkSafe would have something to say about your current situation."

Dan put down the bags and squeezed his hands in and out of fists a few times.

"What can I do?" he asked.

I looked at him. Even if he was willing to mount this terrible tower of wheelie doom, I still didn't think he'd be able to reach the window.

"Do you own a grappling hook?"

He laughed again (*YAY! YAY!* If this had been a different situation, I might have jumped for joy).

"Sorry, no. I can call an emergency locksmith. It's like a hundred bucks per call out though. I've suffered that one before."

"Ouch," I replied, hating the thought of my hard-earned dollars paying for a minute's stupidity.

"Thanks anyway. I think I might keep trying to break in. I'll go and buy a ladder or something."

"OK, well, buzz me if you change your mind and need somewhere to wait for the locksmith. Need a hand down?"

Wait. *Wait.* Was that a direct invitation into his home?! Or was he just offering to let me into the stairwell? I was so busy trying to think of a way to clarify that didn't sound too keen, I almost didn't notice Dan offering his hand up to me.

He is initiating physical contact!

I nearly floated off the catcher. Instead, I reached down for his hand but as I did, he reached up and placed both hands on my waist.

"Is this OK?" Dan asked.

It is more OK than anything that has ever been OK in my entire life. I didn't know the meaning of OK until this was OK, and suddenly OK meant something completely new. I've said OK so many times in my mind that it doesn't make sense anymore. OK, OK, OK. Stop it!

"Yes."

"You'll have to jump. I'll hold onto you."

I tried not to think about how much of me was being revealed as I launched myself towards him. Dan didn't stagger at all as he lifted me easily down until my heels grazed the ground. As he set me down and re-burdened himself with the shopping bags, I felt the absence of his hands on my waist like a burn. Then, with a smile and a "Good luck, Justine", he was gone.

I walked up to the ginger-haired guy at the counter. He was fiddling with a gift card, trying to put it into its cardboard holder but failing miserably. He hadn't noticed me yet, or was pretending not to in favour of fighting his life-or-death gift card battle.

Excellent customer service. Well done, sir.

People were staring at me as they meandered past with their exciting purchases of tap fittings and electrical tape.

Just go and tape things, please! Haven't you ever seen a sexy cop in a hardware store before?

I wanted to do the throat-clearing thing that I'd seen people do in movies, but I wasn't one hundred percent sure if it was a thing that people did in real life or not. I contemplated a "Pssst!" but I settled on leaning one elbow onto the counter in the hope that the movement might catch Hardware Ginger's eye. It worked. He swore under his breath as he frisbeed the gift card under the counter and turned to me, standing there nonchalantly. Except it wasn't really nonchalantly, it was extremely chalantly, as the counter was quite a bit shorter than elbow height and I was bent over it, flashing "Punish Me" to the general public and a good deal of cleavage at unsuspecting Hardware Ginger. He smiled broadly and asked, "What can I do for you, officer?"

I tipped my hat.

Why am I still wearing the hat? I definitely should have ditched the hat.

"Ha ha. I see what you did there. Very good joke."

Hardware Ginger raised his eyebrows and rubbed at his red stubble in an attempt to keep a straight face, clearly no less amused despite my attempt at scathing sarcasm.

"I need a ladder," I said.

He still just stood there, looking at me.

"Is this a stitch-up? My mates hired you, didn't they? I will get fired if you start taking your clothes off."

"I am not going to take my clothes off!" I raised my voice in indignation.

"Then I'm not sure Nate and Jack got their money's worth."

This was going about as well as expected. At least I'd been demoted from mistaken hooker to mistaken stripper.

"Who is Nate?! I have not been paid to take my clothes off! Not since 1996 at least, when my cousin paid me to do a nudie run at our family Christmas. And that was definitely *not* worth the $3.40, thank you very much!"

"Was the 40 cents for GST?"

What is happening here?

This was like one of those dreams you would wake up quite relieved from. I took an audible deep breath.

"I really just need a ladder. I am a legitimate customer with legitimate consumer needs. Please. *Please* help me."

Hardware Ginger still looked suspicious.

"What's the ladder for?"

"To break into an apartment. Also, do you have any grappling hooks?"

The ladder folded down into a reasonable size so I managed to carry it onto the tram and back to my apartment window with minimal sweating and swearing. Hardware Ginger, feeling guilty after realising that I wasn't an early birthday strippergram from his mates, had offered to carry it to the tram stop for me but I had refused out of stubbornness.

A highlight of the trip home had been when, metres away from my place, I'd been hastily passed by a mother practically flying her toddler like a kite for how quickly she was pulling the child along by the arm. She probably feared some of my germs of ill-repute jumping onto her precious daughter. The little girl had pointed at me as she sailed by and announced loudly, "Mummy, that policeman is wearing my skirt!"

I leaned the ladder against the brick wall of my apartment building and looked around.

Who am I looking for?

There certainly wasn't anyone to hold the ladder. I thought about buzzing Dan's apartment on the intercom, but the fear of forever burning "Punish Me" onto his retinas changed my mind. I put a tentative foot onto the first metal step and it felt sturdy enough. Sturdier than the bin-and-mower-catcher combination at least. I gained some confidence and started to climb the rungs, still very aware that the higher I went, the more likely I was to fall to my death. Probably not death, actually. I didn't think it was high enough. Maybe a broken collarbone, a dislocated knee cap, something like that. That kind of thinking was off-putting, so I squeezed my eyes shut and climbed higher.

When I opened my eyes, my head was level with my window, so I hooked my fingertips under the window frame and pulled it towards me. It swung out so quickly that I was thrown off balance and nearly fell backwards off the ladder. I flailed my arms and leaned forward until I was safe(ish) again. My heart was thumping and my hands shaking as I stuck my head in through the open window. The washing machine was just below and I figured I'd be able to drop onto it in one swift, catlike manoeuvre. I climbed the last two rungs to the very top of the ladder and carefully swivelled my body sideways. I held onto the frame and angled one leg in through the open window. I shifted my weight so that I was now straddling my window sill. I fought the urge to throw my hand in the air and yell, "Ride 'em, cowgirl!" Instead, I cautiously balanced myself, pulling my other leg off the ladder and onto the sill.

Now I was facing my bathroom, looking down at the washing machine. It was a bigger jump than I had originally thought. I pulled off my heels and threw them down. They bounced off the tiles below. Dangling my bare feet over the washing machine, I tried to prepare myself mentally. I'd been for an attempted run this week so I was probably at my athletic best. Yes, it was a smallish surface area to aim for, but I was sure I wouldn't overshoot it. Pretty sure.

Crap. Better call Steph for emotional reassurance.

"Hey, it's me," I said after I'd fished my phone from my bra. I gripped the window sill tightly with one hand and pressed my phone to my ear with the other.

"It's early. I'm asleep," Steph said groggily.

"Yes, good point. Sorry. I'm… in a situation."

I could hear her sitting up in bed and Charlie groaning in protest.

"Are you still with that guy?" she whispered, as though he might hear her through the phone.

"No, I left. I'm… I'm on my window sill."

"Your window sill?" she exclaimed, sounding wide awake now.

"Correct."

"On the first floor of your building?"

"Also correct."

"Shit, Justine! I knew you were a bit down after Ben's baby but I had no idea you were so depressed. Please, don't jump! I'll come around right now!"

"No, you idiot! I'm not trying to get out, I'm trying to get in! I left my keys on the kitchen table and I don't have a spare."

Steph let out a relieved breath.

"Did you shimmy up the drain pipe?"

"No. I bought a ladder."

"Of course you did."

"I don't own any grappling hooks."

"You don't? You could have borrowed mine."

She'd clearly put me on speaker because I could hear Charlie in the background saying, "What is happening?! Why the hell are we awake and why are you talking about bloody grappling hooks?"

"Justine is thinking of moonlighting as a vigilante superhero."

"Actually, I can see her in full-body Lycra," came Charlie's muffled reply.

They both laughed.

"Listen, perverts, this is a very serious situation. I need you to pump me up. I have to make a jump."

"From your window sill?" Steph asked.

"Yes. Onto the washing machine."

"You can make that," she said doubtfully.

"That's it? That's your best encouraging speech? Does Charlie have anything to add?"

"He is laughing too hard to say anything."

"I know. I can hear him."

"There are actually tears coming out. The last time I saw him cry was when Hawthorn lost the Grand Final."

"Great. Well, the next call you get will probably be from the hospital."

"Am I your emergency contact?"

"Yes."

"Aww! I love that!"

"Yes, it's very sweet. Well, I better go. I can't sit on this sill forever."

"OK. Just out of curiosity, what are you wearing?"

"Last night's inspired ensemble. The mother of the guy I hooked up with fixed my skirt."

"Amazing. I'll let Charlie know when he's regained his composure. Good luck! Don't die!"

"I'll do my best! Bye!"

Right. That had been entirely unhelpful. I tucked my phone carefully back into my bra and shut my eyes.

No, you fool! Don't shut your eyes! You need them to aim yourself at the washing machine!

The only problem was, I had no idea how to aim myself. I was starting to psych myself out of jumping. Maybe I could make a nice home for myself up here, it was light and breezy and I'd have plenty of bird friends to come and visit.

NO! Just do it! Do it and I'll let you eat that piece of cake in the fridge! I'll even throw in some ice cream, just jump!

That did it. With a deep breath, I pushed away from the window sill. There was a massive thump as my bare feet hit the washing machine and I landed in a crouch on the white surface. For a minute I stayed in that position, shocked and a little impressed with myself for making such a cool landing. Maybe I *could* have a career in superhero-ing. But then, *OWWWWW!* My feet and ankles started to throb horribly. I stepped down tenderly onto the tiled floor and hobbled off towards the kitchen. I'd damn well earned that cake.

After spending the rest of Saturday and all of Sunday nursing not only a hangover, but two possibly fractured feet, I limped into work on Monday feeling like anything but facing 21 bouncy five-year olds.

When it was finally time for the staff meeting at the end of the day, my soul was all but broken from answering questions all day like, "When the moon has a cold, how does it blow its nose?" and "How many fingers does a caterpillar have?" Now I would be expected to coherently answer questions like "What kind of teaching tools do you use to ensure the highest possible outcomes for your students?" and unfortunately "Some felt, PVA glue and a shitload of glitter" was not an acceptable answer. I considered playing the silent, intelligent-nodding game, but the principal, Ruth, who took notes on who had contributed in staff meetings, was definitely aware that I'd said nothing of substance for the past three weeks.

The hour dragged as I attempted to participate enthusiastically but ended up just saying things like "Yes, I agree!" and "Good point!" to other people's ideas. I'd finally given up and tuned out completely when Ruth turned to me, lips pursed and pen poised over her list of staff names.

"Anything to offer, Justine?"

I panicked and blurted out "Assessment data", which was an acceptable answer to 95% of the questions posed in staff meetings, and then held my breath, awaiting her response.

"Excellent, Justine! This is exactly the kind of thinking we need, going forward."

She wrote something on her little list of doom and I imagined she was drawing a smiley face next to my name with the words "Very smart and attractive person". I quietly blew out the air I'd been holding. I'd dodged a bullet on that one. I was only on a year-by-year contract and was hoping to be offered an ongoing position at the school. Which would be important if I ever needed maternity leave. Which I hoped I would sometime before I turned 40.

Geez, I'm planning my maternity leave and I don't even have a boyfriend. I'd better reinstall that dating app.

I'd uninstalled it again after the last terrible date, but maybe if I only swiped right for the guys I really—

"...What do you say, Justine?"

Ruth was looking at me again. *Uh oh.* I was unlikely to fluke a correct answer twice.

Crap, what did she say?

I remembered in high school Psychology, I'd learnt about echoic memory—a brain function that helped you to recall something you'd heard three seconds ago, even if you weren't listening properly. Surely moments like this were the exact purpose for such a handy storage device.

Do your duty, echoic memory!

I waited. Nothing. I had no idea what she'd even been talking about.

"I say... yes. Yep, definitely. Really... just... yes."

She gave me an odd look but still didn't seem displeased.

"OK, great. Thank you. You'll need to be there at 8:30 on Saturday morning to set up. They've given me the name Lachlan as your contact, so ask for him if there are any problems.

Great to have that organised. Thank you everyone, remember…"

But I'd tuned out again, wondering what the hell I'd just surrendered my Saturday morning for.

CHAPTER SEVEN

I smoothed down the too-big apron and surveyed the barbeques.

"Is there a manual for these things?" I asked Ashleigh.

Ashleigh was a perpetually perky first-year teacher who looked like she actually made the most of her gym membership and who'd also been roped into this. Actually, she'd probably volunteered deliberately. She was frighteningly into the whole thing. She'd brought her own tongs.

"I have no idea! I've never done a fundraising barbeque before! How fun! I think they're supposed to be sending someone from the hardware store to show us what we're doing."

Ashleigh motioned to the giant, olive-green building behind us, and I had a flash of last week's early morning visit. Shaking the memory out of my head, I looked down at the barbie again and thought I could probably figure it out for myself. It looked like a push button to light it and dials to turn on the gas and set the temperature. Standard. But I decided that accidentally setting a colleague alight probably wouldn't be the kind of funny incident that you all laugh about at the end-of-year function. I moved away from the barbies and over to an off-balance trestle table, where I began tearing open red-netted bags of onions.

Around us, Hawthorn was busy working itself into a decent Saturday morning bustle. Luxury cars and four-wheel drives were crawling up and down Burwood Road, and people in active wear ducked into cafés, exiting minutes later with steaming coffee cups and crisp paper bags. I reflected sadly on how I hadn't known that this happened because I was rarely awake before 10 on a Saturday morning.

Stupid echoic memory. How could you have failed me like this?

My gaze was caught by a distinct green apron bobbing towards us and I recognised its wearer as the very same Hardware Ginger who'd accused me of being a stripper on the day of the Walk/Break-In Of Shame. Panicked that he might recognise me and mention our last meeting to Perky Ashleigh, I tried to look enthralled with the onions I was chopping.

"Hey there," Hardware Ginger said when he reached us. "I'm Lachlan. Lachie, if you like. I'm just going to show you how the barbies work."

"Oh hi!" Ashleigh perked. "I'm Ashleigh. I just have to, like, zip across the road and get some more bread. Can you show Justine here?"

I looked up to see Hardware Ginger push a copper curl away from his eyes.

"Suits me," he said. "Sound good to you, Justine?"

He was smiling at me in an overly familiar way, like we were sharing a personal joke. I quickly put my head down.

"Fine with me," I mumbled, staring hard at the little onion portions that wobbled on either side of my knife blade.

I love onions. Onions are amazing. I'm just staring at these onions because I love them!

I could feel my eyes beginning to water as I heard Hardware Ginger walk around behind me and stand at the barbies.

"So, you have to hold this button down, while you turn this dial to here and... that's it. Got it?"

"Yep, got it! Thanks!"

I could feel him staring at me. My eyes stung and tears threatened to spill down my face.

"Uh, you didn't even look."

The friendly tone was gone and he sounded genuinely annoyed.

"I know it's easy to figure out, but it's my ass on the line if you burn down the marquee so can you just show those onions some mercy and give me your full attention for one minute?"

I tore my eyes away from the treacherous onions and as I did, the tears saw their opportunity. Two or three drops made a break for my jawline as I looked around at him. Hardware Ginger was still staring at me, but it was difficult to tell if it was a look of recognition on his face or sheer surprise at the downpour. He pulled a cleaning cloth from his apron and offered it to me.

"Here, it's clean. Dab, don't rub. Rubbing will make it worse."

"I know that!"

I didn't know that.

I snatched the cloth from his hand and dabbed furiously at my burning eyes.

"Hold what and turn what?" I mumbled.

Hardware Ginger showed me how to turn the barbie on. It was exactly as I'd suspected. He turned it off again.

"Can you do it now, please? Just so I know that you have got it?"

"This seems unnecessary," I grumbled at him, making deliberately dramatic gestures while turning and pressing. "Why can't you just turn it on and leave it on?"

"Because if I don't show you how to use it and it goes out, then you'll have to come and drag me away from work to do it again for you. And it will go out, mate. They always do."

He turned around and walked away, leaving me with his cleaning cloth balled up in one fist.

Nice one. Great start to the morning.

Cooking sausages actually had quite a calming effect on my mood. It was a warm, windy day and stray blossoms danced up off the car park bitumen, circling our steady flow of customers. My hair waved and flapped around my face as I tonged hot, greasy meat into cheap white bread and let Ashleigh make small talk with the sausage-seekers. The barbie did go out several times, but it was easy to reignite and the time passed quickly in a blur of sweat, sauce and sizzle.

Before I knew it, it was early afternoon and we were being replaced by a couple of our reluctant colleagues, two older women named Ange and Jan, who rolled their eyes as we passed over the tongs (I passed over the school-issued, rust-ridden ones; Ashleigh carefully wrapped her personal ones and placed them back in her bag). I was untying my apron and contemplating an afternoon nap when I noticed a glint of red heading our way.

"I've come to make my donation to East Melbourne Primary School," Hardware Ginger said as he passed me a couple of gold coins over the trestle table.

"You want a sausage?"

I was surprised to see him back again, let alone to be accepting his charitable offering.

"With onions, please. I watched you chopping them in a murderous rage and I don't want their suffering to be for nothing."

I accepted the tongs back from a nosy-looking Ange and retrieved a sausage for him, plopping it unceremoniously into some bread and adding an overly generous helping of onions.

"Sauce?" I asked.

Hardware Ginger nodded so I pumped out a line of sauce and passed the sausage over to him.

"This one's been on the ground, right?" he asked as he took a large bite.

"Don't worry, I cleaned it with this."

I produced his cleaning cloth from my back pocket.

"Dab, don't rub."

I mimed dabbing at a sausage in bread to illustrate my point. To my surprise, Hardware Ginger burst out laughing, sending bits of chewed meat and bread in my general direction. He immediately looked appalled with himself.

"Shit, sorry mate, that's... that was an accident. You just... you made me laugh."

"And paid the price." I answered, but I felt myself smile as I brushed a bit of soggy sausage off my shirt.

"Well, I can't afford to buy you another shirt." Hardware Ginger cupped his hand around his mouth conspiratorially and whispered loudly, "They don't pay a hardware lackey as much as you'd think."

I raised my eyebrows in mock surprise as he continued.

"But the least I could do is buy another sausage. Here."

Hardware Ginger dropped another couple of coins into my palm. I picked up another sausage with the tongs and attempted to drop it into a piece of bread, but somehow missed. I threw my empty hand out as a reflex and caught the snag before it hit the ground. It was hot, really hot, and I flung it back into the air with an exclamation of "Shit! Anus! AH! Balls!" It was at about "Balls!" that the sausage hit the ground with a fatal flop and for a minute we both just stared at it.

"Well," Hardware Ginger broke the silence. "That one was just a polite sausage anyway, I was pretty full up from all the onions on the first one. Better get back to work. Catch ya, mate."

He went to leave but turned around again, his curls flicking up with the sudden movement.

"I have to say though, I wouldn't have expected such colourful language from a teacher... or an officer of the law."

He walked away, leaving me open-mouthed with an empty piece of bread in my hand.

I answered my phone as I jumped onto the tram, dressed in black jeans, black boots and my black-and-white Collingwood guernsey.

"Hey Dad. I'm twenty minutes away."

"Great, I'm nearly at the ground. See you at the gate."

I sat down, buzzing with excitement. The game was set to be a thriller, with the two top teams, also arch rivals, battling it out under the gigantic triangles of white light at the MCG. It was a knockout match, so it was our last chance to make it into the Grand Final. It had also been a while since I'd seen my father, even though my parents lived only an hour away in my hometown of Geelong.

When I got to the ground, I followed the stream of people flowing towards Gate 6. Dad was there, reading a newspaper, with his little wheelie bag at his feet. I knew exactly what would be in that bag: radio, thermos of tea, peppermint chocolate bar and four jackets in addition to the one he was wearing. I was wearing my Spanx again, not for the sake of my figure but for extra warmth. The MCG was often freezing at night, regardless of the season.

Dad looked up, saw me and put down his paper. He wrapped me in a strong, warm hug that smelled like aftershave and mint. For some reason, I didn't want to let him go. It was like I always had to keep it together and be an adult until I saw my parents, and then there was this immediate sense of relief, like I could be a vulnerable kid again. Dad pulled back but kept his arms around me.

"Hey, is everything OK?"

I felt a bit teary but I couldn't really explain it to him.

"I just miss you, Dad."

Why can't every man I meet be as nice as my Dad?

"I miss you too, darl. Excited for tonight?"

I nodded eagerly and he put his arm around me as we walked towards the gate.

"I remember doing this with you for the first time when you were just five. I can't believe you come up to my shoulder now."

"I remember too."

I remembered reaching up for his hand as I struggled along in the heaving mass of people and the feeling of his strong grip keeping me upright. I remembered feeling desperately proud to be by his side. I turned to look at Dad. He seemed shorter now, but his grip was just as strong.

We took our seats and the siren sounded once, twice. The umpire bounced the ball and nervous energy rose in my stomach as the tiny red oval spun into the air. For a minute, everything was silent, then the ball descended to meet a hard punch from an opposition player. The crowd erupted.

"So, what's news—ARE YOU KIDDING ME, UMPIRE?" Dad asked, breaking his chocolate bar and offering me half without taking his eyes off the game. I accepted it and ground the shards of peppermint between my teeth anxiously.

"Not much. I worked at a sausage sizzle for school and—BALL!"

Flecks of chocolate flew from my mouth as we both threw our arms out in frustration, as though the umpire might look up, think "Good point, completely biased crowd members," and call Holding the Ball. Half the crowd exploded in anger after this failed to happen.

"Good on you. Did you use the old Hertz Family method of cooking the sausages?"

"Two minutes on high heat, then medium for 10. Sure did. OH, FOR GOD'S SAKE, KICK IT!"

"Great. STOP MESSING AROUND! Mum said you mentioned on the phone that Ben had a baby."

I waited for the black-and-white-clad player to wipe sweat from his forehead and then break into a run towards the goals. He dropped the ball expertly, with a powerful kick aimed between the two middle posts. The ball spun straight into the right post, bouncing back onto the ground. Dad and I sighed. A point.

"Yeah, he did."

The clock ticked on as the ball was punched, kicked and fumbled up and down the ground. We both just watched the action for a while until Dad spoke again.

"Darl—GET RID OF IT!—we liked Ben enough in the beginning. And I know you two had your difficulties—HE HASN'T GOT IT!—no one's perfect." He turned to look at me. "But I didn't say this at the time and I should have: you deserved so much better than what that bloody idiot did to you."

I leaned forward, my palms on my knees as an opposition player kicked towards goal.

"You have to say that, because you're my Dad."

The ball sailed between the middle posts, as one of our players jumped up to tap it.

"TOUCHED!" we all screamed as we jumped up.

"No Justine, any decent person would say the same. He was a coward. You deserve someone who will stick it out, even when things are tricky."

The umpire held out two pointed fingers. A goal. Dad and I both sat back in our seats.

"I got locked out of the house the other day," I said. "No spare keys. GO! GO!"

"Really? What did you do? GO!"

"Bought a ladder and broke in."

The ball spun through our goals just as the siren went for quarter time. We both stood up, waving our arms and cheering.

"I'm so proud of you," Dad said and hugged me.

On the tram home, after a disappointing loss, I unfriended Ben

October

CHAPTER EIGHT

I could be a multitasking champion when I was motivated. For example, on Sunday morning I was watching a reality dating show, straightening my hair and making an amazing new playlist while waiting for Steph and some of the other girls to arrive for a late brunch. Technically, it was really lunch. But we called it late brunch because it sounded more sophisticated.

The chiselled, muscular, manscaped "Regular Aussie Guy" on TV was strolling along the beach, looking out at the horizon. I spent most of my time watching the show (every week) trying to justify to myself why I was watching it. Clearly, any program which features a guy saying something like, "I'm just going to follow my dreams and enjoy the journey my heart takes me on" is anything but reality. I would be far more convinced if he said, "Yeah, nah, let's check 'em out and see what happens. Should be a bit of fun, eh?"

There was a knock on my door. Weird. Steph usually delighted in the opportunity to buzz and say something inappropriate into the intercom. Someone must have let her in downstairs on their way out.

I grabbed the stray section of hair I was about to straighten and held it over my upper lip like a moustache.

"Hellooo there!" I exclaimed as I flung open the door.

It was Dan. Standing there. Staring at my moustache. The moustache drooped but it was another second before I had the presence of mind to drop it completely.

"This could be the most important moment of my life, the chance to find my soulmate…" came the helpful addition from the bronzed bachelor on TV.

"Oh, hi Dan. I wasn't expecting it to be you. Sorry."

The sides of his mouth twitched as he said, "You should be sorry. Now I'll expect a greeting like that every time I knock on your door."

HOORAH! He's going to knock again! Maybe we can develop a secret knock. And get walkie talkies. And solve mysteries. SHUT UP AND SAY SOMETHING CLEVER!

"OK. Sure."

Nice one. So clever. Points for not mentioning the walkie talkies.

"Anyway, just returning these. I found them on my car windscreen about a week ago. Sorry, I've been meaning to get them back to you, I've just been busy. It was pretty windy on the day I found them and I think they blew off the line. Unless you planted them there."

I followed his gaze down to the offending black material swinging from his index finger. There was a flash of hot pink lettering.

Oh God, oh God, oh no, oh God.

I grabbed the underwear and balled it up, feeling as though the "Punish Me" insignia was branding my palm.

"Ha ha ha ha ha! Ha, no. I didn't plant them. Probably should have buried them, actually."

Dan smiled a full smile, with those amazing teeth.

"I don't know about that. I wouldn't mind seeing them again," he said.

And with that, he did that run-jump down the stairs that really physically confident guys do because they know there's no chance they'll catch a toe on a step and end up riding their own face the rest of the way down.

I was still leaning against the doorframe when Steph's blonde-streaked head bobbed into view. She looked up at me.

"Well, this is a surprisingly sombre reception. I expected you to open the door doing something silly. Wait a minute, is that your underwear you're clutching lovingly to your chest?"

The late brunch went well into the afternoon. The other two girls, Meghan and Lana, both had kids, so we rarely had the chance to catch up properly. They were eager to be filled in on all my recent dating failures and, in return, they told several amusing(ish) anecdotes about their kids.

As I let myself back into my apartment building, I was eagerly anticipating a nap before tackling schoolwork, when my elderly Russian neighbour, Anastasia, sprung from her doorway and nearly knocked me into the wall.

Geez, she is spritely for an old woman.

It really wouldn't have surprised me if she had been sitting at her peephole, waiting for someone to walk by so she could jump them. Although, who was I to judge? If I'd made use of my own peephole, it would have saved me some embarrassment in regards to the moustache incident.

"Justine. Neighbourhood party. You come."

She waved a flyer at me. I had seen it taped to the building door. In fact, I'd read it and thought, *On a Friday night? No way. I have better things to do.*

"Oh, I saw something about it."

I realised I had no idea what date it was supposed to be, so couldn't specifically come up with an excuse not to go.

"I think that, um, I might have, um… I'm doing some... um."

Anastasia just shook her head at me.

"Is next Friday. You come. You bring something."

It was always difficult to tell if she was requesting or commanding.

Just say "No" Justine! You can do it, I know you can!

"OK, yes. Um, alright, yes. I can do that… I think. Yes."

"Housemate come too. You ask."

"I will ask her. Do you know… um… is anyone else from our building coming?"

"They all come."

I found that hard to believe but didn't dare contradict her. I smiled, waved and escaped up the stairs as Anastasia shuffled back into her apartment to wait for her next unsuspecting victim.

The week passed uneventfully, except for the bit on Wednesday where I took my students on an excursion to the open range zoo and one of them had managed to escape from a moving safari bus because she wanted to "pat a rhino". If I hadn't been so petrified of parental retribution, I would have been a little impressed.

On Thursday afternoon, I walked into my apartment where my housemate, Ellie, was ironing her scrubs in her underwear with steam rising in puffs around her attractive features. She could be in a catalogue, advertising irons. Or scrubs. Or steam. Whatever it was, people would buy it. She was the sister of an acquaintance and had moved in about a year ago. We were friendly, but not really friends. It wasn't just the different work hours, I didn't really feel comfortable being myself around her. She was one of those people who had their life together in all the ways I didn't and I got the impression she found me silly. Which was probably an accurate observation.

"Oh hey, Ellie. Are you coming to the Neighbourhood Party tomorrow? Anastasia wanted me to ask you."

"Who's Anastasia?" she asked. "And no, I don't finish till 1am. I doubt the respectable Liberal voters will party on that late."

"They're not all Liberal voters."

"We live in a *very* safe seat. They're mostly Liberal voters."

To avoid getting into an intense political debate, partly because I was too tired and partly because I knew nothing about politics, I rummaged around in the cupboard under the sink for a mixing bowl. I popped up with it in my arms.

"I'm really only going because Anastasia… she's the old Russian woman from downstairs… strong-armed me into it. I said I'd make cupcakes."

"You're too nice."

I sighed.

"I know. I'll save you one."

"No thanks," she said. "I'm doing Sugar-Free September."

That sounds like the worst thing I've ever heard of.

"But it's October."

"I know. I decided to extend it because I felt so cleansed."

I smiled as encouragingly as I could manage and began to gather ingredients. Ellie finished her ironing and went off to her room. I opened the fridge door, which was heavily burdened with wedding invites and baby pictures, and sighed again. I already knew there was no butter in there. No matter how organised I tried to be, I was always short one ingredient. Luckily the shops were only a five-minute walk from our place and I didn't mind the idea of a stroll in the sunshine.

I was on my way downstairs just as Dan was coming out of his apartment, dressed in skins and a footy guernsey. Footy season was over, but there were still social clubs playing matches around our area. The St James Park oval was so close, you could hear the whistles and shouts from our apartment.

"Hey, Justine," Dan said. "How's it going?"

"Good. Just… off to get some butter."

Nice one. Great banter. Now he will remember me as Butter Girl. Although, that would probably be better than Moustache Girl. Or Underwear Girl… Butter Girl it is!

"Oh, cool."

I desperately wanted to ask him about the party, while still seeming nonchalant. Maybe I could just take a leaf out of Anastasia's book.

You come to party. You bring something. You marry me.

As Dan glanced toward the building door, I remembered the flyer.

"Hey, are you and your housemate coming to that Neighbourhood Party thing?" I, Butter Girl, asked casually, motioning towards the flyer as we both began to walk towards it.

Good Justine! Stroke of genius asking about his housemate too. Very aloof. Nice one!

"My mate moved out. I'm between housemates at the moment."

"Oh, OK. Are you looking for someone else, or…?"

Oh geez, did it sound like I was offering myself?

It's all gone wrong! Abort conversation, abort!

"Nah, I don't mind living alone. And I own it so I'm only paying the mortgage, not rent."

"Nice one. Well…"

I couldn't ask him about the party again. It was already obvious enough that I'd asked once and he'd more or less changed the subject. *Shit.*

"Well, I guess I'll see you round then. Again. Sometime." I shrugged at him.

Really smooth, Butter Girl.

"Yeah. I have to work late Friday and then I've got work drinks—boss's orders. But I might drop by the party afterwards if it's still raging. Anastasia promised me her dumplings."

Of course she did. I wish I could promise him my dumplings.

After icing the cupcakes, I slumped dramatically onto the couch. I felt inordinately disappointed about Dan's non-committal response to the party. It wasn't as though a street gathering of mostly senior citizens was ever going to be the ideal place to pick up, but it might have meant a little more time getting to know him. And I wanted there to be a good reason I'd agreed to spend my Friday night there. Now it would just be me and the Liberal voters.

Bugger.

Out of frustration, I reinstalled my dating app. I swiped back and forth for about fifteen minutes, barely registering the faces that fell victim to my ruthless thumb.

Yes. No. No. No. God no. Yes. No. God yes. No.

I suddenly realised the face I was about to swipe *No* to was, in fact, Hardware Ginger. I couldn't believe it. *Lachie, 29.* His first profile pic was him wearing a suit, at a wedding or something, and smiling with his arm around someone who'd been cropped out. I couldn't tell if it was a guy or a girl. It could have even been a large upstanding dog. The next photo was him with a nice-looking woman in her fifties, probably his Mum. Hmmm, interestingly played Hardware Ginger. Some women would definitely think "Awww, he loves his Mum, that's a yes from me!" Some would definitely be turned off by the Mummy's Boy vibe. I didn't know what I thought. She could have been his last girlfriend, for all I knew. The third photo was of him on a skateboard with a grey-and-white kitten draped around his neck like a scarf. Hmmmm.

I shrugged, purely for my own benefit, and swiped. *Yes.* Why not? It was unlikely that he'd do the same for me anyway. I hadn't made any attempts to charm him during either of our meetings. Regardless, I felt quite nervous about it. It was a lot easier to swipe *Yes* to strangers than someone you'd actually met before.

Suddenly, a full-screen notification informed me that I'd matched with "Lachie". My hair felt sweaty against my neck and my heart was pumping forcefully against my ribcage. I didn't really understand it. I wasn't interested in him. Our meetings had been civilised at best, and there certainly hadn't been a spark. Mostly just arguing. I wasn't going to message him. I'd just leave it.

Lachie: If you were a celebrity, what would your rider be?

He'd messaged me straight away. Most guys waited a little while. Or didn't message at all. One night I'd gotten drunk at home and messaged 20 guys that I'd matched with. I'd only heard back from two of them.

Justine: You can ride celebrities now? This is great news. I'm off to purchase a saddle.
Lachie: Do you know what a rider is?

I quickly searched "What is a celebrity rider?" Immediately the answer popped up: "A list of requirements that an entertainer expects for a performance." Now I knew what he meant, I just hadn't known it was called a "rider". I vaguely remembered reading that Mariah Carey had requested 20 white kittens and 100 white doves for her dressing room. I'd spent a lot of time trying to imagine a scenario that didn't end in 20 white kittens chowing down on five white doves each for dinner.

Justine: Of course I do. I was just being witty. It's a set of requests a performer demands before a performance.
Lachie: Just searched it, hey?
Justine: OK, here's my rider: a quality brie cheese, just at room temperature so it's a little bit melty but not yet in wet blob territory... and a six pack of orange fruit boxes.
Lachie: Hahaha. You started off well, but fruit boxes? That's not very extravagant. What if you're a huge star? You can have anything.
Justine: Benedict Cumberbatch.
Lachie: What?
Justine: The brie, the fruit boxes and Benedict Cumberbatch. Just leave him over by the window.
Lachie: OK, good rider. He is the thinking woman's crumpet, I've heard.

Justine: Just searched him, hey? Oh, and glow in the dark stars.

I typed the last part on a whim.

Lachie: Really? That's a good one. Why?

Justine: I had them on my ceiling when I was a kid. They used to cheer me up when I was sad. Anyway, you've obviously thought about this. What's yours?

Lachie: You can't just ask me the same question back, you have to be original and come up with your own question.

I thought for a minute.

Justine: OK then. You die and God says you can be reincarnated as any animal you choose. What animal would it be? You have to give good reasons.

Lachie: I think you've mixed up a few religions there.

Justine: I'm being original.

Lachie: Get ready... A mantis shrimp.

Justine: What is that? I can't be bothered searching it.

Lachie: Only the most badass creature on Earth. They're kind of like crabs. They have these claw things, but they don't do puny little nips with them, they punch with them! Their punch is faster than a bullet. I've read stories where restaurants put mantis shrimps in their aquariums, planning to serve them up, and they've just punched the glass and shattered it! Haha!

Lachie: Also, they have a secret code.

Lachie: Also, they growl.

Justine: OK, wow.

Lachie: I know! Intense, huh? But they're sweet too. They're monogamous and can spend 20 years together.

Justine: You know a lot about mantis shrimp.

Lachie: I just like cool facts.

We messaged back and forth for about an hour, mostly jokes, until I realised it was 11pm and I needed to go into work early to set up in the morning. I could see that Lachie was writing something so I waited before signing off. And waited. He appeared to be writing an essay. Then the little icon that told me he was writing disappeared. Maybe he'd deleted it?

Then:

Lachie: So, I could give you a skateboarding lesson, if you like?

OK. Um. OK.

I had never even stood on a skateboard but I guessed that would be the point of a lesson—to teach me how to stand on it and also potentially how to move it around a bit. I considered his proposal. Although we hadn't exactly clicked during our first few meetings, this conversation had flowed comfortably and he'd even made me laugh out loud a few times. Anyway, why not? It's not like I had anything else going on.

Justine: Sure.
Lachie: Great, I'll borrow a board from a mate and you can use mine. St James Park, Saturday arvo?
Justine: Sounds good.
Lachie: Righto. Catch ya then.

And he was offline. How curious.

CHAPTER NINE

At about 7pm on Friday, I changed into a white shirt and tight jeans, grabbed my cupcake carrier and headed to the church hall at the end of my street where the Neighbourhood Party was being held. My sandals clapped against the cobblestones that lined the road as I passed the milk bar that always seemed to be open, and the bowling club that was usually rowdy with eighty-year olds on a Saturday afternoon and rowdy with twenty-year olds on a Sunday afternoon.

Up ahead, I spotted a small crowd. As I got closer, I could see the street had actually been shut off at this end and there were some kids crowded around a giant block tower, trying to pull pieces out and screaming and laughing as it wobbled precariously. Someone had even forked out for a fairy floss machine.

I reached the gathering and lined up behind several small children waiting to receive some fluffy sugar on a stick from a woman whose grey hair resembled the fairy floss she was spinning.

"For your little one, is it dear?" she asked as she passed me the stick.

I stopped the hand holding the fairy floss on its trajectory towards my mouth.

"Ah yes. It's… she's… over there."

I waved in the direction of a group of families.

"Oh, lovely. How old?"

This was becoming more effort than it was worth. How old was my made up child likely to be?

"Oh, just turned one."

The woman frowned a little.

"One? Oh, I'm not sure that's a good thing to be giving a one-year old."

I was miffed that she was judging my parenting until I remembered that my child was imaginary. I forced a smile and decided to make my getaway.

"Well, she'll probably be getting hungry for her dinner by now, I best go!"

Her brow dipped in deep concern as I turned my back and walked up the stone stairs, through the red brick arch doorway and into the hall. With my luck I'd probably have Child Services knocking on my door tomorrow and insisting I produce a malnourished one-year old. I bit at the cottony strands of fairy floss and felt immediately disappointed. Why had I loved it so much as a kid? It was like eating a sweet beard. I threw the ball of sticky fluff into a nearby bin and headed over to where Anastasia was chatting with the Vietnamese couple from across the hall.

As I half-paid attention to the conversation, I kept flicking my gaze to the hall door, hoping to see Dan standing there, but no one under the age of forty had entered since me. They all probably had fun plans for a Friday night. Or knew how to say "No" to things they didn't want to do.

After forty-five minutes, I felt I'd exhausted all the small talk I could with the people I already knew from the street, and could muster little interest in meeting anyone new. I decided to sneak away stealthily while Anastasia had her back turned.

I amused myself greatly by doing exaggerated tip-toeing out of the hall and was starting to creep down the stone steps when I heard a soft, masculine "Hey."

I looked up mid-creep to see Dan at the bottom of the steps. Even from this distance, the scent of his cologne mixed with alcohol wafted up the stairs and into my nostrils. He was dressed in a navy suit and an open-collared white shirt, with shiny brown shoes and a matching belt. His blue eyes were darkened by dusk, but still distinct in the lingering grey light. He looked behind me to scan the gathering in the hall and, clearly satisfied that he hadn't been noticed by anyone yet, put a finger to his lips and held out his hand to me.

I'd like to claim that I played it cool by hesitating and at least making it look like I was weighing up my options, but my hand was in Dan's before I even knew I'd moved. He led me through the shadows towards home and I was aware only of the heat of his palm against mine and the sound of his shoes on the cobblestones until he was turning the handle of our building door.

What is going on here? Is there a fire and he's an experienced fire warden? Maybe he's leading people out of danger one by one?

I searched for some explanation other than what appeared to be happening and came up with none. So, there was either an unlikely fire threat or… we were going to hook up.

Wait, which apartment are we going to? His or mine? Is he going to ask me?

114

I realised I should have an answer ready, just in case.

DO NOT SUGGEST ROCK, PAPER, SCISSORS, WHATEVER YOU DO!

I may not have been a dating expert, but I knew that no impassioned romantic tryst began with a game of rock, paper, scissors. As I was still bumbling around in my brain, Dan stopped at his door and unlocked it. He was really good at unlocking his door. I always took about three attempts to unlock mine and there were scratches all around the lock to prove it. Dan did it in one swift motion, like he'd been unlocking doors his whole life.

Oh please God, don't let me accidentally compliment him on his door unlocking skills!

It was weird walking into his apartment. It looked exactly like mine, except a boy lived here. Empty protein shakers sat on the bench, a bike was propped against one wall and a TV that looked like it could eat mine was hooked up to a gaming console with bright green game cases stacked on top. I thought we might stop and have a drink or something, but Dan kept a hold of my hand and continued to lead me down the hall and into one of the bedrooms. His, I presumed. It would be a bit weird if he led me into the spare bedroom. No, it was definitely his, there was a photo wall full of pictures of him above the desk. Him and his mates, him and a big, black, slobbering dog, him and his parents, him and girls—*a lot* of him and girls.

Dan finally released my hand and flicked on a desk lamp beside the bed. He put his phone down beside a cuboid speaker and tapped it. Slow, cruisy music floated around the room as Dan returned to where I was still standing by the wall next to the door. He took both my hands in his and then raised them above my head. He ran his hands from my fingertips to my hips, then back up again, via my breasts, and cupped my face, bringing my lips to his so softly I barely felt it.

"What about Anastasia's dumplings?" I murmured.

Who gave you permission to speak, mouth?!

It certainly wasn't my brain, my brain was preoccupied with all the places I wanted to touch Dan. He smiled, my face still in his hands, and stroked my bottom lip with his thumb.

"I can think of other things I'd like to taste right now. But if you want to go back to the party…?"

He moved one hand down to the button at the neck of my shirt and looked right into my eyes.

"No thanks, I had a dumpling. Keep doing what you're doing there."

I licked the tip of the thumb that still grazed my lips, then sucked it gently. Dan smiled *that* smile, then released the button with two fingers. He moved down to the one underneath and undid it too.

Is this really happening? Yes, it is! It is! DO IT!

The third button gave way easily where it strained across my chest and I barely noticed the last two following suit. He was as good at unbuttoning shirts as he was at unlocking doors. He must have excellent fine motor skills.

116

Stop thinking things! JUST DO THINGS!

Dan's hands were flames burning their way across the skin of my stomach and around to my back as he pulled me against him, his mouth soft and strong at the same time as our lips met again. His tongue slid slowly across mine. It occurred to me that I was actually allowed to take his clothes off in real life, not just in my mind, and the thought almost made my knees buckle beneath me.

I pushed Dan's suit jacket over his shoulders and he stepped back to unbutton his own shirt. I felt the air on my bare collarbone as I took a few necessary deep breaths. Dan smiled again as he pulled off his shirt and folded it neatly over his desk chair.

"What are you doing in a suit?" I asked, grabbing his belt buckle and pulling him closer again.

"I'm an accountant."

He kissed my neck.

"You are?! I thought you worked at a gym."

He kissed my shoulder as my shirt slipped to the floor.

"Ha ha! I wish! I just like to work out a lot."

I stopped myself from saying something cheesy like "I can see that", but I couldn't help but stare at the tanned ripple of muscle across his stomach, as well as the enticing bulges of his man chest and triceps and biceps and other bits that I didn't learn the name of properly in Year 12 Biology but appreciated regardless.

"Are you drunk?" my mouth inquired, before I could stop it.

"Not really. I know exactly what I'm doing, if that's what you're asking."

And with that I decided it was time to put my mouth to better use, before it could ask any more questions and ruin everything.

We were lying side by side, facing each other.

"I've wanted to do this ever since I saw you straddling that mower catcher," Dan said, running his hand softly from my clavicle down to my hip, brushing my nipple on his merry way.

"There's nothing sexier than a mower catcher," I replied shakily, feeling drunk myself.

He laughed and rolled me over so that I was on top of him. He slapped the right side of my ass lightly, and then grabbed both cheeks in his hands, pulling me down onto him. I looked down at Dan's soft eyes and chiselled jaw, and I felt crazy with lust. I placed my hands on his chest and moved with him, wondering if it would be possible to do this forever.

Afterwards, we lay side by side again, catching our breath. Before I could start to worry about what would happen next and whether Dan expected me to gather my clothes and head upstairs straight away, he gently turned me to face the wardrobe and put his arm around me, with my ass fitting perfectly into his crotch space and his legs intertwined with mine.

He's a cuddler!

The night had been surreal to say the least and for the first time I had a minute to think about what had just happened. My whole body throbbed with the excitement and shock of it. While I was wondering how I would ever get to sleep, my superpower enveloped me mid-thought.

I slept surprisingly well, considering I had Dan's perfect, naked body stretched out beside me. In my confused waking state, I actually thought I was in my own room, given that I was vaguely aware of the identical layout. But slowly, in burning, delicious pieces, the details of the previous night came back to me. It was like waking from an amazing sex dream.

Shutting my eyes again, I enjoyed the memories, until reality started to poke at me and I realised I was about to be forced to navigate the awkward Morning After A Hook-Up Situation.

Do I get up, get dressed, offer a polite "Thank you very much for everything" and pop my non-existent business card into his palm during a farewell handshake?

Oh no, now that the thought had crossed my mind, I was definitely accidentally going to try to shake his hand while leaving.

Don't do that. Plan something else now, instead!

I could just kowtow out.

Brilliant.

I felt Dan get out of bed and opened my eyes to see him pulling on running shorts and the kind of expensive exercise top that claims to turn your sweat into fairy dust and dispense it back into your bloodstream to increase physical performance.

"Going for a run?" I asked, stretching and feeling sore in pleasing places.

"Brunch, actually, with some friends. But I'll head to the gym after. Here."

He passed me my bra and shirt and I wriggled into them while the rest of me was still concealed under the grey doona.

"I don't know where your underwear went."

"Oh. Ah… It's probably found its way onto your car windscreen."

Dan laughed and grabbed the end of the doona.

"Maybe it's under here!"

He parachuted the doona high into the air, leaving me exposed to the elements… and his gaze.

"You know, I don't have to go to brunch right away," Dan said, his eyes narrowing.

Before I knew it, he had prowled back on top of me and my arms were around his neck.

Oh yes.

My underwear turned up, squashed into the end of the bed, and I dressed slowly, buying time to figure out what to say or do next. I wanted to seem cool and relaxed, but I also really really wanted to see Dan again. And not just in a passing-in-the-hallway kind of way.

"Well, I'd better head off," I said.

"Yeah, I should be going too," he replied.

We walked through his living room and down the hall. We stopped in front of his door. I put my hand on the doorknob, but just as I was about to turn it, there was a knock. I panicked but Dan didn't look worried. I reminded myself that this wasn't exactly a rare situation for him. The supermodel materialised into my mind but I mentally batted her away. Dan looked through his peephole.

Does everyone do that except me?

"Hang on a minute, Anastasia," he called, looking at me with his eyebrows raised.

I cringed, shook my head and stepped behind the door. Dan shrugged and opened it.

"Daneelko," I heard her say from my cosy new hangout. "You very busy last night."

Is she asking him? Telling him? Who knows? What does she mean "busy"? Getting busy? How does she know? Did she hear us?!

"Yes, I'm sorry I didn't make it. You know I was craving those dumplings."

She giggled. *Giggled!*

"Of course I save you some. Here. Heat in micro-oven. Forty seconds."

"You're an angel, Anastasia."

There was a pause during which I was convinced she was patting his cheek.

"How are Maria and Ivan?"

Oh great, Dan was making conversation while I was flat against the wall with his door crushing my boobs and nose.

"They do very well. Very good grades at school. Their mother let them play Australian football this year. I think too dangerous."

"Well, I've been playing all my life and I still have all my important parts."

Even I almost giggled that time.

"I see you soon, Daneelko."

"I look forward to it, Anastasia."

Great, so she'd managed a warm, unawkward goodbye.

Maybe I'll ask her for tips sometime.

Dan shut the door and I saw he was holding a plastic container full of dumplings.

"I don't suppose you'd think about sharing those?" I asked, emerging from my hiding place.

"Not even if you offered me more sex."

He flashed me a smile over the refrigerator door as he placed them inside.

"I've never considered prostituting myself for food items," I said, somewhat thoughtfully.

"There's a first time for everything," he replied.

Then he came over, kissed me on the cheek and said, "See ya", before opening the door. I followed him into the stairwell and we parted, me heading up the stairs, and him out into the perfect Melbourne morning.

I was sitting at my kitchen table eating breakfast when Ellie walked out of her bedroom, rubbing her eyes like a cartoon bear waking from hibernation. She had dark smudges underneath her lower lashes and her usually perfect blonde hair was sticking up on one side.

"Rough one last night?" I asked, my mouth half-filled with cornflakes.

I was *starving* after last night. I'd take a sex workout over the gym any day.

"I got home after my shift and Dan was still at it with some chick," Ellie said, flopping onto the couch.

"*Oh!* Oh. Was he?"

"Oh yeah. Then again this morning. When does that guy sleep? At least this one wasn't a screamer."

I pretended to be really interested in the size and shape of my cornflakes.

"Hmmm, that's good."

"She *was* a moaner though."

I was too scared to look up in case she read "It's me! I'm the moaner!" all over my face.

"Well, at least she had a good time," I said with an attempt at a laugh.

"Oh, she was faking it, for sure."

That startled me.

"Wait, what? How could you tell?"

"Oh, you can always tell," was all Ellie said with a laugh, before she disappeared back down the hall, leaving me with my mouth open and cornflakes dripping out of it.

I'm just waiting near the war memorial, flashed up the text from Lachie on my phone.

Oh shit, it was 1.05pm. I'd totally forgotten about our date. Luckily St James Park was minutes from my place and I hadn't planned anything else for the afternoon except enjoying flashbacks from last night. I threw on my black biker jacket and, out of habit, checked myself out in the bathroom mirror.

Geez, I look like I hardly slept last night.

Which was accurate. But I'd fancied I might be affecting the kind of attractive after-sex glow I'd seen on the supermodel after she left Dan's apartment. That particular memory made me wince, which accentuated the smears of blue-grey under my eyes, along with the deep lines across my forehead, and made me look like a grumpy gremlin. Oh well, no time for makeup, he'd have to take me as I was. Or not take me. I'd already been well and truly taken last night. Maybe I was no longer up for the taking.

Oooh, no. Don't do that. Don't jump ahead to the wedding and babies. It was just one hook-up... So far.

St James Park was a large block of lawn which sprouted English Oak and River Red Gum trees alongside quaint street lanterns. It was split down the middle by colourful garden beds and encircled by a paved track. There was an oval at one end where cricket was played in the summer and footy in the winter, and a war memorial and playground at the other. The park was frequented by fitness groups, professionals on their lunch breaks and tidy-ponytailed mums simultaneously steering prams and sipping lattes.

When I arrived, Lachie was sitting at the top of the grey granite steps leading up to the war memorial, resting his chin between the two skateboards that he held in front of him. He was dressed in a white t-shirt with a blue denim shirt over the top, black jeans and skate shoes. It was weird seeing him without the green apron.

"Hey, Mantis Shrimp!" I yelled.

Lachie's head jerked up and somehow both skateboards went rogue, clattering down the steps and rolling leisurely along the track in opposite directions. Lachie went after one of them, so I stooped to retrieve the other, which was heading towards me anyway. Lachie stepped onto his board while it was still moving and, with a graceful pivot and a few pushes of his foot, wove his way back to me.

"Sorry about that. Ready for your lesson... What do I call you? Officer Sexy? Just Officer? Ma'am?"

"I'm not currently on duty. You can call me Justine," I said as I suspiciously eyed the skateboard I was holding.

The whole idea had originally seemed cool and spontaneous, but now I was having second thoughts. I carefully placed the board on the ground and put one foot on it. It sprung away and continued off down the path.

"I think I've made a mistake," I told Lachie as we walked towards it. "I'm not sure I can master that slippery deathboard."

"Don't worry. By the end of today, you'll be calling it a... a... whizzy funboard?"

I shook my head in disapproval.

"Just trust me," Lachie smiled, offering me his hand. "I'm a good teacher."

"We'll see," I muttered as he helped me up onto the board, holding onto both my hands.

"Alright, try to stand with your feet shoulder-width apart. That's it. And your hips centred… like that."

Now both his hands were on my hips, guiding them. I held my arms out in an attempt to balance.

"OK, that's it, great! You're doing great!"

It didn't escape my attention that I was still only standing on the board and had yet to actually ride it anywhere.

"Now, you're going to push off with your right leg in a minute and put it back here once you've got some momentum." Lachie patted a spot on the board. "Try to keep your back straight and, obviously, watch where you're going."

He looked me over, his hands still on my waist.

"You look really uncomfortable. Do you need to go to the toilet or something before we continue?"

"What?! No! You said to keep my back straight," I protested.

"Oh yeah, I did. Not like that though. Just relax. You'll be fine. Instinct will kick in."

I tentatively placed my right foot on the path and pushed like I'd seen skaters do. The board started to move and my foot dragged along the concrete before I stumbled off. Lachie grabbed my board.

"OK, that was a really great start. You just forgot to put your foot back on the board."

"Oops, I guess I did. Anyway, great lesson, thanks! Want to go for a drink or something?"

Lachie pushed his curls away from his face and gave me a wide smile.

"Uh uh! You're not getting out of this. Think of your students. You make them learn way harder stuff than this and they're five! This will be good for you, being in their shoes. Come on, up you get."

He held out his hand again, but I gave him grumpy face before getting on the board by myself. I'd forgotten he was irritatingly patronising.

Just get through this stupid lesson, then you can make an excuse and go home to daydream about Dan.

I tried and failed about five times, but on my sixth try I managed to remember all the things Lachie had told me to do and suddenly, I was sailing along the path.

Weeeeee! This IS fun!

Lachie appeared on his board next to me, smiling proudly. I couldn't help but feel proud of myself. After a few more goes, I was standing on my board ready to take off again when Lachie put his hands on my waist. We were face to face, due to the height I'd gained by standing on the whizzy funboard. I expected him to say something about my posture, but instead he kissed me.

I hadn't seen it coming so I barely had time to draw a breath before his mouth was on mine. I didn't know if it was the surprise element, or the fact that I was still horny from last night, but the kiss was incredible. It was slow and gentle with no tongue at first. Then he teased me, feigning going to kiss me and pulling away. After that, he softly kissed both my lips separately before finally pressing his mouth wholly against mine. Finally he gently sucked my tongue. The sensation of it sent shocks through my body and I wobbled on the skateboard. I thought Lachie might let me go, but he just held me tighter, steadying me with strong arms. For a few minutes I was in Kissing World, where my brain seemed to turn off completely and I just felt like a mouth without any other attachments.

The sound of children laughing in the playground brought me back to consciousness. Although the school I taught at was a suburb away, I lived in constant awareness that I could run into my students at any time, anywhere in public. What if they saw me making out like a teenager on a skateboard? The thought horrified me and I pulled away quickly.

Unfortunately I broke off the kiss too vigorously and the momentum sent me rolling down the track really quickly. As we hadn't covered braking properly, I had no idea what to do, other than jump off. Which turned out to be a mistake as my feet landed on the track, but the rest of my body kept going, causing me to fall on my face and twist my right ankle in the process. I heard the sound of running feet behind me as I pulled myself into a sitting position.

Shit. My ankle hurt. *Really* hurt. I bit my bottom lip in an attempt to try to stop the tears from falling down my face, but they came anyway. I felt stupid and embarrassed, and wished I could just limp away before Lachie reached me. But there he was, down on his knees in front of me, looking concerned and guilty.

"Are you OK, Justine?"

"You don't happen to have your cleaning cloth handy, do you?" I asked, trying to smile while wiping tears away with an ineffective hand.

"No, but my shirt is clean. And ironed." He grabbed a corner of the denim and dabbed at my eyes. "Are you hurt?"

"My ankle," I said, inhaling sharply with a fresh wave of pain.

"Here, let me look at it. Can I take off your shoe and sock?"

"Uh, I don't usually get undressed on a first date. Especially not in public."

Lachie laughed, taking my foot in his hand and examining it.

"You're a smartass even when you're injured." He shook his head. "Don't worry; I'm not a foot fetish kind of guy. It might be sprained… But I can't really tell with your shoe on."

I nodded and Lachie carefully unzipped my ankle boot and eased it off.

"See a lot of twisted ankles in the hardware store, do you?" I asked.

He looked up at me. His irises were a grassy green with inner rings circling his pupils that were the colour of turned earth.

"I'm a final-year nursing student. The hardware store is paying my uni fees. I've also volunteered as a First Aider since I was in high school."

I was embarrassed and decided to keep my mouth shut for the rest of the examination. Lachie's fingertips were gentle on my skin and for some reason the feeling was almost unbearably intimate, even more than the kiss. Finally, he carefully rolled my sock back on but left my shoe off.

"That's the end of our lesson, I'm afraid. Pretty sure it's a sprain. I suspect you won't let me carry you, but you'll need to lean on me to get home. Then ice it and stay off it for the rest of today and tomorrow if you can."

Kneeling beside me, Lachie pulled my right arm around his shoulders and then carefully helped me into a standing position.

"Now, where do you live?"

I pointed in the general direction of home and we set off in a weird, hobbling huddle, trying to juggle two skateboards and a shoe between us. Surprisingly, conversation was still comfortable and we had covered our favourite movies, music, food and footy teams by the time we reached the oval at the end of the park.

Due to intense concentration, I almost missed Dan, looking as though he'd just finished a run and stretching his legs against the fence. I realised that in my current state, there was little chance of sneaking quietly past. We had to walk right by him to get to my building.

Might as well get it over with. Be casual. Only say normal things. Here goes.

"Oh, hey Dan," I puffed.

So far, pretty normal...

Dan looked up and was clearly shocked to see me. Or shocked to see me draped over Lachie. Or shocked to see me holding a skateboard. One of those.

"Hey, Justine. Are you alright?"

"Ha ha. Oh, yes. Just a flesh wound."

A bit less normal...

"Right."

Lachie shifted his shoulders beneath my arm.

"Um, oh, Lachie, this is Dan, my, uh..."

A flash of Dan kissing slowly down my stomach.

"...Neighbour," I finished.

"Hey, man," Dan said, offering his hand to Lachie before realising that a handshake was going to be physically impossible.

"And Dan, this is Lachie, my, well, um..."

A flash of Lachie gently sucking my tongue.

"...Skateboard instructor."

All in all, more normal than could be expected.

Lachie nodded to Dan.

"Well, I'd better get the patient home. Nice to meet you, mate."

"Yeah, likewise."

Dan returned to his stretches without looking at me again.

"OK, I need to ask you a serious question and I would really appreciate your honesty," Lachie said, as we neared a pedestrian crossing. My stomach dipped.

"How do you feel about piggybacks?"

131

Only when Lachie felt assured that I was comfortable on my couch, with my ankle on a pillow, did he say, "I'm going to leave you now to rest. Don't go breaking into any houses for at least 24 hours, will you?"

We both laughed, but he didn't kiss me again and I felt lonely when the door clicked shut behind him. To cheer myself up, I messaged Steph:

Oh my God, just had my date with Hardware Ginger. It ended pretty quickly after I sprained my ankle. And then guess who we ran into? Hot Neighbour Dan, who I had hot, passionate sex with six hours ago! How do I keep making these messes of my life? XX

I went to put my phone back in my pocket but the message chime sounded while it was still in my hand. That was unusual; Steph was usually slower to text back. I smiled, imagining her reply as I looked at the text.

I think you just made another one.

But it wasn't from Steph. It was from Lachie. Suddenly I realised that I'd been thinking of him when I wrote the message, and instead of opening my message thread with Steph, I'd opened the one with him instead. I had done this before, sent a message to the person I was writing about instead of the person I was writing to, but with minimal damage. This was not minimal damage. The people-pleaser in me was horrified. I couldn't stop myself from reading what I'd just sent to him over and over, feeling more nauseous each time.

132

What do I write to him now?

It wasn't exactly a "Whoops, sorry" situation. Maybe I could get away with a "Ha ha, just joking"? No, there was no way he'd buy that. I couldn't think of anything I could do or say to make it better. I was just going to have to leave it.

Steph was perched on the arm of my couch with her elbows on her knees and her chin in her hands as she leaned intently in.

"So, just to go over it one more time, he said…"

"Nothing."

"And then you replied with…"

"Nothing."

Steph exhaled, blowing her cheeks out and throwing her head back dramatically, which resulted in her nearly falling backwards off the couch.

When she'd regained her composure, she said, "And then you go back to his place for a night… and morning… of—to quote your misdirected text—'hot, passionate sex'?"

"Yup. That's pretty much it."

"Holy shit."

"I know."

We sat in silence for a minute. Steph had come over to sort out some last-minute wedding details, but we had dealt with those swiftly and were now debriefing about my last 24 hours.

"No wonder he has a wall full of women."

"It wasn't just women. There was a dog."

"Still, he's a player, right?"

Of course I'd thought the same thing numerous times since last night. But I still didn't want to hear it out loud. I wanted to hear that he might actually be interested in me.

"Yeah, I guess. But the spooning…"

I knew I sounded too hopeful. Steph looked away, which showed how well she knew me.

"Did he happen to mention catching up again?"

My silence was enough. I started to feel annoyed. I already knew it. I knew it was too good to be true. And she was right, Dan hadn't said anything about seeing me again, even though he inevitably would. But I didn't need it pointed out for me by my best friend. I decided to change the subject.

"So then, yeah, the skateboard date. And the message debacle."

"Right. You didn't say much about the actual date. How was it?"

Between the sprained ankle and the text, I hadn't actually given much thought to the date itself.

"It was… easy. He's funny. He's one of those people who act like they already know you when they've just met you. It wasn't awkward at all. Even after we kissed."

"You kissed?! You didn't say that."

"No, well, I was a bit more concerned with the text. It's not like I'm ever going to see him again."

Steph nodded in agreement. For some reason I started to feel annoyed again. I realised I'd

134

wanted her to contradict me and make me feel like it hadn't been that bad. But she was right again, there was no coming back from that text.

"But the kiss was…?"

"Amazing," I said without thinking. It was in my top five at least.

"Holy shit," Steph said again.

CHAPTER TEN

Sunday night was Trivia and Parma Night with The Boys. Steph and I had lived on campus at uni with The Boys—Rhys, Billy and Li—and we'd all been friends for over ten years, so we knew each other's sordid pasts from start to current. We were terrible at the actual trivia but it was mostly an excuse to catch up. And eat parma, obviously.

Rhys was already there when I arrived. He stood up to hug me.

"Hey Juz! Where's Stephster tonight?"

"Not coming. She's got wedding stuff."

"Oh yeah, it's next Saturday, right? I should probably write that down somewhere."

"Probably," I said, sitting down across from him. "How's life?"

"Good." Rhys replied and then motioned to a jug of beer. "You want some? Nope, I remember," he answered for me. "Fermented dishwater. So, got some good stories for us tonight?"

I looked at Rhys and he grinned.

"Let's wait till the other guys get here," I said.

Li and Billy arrived a few minutes later. There were more hugs all round. Then I filled them in on the last month, which took us well into the first round of trivia. We only got two questions correct out of ten, but The Boys were still merry, with two jugs of beer finished and plenty of laughs at my expense.

"This guy's a genius," Li was saying.

Li was the most successful in our group, dating-wise. He seemed to date constantly, as though it was his part-time job, but never spent more than a few months with the same girl. Billy, on the other hand, was a compulsive monogamist. He'd had back-to-back serious relationships since we'd known him.

"He's got his hands on you pretty much the whole date," Li continued. "So the awkward first-touch terrain has already been negotiated, and then there's the fact that you have to trust him or else you fall on your face—which you achieved anyway, well done for that—and somehow he manages to kiss you in the middle of a family park in broad daylight and not come off as a creep. I repeat, *genius*. Shame you fucked that up royally, I would have loved to meet the man behind the myth to get some ideas."

I rubbed my ankle, which still hurt to walk on but had definitely improved from Lachie's advice. It was just a dull throb now.

"What about The Player?" Rhys asked. It was their definition of Dan, not mine. "He doesn't say a word and Juz goes home with him! Don't you want tips from that guy? What's *his* secret?"

"I know *his* secret," Li said, rolling the dregs of his beer around the bottom of his glass. "He's an impressive unit, right? No normal-looking guy's game is *that* good."

They all looked at me.

"He's actually quite a nice person and—"

They all laughed at me.

"It's not all about the... he also... we have..." I sighed and shrugged. "He's the best-looking guy I've ever seen in real life."

There was more laughter. This wasn't going much better than my chat with Steph.

"Anyway, enough about me," I said, clapping my hands together. "Rhys, what happened with that guy you were sexting? The one who lived within a 1km radius or something? Sounded very convenient."

"Oh, *that*. That did not go well."

"Tell us, tell us," we all chanted.

I felt relieved that the attention had been directed towards someone else's romantic failures.

"Well, I show up at his door, pre-arranged, right? And he opens the door, looks me up and down and says, 'Oh. No thanks. Your pics are better than the real thing.' And then shuts the door."

"What a cock!" Billy said, adding, "And not in a good way."

"I know," Rhys agreed. "Luckily there was another guy interested only another 1km away. Worth the walk."

"Will you go back there?" asked Li.

"Nah," Rhys replied. "His pics were better than the real thing."

We all laughed.

"What about you, Li?" I asked, quickly writing a random guess at the last trivia question. We'd already completely missed two questions in this round.

"Same old roster on rotation," he answered. "Enough variety to stay interesting, but I don't have

138

to waste any time on digital groundwork. Suits me at the moment—work's busy."

I imagined having a roster of men that I could hook up with on a regular basis. During my gap year, I'd been put in charge of rosters at the fast-food restaurant I worked at and I was terrible at it. Two people kept turning up for the same shift. I imagined making the same mistake on my sex roster.

Sorry for the mix-up guys, but you'd might as well both stay now you're here. We'll find something for you to do.

I turned to Billy, hoping he wasn't feeling left out.

"How's Bianca going?" I asked.

"Actually, Bianca and I broke up."

We exchanged looks around the table; none of us had seen that announcement coming. Then we all looked at Billy, waiting.

"I'm actually seeing a new girl, Zoe. She's really great. You guys will like her."

"Of course you bloody are!" Rhys exploded. "Seriously, Bill, have you ever been single in your life?"

Billy looked defensive.

"Yes, I have. Bianca and I broke up at the start of the month. And I've only just become official with Zoe."

"So, a good two and a half weeks of gaming and wanking before settling down again?" Li laughed.

Billy looked at me for support.

"Guys, enough." I said, putting my hands up in a steadying motion. "We're all just jealous because Billy is happy at home while we're still prowling the streets."

"Thanks, Juz," Billy said, looking relieved.

"I mean, so what if Zoe and Bianca hi-fived on the doorstep as one moved out and the other moved in?"

The guys burst out laughing and Billy shook his head at me. I gave him a you-know-I-still-love-you smile. He threw a chip at me and I caught it in my mouth, realising as I did that the trivia round had ended and we'd only answered one question.

I arrived home feeling happy and relaxed, despite the drama of the past couple of days. The Boys always had a calming effect on me. On my way to bed I grabbed the washing basket I'd thrown down by the door after getting my clothes off the line earlier that day. I brought it into my room and pulled out some clean pyjamas. The flannelette embraced me like a warm hug as I changed into them and then threw my underwear and socks into a drawer.

There were a pair of Ellie's scrubs and some of her underwear in there, so I folded them and took them into her room, knowing that she wasn't at home because her car hadn't been in the car park. I left the clothes on her bed and was leaving the room when I heard the mumble of voices from the apartment below. Dan's apartment. It was impossible to interpret any specific words, but there was definitely a low, masculine tone and a higher, distinctly feminine voice.

Leave the room, Justine, I advised myself wisely. *Leave right now.*

I sat down on Ellie's bed, trying to take slow, deep breaths to steady my heartbeat. The voices continued to hum through the floor, occasionally breaking into laughter. More hers than his, I noticed. How long did I sit there? Three, five, ten minutes? I told myself again and again to get up and go to bed, but I was stuck—unable and unwilling to move. Then, the talking stopped. And the noises started. Soft murmurs at first that began to build into moans of pleasure. It was unbearable, not to mention completely voyeuristic, but I still couldn't make myself leave. I wasn't sure my legs would even hold me. The noises were reaching a muffled climax.

How could Ellie tell? I wondered suddenly.

I had no idea if she was faking it. And then, it was over. There were murmurs and laughter again. I finally unglued myself from Ellie's bed and limped back to my room with sharp pains shooting through my ankle again.

Later, I was lying in my bed, not sleeping, when I heard voices outside. My bedroom window faced the apartment car park and I was used to the sound of people coming and going. My window was open so it was easy to hear what they were saying.

"Where do you want to go?"

Any hopes I'd had that Dan had for some reason lent his room to someone else quite literally went out the window. It was definitely him.

"I don't mind," came Mystery Woman's voice.

Don't call her Mystery Woman. That's a really cool alias. She can be Stupid Pants.

"As long as it's not greasy," she added.

Really Stupid Pants.

"Yeah, agreed. I know a place."

I could imagine Dan's muscular arm around Really Stupid Pants as he opened the door for her.

"Great!" said Really Stupid Pants.

And then two car doors slammed and an engine started.

Don't think about it. Don't think about it.

I tried not to think about it for most of the night, until I finally fell asleep.

The weather had been so nice that logically, by Melbourne standards, it had to be followed by four days of freezing, persistent rain. My students didn't get outside to play at all during those days and were almost certifiably insane by Thursday. While I was cleaning my classroom that afternoon, I found that one of them had taken a decent bite out of the cardboard gingerbread house. I sighed and checked my work emails before heading home and found one from Ruth:

Staff Members,
As you know our end-of-year staff function, a picnic lunch at the Melbourne Cup at Flemington Race Course, was decided at the beginning of the school year.

As the date was set early, all staff are expected to be in attendance. Please purchase tickets and BYO food and drinks on the day. I am unable to make it due to prior commitments.

Regards,
Ruth

Oh, wonderful.

At least Ruth wouldn't be there, taking notes on who was making polite conversation and who wasn't. My closest work friend, Nyarout, appeared at my classroom door just as I was shutting my laptop.

"Get the email?" she asked, rolling her eyes.

"Everyone must be there. Except for Ruth," I replied in a whisper and she shook her head.

"She's probably got a dirty long weekend planned with her husband," Nyarout said quietly after a glance over her shoulder.

"No thank you to that visual image," I replied, heaving my laptop bag onto my shoulder. "Have you ever been to the Cup before?"

"Yes, a few times," Nyarout answered, flicking off the lights for me. "But always in Eddie's work marquee. That was awe*some*. This will be aw*ful*. Want a lift home?"

One glance at the grey mess outside the window gave me my answer.

"Yes please. I'm not keen on waiting for a tram in this weather."

We walked to the staff car park together.

"At least we'll have each other," Nyarout said as she pressed a button on her key to unlock her car.

Her backseat was packed with books, folders, laminated posters and various child-made models of indiscernible structures. Similar to what mine would be, if I had a car.

"True," I answered. "At least there's that."

CHAPTER ELEVEN

Steph and Charlie were married at dusk in a garden next to an old woolshed. Steph wore a knee-length red dress with long, lace sleeves and a swirly skirt. Charlie and his groomsmen were in pale blue shirts with suspenders and bow ties, and looked like they might burst into an acapella rendition of "Mr Sandman" at any moment. Candles flickered in jars on the ground around us and everyone ate mini chocolate bars while the witnesses signed the register, an homage to the fact that Charlie had been dressed as a giant chocolate bar at the uni party where they'd met. Charlie barely made it through his vows because he was so choked up and everyone cheered loudly when Steph held up Charlie's hand and yelled, "WOOOO! We did it!" after they were declared husband and wife.

Soon after, I joined the rest of the bridal party who had gathered beneath the nearby gum trees and for an hour we obliged the photographer's requests to "Put your hand there" and "Pretend someone said something funny" as the wet scent of eucalyptus settled in our hair and on our shoulders.

Finally, everyone swarmed into the woolshed for the reception, salivating over the aroma of lamb on a spit. Steph had invited quite a few people from uni who I hadn't seen for a couple of years and several of them asked me, "Are you still with that guy?" I decided that, "No, he cheated on me and just had a baby with the very same woman he cheated with" wasn't a socially acceptable answer, even though asking me about someone who clearly wasn't there seemed to be a socially acceptable question.

After dinner, I looked for The Boys. Billy was sitting at a table with his new girlfriend. They had moved their seats together and she was whispering in his ear. I wondered if Billy had just crossed out 'Bianca' on his original invite and written 'Zoe' on top, like my students did when they made a mistake. Li was dancing with one of the bridesmaids—Steph's sister, Lily—and Rhys appeared to be chatting up a waiter.

I decided to befriend the bottle of red wine placed helpfully by a waiter right next to my place at the bridal table. I was watching people sweeping around the dancefloor to a slow song as I drained my fourth glass, feeling lonely and disconnected, when someone tapped me on the shoulder and said, "You'd better dance with me, before you try to glass someone at my wedding." It was Charlie, with his bow tie untied and his suspenders dangling at his hips.

"I'd be delighted," I said, accepting his hand.

Charlie led me to the dancefloor and put an arm around my waist.

"How are you?" he asked sincerely, looking right into my eyes.

"Oh, today's not about me. Look at this day! This day has been amazing. Does it feel amazing?"

"Yes. How are you?" he asked again.

I rested my dizzy head against his pale blue shoulder and we just swayed back and forth for a bit. Finally, I looked at him again.

"I thought I'd be getting married around this time, too. Steph is my last female friend to settle down. And I'm still single. Really, really single. I'm starting to think it's me."

"It's not you," Charlie said, kissing me on the forehead. "Guys are just idiots. They've got no idea what they're missing."

But he knew he couldn't honestly promise me that I'd be settling down too one day, even though he wanted to, so he just held me and we kept dancing until the photographer pulled him away and I went back to my red wine.

At the end of the night, everyone formed a circle and Steph and Charlie walked around the inside of it, saying their goodbyes, as if they would never see us again. It was my least favourite part of a wedding. It was always so depressing when the married couple left and all their friends and family remained there without them. I stood next to Li, who I'd seen exchanging numbers with Lily, and we waited for the happy couple to reach us. I realised I was swaying when I felt my ear bump against Li's shoulder.

Li turned to me and said, "Are you OK? You look... smashed. And what happened to your dress?"

I looked down at the dark red wine stain which ran from the right boob of the pale blue satin dress, all the way down to the bottom of the skirt.

"My dress wassh thirsshty," I said, hearing the obvious slur in my voice.

"Oh, man," was all Li said.

Finally, Steph stood in front of us.

"Congratulations, gorgeous," Li said as they embraced.

"Thanks for coming," she said, smiling. "If you touch my little sister, I'll give you a free circumcision."

"Noted," he winced.

Then Steph threw her arms around me and said, "I love you so much, friend wife."

I hugged her back, leaning on her a bit for stability. Then, Charlie and Steph were gone and the woolshed full of people somehow felt empty.

"I best be off," I said to Li and then stumbled, falling right on top of him. He caught me and helped me to a table, where he gave me a glass of water and called Billy over.

"You're driving, right?" I heard him ask. "Juz is in a bad way."

Billy said, "Yeah, sure. We'll drop her off."

"I'm nod on your way," I protested. "Issh fine, I'll jusss-"

But Li and Billy were already manhandling me towards the door. *I'll allow it,* I thought. Mostly because trying to organise a ride through an app currently seemed about as possible as solving a Rubik's Cube while finding my way out of a maze in a straightjacket.

I nodded, to no one really, but made sure not to say anything. I was convinced that if I tried, I would definitely refer to Bianca as Zoe. Or the other way round. I couldn't even remember which one was the new one.

As the three of them settled me in Billy's backseat and helped with my seatbelt, I looked out the front windscreen. I watched with tears in my eyes as the wedding car pulled out onto the road and disappeared from view.

I was in front of Dan's door, knocking on it. Billy and Zoe/Bianca had wanted to make sure I got into my apartment safely, but I'd convinced them that I was capable of managing alone. I thought I had sobered up on the way home, but given my current position, I had probably been wrong. Dan answered in just trunks, with a pissed off look on his face.

"Oh hey, Dan," I said. "I didn't expect to see you here."

He stared at me for a minute, taking in the stained bridesmaid's dress, drooping curls and high heels hanging from my hand.

"Sometimes I hang out at my house at 2am," he said dryly.

"So, I just came to say I know you're a player, because your sex with Really Stupid Pants is very loud from my housemate's room. I still hope we can be friends and go for a run sometime. But pssst," I leaned in.

Great, now I was saying "Pssst".

Shit. What the hell am I doing here?

"I really hate running," I continued. "But I like you. That's all!"

I turned to go but walked right into his doorframe.

"Attempt two!" I said, holding up what was probably two fingers as I angled myself towards the stairs.

"Stop it. Come in."

Dan put an arm around my waist and led me inside, helping me to sit down on a chair at his bench.

"I'll get you some water."

"Ssshh! There are probably one or several girls in there. Let them sleep!"

I pointed in the direction of his bedroom.

WHAT AM I DOING?!

He had been reaching up into a cupboard to get a glass, but his almost naked body froze suddenly, stretched out like a bronze statue engaged in an Olympic sport. Finally, Dan turned around to face me. His eyes were like a blue flame in the streetlight from the lounge room window.

"Oh, come off it, Justine! Don't give me that bullshit. I saw you making out with that guy in the park. The skater. That was only a couple of hours after you left my place! So who are you calling a player?"

I sat there, stunned.

"But… you looked surprised when you saw me at the park. I didn't think you saw…"

He scoffed at me.

"I was surprised to see that you were hurt. Anyway, I'm not into drama. Let's just—"

I stood up, walked over and kissed him. I'd had no idea I was going to do it. I was at the dangerously impulsive stage of drunk, where things I did seemed to be happening to me magically. Dan kissed me back for a minute before gently pushing me away. He wiped a hand over his face and looked like he'd just been woken up. Which he had.

"Just go home, Justine."

I felt sad and stupid. I turned around so he couldn't see that I was about to cry.

My hand was on the door handle when I felt Dan's hands on my shoulders. He turned me around and looked down at me. Then he kissed me, hard, pressing me against the door with his whole body. It was a confusing kiss, a bit angry and a bit caring, with his hands in my hair and my hands on his ass. Then he picked me up in one easy swoop, like I was a mop or something. My hair most likely resembled a mop head at that point.

Dan carried me to the bedroom, which didn't actually have one or several girls in it, and placed me carefully on the bed. Then he laid down on top of me, supporting himself with two elbows on either side of my head. He lightly bit my earlobe, then kissed my neck.

"I'm not going to have sex with you when you're drunk," he said huskily into my ear.

"That's lucky because I haven't waxed."

Dan laughed and rolled off me.

"You're something else, Justine," he said to the ceiling.

"Something else from what?" I asked, forgetting what we had even been talking about. Sleep had begun to pull itself over me like a blanket. My eyelids felt like lead as I murmured, "Should I go home?"

"Not if you don't want to. You won't be drunk in the morning."

"I look forward to it," I said and shut my eyes.

November

CHAPTER TWELVE

"Would you like a wine, love?" asked Pops, holding a bottle over my glass.

I shook my head. The memory of my recent hangover was still sharp and pointy in my mind. It had been a while in between Roasts with Pops, but today my whole family was gathered in his little unit, eagerly awaiting the pork we could hear popping and spitting away in his oven.

"Just milk for me. Thanks, Pops."

"You have the taste buds of a ten-year old," my brother, Riley, said as he nodded for Pops to fill his glass with Shiraz.

"But she will have the bone strength of a weight-bearing beast," Pops defended me.

I was dubious about the comparison but appreciated the thought, and smiled at Pops with gratitude. Riley rolled his eyes, which I would have thought was beneath a father of two.

"How are things, buddy?" Dad asked Riley.

In my brother's previous life, he had been a business analyst. Now he was a stay-at-home Dad and his wife, Hayley, worked full time as a barrister. Which was why she wasn't at lunch—she always had a big case coming up.

"Not too bad. Dad, what did *you* think of the Reserve Bank's decision? I just can't fathom why..."

I tuned out.

"Daddy, Daddy, Daddy, Daddy, Daddy," begged my three-year old nephew, Chase, who'd been previously occupied with a miniature farm toy.

I clearly wasn't the only one bored by his father's conversation.

"Manners, Chase," Riley reminded.

"Excuse me, Daddy, excuse me, Daddy, excuse me, Daddy—"

"OK, I get it. Yes, son?"

"Do cows cry?"

"Um... I don't... What do you mean?"

Chase held up a little plastic cow.

"This one is crying."

We all peered at the cow, which just looked like a normal cow. Riley looked very tired.

"Moo-boo-hoo!" Chase wailed, holding the cow in front of his face.

"I think they do cry," Pops told Chase as he returned from the kitchen. He handed Chase a cup of milk and offered me the carton to pour my own.

"Sometimes I used to think they sounded very sad," Pops continued. "But your Gran used to pat their noses and then they looked like they were smiling!"

Chase was very pleased with this, oblivious to the pain in Pops's smile.

"I remember that, Dad," Mum said. "She sang to them too."

"She had a beautiful voice. Like Juzzy," Pops said with glazed eyes.

"Have you done any singing recently, love?" Mum asked, turning to me.

"Only in the shower," I replied. "The opportunity doesn't really come up much anymore."

through my weekly plan when my phone dinged at me. It was a message from one of the guys I'd matched with. His name was Nick and he was one of those guys whose profile photos were all of him topless.

We messaged for a bit, mostly small talk. He was American and a professional dancer, which I found both impressive and arousing. Steph and I had always had a rule that a guy who could dance automatically gained twenty extra points of hotness.

As we were winding up our conversation, Nick asked if I wanted to meet up on Saturday afternoon. I agreed, not feeling as hopeful as I might have a month ago. I brushed my teeth and reread Nick's last message that he was looking forward to meeting me under the clocks at Flinders Street Station.

Going into my room, I had the weird feeling of walking into a parallel universe. I half-expected to see a desk with a photo board above it and a grey doona cover. As I lay down in bed and closed my eyes, I immediately recalled Dan's body, taut and tanned, on top of my own. I rolled onto my side and tried to tap the visions out of my head the way I tried to tap water out of my ear after a shower. I needed to calm down. It was two hook-ups. That was all.

Good night, my sweet prince.

CHAPTER THIRTEEN

I groaned, furious again at the thought that I was spending a public holiday at a staff function organised by a dictator. Still half-asleep, I stumbled over to my cupboard and raked through random clothing items until I found it: my favourite playsuit, white with navy polka dots and pretty frills for the sleeves. I loved playsuits; they possessed all the glamour of wearing a dress, but allowed me to sit on the ground comfortably without sharing my choice of underwear with the general public. This one even had pockets. I stepped into it and almost dislocated both shoulders trying to zip it up at the back. Then I tonged my hair into loose curls and did my makeup while eating breakfast in the bathroom. Finally, I placed the headband I'd decorated over my stiffly hair-sprayed head. It was white, adorned with navy satin roses that I'd "borrowed" from the school art room. I was proud of my ingenuity. I was like a fashion MacGyver.

I met with a group of about twenty other staff at Flemington Racecourse Railway Station and we trailed after the crowd of racegoers towards security, who were checking bags. I walked beside Perky Ashleigh and Nyarout, removing my picnic bag from my shoulder as we neared the checkpoint. Ashleigh suddenly whispered, "Hey guys, check this out!" and opened her own bag, showing us a box of biscuits and a six-pack of water bottles.

"Ah, you've gone all out Ashleigh," I said, wondering what she was proudly showing us.

Maybe that she's on a prison diet?

"The water bottles, dummy! My friends and I always do this. We, like, flip the lids off with a knife so you can't tell they've been opened, empty the water out and replace it with vodka! Super clever, right?!"

"Oh, wow," I said, feeling very old. I had no interest in drinking at a staff function, but if I had, I would have just bought it from the bar.

"Except for the first two," she continued. "They really are water. In case they, like, check them. What do you think?"

I think you are an alcoholic evil genius.

"Ah, yes. Very clever."

"I know, right?!"

Nyarout glanced at me over Ashleigh's head, which was very easy for her, as she towered over both of us, even without the heels. The security guard checked all our bags with a bored, obligatory glance, leaving Ashleigh slightly deflated. She probably could have put the entire bottle of vodka in there, label facing up, and he still would have given her the nod.

We entered Flemington Racecourse and took in the illustrious scene. The grey sky illuminated the immaculate green lawn as well as the pink and yellow roses that bordered the racetrack. Men in fitted suits greeted each other with handshakes, their ties and pocket handkerchiefs obediently straight and flat against their chests. Women were waxed, tanned, curled and compressed into feathers, flowers and frocks, their brightly coloured lips puckering to kiss the air beside each other's carefully contoured cheeks.

I'd been to the races a few times so I knew that as the day progressed it would all descend into a soggy, dirty, drunken shambles, but right now it was the very picture of glamour and prestige.

Maybe this won't be so bad.

We found a spot near the track, put down picnic blankets and laid out our respective lunch offerings. It was quite a spread and the sight and smell of delicious food brightened my mood considerably.

After the food was finished and some of the staff had gone to place bets, I lay back on my elbows, listening to the occasional thunder of hooves as the horses charged past us. The grey cloak of clouds shifted and the freshly disrobed sun toasted my outstretched legs while Nyarout and I argued with a bald, bearded teacher named Greg about which character would be the next to die in our favourite TV series. I was so engrossed in Greg's five-pronged explanation as to why it would be the half-merman brother of the child king, that I barely noticed Ashleigh sprawling herself alongside me.

"Helloooo, Josling," she said, tugging one of my curls and announcing, "Sproing!" as she released the ringlet and it bounced upwards. Then she dropped her hand into my lap.

I sat up and turned to her, surprised by how drunk she was already.

"Hey Ashleigh, um, how many of those bottles have you gotten through?"

"Two!" she said, removing her hand from my lap and holding up five fingers. "No, three! No... dunno. Where's, like... Where's my bag?"

She started shuffling around on her hands and knees on the blanket to look for her bag with her short, red dress flying up around her. I realised I hadn't actually seen her eat anything with the rest of us.

"OK. You just stay there for a minute," I said, holding her arms and gently sitting her down. "I'll get you some water."

I found her bag on another picnic rug and started opening her bottles, sniffing them until I found the actual water. I brought it over and handed the bottle to her. She tried to take it but ended up tipping it all over the rug between us.

"Good boy, Jenson," she said, swaying from side to side and looking like she couldn't quite focus on me. "There's a garden on ya head, did ya know?"

Nyarout and Greg were watching us and some of the other staff had started paying attention too.

"Disgraceful! Really, at a staff function!" said Ange or Jan, I wasn't sure which.

Ashleigh looked like she hadn't heard. She was staring vacantly over my shoulder.

"Ashleigh!" I said, waving a hand in front of her face.

I touched her arm and she crumpled, falling backwards onto the picnic rug.

"ASHLEIGH!" I shook her, but her eyes were shut and she gave no response.

Oh God, is she dead? What do I do? What do I do?!

I took a breath. Her chest was still moving up and down, so she'd just passed out. Nyarout knelt next to me.

"Shit. What a mess," she said quietly.

"Help me get her on her side," I said. Together we rolled Ashleigh to face the racetrack.

Greg ran off to the Medical Assistance Tent to find some help. I shook Ashleigh again, saying her name, but she was out cold. I looked around at the other staff staring at her, judging her lifeless form.

"We've all had drunken experiences that we regret," I said. "She's young."

I felt defensive of her, maybe because of my own recent drunken experience or maybe because they all looked so disapproving. I went to speak to Nyarout, but she had walked away to take a call. I pulled up one of the picnic blankets, sending chips and cheese crumbs flying, and put it over Ashleigh—more because of the revealing nature of her dress than to keep her warm. It was a dry, hot day, which probably hadn't helped her state.

I looked up to see Greg running back towards us. He had a first aid volunteer running along behind him. The man's dark green shirt and pants were distinct against the bright hues of the racegoers, but even more distinct was his red hair.

Oh geez.

Of course it was Lachie.

They both reached us and Lachie immediately knelt down beside Ashleigh, pulling the blanket away.

"Can you hear me?" he asked loudly, and something inside me responded to hearing his voice again. Ashleigh, however, did not.

He pulled open her jaw with one hand and looked inside her mouth. Then he put his hand just below her neck and his ear to her mouth. Finally, he lifted his head, put two fingers on her limp wrist and looked at his watch. I couldn't help remembering the way his fingertips had gently pressed on my ankle and the way his muddy green eyes looked up into mine.

"Can you hear me?" he asked Ashleigh again. "What's your name?"

There was the slightest groan from the back of her throat but she didn't move.

"What's her name?" he asked without looking up. His voice was clipped and serious.

"Ashleigh," I answered him, being the closest in proximity and probably relationship to her.

"Has she fallen or hit her head at all?"

"No, she just passed out. She's been drinking vodka since we arrived this morning."

"Straight or mixed with something?" Lachie asked, picking up her other wrist and checking her pulse again.

"I don't know. I'm starting to think it might have been straight. We weren't really... watching her."

Please don't judge me, I pleaded with him silently.

As though he sensed it, Lachie looked up for the first time and his eyes widened when he realised who he'd been speaking to. Then he gritted his teeth and looked back at Ashleigh.

"Would she have taken any drugs? And does she have any allergies?" he asked, his tone still professional.

"I don't think so. But I'm not sure… about either," I said.

Would someone who brings their own tongs to a sausage sizzle be likely to pop pills at a work function?

"Ashleigh, can you hear me?" he said to her, squeezing her shoulder. "Ashleigh, can you open your eyes?"

She made a sound like a zombie from a horror movie but her eyes remained shut. Lachie turned to his medical-looking bag and pulled out a blood-pressure cuff and stethoscope. He attached the cuff to her arm and held the end of the stethoscope to her inner elbow as he pumped the squeeze bulb in his fist. After checking the gauge on the cuff, he pulled out a radio.

"Altered state of consciousness female," he said into it. "Patient is unresponsive to voice, responsive to pain. Request paramedic support."

Ashleigh made the zombie noise again and I could see her eyelids fluttering. I let out the breath I hadn't realised I was holding.

"What's your name?" Lachie asked her again.

"Assshleee," she murmured as her head began to flop from side to side. "What the f… Who are you? Get off me!"

She was starting to thrash her arms around. Lachie took both her wrists and held them.

"I'm Lachie," he said. "We've met before, at the sausage sizzle. Can you tell me where you are?"

"I'm… Horses."

"Good, Ashleigh, that's good. Do you know what day it is?"

"Ish a bloody holiday… and I'm atta shit work thing."

An ambulance golf cart with a flashing blue light pulled up beside us. Two paramedics jumped out and one of them, a short woman with a high ponytail, knelt down beside Lachie.

"What have we got?" she asked.

Ashleigh's eyes were opening and closing as Lachie explained everything he knew.

"Alright, let's get her back to the tent," the ponytailed paramedic said and the three of them lifted her onto a long blue stretcher that was attached to the golf cart.

Nyarout came over to me and we watched as Ashleigh was strapped into the cart.

"That was Eddie on the phone," Nyarout said to me. "He said he can get us both into The Birdcage."

I could almost feel the fizz of champagne on my lips as she said it. Her husband Eddie did something important in the entertainment industry and it didn't surprise me that he had an invite to the only place worth being at the Melbourne Cup. The

Birdcage was famously filled with fancy food and fabulous people. I'd always wanted to experience it, but had never had the opportunity.

Do it, Justine! Ashleigh is in really good hands and you deserve this.

I looked at Ashleigh, her eyes half open and her strapless dress sliding ominously down her chest.

"I'd better stay with Ashleigh. She might be scared when she wakes up properly."

Nyarout sighed at me and shook her head.

"OK, call me later and I'll get you in. You're too nice, you know," she said as she gave me a quick hug.

"So I've been told."

I returned the hug and then picked up mine and Ashleigh's bags.

The golf cart was ready to take off. Lachic and one of the paramedics were sitting beside Ashleigh but there was still a spare seat next to the driver. I tugged the neckline of Ashleigh's dress up.

"Can I come with you?" I asked Lachie.

"Yep. Get in the front," he replied without looking at me.

I climbed in and we took off at breakneck speed. Not really, it was a golf cart. I could have walked faster next to it.

When we got back to the tent, they did the pulse and blood pressure checking thing all over again. Then a nurse came over and Lachie filled her in using medical jargon I didn't understand. She nodded and talked to Ashleigh for a minute, who was alternating between being really out of it and aggressive outbursts.

"It's likely that she's dehydrated. I think we'll put an IV in. Do you want to do it?" the nurse asked Lachie and he nodded.

I sat beside Ashleigh, not really knowing what to say or do. Finally, the IV was done and the nurse walked away. Lachie looked at me as though he didn't know what to say or do either. I stood up.

"Lachie, I…"

"It was good of you to stay… for Ashleigh's sake, I mean," he said and then went to walk away.

"Wait!" I said.

What am I going to say?

"I'm sorry."

Lachie stopped, his face blank.

"We don't have to talk about this," he said quietly, scratching the back of his head and refusing to make eye contact.

"I know. Just, please, I really am so sorry. That message was terrible. I am terrible for sending it, even if I didn't mean to send it to you. I'm so ashamed and I promise, if I could do anything to fix it or retract it or if I could think of *any way* to make it better, I would. I'm so sorry."

I looked down at my dusty high heels, suddenly struck with the realisation that I'd never said anything like that to Ben at any time throughout our four-year relationship. There had been plenty of times when I should have, but we'd both always just ignored the things that poisoned the air between us and hoped that they would magically dissipate.

I looked up at Lachie. He shrugged his shoulders but still said nothing. I had hoped he would say, "That's OK" but it didn't look like that was going to happen.

This is why I never do it.

"I appreciate your apology," he said finally and then walked away to check on one of the other drunkards.

Wanting to do something, anything else but be in that stuffy tent with him, I took Ashleigh's phone from her bag and walked outside, grateful for the cool breeze that greeted me.

My body felt tight with tension. I shook my limbs and unlocked Ashleigh's phone, which luckily didn't have a password. After some light stalking, I found a number for someone named Oscar who seemed to be her boyfriend. I called him and explained the situation. Oscar sounded frantic with worry but I was able to calm him enough to give him directions to come and pick her up.

When I returned, Ashleigh was sitting up and Lachie was crouched beside her.

"Hey, Justine," she said, attempting a smile.

She looked terrible; her eyes were bloodshot and her naturally tanned face was pale and blotchy.

"It's Lachie! From the barbecue. You dropped his sausage."

She touched him on the shoulder like they were old friends and he smiled at her. I hadn't realised just how worried I'd been about her until then. I let out a breath and tears came to my eyes.

"Yes, Ashleigh, I remember," I said, taking a seat on the other side of her. Lachie still seemed to be avoiding eye contact, not that I was desperately trying to catch his eye.

"Justine," she said, still with an obvious slur to her voice. "I don't get playsuits. Like, how do you go to the loo?"

"Oh... um... well..."

"Because," she continued as though she was just warming up. "You can't lift it up. So you, like, have to unzip it and pull it down, right?"

"You should really get some rest," I said, very tempted to squeeze her lips shut with my fingers.

Lachie didn't even have the decency to walk away or pretend to do something else. He just sat there, not looking at me.

"So you're just sitting there naked. Right, Justine? Are you naked on the loo?"

"OK, yes, that's right, Ashleigh! It's not ideal. It's rather cold at times."

Kill me.

Luckily, at that moment, Oscar arrived, looking about nineteen. He thanked me as I moved aside so he could sit with Ashleigh. She looked extremely relieved to see him.

Once Lachie had removed the IV and checked Ashleigh's blood pressure and pulse again, he offered to help Oscar walk her out to the car. As they passed, Lachie nodded at me as if to say, "We're done here."

I left the tent and watched as people streamed out of the gates. The last race was over and I decided there would be no point to calling Nyarout to see if I could still meet her in The

Birdcage. I didn't think I had the energy for it anyway. The drama of the day had completely drained me. Remembering Lachie's last, cold nod, I shouldered my bag and started off for the station.

CHAPTER FOURTEEN

I looked up at the clocks above my head and then checked my phone. He wasn't late; I was slightly early. He might have already been there for all I knew. Flinders Street Station was an obvious landmark, but a terrible place to meet. It was so packed with people, I wasn't sure if I'd even pick him in the crowd. There definitely weren't any topless men walking around, so that ruled out recognising him from his profile pictures.

Ashleigh had been absent from school the day after the Melbourne Cup, maybe from a hangover or maybe from embarrassment. But she'd come into my classroom the following afternoon while I was cleaning tables.

"I just want to say I'm sorry for what happened, Justine," she had said, looking incredibly uncomfortable and twisting her hair around her finger. "It was so stupid, that's never happened to me before. I can't believe I was one of those drunk, messy girls and everyone saw me and, like, now they're going to think I'm…"

She had looked as though she was going to burst into tears.

"It's OK," I said. "Don't worry about it. We've all been that girl. I'm glad you're alright."

"Well, thank you for, like, what you did for me. Can I please give you a hug?"

Oh, I really don't think that's necess—

She had come over, put her arms around my neck and held me close.

OK, this is happening.

I'd put my arms around Ashleigh and tried to keep my cleaning sponge out of her hair as she squeezed me tightly. When she pulled away, she had looked relieved and I realised it hadn't been easy for her to come and talk to me. After my conversation with Lachie, I completely understood.

Ashleigh walked towards the door but stopped again as she reached it.

"What about seeing that hardware store guy again? Coincidence, huh? He's really sweet though. I don't really remember, like, much about the day, but I remember he was great. And he's a bit cute, hey?"

I checked the time again. Yes, my date should definitely be here somewhere if he was on time. I scanned the crowd again, this time looking for anyone who looked like they were waiting for someone. That narrowed it down to about a hundred people.

Why is this such a popular meeting spot?!

I had run into Dan that morning. I hadn't seen him since the morning after our last hook-up and suddenly, there he was, coming into the building as I was going out. I'd almost forgotten how beautiful he was, with his deep-sea eyes and Adonis body, until he materialised in front of me. He'd taken in my tight, ribbed jumper, my short, black skirt and my knee-length suede boots. I wondered if I'd made a mistake in deviating from the usual dating uniform.

"Heading out?" Dan had asked, leaning on the door frame and forcing me to awkwardly continue to hold the door open for both of us.

I'd considered leaning against the door in a cool way, but couldn't risk the likelihood of it swinging away from me as soon as I placed weight on it.

"I am, actually. Heading in?"

Little lines crinkled neatly beside his eyes as his cheeks rose in a wide smile.

"You look nice. Hot date?"

"Yes, actually."

What are you playing at? Kiss me. What I mean is, please move aside.

His eyebrows had risen in mock surprise.

"In the afternoon? That's... interesting."

What's happening here? What are you implying? Kiss me. What I mean is... KISS ME!

"Yes, well, he's a dancer so he probably works nights," I'd said.

That seemed to shut his smug face up for a minute. I figured that he must also be aware of the twenty hot points rule.

"Anyway, I don't want to be late, so I'd better go."

Dan had moved aside slightly and motioned with his hand for me to go through, ensuring that I had to walk rather close to him to get by. As I passed him, he stopped me with a gentle hand on my arm. I could feel his breath in my hair.

Mmmm, breath hair.

"You know where to find me if he's no good," he said quietly.

I felt shivers run up my arm and tingles zing from my stomach to my lady bits.

Forget about this date! Take me now!

"I think I do. Which number apartment again?"

Dan smiled again, looking right into my eyes. Then he dropped his hand and walked towards his door.

It took me the whole tram ride into the city and some deep breathing to settle the adrenaline from having him touch me again. And now here I was, under the stupid clocks, waiting.

"Hey there. Are you Justine?" someone said in a rich American twang.

I had been so deep in thought that I must have been gazing at him vacantly as he approached me.

Nice one. Great start.

"Hi, Nick?" I said, looking at him properly for the first time.

Nick was good-looking. Really good-looking. I would have been very impressed if I hadn't just had Dan's face stamped on my inner eyelids.

Nick gave me a kiss on the cheek and pulled me towards him in a hug. He smelt amazing, like a department store at Christmas time. As he hugged me I could feel the hardness of his body beneath the thin grey t-shirt he was wearing. He didn't seem appropriately dressed for how cold it was supposed to be, but maybe he was new to Melbourne.

As we walked along St Kilda Road and chatted about how Nick missed his home in California but planned to stick around in Melbourne for a few more years, I realised I actually had no idea what this date was going to involve. We hadn't discussed it.

"So, do you know where we're going or are we just walking and expecting the other person to take the lead?" I asked.

Nick laughed—a loud, uninhibited sound that both surprised and delighted me. I hadn't thought it was the greatest joke, but I'd take it.

"I wanna take you somewhere," he said, taking my hand. I was surprised by his forwardness so early in the date, but he'd given me no reason to feel uncomfortable so I decided to go with it.

"I've lived in the city for three years now," Nick continued. "So I pretty much know my way around."

"Sounds good to me," I answered.

Dates were always awkward and unpredictable, but I felt at ease with Nick. *Ha!* I thought at Dan. *I will not be knocking on your door tonight, you arrogant—*

"You like tea, right?" Nick asked, a questioning look in his dark-lashed, almond-shaped eyes.

"Sure."

Not really, but maybe you could change my mind.

"Great, because I'm taking you to my favourite place. I even have a 'usual' there." He laughed. "Does that make me a *wanker,* having a 'usual' tea?"

He accentuated "wanker" with a failed attempt at an Australian accent.

"It doesn't, but your British accent might."

He laughed again and shoved me gently with our joined hands, then pulled me back towards him. We were walking across Prince's Bridge, with the Yarra flowing gently beneath us. I looked towards Southbank, my eye caught by the glint of gold from the top of the Eureka Tower. I loved this view of the glassy skyscrapers that lined the wide banks of the river.

We took the cement stairs at the end of the bridge down to the Southbank walk and Nick kept hold of my hand the whole time. He laughed at my jokes and teased me about my football team choice, saying, "The first thing I learned when I moved here was not to root for Collingwood because everyone hates them, except the people who are crazy for them, like the Yankees."

We reached the Silver Dragon Tea House and Nick dropped my hand to hold the door open for me. I didn't need doors opened for me, but appreciated the thought and thanked him as I walked in. I was greeted by the smell of freshly brewing tea as high, wistful notes from Chinese musical instruments swooped down from a speaker on the wall.

When the women behind the counter saw Nick walk in behind me, they started nodding and smiling. He put his arm around my shoulders and pointed at the menu on the wall.

"Those are all your choices," he said. "Go nuts."

The list was extensive and I really couldn't tell one tea from another.

Don't panic and order milk.

"Um, care to recommend something?"

"You bet!"

Nick approached the counter and was greeted warmly by a woman almost half his size. He said something which caused her to giggle and nod. After he'd ordered, Nick directed me to a table by the window.

"I like to watch people walk past and try to guess what they do, who they're with, that kinda thing," he said as we sat. We played his guessing game until an ornate silver pot of tea came out, fragrant and steaming.

Nick poured us both a cup and held his up in a "Cheers" motion. I returned the gesture and drank. *Oh. Yuk.* It tasted like a scented candle.

"Delicious," I said and Nick smiled at me, then sipped from his own cup and closed his eyes, obviously savouring the moment.

How much do I need to drink to make it seem like I'm enjoying it?

The answer was two cups. When we stepped outside again, I felt hot and sloshy.

"Hmm," Nick said, looking around. "It's way colder than I thought it would be. Seriously, what is it with you guys's weather? It's nearly summer."

"Welcome to Melbourne," I answered. "We could go into the casino? It will be warmer in there."

"Nah," he said. "I live right near here. I'll just grab a sweater from home, if that's cool with you?"

I looked around. We were in one of the most expensive areas of the city. Where did he live?

"Yeah, no worries," I said.

Flashing me a smile, Nick took my hand again and we'd only walked about one hundred metres when we turned left. Then he stopped in front of the Eureka Tower.

"Here we are! Home, sweet home."

I laughed, thinking he must be joking, but his face was straight.

"Wait, you actually live in the tallest building in Melbourne?"

I'd read somewhere that a one-bedroom apartment in the Eureka Tower could rent for around $3000 a month. Nick shrugged and continued towards the building.

Am I on a date with Batman?

We walked through a side entrance, away from where the general public entered for the Observation Deck, and went to a set of private lifts. Nick hit the arrow pointing up and then turned to me with a smile.

"You're not afraid of heights, are you? I'm on the 22nd floor," he said, pulling an access card from his back pocket.

"No, I'm good," I replied as I stepped into the lift in a daze.

The bell dinged for the 22nd floor and Nick stood in the way of the automatic doors as he motioned for me to walk out before him. I tried not to think of him as Willy Wonka and me as Charlie, mostly so I wouldn't accidentally burst into a song about golden tickets.

I followed Nick down the hall to a door where he swiped his card and a little green light flashed. He grandly pushed open the door to an air-conditioned apartment, where a stunning view of the city greeted us from ceiling-to-floor windows. I didn't know a whole lot about furniture, but I could tell that his was expensive. There was a heavy oak coffee table which held a coffee-table book that was open to a double-page spread of glossy, black-and-white photos. None of my friends had a coffee table, let alone a coffee-table book. There was art that I didn't understand hanging on most of the walls and a projector fixed to the ceiling above a dark leather couch that faced a roll-down screen.

He must be a really, really good dancer.

"Come on," Nick said, taking my hand again. "I'll show you my room while I get that sweater."

I had been so overwhelmed by the thought of him actually living here, that I hadn't really considered what had taken place. He'd invited me back to his place and I'd agreed. This wasn't my usual modus operandi for first dates. I was happy with hand-holding and maybe a kiss goodnight. Instead, I was on my way into Nick's bedroom at 1pm in the afternoon.

Well played, Batman.

The bedroom had the same wall of windows as the living room, but these ones slid open to a balcony. On the other side of the room, the doors to his wardrobe were all mirrors. It made the whole room feel as though it was made of glass. The bed itself had way more cushions on it than I imagined could be practical and there was a black, padded chair in the corner.

Nick slid open one of the mirrored doors and rifled around on a shelf. I couldn't help but notice that there were several plastic-bagged items hanging in his wardrobe, like the ones you get from a dry cleaner. I could only see the first outfit, but it was black, vinyl pants with a navy, sleeveless shirt, which had a fake police badge and tie attached. There were handcuffs hanging off the coat hanger.

What the... I thought, but then reminded myself, *Don't judge, you have a similar outfit hanging in your wardrobe.*

Nick saw me looking and grinned.

"One of my work costumes," he said. "Do you want to see the others?"

He grabbed a black jumper from the shelf, pulled it over his head and then started flicking through the plastic bags.

"Sexy firefighter, sexy postal officer, sexy pilot, sexy politician... That's a bit of a niche market. I don't get many requests for that one."

"So, when you said you were a dancer, what you meant is that you're a..."

"Exotic dancer. Yeah. I know, crazy, right?"

So now I had gone from being mistaken for a stripper to dating one.

"Yeah, crazy. What... uh... How does it work?"

"I have a regular show in the city but I also do a lot of private events, because the cash for them is insane. I work in IT during the day. Come on, let's check out the view."

He shut the wardrobe and crossed the room, flicking up the lock of the balcony door and pulling it open. I stared at my reflection in the wardrobe for a minute as my brain desperately tried to catch up. Then I followed Nick out and stood beside him at the balcony railing. My racing thoughts were stilled for a minute by the breathtaking view. I felt the wind dance my hair around my shoulders as I watched a helicopter land on top of a building.

"So, what are your passions in life?" Nick asked, turning to me.

I was taken aback by the question, considering that before the stripper revelation we'd erred on the side of small talk.

"Uh... I like footy, which you already know, unless we're losing, ha ha! Baking too, I like to bake. Mostly because I like to eat what I bake," I babbled, uneasy about the direction this conversation might head in once I gave him a chance to talk. It felt like he might be about to try to sell me a timeshare or involve me in a pyramid-scheme.

"No, I mean, what do you *love*? Why do you get up in the morning?"

I assumed "Because my alarm clock said I had to" was not an acceptable answer.

"I really love to sing. But I don't do it much anymore."

Nick looked into my eyes suddenly, intensely. He put both his hands on my shoulders.

"Yeah, *exactly*! You see?"

I had no idea what point he had apparently just proved so I waited for him to continue.

"Most of us have these passions as kids, then we grow up and stop doing the things we really love and just do things to make money. I wrote all about really living your passions in a book I published."

"You had a book published?"

"Self-published. It's an eBook. You gotta make these things happen for yourself. Ain't nobody gonna realise your dreams for you!"

"OK, uh, cool. What's it called?"

"Stripped Down," he said. "The Real You. For Real."

"Uh, great title."

I was in the dark as to whether it was all part of the title, or if he was just saying "For real" on the end for emphasis. Nick took his hands off my shoulders and gestured excitedly as he continued.

"Yeah, I mean, my passion is my dancing. It's not just my job, it's my craft, my art. People think stripping is like, you just take your clothes off. But it's not. A whole lot of work goes into the scripts, the concepts. At the moment I'm developing my own show. Wanna hear about it?"

Um, no.

"Yes."

"OK, well, women come to strip shows wanting to be like, sexually stimulated, of course. But what men don't realise about women and what women don't realise about themselves, is that they need to be *intellectually* stimulated first and then the rest follows, right?"

Um, no.

"Right."

"So, I'm writing a show that begins with me performing a monologue from Hamlet. The one with the skull, right? And then... *BAM!*"

I jumped back as his hands flew into the air.

"I pull off my puffy shorts and I'm just in a G-string. And the chicks go wild for it!"

"OK, yeah, I kinda see where you're..." I had no idea how to finish the sentence but I needn't have worried as he wasn't done.

"And then, I've got this other idea where I'm performing Homer's Greek tragedies and I take off my toga to Zorba's Dance. And then for the finale, I'm Icarus, with wings and shit, high up on a wire. As some epic music plays, I start dropping my clothes on the audience. Because it's hot near the sun, right?"

His eyes were blazing with excitement. I felt a sort of hysteria start to bubble inside me, as though the tea in my stomach had become carbonated. It rose to my chest.

Oh no, it's laughter!

I was about to laugh. I coughed, desperately trying to hide the fact, and then covered my mouth, wondering if I should shove my whole fist in there. Nick saved the day by turning his back on the view and walking to the balcony door. I took some desperate breaths, trying to think of unfunny things to calm myself.

Death at sea. Orphaned kittens. No-Sugar September.

"I'll give you a preview of a routine I'm working on," he said, turning his head and winking at me as he stepped back into his bedroom.

I was both horrified and a little bit curious. I couldn't think of a polite way to decline his offer anyway.

OK, this is happening.

I followed Nick as he pulled the padded chair into the centre of his room.

"You've always gotta check the chair before a performance," Nick was saying. "People don't realise the logistics of it when they book you for a party. But it can't have arms on it, because you've gotta straddle it. And it's gotta be strong enough to hold two people. Don't worry this one definitely is—tried and tested."

He patted the seat and winked again.

Ew. Did you clean it afterwards?

I sat down. Nick pressed a button on a remote that sat on his bedside table. Music started playing, I had no idea where from. Then he began to dance. I had to give it to him, he was good. He could move his body in very impressive ways and I was actually quite enthralled until he straddled me and began to roll his crotch in the direction of my face.

AH! Where do I look?!

I remembered reading a book once where the main character had struggled to decide on an appropriate facial expression when she was being serenaded with a guitar. This was like that, but three thousand times worse. What facial expression should you do when someone is thrusting at you rhythmically to music? Thankfully, the music changed and Nick danced off me again and back towards the bed.

"Come here," he said in what I imagined was his stripper voice but was a bit more like a serial-killer-on-the-phone voice. "You bad, bad girl."

I stood up, mostly because I didn't want to encourage Nick to start dancing on me again. He gyrated towards me and pulled me to him. We started to move together, which was less awkward at least, and he kissed me passionately. He turned us around rather expertly and danced me towards the bed.

No, I thought. *I don't want this.*

"Can I use your toilet… uh… bathroom?" I asked.

Nick looked immediately put out, breaking character with a sullen look as I pulled away from him. I imagined his "craft" was usually rather effective with the ladies. But he recovered himself quickly.

"Sure, it's just through there." He pointed to a door off the bedroom.

I smiled briefly and exited the room. The bathroom was spotless and there was a reed diffuser on the black marble sink. I looked in the mirror because it was what people in movies did when they were having a dilemma. My face looked helplessly back at me.

The problem was that I was bad at saying "No" at the best of times, let alone in intimate situations like this one. At least I had a few minutes to rehearse what I was going to say.

Nick, I've had a very nice time, but I've only just met you and I'm not really comfortable having sex with you already.

I hadn't heard it out loud yet, but I was pretty confident it sounded like something from a video about puberty that was made in the eighties. I tried to think of something more casual.

Hey Nick, can we cool things for a bit? Maybe get to know each other first?

That sounded better. It would have to do, I couldn't spend much more time in the toilet without it being weird.

OK, here goes.

I realised I hadn't actually gone to the toilet yet and did need to quite badly. I pulled my pants down and saw a smear of blood on my underwear.

It's a miracle! Thank you God… or whoever the patron saint for menstrual cycles is.

I emerged from the bathroom.

"Hey, Nick. Uh, bad news, it's that time of the month. So sorry!"

I shrugged in a "That's life" gesture, probably appearing way too happy about it. Nick looked entirely deflated. He probably thought I'd made it up but I decided against offering proof.

We said goodbye at the door. Nick didn't even offer to see me to the lift, but he did say, "It was nice meeting you," before brushing my cheek with a kiss.

I messaged Steph, who was still on her honeymoon, about the date on the way home—checking three times that I was definitely sending it to her. I felt giddily glad to be outside and free. I would never look at the Eureka Tower in the same way again.

I hesitated at Dan's door when I arrived home.

What would I say? I thought. *My date was a stripper, can I have a hug?*

I thought of his unbearably over-confident face when I'd spoken to him earlier. It wasn't like I could have sex with him either. I headed up the stairs and straight to the shower.

I was sitting on the couch in my comfiest pyjamas—multitasking again by eating a block of chocolate, cuddling a hot water bottle and watching a rom com—when there was a knock at the door. That was weird. With Steph away, I couldn't think of anyone who might just drop in. Maybe Anastasia needed something. Oh, I really didn't feel like being coerced into helping her right now.

What if she has an emergency?

I thought seriously about ignoring it, but my conscience dragged me up off the couch and over to the door. I looked through the peephole.

Oh shit.

It was Dan. I looked down at my chocolate-smeared love-heart pyjamas that said, "If you think I'm fun, you should see me when I'm sleeping" across the chest. I wasn't even wearing a bra. Dan looked like he was about to walk away and I realised I was just staring at him through the peephole like a creep. I opened the door.

Dan stood there looking at me for a minute and then, *that smile.*

"I have seen you when you're sleeping. I wouldn't say *fun* exactly. You drool a bit. Date ended early?"

"No. It was an afternoon date, so it went for a normal amount of time."

What are you doing here?

"I brought beers. I thought we could hang out for a bit," Dan said, holding up a six pack of the same craft beers Fluffy Aidan favoured.

"How did you know I was home already?" I asked, not moving aside to let him in yet.

He sighed and then muttered something like, "I heard you singing."

"Oh, OK—wait, *what*?!"

I felt even more than the usual Dan-induced amount of nervousness.

"I can hear you singing in the shower when my bathroom window is open."

"Right. Interesting," I said, horrified.

How long has this been happening? I thought, realising immediately that the answer was *always*. For the whole two years we'd lived in the same building. When I sang in the shower, I imagined I was performing to the entire crowd at Rod Laver Arena, not *Dan.*

Dan shrugged, causing the beers to clink together.

"I never told you because I thought you might stop if I did and I like it. Am I allowed in?"

Had anyone ever refused Dan entry to anything?

"Of course, and thanks for bringing…" *Fermented dishwater.* "Beer."

We sat side by side on the couch. Dan put his knee up on a cushion and stretched his arm across the headrest. He looked so comfortable, it could have been his couch. It actually could have been his couch, because at that moment I would have given it to him if he'd asked for it.

"What are you watching?"

I looked at my TV. The rom com was paused on a close-up of the main couple who were about to kiss.

"Just porn," I answered as Dan opened a beer and handed it to me.

He laughed and shook his head.

"Ah, rom coms. I've actually seen this one. It's the one where they have to pretend to be a couple and end up being a couple. Who saw it coming?" he said, opening his own beer.

"Hey," I said. "You ruined the end for me."

"Oh, come on, they're all predictable."

He "Cheers"ed me and then took a swig from his bottle.

"Then why did you watch it?" I asked, taking a sip that wasn't really a sip but I still hoped it looked like a sip. Even pretending to drink beer was gross. Worse than the tea.

"It was on a date."

"Oh."

We were silent for a minute while Dan took another swig and I picked at some chocolate on my pyjama pants.

"How was your date?" he asked.

I won't tell him anything specific. I'll just make it sound like a successful, attractive man enjoyed my company for the afternoon and I left him wanting more.

"He was a stripper who'd written a self-help book. He took me back to his apartment in the Eureka Tower and gave me a lap dance. He is creating a Shakespeare-themed strip show because apparently that's what women really want."

Dan stared at me for a minute, as though he was trying to figure out if I was joking, and then when my face remained serious, he burst out laughing. And laughing. And laughing.

Oh calm down, lots of people have had that happen to them.

"The situations that you end up in, Justine. Pure gold!"

"My best friend always says that someone should write a book about my life."

"They probably should," Dan said, still chuckling. It seemed my date story had broken the ice.

"Well, come on then, let's watch the rest of this movie. I can't remember what happens. Except for that they definitely get together."

192

I threw a cushion at him but pressed play.

The movie was just finishing when Ellie walked in. She saw Dan first and just stared at him, then back at the door, like she might have walked into the wrong apartment. I popped my head up over the couch.

"Hey, you're back! How was work?"

I knew I sounded excessively cheery, but I was trying to compensate for the weird situation.

"Uh, it was OK. How was your date? Hi Dan."

She was not attempting to compensate for the weird situation in any way.

"Hey Ellie, just popped by with some beers," Dan jumped in helpfully. "I thought it would be nice to get to know you guys better, since we see each other all the time. Want one?"

She looked at the beer distastefully and shook her head. I was immediately jealous of her.

"No thanks. I've been doing dry July since July."

"Wow," said Dan. "I'm not a massive drinker myself. The body is a temple and all that. But I figure the good stuff in the smoothie I drank earlier neutralises the alcohol, right?"

I laughed loudly, even though it wasn't a hilarious joke. Or maybe it wasn't a joke at all.

"I won't go into the science of it," Ellie answered, looking confused. "But alcohol doesn't actually work that way. Anyway, I'm off to bed. I've got an early one tomorrow."

"Woah," said Dan as her door shut. "Tough crowd."

"Tell me about it. Just imagine if she *had* gone into the science of it," I said, realising the credits were rolling and I'd missed the final, getting-together scene. Now I felt awkward again.

"So, how did you let your date down gently?" Dan asked.

"Ah…"

Say, "I told him I'd left my cat in the oven." Say anything but—

"I told him I had my period."

Damn it! Anything but that.

"Were you lying?"

"Actually no, I really did get it," I said. "It was a miracle."

Dan laughed.

"Well, I'd better leave you to get some rest and… ah, drink lots of fluids or whatever. You can keep the rest of the beers."

I appreciated the thought, even though he seemed to have confused a period with the flu. He leaned forward, put his hand on my cheek and kissed me on the mouth. Then he got off the couch and went out. I could hear him whistling in the hallway.

I suddenly missed Steph intensely. I needed her here, to help me figure out what my feelings were and analyse everything that Dan had said and done since her wedding. I'd kept her updated through messages but it wasn't the same.

My phone chimed to say I'd received a message. I wondered if Steph had somehow gotten

194

the vibe that I needed her. I checked who it was from. It was a picture message from Nick.

Uh oh.

Against my better judgement, I opened it. It said:

this is what ur missing out on babe

And there was his penis, staring me right in the eyes. I refilled my hot water bottle and went to bed.

CHAPTER FIFTEEN

I woke up to my ringtone. I'd been dreaming about Dan and automatically put my hand out, thinking that he'd be there. My fingers closed on cold pillow. I smacked at the bedside table in an attempt to shut my phone up and, finding myself unsuccessful, fumbled around while groaning until I got a hold of it. I swiped clumsily at the answer button, only managing to get it on the fourth try.

"Mmmello?"

"Justine? It's Lachie here."

Lachie? Lachie!

"Uh, hey Lachie."

I tried to sit up but I was tangled in sheet and landed back on the pillows with a *fwumpf!* I felt disoriented. Our last interaction had been incredibly uncomfortable, so why was he calling me?

Who even calls anyone these days?

The only people I spoke to on the phone were my parents and strangers asking for money.

Does he want some money?

"Hi. Sorry if I woke you up, I know it's early. Listen, did you mean what you said?"

I searched my sleepy mind for the answer to that conundrum.

What did I say?

I shook my head, trying to clear the fog.

"That you're naked when you go to the toilet in a playsuit? Yeah, I mean, sometimes you're wearing a bra, it depends on the cut of the—"

"No, sorry, I meant when you said you'd do anything to fix things between us?"

196

"Oh… Yes, I did. Wait, you don't want me to take a hit out on someone, do you?"

I kicked off the sheet and sat up, stretching out my free arm.

"Do you think if I was in the habit of knocking people off who've wronged me," Lachie said. "That *you'd* still be standing?"

I couldn't tell over the phone if his comment was meant to be scathing or teasing.

"Yes," I said, rubbing crusty sleep from the corners of my eyes. "I have catlike reflexes."

"That's actually very relevant. Also, you told me you like footy."

"I do… Why?"

"Great!"

I didn't like where this was going and wanted to make an excuse. But even if I wasn't a hopeless people-pleaser, I'd told him I wanted to make things right after my horrible mistake. I couldn't just brush off the first opportunity.

"Yes, I'm free. Why?"

"I desperately need a female…"

I decided this wasn't the time for obvious jokes.

"OK, well, I qualify, I think. *Why?*"

"For the social footy team I captain. One of our female team members is sick. Can you fill in tonight?"

NO! I WILL NOT BE PLAYING ANY SPORT! I don't have a mouthguard. Or coordination.

"Of course, that's fine. What time do I need to be there?"

Lachie filled me in on the details and then we said goodbye and hung up. I pulled the covers back over my shoulders and tried to return to my dream, but I was too full of nervous energy.

I liked the thought of things being resolved with Lachie, even though I wasn't exactly sure why, considering I couldn't really even call us friends. But I didn't like the thought of him seeing me fall over a lot, which was now very likely. I had never enjoyed sport as a kid. I'd been more into artsy things like singing and drama. I enjoyed footy purely as a spectator, although my Dad had insisted I learn the basics of kicking and handballing with my brother. My feelings about participating in sport were summed up by a game of basketball I'd been forced to play in Year 6. I'd ended up with a concussion and I wasn't even on the court.

I sighed mentally.

I'd better go and look up the rules.

Glenferrie Oval was tucked into a leafy spot just behind Glenferrie Road. The grass was patchy at this time of year but the spectator stands, which had presumably held a decent home crowd when the Hawthorn Hawks had played there years ago, were still well-maintained. I rocked up about 10 minutes before the game was supposed to start. The oval was only a five-minute walk from my house, but I'd stalled the whole way, dreading the imminent humiliation.

Lachie had told me to wear comfy clothes, so I'd inhaled and squeezed into the only active wear I owned—a clingy t-shirt and black leggings.

I'd thrown an oversized, old uni hoodie on over the top. It wasn't a flattering outfit, but my only other options seemed to be my dating uniforms.

I stepped into the stands and surveyed the ground. Two people dressed as umpires were marking out a rectangular shape on the oval with bright orange cones and there were quite a few people in footy gear standing around, talking and stretching. Lachie spotted me and ran over. He was wearing a green guernsey with a red sash, white footy shorts and a black backwards cap which pressed his curls tightly against his head.

"Hey mate, you made it! Thanks, I really appreciate it."

He tossed me my own red-and-green guernsey.

"Throw this on, then head over when you're ready. We're pretending to warm up but we're mostly messing around. Don't worry, none of us take it too seriously."

Lachie started to run back in the direction of the oval and I felt a rising panic. I hadn't played a game of organised sport since high school, and even then I didn't know what sport it was. While I was playing it.

"Lachie, wait! I don't know anything about social footy."

This was still true, even though I'd spent the afternoon looking it up.

"What... What do I do?"

"Oh, you'll pick it up. It's just touch so no tackling or anything."

Oh thank God, I hadn't even considered tackling.

"I've put you in the forward zone with me," Lachie said, pushing a flattened curl away from his forehead. "Just try to get the ball and kick it through the goals. You'll be fine, mate."

He marked a footy that had been kicked to him by his teammate and ran off, handballing it to someone else. I felt my eye start to twitch. I looked back in the direction of my apartment, seriously considering making a break for it.

I'll just say I felt faint—which is true—or maybe that I had a minor stroke. Which also might be true.

Reluctantly, I removed my hoodie and hung it on the fence. Then I pulled the guernsey, which smelt strongly of washing powder, over my head.

High-pitched, irritating laughter assaulted my ears just as my head popped out from the neck of the footy jumper. I searched the field to investigate its source, expecting to see a bunch of teens drinking energy drinks, and discovered it was coming from a couple of women in "my" team. They were chasing Lachie, dodging towards him and then darting away again, trying to pull off his cap. I was fascinated by the sight. I couldn't believe these women, who were at least their late twenties, were utilising such an overt teenage flirting ritual. Eventually, a silver-blonde-haired woman succeeded and placed the cap on her own head, parading around by swishing her hair and hips in unison. De-capped, Lachie's hair blazed in the low sun setting behind him.

I watched as he continued to run around with the rest of the team, kicking and passing, occasionally stopping to give someone a noogie, or to fake-tackle them. He kicked a ball straight into a goal post and laughed off the silver-blonde's teasing while running around with his hands in the air in mock-celebration.

Lachie looked up and caught my eye. He slowed, dropped his hands and beckoned for me to join them. One or two of the women followed his gaze to where I was standing. Lachie said something to them and they laughed uproariously, making me feel even more nervous and self-conscious. I made my way over to them.

"Hey, mate," Lachie said.

Mate, mate, matey, mate. I get it. I've been friend-zoned.

"I was just saying that you're probably going to offer your services to the other team after seeing that pathetic effort."

"Not really," I shrugged and he cocked his head, as if he was waiting for the punchline. "I think you have to have some serious skill to hit a target that slim. You must have been aiming for it, right?" I said.

Lachie smiled widely at me and a few of the other guys chuckled.

"Don't make me regret drafting you," he joked and handballed a ball in my direction.

The ball bounced off my left boob and onto the ground. So much for my catlike reflexes. Lachie winced.

"Sorry about that," he said. "But don't worry, it's only a forty-minute game."

FORTY MINUTES?!

"Let me introduce you to the team," Lachie continued, either not noticing or ignoring my shocked expression. "Everyone, this is Justine, our gallant replacement for Fee. Justine, this is Remy." Lachie nodded to the silver blonde as he retrieved his cap from her head.

"I'm vice-captain," Remy said, picking up the ball my boob had dropped.

As she straightened up, she flicked her silver tresses away from her elven face. She had bright-green upturned eyes which stared unapologetically into mine and her mouth was a love-heart shaped pout above her angular chin. She was clearly unimpressed by my presence, but she was also adorable. I just wanted to go *boop!* with my index finger on her cute little nose.

"Nice to meet you," I said to her, even though I wasn't sure if I meant it.

Remy turned to Lachie and threw the footy into the air, attempting to kick it in his general direction as it came down. Lachie chased after the ball as it bounced away to his right. A guy about my height with a fashionable blonde comb over and dark stubble held his hand out to me.

"I'm Nate, a fellow forward. I reckon you, me and Lach are going to dominate that zone tonight."

I shook the hand Nate offered me, trying to look relaxed as he continued to introduce the rest of the team. Lachie joined the coin toss with the other

202

captain, an uncommonly tall guy in a yellow guernsey with blue stripes who made Lachie look like a hobbit. The coin landed, Lachie nodded and gestured to one end of the oval and then we were taking our places on the coned-off field.

There were six people in the forward zone to start with but once play began, Nate and Lachie seemed to disappear, leaving me in front of the goals with an opposition player. She was friendly and also a teacher, so we got chatting about work until suddenly the ball was bouncing within a metre of me. I had the urge to run away from it, but remembered vaguely that that was not in fact the aim of the game. Before I could take a step though, my opposition player had scooped it up and handballed it off to her team. Away it went, travelling down to the other end of the field.

The game continued in that fashion, with me panicking every time the ball came near me. Lachie and Nate both kicked goals, but the opposition kicked more. When the whistle blew for half-time, I was yet to touch the ball. The teams divided into separate huddles.

"They're killing us," Remy complained as we crowded together in a tight circle. "Maybe a change of positions? Someone more... proactive in goals?"

She flicked her searing green light bulbs in my direction. My heart pumped rapidly and my face flushed with heat.

"We just need a little more strategy," Lachie ignored her. "Nate, maybe if you..."

I tuned out as he went on. I probably wouldn't have understood it even if I wanted to.

What am I doing here?

I felt unable to bear another twenty minutes of failure. The huddle broke up and my teammates drifted back to their positions. Lachie came up to me in front of the goals as I looked back in the direction of my apartment again.

"Are you doing OK?" he asked, locking eyes with me.

"I think you'd be better off without me playing," I replied, trying not to sound like I was throwing myself a little pity party but failing.

"Remember the skateboarding… Sorry… Slippery deathboarding?" Lachie said as the umpire held the ball up, ready for the centre bounce.

"Yes," I said, surprised he was bringing up our date. "When I hurt my ankle?"

Why did I say that? I could have said, "Yes, that kiss was in my top five."

"Before the ankle," Lachie went on with a wince. "You didn't think you could skateboard and then you actually tried and you did it! I get that this might not be your thing and I don't care if we win because it's just a game. I'm just asking you to actually try. Please?"

I felt furious.

I am standing on this stupid field in your stupid guernsey, tolerating your stupid vice-captain and feeling stupid. I. Am. Trying.

I nodded at him sullenly as the umpire bounced the ball. Lachie jogged back to his opponent and I looked around for mine. She was off chatting with one of my teammates, touching him on the shoulder and laughing about something he'd said.

This is probably an excellent way to meet guys, I thought. *Shame about the having-to-play-sport bit.*

I took a deep breath.

Twenty minutes to go and counting.

The defence was strong for both teams in the second half but my team had somehow regrouped and slowly started to come back, still with no significant assistance from me. I noticed that Remy had plenty of possessions but no idea what to do with the ball once it was in her hands and kicked it to the opposition at least twice.

I watched the play surge back and forth for a bit, like a tug-of-war. I saw Lachie check his watch, and then motion with two fingers to me and Nate. Two minutes. As far as I could tell, we were now only a goal down.

Suddenly, the ball was spinning high above our heads, then swiftly descending into our zone. Lachie caught it with two hands in the air and dodged his charging opponent, kicking it sideways towards the goals, right near where I was standing. As it bounced closer, I could see that it wasn't going to make it through. My opponent had rightly deemed my threat level low and ditched me to guard Nate. With two people tagging him, there was no way Nate would get there in time.

If I can just get a toe to it.

I ran towards the ball and stretched out my foot, sticking out my tongue in concentration. I felt my foot connect with the side of the ball. I stopped, stunned, as I watched it roll between the two middle posts. Everyone was silent for a few seconds. Then the goal umpire pointed her two index fingers towards me.

"GOAL!" I heard Lachie yell from somewhere and then he was right in front of me. He put his hands on my waist, lifted me high into the air and spun me around. I was shocked by both his strength and balance, and also by the fact that *I* had actually managed to kick a goal. The rest of the team were cheering with excitement and ran to join us as Lachie returned me to the ground. They all patted my back and ruffled my hair, but at least no one took it upon themselves to smack me on the ass.

"Why are they so excited?" I asked Lachie. "We only evened up the scores."

"In social footy, a goal from a female counts for nine points, not six!" Lachie cried joyfully, high-fiving Nate.

A whistle blew and everyone returned to their positions, remembering it wasn't quite the end of the game. The ball came spinning through the air, back towards our end. Feeling newly confident, I ran towards the footy, knowing that I could mark it if I didn't take my eyes off it.

Nearly there.

Suddenly I felt a *whumpf* as all the air seemed to leave my body. I crumpled to the ground, gasping. I was vaguely aware of the sound of a whistle and the concerned chatter of people crowding around me. Then Lachie's face was right next to mine.

"I wasn't watching, what happened? Can you talk?" he asked gently.

I tried but found I was still completely out of breath. The pain in my stomach brought tears to my eyes.

"She ran into me when we were both going for the ball," I heard Remy say with a cold bite to her voice. "I was just about to mark it."

Lachie took my arm and helped me into a sitting position.

"Listen to my voice," he said quietly. "You're winded. I need you to breathe in through your nose and then out through your mouth. Take some breaths for me."

I inhaled through my nose, feeling the pain throb through me again, and then shakily exhaled through my mouth. I did it a few more times and began to feel better, although the hurt and bewilderment were quickly replaced by embarrassment.

I blame YOU, sport!

I allowed Lachie to help me stand. I still felt a bit disoriented but our team seemed to have resumed their celebrations, having won the game by three points. They all—except Remy—patted my back again and then went to shake hands with the opposition. Lachie remained by my side.

"You can go and do… captain things. I'm OK. I've got my breath back," I said to him, gently extracting my arm from his hands.

"I feel… responsible," Lachie said, not letting me go. "It looked like you took a hard hit. You were amazing, though. Thank you."

There was genuine respect in his eyes.

"Yo, Lach, Justine! Are you guys coming for a bite to eat?" Nate yelled to us.

I shook my head. I still had my school planning to do. I'd spent so much time researching social footy, I hadn't had the chance to get organised for the week ahead.

"I'm going to give it a miss this time too," Lachie called and then turned back to me. "I'll walk home with you. I live on Burwood Road so I'm on your way if you go via Glenferrie Road?"

"Yeah, sure."

It wasn't the shortest way home, but it wasn't very far out of my way.

"Cool. You start walking and I'll catch up. I've just gotta say goodbye."

I waved farewell to the team, then pulled off my guernsey and handed it to Lachie, who accepted it with a smile and then walked over to where the others were gathered. I started to head over to where I'd hung my hoodie on the fence. As I walked, something in the stands caught my eye. Another footy team were gathered there, dressed in pink-and-black striped guernseys, probably waiting for the next game. From this distance, he was just a muscular silhouette amongst them, but I'd reminisced about his body enough to have committed it to heart. It was Dan. My automatic Dan-in-the-vicinity response revved up—my heart rate accelerated and my stomach danced.

Does he know I'm here? How much did he see? Did he see my goal? Did he see Lachie lift me into the air? Did he see me fall into the dirt?

It made sense. I knew Dan was a footballer and now that it was off season, it followed that he might be a part of a social team. But seriously, did he have to be there? At that particular oval? At that particular time? I was staring into the stands, so I hadn't noticed my opponent approach until she was right beside me.

"Hey," she said. "Are you alright?"

"Yeah, I was just a bit winded," I smiled at her. "You can probably tell I don't play a lot of sport. I'm not very coordinated."

She looked at me strangely and said, "Your coordination had nothing to do with it. The umpire missed it but I saw it. That girl from your team, she dropped her shoulder at the last minute. There was no way it was an accident, she was aiming for you. I just thought you should know what your own teammate did. Nice to meet you."

She walked back to her friends, leaving me with shivers. It was all a bit too much. I wanted to be home, cosy and unmolested by crazy silver-blonde elves. The only problem was that I had to walk right up to Dan's entire football team to retrieve my hoodie.

Breathe in through your nose, then out through your mouth.

As I neared the group, it became evident that they were all *very* attractive people. I suddenly had a terrible thought: was one of the women Really Stupid Pants?

No, don't think about that. Just get through this.

My nerves prickled at my skin as they all started to turn their heads, noticing me approaching them. Dan looked up from his conversation with a woman with shiny chestnut hair and a very convincing fake tan. I couldn't tell if it was the first time he'd realised that I was there or not. What would he say to me? Would he tell his friends about me straddling the mower catcher as a fun anecdote? Or maybe the stripper date? What would he introduce me as?

Oh no. Here goes.

Dan flicked up his index finger at me with the slightest nod of his head and then went back to his conversation.

Seriously? That's it?! YOU HAVE BEEN INSIDE ME!

My face burned with fury and embarrassment as I snatched my hoodie off the fence. One of the other guys even said, "How ya goin'?" and he was a complete stranger! I mumbled a response and then hurried away with my head down.

I pounded my anger into the footpath as I walked and was almost at Glenferrie Road by the time Lachie caught up with me.

"Slow down, speed demon," he said, puffing.

He'd swapped his guernsey for a zip-up jacket and a backpack but was still in his footy shorts. We walked along, side by side, turning right onto Glenferrie Road—a perpetually busy street with trams, trains and cars all providing a soundtrack of *clacks*, *honks* and *dings*. Cluttered shop fronts jostled for attention from the mixed clientele of poor students and rich professionals, with the aromas of several different restaurants fusing together and greeting us in mouth-watering waves.

"Ah, that smells good," Lachie said after inhaling audibly.

"Which one?" I asked, looking up and down the street.

I was starting to feel hungry myself, now that the sharp rage in my stomach had dulled slightly.

"I don't know, but I want whatever it is. What do you feel like?" he asked, without even querying as to whether I wanted to eat with him.

"Anything," I said honestly.

"If you had to choose one?" Lachie gestured in a wide arc.

"I'm happy with whatever you want," I shrugged.

We'd stopped walking and were just standing in the middle of the footpath, facing each other. People had to walk around us to get past.

"You have to have some preference though," Lachie pushed. "Just pick one."

"Fine!" I said, exasperated. "Thai!"

"Nah. I don't feel like Thai," he said.

I looked at him with my eyebrows narrowed in disbelief.

"Ha ha! I'm just kidding!" Lachie laughed. "I love Thai!"

We ducked into the first Thai restaurant we passed and sat across from each other in mismatched plastic chairs at a wonky table. Over massaman curry and coconut rice, Lachie talked about being raised by his single mother, a nurse who he idolised. He had two sisters, one older and one younger, he liked movies from the 40s and music from the 70s, and he was definitely a cat person. He added that he'd considered getting a tattoo many times but probably wouldn't because he hated needles.

"Getting them, that is," he said. "I love giving them. It's fun."

"You're sick," I said. "What tattoo would you get?"

"I don't know," he said, sucking lemonade through a stainless steel straw he'd produced from his backpack. "Probably Chinese symbols that said something like 'Get Your Petrol Here', but I'd tell everyone it said 'Live for Peace' and only I'd know the truth. What about you? What would you get?"

I stirred the remains of my curry and watched the sauce wash over the scattered grains of rice.

"Something to do with the ocean," I answered.

"Really? Why?"

"I grew up near the Great Ocean Road. The ocean has always… calmed me. I feel like when I'm there, my thoughts slow down to match the rhythm of the waves."

I suddenly felt embarrassed, realising that I'd just said something out loud that was extremely personal and massively cheesy. But Lachie just smiled and nodded.

"I get that," was all he said.

After dinner, we continued our walk along Glenferrie Road, with our stomachs now pleasingly warm and full. As we turned right onto Burwood Road, Lachie casually said, "So, how's the dating going, mate?"

Is it awkward if I tell him the truth?

He hadn't given any indication that he might be still interested in me. So I recalled the details of the date with Nick, deliberately embellishing them to prolong his laughter, but leaving out Dan's visit at the end.

When he finished laughing, Lachie said, "So, you'd be keen to see him again soon. He's clearly a catch."

"Well, he certainly thought I was," I said as we stopped at a set of lights. "Because that night he sent me a dick pic. Seriously, why dick pics? Do you send them?"

"Yeah heaps, but never of my own," Lachie replied, pressing the silver button. "Hang on, is this a subtle request? Alright, the answer is yes, only because you won us the game. But I draw the line at autographing it."

I laughed as the little green figure lit up, beckoning us across the road. Then I continued on my rant.

"I've just never heard a girl say 'Then he sent me a picture of his penis and I could not resist him.' I don't get it. What kind of success rate could they have? They are the worst element of dating today."

"What about catfishing?" Lachie asked.

"It's fine. I love a good mystery."

"Ghosting?"

"Not exactly noble, but an efficient way to avoid awkward conversations."

"OK. Fair enough," Lachie conceded. "But what if the lighting is really good on the picture? I mean, if I had to say what my best angle was…"

We both laughed and suddenly he was stopping in front of a cluster of newly built units.

"This is me," he said. "Um, here, I meant to give you these. To say thanks for filling in today."

He handed me a bunch of paper tickets from his backpack.

"My mate is running this Covert Cinema thing, so he gave me a few freebies for my friends. It's really cool. You get given a theme and a location, then you dress in the theme and just show up—the rest is all a surprise, including the movie you're going to see. This time the theme is Roaring Twenties. Anyway, it's on New Year's Eve, so you've probably got something on."

"I don't," I said quickly, putting the tickets carefully in my hoodie pocket. "New Year's hasn't really been much of an event for me since I got old and boring. I'm free. Thanks. It sounds fun."

There was a weird moment where it looked like Lachie wanted to hug me. I tried to avoid any awkwardness by giving him a jolly wave, but, because we were standing quite close, I ended up waving right in his face and almost brushing his nose with my palm.

"Catch ya then," Lachie said, turning to go.

It occurred to me that we didn't really have a reason to see each other again until New Year's. And he hadn't even said if he'd be there. Maybe he was just promoting the event for his mate.

"I'll be at Covert Cinema," Lachie said, reading my mind as he turned back towards me. "But maybe in the meantime you'll need to break into your place again. I'll order in some grappling hooks just in case."

Then he smiled and walked away.

CHAPTER SIXTEEN

On Friday evening I was sitting on the ground, copying a picture of a rainbow serpent onto a large white piece of paper, when my intercom buzzed. I picked up the receiver.

"What are you wearing?" a voice whispered breathily into my ear.

"Nothing, as I've been expecting you," I replied in my huskiest voice, pressing the little button with a picture of a key on it.

About thirty seconds later, Steph was throwing herself into my open arms. I hugged her tightly and she squeezed me back. When we broke apart and she stepped back, I said, "Did marriage make you hotter? You look amazing."

Her hair was beach-wavy and her dyed blonde streaks had lightened further under the Fijian sun. She was wearing a bright blue dress that showed off her tanned legs.

"What can I say, it turns out having no responsibilities and lots of sex is really good for you. Who knew?"

She went and plonked herself down on the couch.

"Er, speaking of, what is that phallic symbol?" she asked, pointing to my serpent.

"Oh. I haven't drawn the eyes yet. It's a rainbow serpent, for school."

I rolled it up and put it aside.

"Oh good, I thought maybe you'd discovered art therapy as a solution to your dating woes. Now, quick recap of what I've been away for:

drunken drop-in on Neighbour Dan and a morning bang, unsolicited strip show from Nick the Dick, Neighbour Dan brings over beers and pashes you, dick pic from Nick the Dick, and then, the most unbelievable part, *you* played *sport*?"

"That's the gist," I said as I pulled chocolate biscuits from the cupboard and tore them open.

"God, I've missed you."

"I've missed you too. I have no idea what my feelings are."

I filled Steph in on all the tiny details I hadn't bothered to message her while she munched thoughtfully on a biscuit.

"Wait," she said as I took a breath and a biscuit for myself. "So Hardware Ginger—or is he First Aid Ginger now?—is back on the scene? I didn't see that coming."

"Not really *on the scene.*" I said, remembering the potential-hug-turned-face-wave. "We're friends, I think. He calls me 'mate' all the time."

Steph screwed up her nose while picking off crumbs that had stuck to her lip gloss.

"So then, what's Neighbour Dan's deal? Is he ghosting you or what?"

"I don't know. But the fact is that I can't control him or his emotions, so I need to find happiness from within myself," I said wisely.

She looked at me suspiciously.

"Have you been reading horoscopes again?"

"No, but I'm listening to a lot of positive-thinking podcasts."

"Makes sense. But seriously, *what is his deal?*" she asked again, reaching for another biscuit.

I sighed and looked at her hopelessly. In truth, that question had being playing on repeat in my mind all week.

A student had begged me to hold a funeral for a dead bird he'd found in the schoolyard. *What is Dan's deal?* I'd thought as I said the eulogy.

Anastasia had gotten me to stand on a chair to remove a foam dart from her ceiling that her grandson had shot up there. *What is Dan's deal?* I'd thought as I dropped it down onto her lino.

Pops had called me to arrange another Sunday Roast. *What is Dan's deal?* I'd screamed in my mind as I added the date to my calendar.

"Let's go and meet The Boys," Steph said, wiping her hands on her dress. "They sent me the name of a place on Swan Street."

That perked me up. Swan Street never disappointed, in food or atmosphere.

As we headed down the stairs in single file, I heard one of the ground floor doors opening and Dan's dark hair emerged just below the metal banister I was holding.

What is Dan's deal? reverberated around my head.

I didn't want to see him but short of carefully turning around and tip-toeing back up the stairs (which was definitely not beneath me), I couldn't avoid it. Dan looked up and saw me descending as he pulled his door shut behind him. He leaned on it casually and smiled up at me.

"Hey there," he said. "It's the footy star."

218

I glanced at him and then looked away quickly, knowing I had no defences with which to shield myself from his stunning smile.

"Hey, Dan."

I kept walking as Steph greeted Dan politely behind me. I opened the door and caught a glimpse of his deflated face in the glass reflection.

Good.

The Boys were already seated upstairs when we got to the restaurant—a burger joint which boasted slow-cooked meat and cold cider. It was stuffy with the combination of many warm bodies and frying meat, and abuzz with chatter. The Boys and Zoe were already seated in an upstairs mezzanine, visible if Steph and I craned our necks from the lower level. We held our dresses against our legs as we climbed the stairs and were met with cheers and hugs as we approached the table.

After we had all consulted each other on menu choices and ordered, Steph filled us in on her honeymoon, which she described as "Weeks of doing nothing but lying on the beach and loving the shit out of each other." I was jealous, in a happy-for-her kind of way. The food came and the banter ceased as we all savoured the hot, dripping bread rolls of pleasure. Then conversation ramped up again, turning inevitably to our love lives. I told the Nick the Dick story for the sixth time and the resulting laughter earned us disapproving looks from the table of middle-aged diners beside us.

"OK, I've got one," Li piped up once the laughter died down. "I've been texting this chick for a while and I'm bored one night, so I take her out. We're having a few drinks at a bar and she's on her phone most of the time. Then she says her friend's going to join us. The friend arrives and suddenly it's like it's their date, both of them are pretty much ignoring me. Karaoke starts, so they go off and do a duet, leaving me with their handbags. I can't leave, because I've got all their money and shit.

"Anyway, when they come back, my 'date'," he motioned with air quotes. "She says, 'Let's go back to my place'. I'm thinking maybe she means all three of us, but the friend stays, so it's just me and her again. She's been drinking the whole time, so she's pretty off her face by now. I'm thinking she's way too drunk, so I'm about to make an excuse to leave, but she says..."

He took a sip of cider and we all stared at him, hanging on the next line. He was clearly enjoying the suspense and made a show of wiping his mouth with the back of his hand before he continued.

"She says, 'Wanna play Super Nintendo?" Fuck yeah, I do! So she fires up Mario Kart and we start racing. Then I notice her car—she's Bowser—is just ramming into a wall over and over. I look at her and she's fallen asleep on her controller. Snoring and everything."

"So... What did you do?" Billy asked, putting his arm around Zoe.

"I did what any self-respecting man would do," Li said. "I played until I won the championship and then I went home."

Steph's car that she'd had since uni was parked on the street just outside my apartment. When we reached it, she opened the passenger side door and pulled out a paper bag, which she passed to me.

"It's your souvenir."

I put my hand in and pulled out a bracelet made of aquamarine glass beads. There was a tiny wooden turtle charm hanging off it.

"Thank you. I love it!" I said, putting it on.

The little turtle danced around as I turned my wrist to see the bracelet in the street light.

"Well, I know you love the ocean and the turtle is the Fijian symbol for wellness and peace. Also fertility."

"OK, well, I'll just take the first two for now."

Steph stared down at the keys in her palm for a minute before closing her fist around them.

"Are you alright, Justine? Things have been a bit… full-on for you."

She looked at me with the face of a friend who already knows the answer when they ask after your welfare. My eyes filled with tears.

"I just… I just want to be settled, Steph. I don't want to be single anymore. I want what you have. I just want to find… him."

"I know Juz, and you will. I know you will."

She put her arms around me and I felt my tears drip onto her bare shoulders. We stood like that until I'd composed myself.

"I'm so pumped for Spa Day. It's only two weeks away now," Steph said, referring to the trip we took every year to a thermal hot spring on the Mornington Peninsula. "I booked the Soak and Rub package for us before I left for Fiji."

"I can't wait to just catch up and chill out," I said, feeling tired of life in general.

Steph nodded, gave me a final squeeze and headed home to her husband.

I woke up early to my alarm. For some reason, Past Justine had decided to book a 9am wax so that she could use the rest of Saturday to do washing, exercise and get her life together. Past Justine really was a bossy, self-righteous bitch sometimes. She didn't buy junk food at the shops because she was trying to be healthy and she also unfriended people on social media that I now wanted to stalk.

I wriggled into my denim shorts and a black t-shirt with a French phrase on it, then walked down the street to my waxing place. I was sitting in the waiting area when my phone chimed. It was a message from Lachie.

Sorry, I know you were hoping for a dick pic. Just wondering if you're around this arvo to hang out? Hope that's not weird. Let me know.

I was around, as it happened.

Sure. When and where? Please leave all skateboards and other sports equipment at home.

He texted back St James Park with a smiley face. Ah, the smiley face. So many meanings in one stupid little yellow circle. I didn't have time to

222

analyse it though, because a woman came out and called my name. She wasn't my usual waxer. My usual waxer, Aisha, was a funny, empathetic woman who knew my whole dating history. We'd discuss the hopelessness of men while she literally tore strips off me. I trusted Aisha with my secrets as much as I trusted her with my lady bits. But this new woman was twitchy and nervous-looking.

"Hi, uh, I'm Kelly. Er… Aisha's not well today so I'm filling in. I hope that's, uh… OK," she stammered as she led me into the waxing room.

Twitchy Kelly left me to remove my shorts and undies, then returned when I was lying on the table. I watched her stir the container of wax with a wooden stick, drop the stick onto the floor, then fumble for another one.

"Can I get you to… uh… get on your… er… hands and knees please?" she asked.

This was a new request. I usually just held my legs in the air. I didn't protest though, assuming that, despite appearances, she was a professional and not someone hired from a temp agency for the day.

I got into a crawling position and with no further warning, Twitchy Kelly was smearing wax along my inner butt cheeks, with some of it splattering onto my thighs and calves. She slapped strips onto the wax and then hastily pulled on them, one at a time, ripping with the hair grain instead of against it.

"YEOOWWW!" I yelled, clenching reflexively.

"Er… sorry about that. Um, could you turn over now?"

Nope, I'm good, that's enough for today!

I tentatively laid on my back, eyeing Twitchy Kelly as she stirred the wax again. I couldn't be sure, but it looked like her hands were shaking. The temp agency theory was gaining momentum.

Get out Justine, while you still have any lady bits left!

But I couldn't leave. What would I say? Well, most people could probably come up with a decent excuse, or would just say, "Don't touch me again, you sadist." But not People-Pleaser Me.

Twitchy Kelly was at it again, slopping the wax all over me like a kid with craft glue when there are no adults watching. Then the strips again. *Rrrrriipppp.* I bit my bottom lip. It was no less painful for the fact that I was prepared for it. Tears sprung to my eyes and ran down my cheeks. *Rrrrriipppp. Rrrrriipppp.* Aisha would usually do two at a time to minimise the pain, and she always pulled upwards, but not Twitchy Kelly. *Rrrriiipppppppp.*

"All done!" she announced a little hysterically, as if she was as relieved as me.

I looked down.

Oh God, what have you done?

It was all gone. I usually went to Aisha for a downstairs tidy up, but thanks to Twitchy Kelly, I was now as hairless as one of those stupid-looking, allergy-free cats.

224

"And now for your legs," she said, stirring her little pot again.

Oh, please no.

I cringed through the leg wax, which was not quite as bad as the Brazilian XXX one she'd given me, and was relieved when Twitchy Kelly started rubbing a strong smelling moisturiser on my legs. It was really thick, different from the one Aisha used, but at that point I was so relieved the waxing part was over, she could have been rubbing Vegemite on my legs for all I cared.

I paid at the counter, feeling the deep injustice of having to part with money for the sake of that merciless torture. On the walk home I was still smarting from both the physical pain and the emotional trauma, when my phone rang.

"Juzzy. I need a favour," Riley said in a hurried tone.

Hello, brother. I'm good, thank you.

"OK, ah, what is it?"

We both knew I was going to say "Yes" anyway, so I don't know why I bothered to ask for details.

"I need you to take the kids for an hour or so this arvo. Hayley is working and my car's playing up, so I have to get it to the mechanic. Hayley will drop them off on her way to work. We just need you to take them to the park or something for an hour?"

"Oh, um, I have a…"

Not a date.

What is it exactly? A matey-type hang? Can I say, "Sorry, I have a friendship hang"?

"Please, I'm desperate. No one else can do it and I need my car. Please. Chase is really excited to see you. I'll put him on."

"No, that's really not—"

"Hi, Teeny!" Chase's excited little voice piped up. "I went looking for emus, but I didn't find any, so I played in the sand for a bit, but then I went looking for emus again in case they wanted to play in the sand too."

"That's great, Chaser. I think emus would love the sand. Is Daddy still there?"

"Yes, here he is, Teeny. See you at the park sooooon!"

"Emotional blackmail is low, Riley." I scolded.

"I told you, I'm desperate. Outside your place at noon?"

I was meeting Lachie at 12.30.

"OK, fine. See you then."

At 12.15 Hayley was extracting two tired-looking kids from her four-wheel drive and dumping them into their double pram. She looked exhausted herself. I helped her strap them in and then retrieved their favourite soft toys from the car.

"Thanks, Justine, we really appreciate this," Hayley said, massaging her temples. "They're both due for a nap so if you walk around with them, they'll probably nod off."

"No worries," I said, returning Isla's happy smile and touching her cheek. "Any idea when you'll be able to pick them up?"

"Shouldn't be longer than an hour," Hayley said, looking doubtful. "As long as the client is on time."

She bent to brush each child's forehead with a kiss.

"Be good. Thanks again, Justine!" Hayley said and then was gone in an exhale of exhaust from her giant car.

"OK, niblings," I said. "Let's ride!"

I made zooming noises as I powered the pram forward towards the park. Both kids squealed excitedly as I took unnecessary corners sharply, causing them to flop from side to side.

"And they made it! Champion rally drivers!" I announced as we crossed the finish line, which in this case was the pedestrian crossing leading to St James Park.

Both kids clapped and cheered loudly. I could see Lachie leaning against the fence of the oval, with his backpack resting against his leg. He was wearing an open-necked, short-sleeve shirt in red and black tartan with camel-coloured shorts. He looked up and waved to me.

"Cute kids," he said as I approached him. "Are they yours?"

"One of them could be, we're still awaiting DNA results," I said. "And the other one I found on the side of the road. Want one?"

"Better not, I've already got several at home. They do my cooking and cleaning."

"You're like a modern day Snow White," I said, handing Isla back the toy bunny she'd dropped. She put one of its ears into her mouth.

"I've got the skin for it. And the perfectly pitched soprano voice."

"Really?" I asked.

"No, I'm a terrible singer. The rest is true."

Lachie knelt down in front of the pram.

"They're my brother's kids," I said. "He threw them at me at the last minute. But they're really great."

"Hey guys, I'm Lachie. Those are some cool friends you've got there. What are their names?"

After Chase had not only introduced both toys, but also explained their favorite foods, as well as their hopes and dreams for the future, he held his little tiger close to Lachie's face.

"Nice to meet you, Lachie. I like your bright hair," Chase said in a gruff voice.

Lachie shook its paw. Then Chase put his thumb in his mouth and held the tiger close to his face. Isla already had her eyes shut.

"Mind if we walk? So they can sleep?" I asked Lachie.

"Sounds perfect," Lachie said. "Let's take the river trail."

We set off—probably looking like the picture of a perfect nuclear family—following the path through the park and then out the other side. We crossed the river onto Bridge Road in Richmond, and walked along a winding track down to the Yarra River Trail. The Yarra lay in front of us, murky and still, like a long stretch of muddy puddle.

"I don't trust the river when it looks like that," I thought out loud as I steered the pram left and we began to follow the walking track.

"What do you mean?" Lachie asked.

"It's creepy, like there could be anything in there and you wouldn't know."

I snuck a peek in the pram. Both kids were already fast asleep.

"Oh yeah? Like what sort of thing?" Lachie asked.

He stopped to smell the leaves of a eucalyptus tree with thin, drooping branches that trailed along the opaque surface of the river.

"I don't know, I haven't thought of anything specific. A dead body."

"Once the gasses built up and inflated the body tissue, it would eventually float to the surface," he said matter-of-factly.

"A stolen car, then."

I pushed out the pram's canopy so that it shaded both children. Although the sun was snuggled into a doona of clouds, it was a hot and sticky day. I could already feel sweat beginning to bead on the backs of my legs.

"It's not deep enough. I'm pretty sure you'd see some part of a submerged car."

"I don't know! A sea monster!"

"It would make huge bubbles. Also, to my knowledge, sea monsters are partial to salt water—with the exception of Loch Ness, of course."

"You just have an answer for everything, don't you?"

"What?" Lachie laughed. "I'm just trying to help you solidify your arguments before you write a strongly worded letter to Melbourne City Council requesting that they drain Melbourne's most significant natural landmark."

"I just prefer my water clear, that's all."

We walked in companionable silence for a bit, with Lachie occasionally slowing to retrieve bits of rubbish from the undergrowth, which he deposited into a bag that he'd produced from his backpack.

"You're really into the environment, aren't you?" I asked.

"Just imagine if every person did the tiny amount that I do," he replied with a shrug.

As we continued along the path, Lachie talked about the six months of medical volunteering he'd done in South America and about his time as a snowboard instructor in Canada. His stories were fascinating and I didn't realise how much time had passed until we reached the stairs that led up to Burnley Street.

"Will we turn around?" Lachie asked. "Head back home?"

"Sure," I answered, checking on the kids.

Neither of them stirred. I would volunteer for this kind of babysitting any day.

"Here," Lachie said, putting his hands on the pram handle. "My turn to drive."

I took my hands away and shook my arms out as we did a U-turn and headed back the way we'd come. Lachie pointed to a tiny dock across the river, where there were two chairs set up and a wooden rowboat was tethered to a post. A massive red brick house loomed on the bank above it.

"When I live there—" Lachie began.

"When you somehow have millions of dollars to spare, you mean?"

"When I live there," he continued. "You can come and visit me and we can sit on those chairs and discuss all the things that could be lurking at the bottom of the Yarra."

"Won't your wife mind?" I asked.

For some reason I was thinking about our kiss and the way he'd teased me and sucked my tongue. I felt a shock of sexual electricity suddenly awaken certain parts of my body.

Ask him to do it again, my brain piped up.

"No, she won't see you as a threat. Not once I explain how I made you sprain your ankle by kissing you on our one and only date, and then you retaliated by messaging me about the great sex you'd had with another guy."

His tone was light and joking, but the comment pierced my skin, stinging me. I would have preferred he call me "Mate".

"Too soon?" Lachie asked, sensing my discomfort.

"No, it's… it's fine. I love reminiscing with you. Like about the time you spat your sausage at me."

Lachie laughed. The zoom and thump of cars on the overpass above our heads reminded me suddenly that we were in the city, not out in the Australian bush somewhere.

"Not my smoothest moves," he agreed, good-naturedly.

We were quiet for a little while, listening to the screeching and tweeting of unseen birds. A team of four school kids in a long rowing boat pulled into view on the river. We could hear their cox calling to them, his voice breaking distinctly on the "Row!" command. I saw Lachie cringe.

"I feel his pain," he said, "I was working on a drive-through when my voice was breaking. One of the girls I worked with teased me because I once said 'nuggets' all high and squeaky, so I used to try to avoid saying it, which was pretty impossible. I hated it."

I smiled, trying to imagine a self-conscious, fifteen-year old Lachie. He steered the pram right and we emerged onto Bridge Road. Then Lachie asked me if I had any funny stories from teaching and we laughed about those until we were back in St James Park. The wind whipped up as we strolled the path and I felt the gust, hot and bitey with dust and tree debris, hit my legs.

"I'll walk back to your place with you," Lachie said. "It's on my way anyway. Then I'd better go home and prepare for my rounds tomorrow. I'm at the Epworth in Richmond this time, which is good. Just an easy tram from home."

Hayley was already waiting outside when we got there. I was slightly disappointed, mostly because I'd been hoping Lachie might actually hug me goodbye this time, and it seemed far less likely with her standing there, watching.

"Hey Justine," she said. "What's up with your legs?"

I looked down. My legs were brown with dirt and had little bits of leaves plastered to them. The covering was so thick, I looked like a Wookie.

Really? Haven't I suffered enough?

"Oh no! I got a wax this morning and I think the moisturiser she put on has mixed with my sweat and become something of a glue…"

I ran a finger through it, leaving a streak of exposed skin, and looked at Lachie, who looked back at me sympathetically.

"Sorry, I didn't notice or else I would have said something. Anyway, I'd better go," he said. "Thanks for the walk… and…"

He looked at Hayley and hesitated.

"I'm around later, if you want to chat or whatever," he said quickly.

Lachie hoisted his backpack and smiled at Hayley before walking off. A panicky frustration rose and clotted in my throat as I watched him walk away. I tried to swallow the thick lump of disappointment that our time together had ended so abruptly.

"Here you go," Hayley was saying, handing me a wipe that she'd produced from beneath the pram. "Now, I'm going to attempt to transfer the kids to the car without waking them. Want to place bets on whether it works? Also, who was that?"

"Just a mate," I replied and began to clean my legs.

CHAPTER SEVENTEEN

"I'm heading out for the night," Ellie said as I came out of my room.

She was adjusting her black singlet in the bathroom mirror. I almost asked her if she had a date, but couldn't imagine a conversation that didn't end in her telling me she was doing No-Sex November or something like it.

"Have a good night!" I called, walking down the hallway. I laid down on the couch, put my feet up and looked at my phone.

No messages, no plans.

It was Saturday night. This was sad. As the door shut behind Ellie, I started flicking through my phone, checking my list of friends to see who might be available to hang out. Steph was sick, so she was out. I came to Lachie's name. He had said he'd be around. I looked around the room, as though trying to prove to myself that I didn't have anything better to do. Satisfied with my assessment, I pressed on his name.

I'll just message him something casual.

I'd spent about fifteen minutes trying to think of something casual when there was a knock at the door. Maybe Ellie had forgotten her keys. I got up and looked through the peephole with my hand on the doorknob.

Dan was standing there with his hands in his pockets. I slowly took my hand away.

Stay silent, like a stealthy ninja.

234

"Justine, I can hear you shuffling around. Please open the door. I saw Ellie on her way out so I know it's you."

Well, even stealthy ninjas probably shuffle around a bit, I consoled myself. *I'm still not opening the door.*

"I can just imagine you," he continued. "Creeping through your peephole."

He looked straight at my creephole as he said it, spotlighting me with his blue eyes. I jerked my head backwards and was thrown off balance. My sandals made a distinct clapping sound on the floating floorboards as I regained my balance. I sighed and pulled open the door.

Dan was wearing fitted black jeans and a dark maroon, V-necked t-shirt that showed off the top of his chest muscles. His hair was wet as though he'd just showered and his familiar scent disoriented me like a drug.

Take me now.

"What's up, Dan? I'm quite busy at the moment."

He looked behind me, where clearly nothing was happening. I hadn't even had the good sense to open my laptop or turn on the TV.

"I didn't think you were going to make this easy. Listen, I get it, I was a bit of an ass the other day. I should have introduced you to my mates. Sorry. All good?"

He stuck his hand out, tilting his head and smiling at me. He really was sex personified. I could almost feel his outstretched hand on my body, caressing my—

NO! Be strong, Justine!

"Ok, sure, Dan. Is that all?"

I shook his hand formally and dropped it. My palm tingled.

"Justine… come on…"

That smile.

I felt it wash over me like a warm bath.

Must… be… strong…

"Dan, I don't really feel like… whatever is going on here." I motioned between us. "So, thanks for visiting. Good night."

I went to shut the door but he stopped it with his hand. His face was straight, serious.

Oh my God, this is the reality TV moment where he says, "This could be the most important moment of my life, the chance to find my soulmate."

"I think you're hot in your pyjamas, even when they're covered in chocolate," Dan said.

Close enough.

I stopped pushing, my hand frozen on one side of the door and his on the other.

"And I was worried about you when you hurt your ankle… and when that chick flat out hip and shouldered you. And I think you're funny. And I like that you bought a ladder to break into your own place. And I guess… I like you."

He ran a hand through his damp hair and then produced a little black stick from his back pocket.

"You filled a USB with dick pics?"

Dan laughed and shook his head.

"Actually I downloaded four different rom coms onto it. I'm willing to watch any or all of them

236

with you and I promise not to give away the endings, even though I will definitely think less of you if you can't guess them."

I stood there, unmoving. Dan looked uneasy and unsure for the first time since I'd met him. Hot blood pounded in all my bits. Then I stepped forward and put my arms around his neck.

Is this a good decision or a bad decision?

Dan pulled my waist towards him and we kissed. It was different this time. His touch was urgent, almost needy. Dan's tongue met mine as his arms closed all the way around me, squeezing me against his hard chest as he kicked the door shut. He walked me backwards mid-kiss and we somehow managed to fall safely onto the couch, with Dan landing on top of me. He pulled my t-shirt out from where it was tucked into my shorts and ran his hands up my body. I held my arms up as Dan pulled off the t-shirt and then my bra with unnerving competency. Then he grabbed the neck of his own t-shirt and pulled it over his head, revealing the glorious ripples of his chest and abs.

Good decision. GOOD DECISION!

"Wait," I said. "Let's go to my room. I don't know where Ellie's gone or how long she'll be."

"Oh, she's out with friends for dinner and then going to the movies," Dan said.

"Right… OK… Well, great. But still, my bed is more comfortable than the couch."

Also, I bought it with my ex and don't want to be reminded of him at any stage during sex with you.

"Suits me." He stood and his shirtless form sent fresh tingles down my stomach.

Dan held out his hand and I took it, holding my t-shirt and bra in front of me with my other hand. He interlocked his fingers with mine and we walked down the hall to my room.

"Woah, this is a bit weird," he said, taking in the flowery doona cover and pastel-coloured candles. "It's just like mine. Except with different stuff."

"I know!" I said, glad it was relatively clean. His had been spotless.

Dan held me close again, his teeth and eyes bright in the low light and his chest warm against me. His fingers were still entangled with mine so he undid my fly with his spare hand, again with unsettling ease, and my shorts dropped to my feet. I stepped out of them as he ran his thumbs around the inside of my underwear waistband.

"Wait! Do you have... protection?" I asked, a little breathlessly.

"Oh shit... No, I'm all out. Don't you... have anything?"

NOOOOO!!!

"No, I don't."

"Oh."

His hands trailed off and he stepped back. There was a distinct bulge in his jeans which would have amused me if I wasn't so turned on.

Justine... make a good decision...

"I'm on the pill and I just finished my period so... the chances are pretty miniscule."

Unless the fertility turtle becomes involved.

238

I shrugged at Dan, yearning to feel his body blazing against mine again.

He looked at me as if he was battling with his penis in his brain. Then he closed the gap between us, unzipping his fly and kicking off his shoes and jeans as he kissed my mouth and neck.

Good to know that he can multitask too.

"Wait a minute…" I said.

"Fuck, what?!" Dan said in a voice that was rough with lust. He broke away from me again and ran a hand through his hair.

"I had a wax today and the waxer was er… quite liberal with the wax. Just letting you know that it's a little breezy down there."

Dan smiled the most devious smile I'd ever seen that wasn't on a cartoon villain and lifted me with one arm around my waist. I wrapped my legs around him as he kissed me, his tongue sending tiny shocks down my limbs to my toes and fingertips. I had the vague sensation that I'd been planning to do something but the flickering thought disappeared as quickly as my underwear as I tumbled backwards onto my bed.

Pale light shone through my blinds as I snuggled down into the warmth of our sex-nest of mussed sheets and dented pillows. Dan groaned softly beside me, throwing his arm over his eyes. I put my hand on his chest, still astounded by how firm it was. He rolled towards me, pulling me closer.

"Mmm. Morning," he mumbled.

"Good morning."

I needed to pee quite badly, so I savoured his embrace for one more moment before I extracted myself, rolling ungracefully out of the bed. I threw on my silky dressing gown and carefully opened the door, peeking into the hall. I hastily padded to the toilet but Ellie's door opened just as I was stepping onto the cool bathroom tiles. She stood in her doorway, stunning in black active wear and neon orange sneakers.

"Oh, morning Justine. This is early for you. Want to come for a run?"

She was being polite; she knew my answer would be a slightly more articulate version of a raspberry noise.

"Oh, no way. I mean, no thanks. I'm heading back to bed. You seem… fresh. You must have been late last night. I didn't hear you get in."

"Yes, I was. But I slept so well! Dan is usually at it on a Saturday night, but last night—nothing! My sleep tracker said I had more REM sleep than any Saturday for the last five months. I guess even a guy like that has to take a break sometimes."

She laughed at what was apparently her attempt at a joke. I hoped I wasn't as deep a shade of red as I felt.

"Ha ha, yes, good point. He does… he must… He was probably doing a Sudoku instead. Anyway, must pee, enjoy your run!"

I quickly hid myself in the toilet and didn't come out until I heard her leave. When I returned to my room, Dan was sitting up in bed, scrolling through his phone.

When he looked up and saw me undoing the tie on my dressing gown, he said, "Just stop, Justine. Even a guy like me needs a break sometimes."

"Oh shut up, you whore," I retorted, joining him back in bed.

"Just working on this Sudoku," he answered.

I looked over to see him flicking through news headlines. I flopped back onto my pillow and as I did, I accidentally hit the "Over-Analyse and Panic" button in my brain.

What exactly is happening here? Did his little speech last night mean anything? Or is this time the same as the other times? Am I just a convenient hook-up because I'm only a flight of stairs away? Is he thinking about messaging Really Stupid Pants right now while he's in my bed?!

I probably should have asked him last night, but I had been wearing lust-induced blinkers.

"Can I ask you a question?" I said suddenly. "Just to… um… clarify something?"

Dan stopped scrolling and looked at me.

"That depends."

Not exactly encouraging but I ploughed on.

I hate these games.

"Uh, well, if someone messages me on my dating app tonight, am I still… free to go out with them?"

There, it's out. Now quickly run out of the room and hide in the bathroom again until he leaves.

"Well, that's up to you, but I uninstalled mine before I came here last night."

He went back to scrolling. Nervous excitement fizzed inside me.

Stay calm.

"That was presumptuous," I said.

God, I'm cool.

"I've had enough of the apps. Like I said, I didn't really expect you to let me in," Dan answered, not looking up.

"Would you have kept trying if I hadn't?"

"To a point."

"So again, to clarify, I'm your…"

Less cool…

"I don't like labels, but you can call it what you like."

I'M HIS GIRLFRIEND! WEEEEEEE!

CHAPTER EIGHTEEN

I'm not single anymore was my first waking thought on Monday morning.

I swished the delicious idea around in my mind. Obviously I'd messaged Steph as soon as Dan had left on Sunday morning and she'd messaged back a whole paragraph of smiley faces and love hearts. I'd wanted to call my mum, but decided to hold off until I had at least seen him again and made sure he hadn't changed his mind.

I floated onto the tram to work, heading to my favourite seat near the back. A luminescent flash of copper stopped me. Lachie's hair, shining in the sun from the window, was flopped over his forehead as he appeared to be concentrating intently on a text book. He was wearing a white shirt and a lanyard that said "Student Nurse" in bold letters. Part of me wanted to keep walking without alerting him to my presence, although I wasn't exactly sure why.

"I'm flattered but stalking is illegal you know," I said, sitting in the seat across from him.

Lachie looked up and smiled widely when he saw me.

"Well, technically I was here first, so that makes you the stalker," he replied.

"Sounds like something a really crafty stalker would say," I said, lifting up the textbook in his lap so I could read the title.

"*The Survival Guide to Nursing,*" I read aloud. "A riveting read, I presume?"

"It's no Marvel comic, but it has its moments. How are you? How was the rest of your weekend?"

Well, the sex-nest was a highlight.

"It was good. Um… yeah, I'm sort of seeing someone now."

Why did I say that?

I felt like it was important to disclose, for some reason. Lachie rummaged around in his bag and pulled out a highlighter, then returned to his textbook. I didn't know what reaction I'd expected, but it wasn't that.

"That's great, mate, congrats," he said finally, pulling the lid off his highlighter. "Who is it? The stripper?"

I laughed, a little too loudly.

I don't want to tell you, I suddenly realised. *Why did I start this?*

"It's Dan, who… ah… you met. At the park."

For a minute I thought he might bring up the message blunder again. Apparently this conversation still had the potential to become more awkward.

"I'm happy for you," Lachie said, highlighting a passage in his book.

I didn't know what to do. Should I pull out my own book? Go and sit elsewhere? Stand up and yell out "TRAM CONGA!"? I looked around at the early-morning passengers swiping drowsily at their phones. I didn't think I'd have many willing conga volunteers.

"You busy tonight?" Lachie suddenly asked.

"Do you need another fill-in for footy? Because if so, yes, I am extremely busy."

"Ha ha! No, I've just got nothing on and I get bored easily. My mates say I don't know how to sit still."

"Wait, you mean the skateboarding uni student who works at the hardware store and volunteers in his spare time has nothing on tonight? This is outrageous!"

He laughed and shrugged.

"It is a rare occasion. Want to hang out? Maybe walk along the river again?"

"Are you going to make me pick up rubbish?"

"No, but I might make you watch while I do."

"Saucy. OK, I have a meeting after school but I'm free after that."

"Great. I'll text you."

We're just friends, I thought loudly to myself as I got off the tram at my stop.

I just told him I have a boyfriend, so it's clearly another friendship hang.

But regardless of how many times I repeated it in my mind, I still had the distinct feeling that I'd agreed to a date with someone who wasn't my new boyfriend.

Nyarout, Ashleigh, Greg and I were all gathered in my classroom, attempting to write a risk assessment for our upcoming excursion to the Royal Botanic Gardens. So far we'd discussed our weekends, new developments in TV shows and the food place that had opened nearby. I had stopped myself several times from interrupting the discussion by yelling, "I have a boyfriend now!" at them. I was actually supposed to be scribing but my fingers had been idle on my laptop keyboard for over fifteen minutes.

"What have we got so far, Justine?" Nyarout asked hopefully.

I looked at the blank screen.

"Um, Addie might lick a tree and get tongue splinters. Will could perform that impromptu somersault trick he's fond of and end up in the ornamental lake. Lulu and Greta are likely to wander off, but with any luck they'll leave a trail of nut-free, dairy-free, gluten-free muffin crumbs." I took a breath. "Ultimately, we may need a rather large, chew-proof rope to secure the lot of them."

I wonder if they sell those at the hardware store, I thought absently.

Finally, we managed to write enough for the risk assessment to be legally acceptable. I walked out with Nyarout.

"Guess what?" I said excitedly, unable to hold it in anymore.

"Ooh, what?" she asked, zipping her laptop bag.

"I'm seeing someone!" I exclaimed. "We made it official on the weekend."

"That's awesome! Show me a pic!" Nyarout said, looking genuinely excited for me.

She was well-informed on my dating history, give or take a few of the more personal details. I went to take out my phone and then stopped. Dan and I were definitely not at the stage of taking selfies together and I still didn't have him as a friend on social media.

"Oh," I said. "I don't have any. Uh, take my word for it that he exists?"

Nyarout laughed.

"Invite him to Greg's going away drinks on Friday, and then I can see him for myself!"

"OK, I will," I said, thrilled with the idea of showing Dan off in public.

When I got home, I showered quickly, changed out of my work clothes and headed out again to meet Lachie. I was excited to see Dan arriving as I came down the stairs, but he was on the phone. It was a bit strange because I didn't know if I was allowed to kiss or hug him in public yet. I decided to let him take the lead.

Dan smiled, waved at me and said, "Just a minute, man." He put his hand over the phone and held it at his waist as he kissed me on the cheek and said, "Hey, gorgeous" into my ear. "I'm really busy this week, but I'll come and see you Friday night after work drinks and we can have brunch on Saturday. Sound good?"

You're too busy to see me all week? I literally live on top of you.

I smiled.

"Sounds perfect."

Lachie and I went for our walk and then I came home and had a late dinner. I had suffered some serious chafing during the walk and when I sat down to pee, it stung. I prodded my lady bits to make sure everything was normal down there and my finger landed on a hard, sore lump.

Oh, crap, what is that?!

I grabbed a compact mirror and had a look. There it was: a shiny, angry looking thing surrounded by a bumpy rash. I told myself it was nothing, just the result of wearing lacy underwear instead of cotton ones in case of unexpected sex opportunities with my boyfriend. Regardless, I went to bed slightly concerned. It crossed my mind to ask my only nurse friend if it was something to worry about, but I ruled out texting *I have this red lump and an itchy, burning rash* to Lachie.

There was no point to it, but I couldn't help punishing myself with the thought again and again.

I never should have had unprotected sex.

It had seemed like a sound decision when Dan was half-naked in front of me. Now it felt like the worst decision ever. It's not like I hadn't known that he had a lot of sex with a lot of women.

What was I thinking?

I was tempted to ask Dan about it, but of course I didn't have his number, so there wasn't much I could do, short of knocking on his door and saying, "Hey babe, did you happen to give me an STD?" I decided if it was still bad in the morning, I'd make an appointment with my gynaecologist, Dr. Stacey.

It was still bad in the morning, so I made an appointment for that afternoon. Lachie was on the tram again and we spent the ride laughing about a customer he'd had at the hardware store who couldn't understand why he wasn't allowed to trial a bin for two weeks and then return it. I suspected most of the story was made up to amuse me, but Lachie created an excellent character with a Scottish accent who was highly concerned about whether or not his bin would stink after holding haggis leftovers for six days.

The mystery lump was throbbing painfully by the time I left school for my appointment. I thankfully didn't have to wait long before Dr. Stacey showed me into her room. There was a freckled girl who looked about eighteen sitting there.

Is it Bring Your Daughter To Work Day?

"This is Vikki," Dr. Stacey said, gesturing with her long fingers. "She's a medical student. Do you mind if she sits in?"

Dr. Stacey sat down across from me. I glanced at Vikki, who looked bored and scared at the same time.

Sure. Would anyone else in the building like to view my vagina?

"No worries."

"What seems to be the problem?"

"Ah... I have a very sore lump and rash on my lady..."

Don't say lady bits to a doctor!

"Vulva."

"OK. And have you had unprotected sex?"

How did you know?! Are you a wizard?

"Yes, a few days ago. I didn't... I don't usually... I just... just once."

"It really only takes once. You should always use condoms, even if you are on the pill. Especially if you have had multiple partners?" Dr. Stacey asked me, peering over the top of her glasses as if she was certain that I'd had multiple partners.

Not at once!

"Well, yes, um, sort of. There have been, ah, a few."

Vikki stared at me as if she'd suddenly become interested in her job.

Oh shut up, Vikki!

"Well, let's take a look. Take off your pants and hop up on the table."

Dr. Stacey showed me to the padded bench covered in disposable cloth and drew the curtain around me while I pantsed myself. Then I lay on the table while she and Vikki gathered around my lower half.

"Right, OK, I see. Look just here, Vikki," Dr. Stacey prodded me gently. "Now, if it was chlamydia we'd be looking for…"

She went on to list a variety of uncomfortable-sounding symptoms and then continued through the symptoms of several other STDs while I felt increasingly sick and panicked. Once again, I lamented Past Justine's rubbish decision-making. Sometimes she really ruined things for the rest of us.

Finally, Dr. Stacey said, "But what we're actually looking at here is a badly infected ingrown hair. Looks like you may have had a wax recently, Justine?"

The wax that keeps on giving.

"Yes."

"Well, I'll give you some antibiotics for this. Also, I think you might have had an allergic reaction to the wax and that's what's caused the rash. It's a pretty sensitive area to be smothering in hot liquids."

Vikki nodded seriously in agreement.

SHUT UP, VIKKI!

When I was fully clothed again, I sat across from Dr. Stacey as she wrote me a prescription.

"I see you're going to be 32 in May, Justine. Are you hoping to have children one day?"

"Oh... yes. One day."

"It might be a good idea to consider this then."

She handed me a pamphlet called *Freezing Your Eggs: Your Future On Ice.*

"A female's fertility will naturally start to decline in her 30s, and that speeds up after 35," Dr. Stacey said, more to Vikki than me. "Many women over 30 who aren't in a position to think about having a family will freeze their eggs to give themselves the possibility of having children later."

Vikki nodded again, looking at me like I was a cautionary fairy-tale. I wanted to jingle my bracelet at them both and say, "Don't worry, I've got it covered. I have a fertility turtle."

But instead I accepted the pamphlet and said, "Thank you, I'll think about it."

I looked at my bedside table in satisfaction. I'd stocked all three drawers with two boxes of condoms each. The checkout person at the chemist had given me a shocked look in regards to my bulk purchase, but I didn't care, I wouldn't be facing a condom drought again anytime soon.

It was 6.30pm on Friday and Dan had said he would see me after work drinks. I didn't know what time that would be, but whenever it was, I'd be ready. Once again, I cursed my inability to text him. I had skipped Greg's drinks in favour of going home to have a long bath so I'd be clean and relaxed when Dan arrived. Then I'd planned for the coming week so we could spend most of the weekend together if he wanted to. After that, Pops had rung to book me in for a Sunday roast.

"Your mother said you have a fella now," Pops said.

Damn sneaky spy, I thought.

I'd had a moment of weakness after my depressing gyno appointment and called to tell her that Dan and I were a couple.

"Yes, Pops, I mean, it's very new and I don't know…"

"Bring him to lunch, love," he said. "There's always room for one more."

Now I was floating aimlessly around the house, looking for things to do to kill time before Dan arrived. A bouncy ball of nervous energy ricocheted off the walls of my stomach as I cleaned the bathroom, plucked my eyebrows, changed the sheets on my bed and finally plonked down on the couch. 9pm. Still no Dan. I clicked on the TV.

"She has an amazing spirit and I've loved the time we've spent together, but my heart is taking me in another direction and I just couldn't forgive myself if I didn't follow it," the polyamorous bachelor on the TV recited, sounding bored by his own revelation.

I watched until it was over and then put on one of the rom coms from the USB Dan had left me. At 11pm I decided to head to bed. I retreated into my doona, feeling desperately dejected and hurt that he wasn't there beside me. I couldn't imagine falling asleep with the hard lump of disappointment that had settled in my oesophagus, but suddenly I was dreaming.

I dreamed that the spiteful, silver-haired Remy was repeatedly kicking a footy against a wall and when I looked at what she was aiming at, it was a collage of enlarged copies of my pictures from my dating app.

When I woke up, I realised the thumping of the football on the wall was actually knocking on my apartment door. I dragged myself out of my bed, convinced in my disoriented mind that I would see Remy's face through my creephole.

But it was Dan, with his shirt collar open and his hair mussed. When I opened the door, he smiled and before I could say anything, he was kissing me. The taste of beer and mint filled my mouth as his hands found their way under my pyjama shorts. I pulled away from him.

"Are you drunk?" I asked, not really sure if I would feel more annoyed if he was.

"A little," Dan admitted. "But don't let that stop you from taking advantage of me."

He ran a hand through my hair and kissed the top of my head.

"I'm sorry I'm so late. I flew in from Sydney this afternoon and went straight to drinks. I had to debrief with my boss about the trip."

"You were in Sydney this week?" I asked groggily, leaning against him and breathing in the enticing smell of sweat, spirits and cologne.

"Yeah, for a few days. I told you I was busy. I go back and forth a fair bit for work. Come on, let's go to bed."

Dan put his arm around me and we walked back to my room, bumping into the walls of the hallway which wasn't really designed for two people abreast.

"Look, I even came prepared this time," Dan said. He stepped into my room ahead of me and pulled a condom from each of his pockets.

"I'll see your two," I replied, climbing over my bed and opening my drawers to display the shiny, black boxes. "And raise you 70."

Dan laughed and threw the little square packets over his shoulders.

"I hope you realised I would see *that* as a challenge!"

He laughed as he stepped out of his shoes and launched himself onto my bed.

AH! There's a boy on my bed and he's acting like he belongs there!

When I finally fell asleep again, it was with Dan's fingers in my hair and my hand on the perfect curve of his thigh.

CHAPTER NINETEEN

"Rise and shine, Sleeping Beauty!" Dan chirped at me. "We're going to brunch, aren't we?"

He pulled the covers down, uncovering my naked, curled-up form. I moaned and raised my head slightly. He was already fully dressed in his clothes from last night, his shoelaces tied and everything.

What is wrong with you? It's Saturday.

"Not at 6am. I'm sleeping."

"It's 9.30," he said.

"Well that's not brunch, that's breakfast."

"I'm going to go downstairs to get changed. Get ready. I'll see you at my door in five."

"Ugh. I'll see you in 20. And that will be pushing it," I mumbled at him.

Dan smiled widely, undeterred from his infuriating positivity.

"You're cute when you're grumpy," was all he said.

"I'm grumpy when I'm grumpy," I grumbled at his retreating form.

30 minutes later I was dressed in a button-up green dress with a high neck and no sleeves. I flapped down the stairs in my sandals, where Dan was leaning casually against his door, scrolling through his phone.

As I approached, Anastasia's door opened and she made it to Dan first. She held up a little cotton-wrapped package and beamed at Dan as he accepted it. Then she brought her hand up to pat the shadow of stubble on his cheek.

"You good boy, Daneelko. I make you some cottage cheese."

Dan touched her arm appreciatively. Her smile, which had already been in full beam, somehow widened.

"You know I love your cheese, Anastasia," he said.

I went to stand beside Dan, forcing a smile at her in greeting. She took her hand away from Dan's cheek and looked up at me.

Should I present my cheek for a pat?

"That skirt is too short, Justine. You will catch cold in your kidneys," she said before shuffling back into her apartment.

I could feel Dan's shoulders shaking beside me.

"Don't," I said, opening the building door for us both.

"I won't."

But he was laughing audibly now and when he looked back at me, there were tears clouding his blue eyes.

"That skirt *is* too short, Justine," Dan said when he'd composed himself, pulling me closer and running his hands down my lower back.

My body tingled with electricity as he leaned in and kissed me softly on the lips. Right there in front of our building. People were walking their dogs past us. The dogs might have been staring at us kissing, if they liked that sort of thing, which they probably didn't. They were more into the bottom-sniffing and licking. The electricity seemed to fizzle as I tried to suppress a visual image of Dan and I sniffing and licking each other's bottoms.

I snorted and Dan drew back to look at me.

"What? What are you thinking about?"

Oh! Oh no! Lie lie lie lie.

"Just dogs."

Dan looked justifiably confused and a bit disappointed.

"Right. Fair enough. Come on then, we'd better get going."

We'd been waiting in a brunch queue for ten minutes. This was a new experience for me. If Steph and I ever came across a brunch queue, we'd just choose another place. But Dan insisted that this was the best brunch place in Hawthorn so here we were, standing around with the sun warming the tops of our heads like toasted crumpets. We weren't even lined up at the restaurant door, as the restaurant itself was on the rooftop of a building. Instead, we were waiting in the foyer to get in a lift that people were being shown into a few at a time. We were the fifth couple in the line when suddenly a tall, well-built man in his forties who'd emerged from the lift seized Dan with an arm around his neck, choking him.

"What are you doing here, Daniel, you son of a bitch?" the man boomed, his voice even more imposing than his figure.

"Get off me... you big bastard," Dan managed to cough out before the man finally released him. Dan rubbed his neck as he said,

"Justine, this is Rosco. He owns this overrated establishment."

They did pretend boxing at each other for a minute.

Am I supposed to join in? Should I throw a left hook at Rosco as a greeting?

"Daniel, I've told you before," Rosco said, finally throwing an arm around Dan. "You don't wait in line here. You let me know and I'll come and get you. Don't you want to impress your... friend here?"

Rosco put an arm around both of us and I felt like I was carrying a log on my shoulder. Then he led us to the woman whose job it was to let people into the lift and simply said, "Look after this guy," before disappearing outside.

"What was that about?" I asked, feeling a little dazed as we walked straight into the lift.

"My company does his taxes," Dan said as we were shown to a table on the balcony and given menus.

"We're good to order," Dan said to the waiter, who nodded and waited expectantly.

"You have to get the muesli here," Dan said, looking at me. "I swear it's the best thing on the menu."

"Ah, OK, sure," I agreed as the waiter almost forcibly removed my menu. I had been in the middle of reading a mouth-watering description of French toast drenched with maple syrup, topped with mascarpone, pistachio crumb and something else that I would now never know.

Our waiter left and returned in about ten minutes with a wooden board for each of us. On the board was an empty bowl and several smaller bowls lined up next to it. As the board was set down in front of me, I saw that each little bowl was filled with something different. The first was rolled oats, then almonds, grains, sunflower seeds and finally, tiny flakes of dried fruit.

"Deconstructed muesli," the waiter announced grandly and then disappeared again, returning with a small jug of yoghurt for each of us.

"Enjoy your meals."

I stared at my "meal".

AH! What is this?

I watched Dan shake a specific-looking amount from each little bowl into his big bowl and then pour yoghurt over the top. I tried to appear deliberate in pouring out my own little bowls, but ended up just tipping everything in. Then I took a mouthful.

Ugh, it tastes like muesli.

"Isn't it great?" Dan said, watching me. "I love being able to control the ratios of what goes in. It's genius."

"Yes, it is. It is genius."

Actually, it's muesli.

We sat in silence, munching. Dan opened up a newspaper that he'd grabbed from the front counter.

"Can I have your number?" I blurted out, nearly spraying seeds and dried fruit across the table.

"Sure," Dan said, turning the page of his paper.

He recited his number while I tapped it into my phone.

There. Saved. That feels good.

"Ah, do you want mine?" I asked, putting my phone away again.

"Why?" he asked, turning another page. "I know where you live. Anyway, I'll have it once you call or text me."

It was sound logic. But it felt weird.

Dan insisted on paying for both our brunches, and then Rosco reappeared and insisted that Dan didn't pay for anything. We exited the lift and walked down Burwood Road and Dan took my hand. As we walked along, and I noticed how people turned to look at Dan as he passed them, I felt like the sun was shining out of me instead of on me. I felt so happy that I barely noticed that I was still hungry.

By 2pm, I had definitely noticed. So when the pancakes arrived, I just stared at them for a minute, salivating. Then I touched them to make sure they weren't a mirage. The golden pillows bounced back from my poke and my fingertip came away coated in sticky salted caramel.

On our way to Mouth Feels, I'd recounted the traumatising deconstructed muesli experience to Steph, who'd responded with a disgusted expression and retching noises.

"Have you ever faked an orgasm?" I asked Steph after we'd eaten and our plates had been cleared away.

"Nah, why would I do that?"

"I don't know… Because it's going on too long and you're ready for it to finish?"

"Then I'd probably say, 'We're done now.' I don't want a guy to think he's getting it right when he's not. Especially because I'm only having sex with Charlie now and it wouldn't benefit me to make him think I like something I don't. Then I'd be getting the same shit effort for forty years. Also, I'm not a people-pleaser like you." She said the last bit with love.

"Good point."

We both sat back in our white patio chairs and Steph groaned as she clasped her hands over her belly.

"Food baby?" I asked, happily patting my own inflated stomach under my t-shirt.

"No, a real one," she said.

"Ha ha!" I laughed loudly. "Can you imagine if someone really announced their pregnancy to their best friend like that?"

"I did. It is… A real one, I mean." she said, her face suddenly very serious.

I sat up straight, ignoring my stomach's immediate protests.

"Wait, what?!" I asked, feeling panicked.

"Well, I've been waiting all through brunch for the perfect segue. I took what I could get."

I tried not to think about the time I'd seen someone fall over on a segway in Paris. The memory always made me laugh at inappropriate times.

"But… I thought you guys didn't know if you wanted kids?" I asked, trying to process her news.

"We didn't. But looks like we're getting one. Ugh, *having* one, I guess." She rolled her eyes. "Honeymoon sex is apparently *really* potent. I'm freaking out Justine, I'm gonna have to be in one of those club things where they just talk about their babies all day and when they're not doing that, they're sending each other pictures of their babies on their phones. I don't want pictures of other people's babies on my phone!"

"I don't think that's exactly how mothers' groups work…" I tried to reassure her.

"And my abs. They're gone forever. I'm going to be massive. I'm only five weeks or something and I already want to eat the world. Hold me!"

I got up and went to her side, kneeling down to hug her.

"Congratulations, friend wife," I said, tears coming to my eyes. "I can't believe we're having a baby."

"The other bad news is," Steph continued after I returned to my seat. "Now that I'm knocked up, I can't do Spa Day because the hot water might boil the baby or something. I'm so sorry! I cried when I found out. I've already called them and they said they can't refund us, but I can transfer the booking. I thought you could make it Sexy Spa Day and take Dan instead? I'll still pay my half."

I was sad, but also a bit excited about the prospect of Sexy Spa Day.

"That's OK, of course I understand. And don't worry about it, I'll pay you the full amount. Bring on Sexy Spa Day!"

When I got home, I knocked on Dan's door. He hadn't said what he was up to for the rest of the day, but I was keen to organise Sexy Spa Day so I'd have something exciting to get me through the week of teaching. He didn't answer or come to the door, but Anastasia popped out in her usual terrifying way as I stood there.

"Justine. You come in."

I followed Anastasia into her apartment, assuming she had a job for me, but she motioned for me to sit down on the multi-coloured crocheted rug that covered her couch. I sat. She shuffled over and sat beside me.

"Daneelko, he is good boy. He remind me of my son. Still in Russia."

She looked so sad that I almost hugged her until it occurred to me that she must have seen Dan and I kissing and was probably about to tell me not to besmirch her precious Daneelko.

"Daneelko is good boy, but he have many girls. You should be with boy who just have you."

She waited. I waited.

Was that a question?

"He may have dated quite a few women. But now he's just dating me. I know he—"

"He is special boy. But he is hard to know," she cut me off.

I started to feel annoyed. Why was Russian Oprah ambushing me with this?

It's none of your damn business!

"Thank you for your concern, Anastasia. I'd better go."

I stood up and left, feeling guilty but proud of myself for not agreeing to break up with Dan immediately just to please her.

I entered my apartment to the buzzing of the intercom. Steph had said she would drop by to pick up a top I'd borrowed from her after she'd done some shopping on Glenferrie Road. I picked up the receiver.

"Is this the hooker I ordered?" I said huskily into it and followed the question with some deep breathing.

"It is if you're going to start paying me," Dan's voice replied.

"Wrong number!" I said and hung up the receiver in panic.

Calm down. He's your boyfriend. He's going to have to get used to the stupid things you do. Like how you're now doing Irish dancing in an attempt to distract yourself from what just happened.

The intercom buzzed again.

"Hello, this is Justine speaking," I said in my best phone voice.

"Did you just hang up on me?" Dan asked.

"No, it wasn't me. You must have buzzed Anastasia by mistake."

I could hear him laughing from outside my window, as well as through the receiver.

"How can I help you?" I asked.

"Can you let me in please? I forgot my keys."

"Oh, sorry, no," I said. "You'll have to use a ladder like the rest of us."

"I live on the ground floor."

"Oh, yeah."

There was a silence.

"I'm still outside."

I quickly pressed the buzzer and hung up the receiver. I decided to go down and meet him.

When I got downstairs, Anastasia was handing Dan a key. He'd obviously just been for a run and sweat glistened on his bulging man chest above his low-necked singlet. He thanked Anastasia, took the key and opened his door in his efficient way. He cocked his head for me to follow him in. I could feel Anastasia's eyes boring into me as I went in. Dan shut the door behind us and pressed me against it, kissing my neck.

"Hello there," I said.

"Hello there," Dan replied, releasing me and dropping the spare key onto his bench. I could feel his sweat, damp on my dress.

"Anastasia has your key?" I asked, glad that I'd refrained from adding, "Maybe she should be your girlfriend."

"Yep, gotta have a contingency," Dan said. "I'm gonna make a smoothie. Want one?"

"Sure."

I watched him throw a whole lot of powdered things into an expensive-looking blender with a banana and some almond milk. He pulsed it a

265

few times and then poured two tall glasses, handing one to me. I took a sip.

No! Bad! BAD SMOOTHIE!

"Mmmm, it's delicious," I said, shutting my eyes in an attempt to shut out the taste.

Why do you hate me so much, Smoothie?

"Oh great! This mix isn't for everyone. It's all raw ingredients."

"Well, it is for me!"

It is not for me! The smoothie and I are not friends. I don't want to be in the same room as the smoothie.

"I'll get you the recipe then. The secret ingredient is bee pollen."

Bee pollen? How do I acquire that? Do I milk a bee?

"You can get it from health shops."

Shit, did I ask about milking a bee out loud?

"Great!"

I put the bad smoothie down and put my arms around Dan, hopefully making it seem like I loved the smoothie but just couldn't resist his magnetism.

"So... me and my best friend, Steph, who you've met, do a Spa Day every year at the Dromana Hot Springs. We get massages, have a nice lunch, that sort of thing."

"Sounds romantic."

"Yeah, but she just told me she's pregnant. So she can't do it anymore, something to do with the water temperatures and pressure points, I'm not sure..."

You're rambling! Just ask him!

266

"Anyway, we were supposed to do it next weekend and can't get a refund. Do you want to come with me instead?"

"Sure, sounds great."

"Really?"

"Yeah, I could use a good sauna session. Flick me a reminder text later in the week. I'm in Sydney again so probably won't see you till Friday. Now, I'm gonna have a shower. Wanna come? You can sing for me."

"That's not going to happen."

"OK then, if you wait here, I'll—"

"I meant the singing is not going to happen. The shower is definitely happening."

CHAPTER TWENTY

On Friday morning I was beside myself with excitement for Sexy Spa Day. I skipped onto the tram, tripped on the first step due to the skipping, then happily bounced back up and skipped down the aisle to meet Lachie. He was sitting in our usual seat, reading.

"Good morning!" I chirped at him.

He made a show of shutting his eyes, rubbing at them and then opening them again, really wide.

"Justine? Being perky in the morning? I don't believe it. Go back and get her. I'm frightened."

"I am often very jolly in the morning."

"You think that because you think the morning starts at 11.30am."

"OK, that's true. I'm just glad it's Friday."

I had sent Dan a text the night before to remind him about Sexy Spa Day. He hadn't written back yet.

"I hear ya. OK, I've been thinking about what we were talking about yesterday—would I rather be an animal who can talk to humans or a human who can only talk to animals? I want to clarify a few things…"

Lachie opened his mouth to continue but I was distracted by my ringtone. Dan. I grimaced in apology to Lachie, who shrugged and went back to his book as I swiped to answer.

"Who is this?" I said, smiling to myself.

"It's Dan."

His voice was even sexier on the phone than in person.

"I know a few Dans," I replied.

"Oh, I think you'd remember me," he said and I felt a fresh wave of excitement shiver through me. "Listen, I've got some bad news. I totally forgot I've got a Buck's Trip this weekend that I committed to ages ago. My mate just reminded me. Sorry about that. I hope you can find someone else at short notice."

I didn't say anything as I felt all my excitement slowly drain away.

"I'll make it up to you, I promise," Dan said.

"OK. That's OK," I said mechanically.

Lachie looked up from his book with a concerned look on his face.

"I'll still see you tonight," Dan said, sounding unsure.

"Yeah, OK. See you then."

I hung up.

I tried not to cry, aware of Lachie's worried eyes on me.

"Hey," he said quietly. "Are you alright?"

Kindly asking someone who is not alright if they are alright is undoubtedly the best way to make them cry. Tears began to drip down my cheeks.

"I'm just really… disappointed," I said, trying to steady the waver in my voice. "Dan and I were supposed to go to the Dromana Hot Springs tomorrow. It's all booked and paid for. I won't be able to find a replacement at this short notice. Who's going to have no plans on a Saturday?"

"Um, me. Sort of," Lachie said, offering me some gauze from his medical kit.

I wiped my face with it. It was pretty ineffective compared to his cleaning cloth, or even his shirt, but I felt a bit better.

"You're free this weekend? Why? Shouldn't you be skateboarding up a mountain or something?"

Lachie smiled.

"I have a camping trip with friends on Saturday night; we're going to check out the supermoon. But it's at my mate's property in Main Ridge. That's on the Mornington Peninsula, not too far from Dromana. So it's perfect. I can come with you and then head there after."

"Are you sure?" I asked.

I started to feel a bit better. A day with Lachie would be fun, at least. Better than sitting at home feeling angry and deserted, and much better than wasting the hundreds of dollars that Steph and I had already paid.

"Positive. I can even drive us, if you want. And then drop you at a train after."

"OK, let's do it. I'll pick the music."

"No way."

"We'll see. Would about 9am suit you to pick me up?"

"I'll be there."

That night there was a knock on my door at 5.30pm. I looked up from the biscuits I was making as car snacks for Lachie and I.

Precursory creephole glance. Dan was standing there with a large bunch of flowers in his hand. I looked down at my apron that was printed with a Christmas elf's costume.

Who cares? I'm angry with him anyway.

I opened the door. Dan tried to keep a straight face but failed.

"It's still November."

He was smart enough to put his hand over his mouth to hide the smile.

"Only just," I retorted. "And it's also the only apron I have."

"Are you naked underneath it?"

"No..." I looked down just to double check. "No! I'm wearing a boob tube and short shorts because I just put on fake tan. Are those flowers for Anastasia or me?"

"They're for you."

He held them out to me.

"I really am sorry. I will still pay for half and you can go by yourself. Or if you don't want to, I'll just pay the whole lot. I never meant to..."

"I found someone to go with," I said before I could stop myself.

Uh oh. This could go very wrong very quickly. Time for a smooth topic change.

"Um, so, about that bee pollen—"

"Who?"

Give him a fake name!

"Lachie."

"Who's Lachie? Wait... the ginger guy? Lachie the thirty-year old skater from the park?"

"Yes, but—"

"From the footy match? You are kidding me."

I wondered if it would be a good time to put my hand out to accept the flowers. Dan's face said no.

"We're friends. We take the tram together in the mornings. Tram friends."

"Tram friends who sometimes have dirty spa weekends together?"

Dan was starting to raise his voice. I opened the door wide and motioned for him to come in. With my luck, Anastasia would be knocking on my door any minute offering to mediate.

"It's not a dirty spa weekend. You might remember it was originally meant for me and my *friend*."

"Yeah, a chick who you haven't kissed."

"I have actually. For free drinks at a uni function."

"That's not the point," Dan said but he looked as though he'd forgotten what the point was.

He shook his head and walked in. As I shut the door, I suddenly remembered that I was supposed to have the upper hand here. *He* was the one who'd let *me* down. Also, this was pretty jealous behaviour for someone who still wasn't referring to me openly as his girlfriend.

"So you haven't kissed any of the women you hang out with, Dan?"

That shut him right up, which was a shame as I'd been hoping he'd say that he definitely hadn't. I didn't enjoy the thought that Really Stupid Pants could be in his close friendship circle.

"I was supposed to be going with *you*, remember?" I continued. "But you cancelled at the last minute and Lachie happened to be free. So stop acting jealous, give me my flowers and let's try to enjoy our night. Or you can leave if you want."

Wow. Didn't know I had that in me. I'm badass when I'm a Christmas elf.

Dan ran a hand through his hair and then handed over the flowers, less than enthusiastically. He sat down, reaching over to the glass bowl in the centre of the table and pulling out a decorative rock. He began turning it around in his hands as I put the flowers into a glass vase of Ellie's.

"Yeah, right. I'm sorry," he said, finally. "I don't... I've been single for a long time and... that threw me."

"I understand. I'm making bikkies, if you... You probably don't eat bikkies."

"Not really."

We were both quiet as Dan watched me finish rolling the dough into balls. I kept wanting to do silly things to break the tension like throwing the rolled balls at him and yelling "Dough fight!" or putting two of the dough balls into my cheeks and talking like Marlon Brando in *The Godfather*. But I decided it was unlikely that either option would be well received, so instead I focussed on flattening the bikkies and getting them into the oven without burning myself. Then I sat across from Dan at the table.

"Uh..." I started, trying to think of something to say. "If you could be reincarnated as any animal, what would it be?"

"Easy—lion. King of the jungle, top of the food chain."

He threw the rock into the air and caught it.

"Oh yeah, of course."

"What about you?"

Dan finally looked at me as he returned the rock to where he'd found it.

"I don't know…" I'd never actually thought about my own answer to the question. "Maybe a bear. They get to sleep a lot."

"Want to watch a movie?"

"OK, sure."

We chose a mindless action flick and sat side by side on the couch, not quite touching. After the third bomb blast, Dan put his arm around me and pulled me close. I lay my head on his shoulder. I remembered thinking that once I had a boyfriend, I wouldn't have any problems anymore. It wasn't turning out to be the case.

December

CHAPTER TWENTY-ONE

Dan was gone when I woke up. The Buck's Trip was beginning with a 7am bike ride around the city.

He must have some fun friends, I thought as I patted around at the back of my wardrobe shelf for my bikini. As I pulled it out and was greeted by a faint whiff of old chlorine, it occurred to me that Lachie was going to see me in my bathers. This was a new level to our friendship that I hadn't properly considered.

I shook away the thought as I stepped into the bottoms and tied on the halter-style top. I looked in the mirror. My bikini concealed less than my underwear did.

Who cares? I thought. *He won't be looking.*

I pulled on some short black shorts, a white t-shirt that tied up at the front and my transparent beach kimono with purple flowers. I walked into the living room just as Ellie was getting back from a run. She detached her earphones from her phone as I reached into my food cupboard.

"I ran into Dan this morning," she said.

My back was turned so I couldn't see her expression.

"Oh, did you?" I asked casually, tipping cereal into my bowl and hoping that she meant she'd seen him downstairs.

"Coming out of your room."

Tell her he was just borrowing a... a... packet of condoms? No! A pair of heels? WHAT

"Yeah, we're, um... kind of seeing each other."

I turned around to see her mouth drop open.

"Oh... How long have you..."

Her attractive features distorted into an expression of both realisation and disgust.

"Please don't tell me... I don't want to know if I heard... Ugh."

She wrinkled her nose and pursed her lips as if she had a bad taste in her mouth.

"OK," I said.

"Just..." she began awkwardly. "Protect yourself around him, Justine."

"Do you mean that in your capacity as a doctor? Like safe-sex wise? Because I could have used that advice a week ago! Ha ha!"

Oh God, what am I saying?

Suddenly, I had a horrible thought.

"Wait, have you hooked up with him too?"

She gave me a look like I was the stupidest person in the world, which given my previous ramble, I probably was.

"I'm gay," she said, as though she was talking to a child.

"Oh yeah, that's right. I knew that!"

I had no idea!

"I've just known plenty of people like him. Be careful."

With the most uncomfortable conversation in the world apparently over, Ellie walked quickly towards her room.

Why is the whole building set on warning me against my boyfriend?

I didn't have time to think about it because a quick glance at my phone told me that it was a minute past when I'd agreed to meet Lachie outside.

I emerged from the building a few minutes later. I suddenly felt silly and embarrassed about my little plastic container of bikkies. I stood on the footpath and looked up and down the street, scanning the twenty or so parked cars that lined it.

Is Lachie in one of them?

I looked over my shoulder, sussing out a bush behind me that sat in front of the mailboxes. I could just throw the bikkie container in there and then pick it up when I got home. I began to casually swing my arms back and forward, getting ready to drop the container, when there was a *beep beep* from a little red hybrid car about twenty metres away.

I quickly shoved the container under my arm and began to walk towards the car, trying to subtly peek through the windscreen to make sure it was Lachie, just in case I was about to accidentally get solicited again. I caught a glimpse of his wild curls. I opened the door and slid in, with the feeling that getting in his car was in some way a change to our relationship.

"Hey, mate," Lachie said. "What's in the container?"

He peered closely at the Tupperware tucked conspicuously under my arm.

"Did you make biscuits?"

278

Oh my God, why didn't I just get rid of them when I had the chance? YOU'VE RUINED EVERYTHING, STUPID BIKKIES!

"Uh, yeah. Well, not for today... I had them left over from... something else."

"I love biscuits. What kind?"

I felt warm inside.

"ANZAC."

"The best! This might sound weird but it kind of looked like you were about to throw the container away."

I forced a laugh.

"Ha ha! What a notion!"

Lachie gave me a justified strange look.

"Well, can I have one please?" he asked.

"Now? OK."

I pulled off the bright green lid and Lachie spent a few seconds with his hand hovering over the container, finally choosing the biggest bikkie. He put it in his mouth and then pulled out onto the road.

We argued for a bit about music until we agreed on a radio station. We'd been driving for about fifteen minutes when my phone rang.

"It's my mum," I said. "Do you mind if I answer it? I always answer when it's my parents in case it's an emergency, which it never actually is."

"I'll allow it this once because you brought biscuits. Which taste amazing, by the way."

"Hi, love!" Mum greeted me. "I can't talk for long, I have my new sewing circle today. Oh, Justine, you wouldn't believe what they call it. It's called a Stitch and..." She dropped her voice to a barely audible whisper. "Bitch… Can you believe that?"

"Yes, I can," I whispered back.

"Hi, Mum!" Lachie yelled cheerfully.

"Oh, hi Dan!" Mum yelled back, right into my ear, and then more subduedly, "Are you two on your way to the spa then? How exciting!"

"It's not Dan," I said with an involuntary wince.

I hadn't quite gotten over the disappointment of it and certainly didn't feel like explaining it to my maternal KGB agent.

"He couldn't make it after all. Lachie filled in at the last minute."

"Oh," she said, sounding confused. "Who's Lachie?"

"A mate," I rushed to avoid further questioning. "So, what's up?"

"Here, your father's here. I'll put him on speaker."

"Who's Lachie?" Dad said.

"A friend, Dad."

"I was friends with your mother once," Dad laughed. "And some of her friends too!"

Oh shut up with your parent porn!

"Alright, calm down," I said. "I think Mum rang for a reason?"

"We love our daughter, isn't that a good enough reason for us to—" Dad began.

"No, I did actually," Mum broke in. "I was wondering if you and Dan will both be having Christmas lunch with us this year?"

"I will. I doubt Dan will… but I don't know. I'll ask him."

"OK, you ask him. You know we're always welcoming of new people."

"Yes, I know you're always welcoming of new people," I recited, having heard it many times in reference to the men I was interested in.

"Well, we'd love to meet him, love. At Christmas or otherwise. So happy that you're happy. Well, I'd better get to my Stitch and… what have you."

"OK, bye!"

"Bye!" they both called out.

When I hung up, I turned to Lachie, who was polite enough to pretend he hadn't listened to the conversation.

"How did such a delightful, innocent woman end up with an inappropriate daughter like me?" I asked him.

"Maybe she's not as innocent as you think," Lachie said, grinning.

"Yuk. Thanks for that," I said.

"So," Lachie said, with a glance at his phone which he'd attached to a dock on his windscreen. "Apparently we've got another hour to go. Care to fill it with some more of your excellently entertaining dating stories?"

"OK, but I'm going to need a bikkie," I said, pulling open the container again.

Lachie reached over and took another one, brushing my fingers with his knuckles.

As we drove, I told him about the past three months: the movie date with Fluffy Aidan and his weekly shop, the cheese and leg-molesting John and breaking up with my one-night stand's mum, Lyssa. I left out the bits with Dan in them, rationalising that he probably wouldn't find them funny.

"And the Nick the Dick story you already know," I finished, noticing that during my anecdotes, the gritty, suburban landscape had given way to green paddocks and sprawling vineyards behind grand sandstone walls. Lachie was wiping away tears. He'd been highly amused by my story time.

"You know, I wouldn't believe these stories were true if you weren't here beside me telling them," Lachie said, his voice still light with laughter. "But I'm guessing they're not as funny when you're in the moment?"

"No, not really," I admitted. "I probably go along with things when I shouldn't. It comes from being a hopeless people-pleaser and also loving the idea of being adventurous and spontaneous. There's often a bit of bad luck and alcohol involved too."

"Do you feel safe when you date? It sounds like you've met some creeps. Do you have one of those alarms on your keys?"

"I try to make sure I meet them in a public place. I always let Steph know where I'm going and when I get home. Also, I have a torch."

"A torch?"

"Yeah. A creeper torch."

"Which does what?"

"Uh, well, if I was scared I could shine it in someone's eyes. It's very bright. Or, it's metal so I suppose I could hit them with it. I don't know... my

Dad gave it to me for safety. I don't really know why. Maybe he meant safety like just if it's dark and I can't see."

Up ahead I could see the blue-grey haze of hills as we neared the turn-off to Dromana. Lachie flicked on his indicator and a few minutes later the ocean emerged beside us—vast, blue and still. I directed him to the spa and the familiar wooden fence greeted us with its sign, "Welcome to Dromana Hot Springs—Your Relaxation is Our Pleasure."

"Can we bring the bikkies?" Lachie asked as we pulled our bags from the car.

"I don't think it's that kind of place," I answered, not always able to tell if he was joking.

We were greeted at the main desk by a woman with hazelnut-coloured ringlets and a voice like flowing water. She introduced us to a man with blonde hair and blonder eyebrows, saying, "Jeremy will explain the spas to you. Come back here about twenty minutes before your massage at 1pm."

Jeremy motioned for us to follow him and stood at the door to the change rooms.

"Welcome to your little piece of paradise for the day," he said, sounding suspiciously like a reality television bachelor—bored and unconvincing. "Everything is designed to ensure your relaxation. Through here you'll find our newly renovated unisex change rooms. With the Soak and Rub package, you have access to our Float Away Room, which holds our special floating spas. Enjoy your day and see one of our friendly staff if you have any questions."

283

Jeremy hastened away before we could ask any questions. Lachie pushed open the door to the change room.

"What luck," I said. "Usually I have to pretend to be a man to get into the male change rooms."

A man near us with a sun-weathered face and sizeable paunch looked at me suspiciously and then pulled his towel tighter around him. I heard Lachie snort beside me and then try to turn it into a cough.

We went into side-by-side cubicles. It was weird to imagine Lachie nearly naked right beside me. I pulled off my kimono and t-shirt, then stepped out of my shorts. I wrapped my towel around my waist, feeling ridiculously self-conscious. I heard Lachie's change room door open.

Here goes.

"Did you just say, 'Here goes'?" I heard Lachie ask.

"What? No."

Yeah, I did.

"Yeah, you did."

"Well, I'm a little bit nervous. I'm not wearing much."

"Mate, I'm wearing less. Don't worry about it. I promise to keep my eyes on your eyes at all times."

Feeling slightly better, I unlatched the door and stepped out. True to his word, Lachie only looked at my face. I couldn't help but look down at him though. He wasn't muscled like Dan, but there was still some pleasing definition there.

Maybe I should take up skateboarding and social footy to keep fit... Ha ha ha! No!

"Hey mate, can you sunscreen my back for me?" Lachie asked, handing me a white tube.

"Would you stop hitting on me just because we're in a communal change room?" I said, feigning outrage.

He laughed and turned around.

Over his shoulder he said, "What can I say? It's the Curse of the Ranga. Gotta protect my delicate skin."

I squirted some of the thick white cream into my palm, trying not to giggle like a three-year old at the resulting sputtering noise. I ran my hands across Lachie's broad shoulders with freckles scattered like stars across them. I felt my heart rate increase as I spread the sunscreen down his back to the waistband of his board shorts. I smoothed more sunscreen along his sides, tracing the lines of his body, with my mind wandering.

Don't be such a creep! Act like a professional!

I wasn't sure how a professional sunscreen applier would behave but I imagined I was doing a good job until Lachie said, "OK, you can stop now. I think my skin is starting to wear away."

We spent the morning soaking and floating until our fingers and toes resembled sultanas. Lachie talked about his sisters and how he was scared to introduce girls to them because of how protective they were, especially the younger one. He talked about his mother and how hard she'd worked to make sure he'd never felt the absence of his father. He talked about his cat, Galileo Figaro, and how she would hiss at birds through the window but then cower from them if she was put outside.

Then we walked outside, past the sauna and plunge pool and up a winding stone path to my favourite spot—a thermal spa on top of a small hill, with a view of grassy paddocks, dotted with sheep. The spa was completely empty and we both dropped our towels and dipped our feet in, feeling the warm water lick at our toes. I lowered myself in carefully and then Lachie jumped in beside me, deliberately showering me with hot droplets. I lay my head back on the stone ledge behind me and closed my eyes, listening to the gentle call of birds and feeling like I could drift off to sleep. Suddenly, I lifted my head.

"Hey Lachie?"

"Mmmm?"

His eyes were shut and he'd sunk so low in the pool that the water lapped at his chin.

"Can you tell when a girl's faking it?"

He opened his eyes.

"Faking being a man so she can sneak into the male change rooms? Yeah, it's usually obvious because of the small hands and feet, not to mention the fake moustache. Also, the boobs can be a bit of a giveaway. Lucky you didn't have to do that today because—"

"Ha ha. No. I'm asking you a serious question."

"OK," Lachie sat up and wiped the dripping water from his chin. He moved his neck from side to side as though he was stretching it out. "Well, I'd like to think so but I guess I wouldn't know, would I? To be honest, I've only had one girlfriend and that was for a long time. We only broke up two years ago and it took me a while to start dating again, so I'm not quite as experienced as you are on the whole scene. Those stories you told actually made *our* date sound like it wasn't that bad."

"It was the best date I've ever been on," I blurted out.

It was true and I was even including the deconstructed muesli date with Dan. Our eyes met but I looked away. In my peripheral vision I saw Lachie check his watch. He cleared his throat.

"Well, it's 12.30pm. Want to head back for our massages?"

We returned to the change room and showered, wrapping ourselves in the fluffy white robes we'd been supplied with. Feeling too weird about the thought of being entirely naked under my robe, I put my bathers back on as well. Then we returned to the main desk.

"Welcome back," said the woman with the ringlets. "I hope you've had a relaxing morning. If you'd like to follow me, I'll take you into your room."

Room. *Room?*

Our spa-issue thongs clicked against our heels and the sound echoed down the corridor that Ringlet Lady lead us into. She stopped at an open door and beckoned us into a warm room where a stone water feature was bubbling away in a corner and the air was sweetened with the scent of orange and vanilla. There were two massage tables set up in the centre of the room, laid with towels.

Oh no.

"I'll leave you two to get ready. You can remove your clothing except your underwear, lie face down on the table and cover yourselves with a towel."

The door shut almost inaudibly behind her. Lachie and I stood staring at each other. I suddenly realised what must have happened.

"Oh God, I'm so sorry. My friend Steph must have booked a couple's massage for me and her as a joke. It's the sort of thing she would find funny. And then I was supposed to be bringing Dan so she wouldn't have thought to change it…"

I let out an awkward laugh.

"It's fine. It *is* funny," Lachie said. "And it's not like they're going to make us hold hands during the massage."

"Oh, I hadn't thought of that," I said. "Are you sure they won't?"

I was becoming a bit hysterical with nervous tension.

"If they do, we'll tell them we're Fundamental Christians and we can't hold hands until we're married."

"Deal. Could you… um… turn around?"

"Oh, yeah, of course."

He turned to face the wall and I did the same.

I pulled the halter strings of my bikini over my head. Then I tugged at the bow at the back, which I'd tied rather tight to avoid any nipple slip incidents. The strings didn't budge. I yanked again and suddenly the whole bikini top *sproinged* away from my body and hit the water feature, causing it to wobble precariously. The rogue swimwear ricocheted, landing with a splat on the floor at my feet. I ducked to retrieve it and whacked my head on the massage table as I stood up again.

"*Shit!*" I hissed and Lachie whirled around.

"What happened?! Are you alright?" he asked, concerned.

"Yes! NO! Don't turn around!"

I flung my arms across my chest.

"Ah! I forgot! I'm so sorry!" he cried, slapping the hand that wasn't holding his towel around his waist over his eyes with considerable force.

Considering the angle, he could have only caught a glimpse of side boob. I quickly lay down on my table and put my face into the head hole in an attempt to muffle the embarrassed giggle that escaped my throat. Lachie began to chuckle as he sat down beside me, shaking his head.

When our masseuses walked in, we were both lying face down, covered with towels and in hopeless hysterics.

"I remember when my husband and I used to laugh like that," I heard one masseur murmur to the other.

"I'm Lina," my masseuse said as she gently uncovered one of my legs and spread warm, silky oil from my thigh to my ankle.

Mmmm... That feels nice... I can't believe Lachie just saw my side boob... Shut up, don't think about that. Enjoy the massage. It brings a whole new meaning to offering him my bikkies... Stop it, enjoy the massage.

Lina pressed my heel with her thumb and then covered my leg again, moving onto the other one.

Should I tell Dan about the side boob incident? No, I don't think so. It's not like it's cheating... Unless I liked it... Did I like it? Don't think about it. Back to the massage, it's so relaxing.

Finished with my legs, Lina pulled down the towel from over my shoulders and tucked it into the waistband of my underwear. The thought of Lachie lying similarly exposed and just an arms-length away made my skin tingle.

No, that's just the massage doing that. Stop thinking about anything but the massage... I wonder if you can keep referring to someone as "Mate" if you've seen their side boob? Oh my God, stop it!

"How's the pressure?" Lina asked softly.

"Mmm, really good thanks," I murmured into my head hole.

It is *really good, so I can just forget about everything else and enjoy the... I wonder if Lachie's enjoying his massage?*

Lina's palms glided down my back and then up again. I shivered. She began to knead my shoulders with her slippery knuckles.

Do masseuses ever massage their partners or does it feel too much like work? Like chefs who never cook dinner because they've been cooking all day. Lachie's going to be a nurse. I wonder if he'll get sick of giving sponge baths to patients and never give one to his partner when he gets home. What am I talking about? Who gives a sponge bath to their partner? Creep alert. Great, now my eyes are open. Shut them and ENJOY THE BLOODY MASSAGE!

"I'm going to leave you now," Lina said, pressing the towels back into place on my body. "When you feel ready, sit up slowly and have some water if you like. I'll leave some just here."

I heard Lachie's masseuse speak to him in similarly soft tones. Then both women left and we were alone again. Mostly naked, lying down, side by side. I lifted my head up. Lachie's was still down in his own head hole. He'd probably just tuned out and enjoyed his massage. Then he lifted his head and saw me staring at him.

"How was it?" he asked in a deep, throaty voice.

"Really good. But... I was a little distracted."

"Me too."

I waited for him to elaborate but he didn't, so neither did I.

"Uh... how do you want to do this?" he said, after a pause.

"I'll turn around so you can get changed and then you do the same," I said, pulling my towel around my chest and sitting up to face the wall.

A few minutes later, Lachie said, "Your turn."

I quickly checked to make sure he was facing the opposite wall and then rushed to get dressed again, silently begging all my clothing items to behave themselves this time. We managed

291

to leave the room without further incident and headed to the sauna.

After we had sat in comfortable silence for a little while, Lachie turned to me, his freckled nose dripping with sweat. I realised we were sitting rather close. I studied his face. His jaw was on the angular side but was softened at the edges by his ginger stubble. His nose was slightly crooked and his lips looked a little dry... but he was attractive, even though I couldn't quite figure out why.

"Well, we should probably think about heading to the train station now, so you're not travelling back too late," Lachie said, breaking into my assessment of his face. "We could grab an early dinner if you want. We kind of skipped lunch."

"Bikkies are a sort of lunch."

"Amen," Lachie said as he stood up.

The breeze was cooling on my damp skin when we emerged from the spa into the carpark. Lachie's car was stifling from the hot day and he wound the windows all the way down as we drove the coastal route to Frankston. I was enjoying the cool wind on my forehead and the summer pop blaring from the radio and it wasn't until Lachie said, "Wow, you've got a great voice!" that I realised I'd been singing out loud.

"Oh. This old thing. Thanks."

"You never said you could sing. Are you in a band or something?"

"No. I used to sing... not professionally, just at casual things. But I don't really anymore. I don't know why. I just sort of stopped."

"Do you miss it?" Lachie asked.

"Yes, a lot," I admitted.

He nodded. We both fell silent until we were parking across the road from Frankston train station.

"What do you feel like for dinner?" Lachie asked.

"Oh no, we're not doing this again. It's your turn to pick."

He smiled and rubbed his stubble.

We ate noodles from boxes and then walked back towards the station. When we got there, I looked up at the train schedule screen, which was displaying an ominous "Please Listen For Announcements" message. I noticed a crowd of people gathered around a sweaty gentleman in a hi-vis vest. I pointed the group out to Lachie and we walked over to catch the end of his speech.

"...Incident on the rails. All services are terminating at Mentone. Replacement buses are being arranged as we speak, but there will be a possible two-hour delay. We are responding as promptly..."

His hands flew about frantically as he spoke, as though he was a magician trying to use sleight of hand to distract the disgruntled commuters from what he was actually saying. It wasn't working.

"How are we supposed to get home?" one woman threw out angrily.

"This is just typical of you blokes!" a man added, almost spitting out his lit cigarette.

"I have a meeting with my dealer—my mother, I mean—that I can't miss!" whinged a thin teenager with stringy hair.

Lachie pulled me aside.

"What do you want to do? It's going to get dark soon. I don't like the idea of you on this train line at night, creeper torch or not."

"I could just book a ride on my app," I said doubtfully, knowing it would probably cost about a week's wage to get from Frankston to Hawthorn.

"No," Lachie said. "I'll drive you."

"No way. You're not missing your camping trip because of me. You already did me a huge favour today."

"Then…" He hesitated. "Come with me."

"What?"

"Come camping. There's always plenty of room and food. I can lend you warmer clothing and bring you home tomorrow morning. You said you liked the idea of being spontaneous and adventurous…" He shrugged. "Don't do it just to please me. Only come if you want to."

No. I'll just say, "Thank you, but no."

"OK."

CHAPTER TWENTY-TWO

When the sign saying "Main Ridge" appeared, I began to feel nervous. Lachie turned down a dirt road that was crowded by bush on both sides and as white-grey branches swiped at the car, I realised that I had agreed to hang out with a bunch of people I'd never met for the night. What if crazy elf Remy was there? She'd probably challenge me to a duel to the death while everyone else toasted marshmallows.

And what will my boyfriend say?

I decided I'd better inform Dan of my plans in the interests of full disclosure. I quickly drafted a message.

Hey, hope you're having fun. Just letting you know all the trains were cancelled so I'm camping with Lachie's mates. I'll be back late tomorrow morning if you want to catch up.

Kisses or hugs? How many of each? None? Maybe "Cheers" on the end? Ugh, I might as well call him "Mate". I added one lowercase kiss and hit send. Just as I did, Lachie pulled into a long, narrow driveway. In the smudgy dusk, I could just make out a little farmhouse in the distance. Lachie told me his mate had inherited it and fixed it up himself.

As we pulled in next to a four-wheel drive covered in brown dust, I could see a group of about ten people milling around the back of the house; some lounged in a circle of fold-out chairs and others were heaving eskies onto a rickety-looking wooden table.

"Should I bring the bikkies?" I asked, wondering if there'd be enough.

"No way. They're too good to share," Lachie said, getting out.

I followed him to the boot and watched him pull on a black hoodie he'd found in there. Then he retrieved a big red-and-white overnight bag and threw it over his shoulder.

"Come on," he said.

Lachie looked for a minute as though he was about to take my hand and then, as though he'd just realised it himself, turned and quickly walked off ahead of me. It had been an oddly intimate day and I was feeling rather confused myself.

I followed a few steps behind Lachie, trying to gather my courage.

List of things not to mention to Lachie's friends: he thought I was a stripper, he spat his sausage at me, I concluded our date by sending him a text about having sex with another guy, he had to put an IV in my drunk, belligerent friend, I've sustained two injuries in his presence and today he got a glimpse of my side boob. Got it.

"Hey everyone!" Lachie announced loudly to the group as we approached, interrupting an argument that, judging by the participants' gesturing towards the surrounding bush, seemed to be about gathering firewood.

Everyone turned to look at us and a loud cheer went up.

296

"We were beginning to think you'd stood us up!"

I recognised Nate as he came forward to shake Lachie's hand. Lachie pulled him in for a hug.

"I told them there was no way you'd miss this. You're too much of a nerd."

A short woman with straight blonde hair and bright, chocolate-coloured eyes ducked under Nate's arm, which he immediately drew around her.

"You know Nate already," Lachie said. "This is his fiancé, *Fiona*."

He pulled her away from Nate with an arm around her neck and ruffled her hair. Fiona ducked away and punched Lachie lightly in the stomach. He pretended to be winded.

"It's Fee," she said to me. "And I'm also his sister, even though the ginger knob doesn't like to admit it. What's a nice girl like you doing with a peenbag like my brother anyway?"

"And that's why we call her No Filter Fee," Lachie said affectionately.

He hoisted his bag further up onto his shoulder and pointed in the direction of the rest of the group.

"That's Jack, we're nice to him because this is his place, and his girlfriend, Bella. That's Pete and the Tims." He pointed to three guys who all waved at the same time. "Jacqui, Gaz and that guy over there is Sprinkles. Everyone, this is Justine."

They all smiled at me. I felt incredibly conspicuous with everyone looking at me at the same time.

Do not accidentally break into song.

"You didn't answer my question," Fee said, interrupting the introductions. "How do you two know each other?"

"He thought I was a stripper," I said at the same time as Lachie said, "I spat my sausage at her."

Fee stared at us. A few people laughed and then general activity seemed to resume.

At least we didn't mention the side boob.

Jack, a guy with trendy stubble and a man bun, embraced Lachie in a big bear hug.

"Grab a drink, guys," he said, shaking my hand and giving me a kiss on the cheek. "There's cider and beer, Justine. Lachie, plenty of soft drink too, mate."

Lachie nodded in appreciation and we walked over to the esky-laden table.

"Beer, cider or soft drink?" Lachie asked me.

"Cider, please. Why did Jack mention the soft drink to you? You're not driving anywhere tonight, are you?" I asked.

"No. It's because I don't drink alcohol," Lachie answered, retrieving two cans. He passed the cider to me and kept a lemonade for himself.

"Really? Not at all? Why not?"

"My father was an alcoholic. I don't remember much about him, but what I do remember is enough to put me off the stuff for a lifetime."

I worried I'd brought up a painful topic, but Lachie's face remained neutral and I imagined he'd had to answer the question plenty of times. We

298

clinked our cans together and drank. I appreciated the cold fizz in my mouth and throat for a minute.

"Oi! Go make yourself useful and get some firewood!"

Fee appeared behind Lachie, pushing him in the back so that he stumbled forward. He looked at me and then at Fee.

"Is that alright, Justine? Will you be..." He trailed off, looking even more unsure than I felt.

Fee continued to push him but Lachie dug his heels in. It looked rather amusing. She barely came up to his shoulder and was putting her full weight against him. Her feet began to slide in the dirt.

"She's a big girl. For fuck's sake, what are you worried about? I don't bite."

"Actually, I have the scars to contradict that statement," Lachie said, rubbing his arm as if reliving the memory.

"It's fine," I said, not wanting to hold him back around his mates, even though I was a little terrified of his sister. "Go. Fee can tell me about all the embarrassing things you did when you were a kid."

Lachie looked even more unsure but shrugged and walked off in the direction of where Gaz, Bella and the Tims were heading into the bush.

When Lachie was out of earshot, Fee said, "I know I've only spent three minutes with you but I already like you better than the last one. Come on, help me set up the fire drum."

"The last one?" I said as I followed her to the dusty four-wheel drive.

Fee hoisted open the boot where a large steel barrel lay on its side. Fee got into the boot and crouched behind the barrel. She rolled it towards me and between us we lifted it out.

"He hasn't told you about his ex?" Fee asked, jumping down from the boot.

We each hoisted a side of the rim of the drum and began to walk back towards the campsite.

"The vicious bitch," Fee said bitterly. "They were together for ages and then she broke his heart. Hooked up with his now ex-mate, Corey. Because she's a vicious bitch."

Fee shivered in disgust.

"Watch that rock there," I warned.

We stepped around the rock and settled the drum in a patch of grass in the middle of the chair circle. Fee dusted her hands off on her khaki shorts.

"They got together when they were teenagers. They met through dancing."

"Dancing?" I asked, wiping my own hands on my shorts. "Like out at a club or something?"

Fee looked at me, eyes wide, as though she had finally said something she regretted. She sighed in resignation.

"No, not like pumping a fist in the air, shuffling from foot to foot dancing. I mean proper, professional dancing. Lachie's amazing. He started when we were kids and by his teens he was winning competitions. That's why he deferred uni, because he was getting so much work dancing. His ex too."

"Wow, I didn't know that," I said.

Really, I shouldn't have been surprised. He seemed to do everything else. *Twenty hot points,* my brain reminded me annoyingly.

Fee grabbed my arm suddenly.

"Please don't tell him I told you that. He doesn't talk about it much. He stopped accepting the work after she cheated. At first, I think he was worried he'd run into her."

My emotions were split. I felt guilty for listening to gossip about Lachie that he had clearly chosen not to tell me, but I was also completely fascinated. Lachie had always been so open and honest when we talked; it had never occurred to me that there might be things he'd deliberately omitted.

"The worst thing," Fee said as she flopped into one of the chairs. "Is that for some reason he let her snake her way back into his life. He's never seen Corey again. But Remy, well, she's on our fucking football team. Even made herself vice-captain. Lachie's just too nice. I think he's trying to prove he's the opposite of our asshole father. So now not only does he see that fake-haired, fake-everything psycho bitch every week, I have to as well. Luckily she couldn't weasel an invite here. None of us can stand her."

I sat down beside Fee, suddenly feeling cold and uncomfortable. It made sense. Remy had been ludicrously territorial towards me. But for some reason, I hadn't even considered that her and Lachie might have a history.

"She hip and shouldered me when I filled in," I blurted out, knowing that I shouldn't be saying anything. I couldn't help myself, Fee's openness was contagious.

"Ah, so that was you who replaced me when I was sick? That doesn't surprise me, by the way. Vicious bitch. Does Lachie know?"

"No, I didn't tell him. I only found out she did it on purpose from a girl on the other team."

Fee just shook her head.

There was a buzz of noise that heralded the return of the firewood-collection party and the fiery halo of Lachie's hair caught my eye. He was laughing about something. He looked so happy.

Why Remy?

I just couldn't see him with someone like her. I understood that he'd let her back into his life, though. I'd missed Ben's company so much after we broke up, that I knew I would have stayed friends with him if he'd wanted to.

Several of the group began to lend a hand with building the fire, which mostly seemed to involve arguing about what formation the wood should be laid in.

"Alright Lach," Jack said after a small flame finally appeared. "Where's that fancy telescope then?"

Lachie looked up from where he was crouching next to the drum, prodding a long stick through one of the holes.

"In the car. Want to help me grab it, Justine?"

"Sure," I said, standing up from where I'd been happily drinking cider and spectating the fire construction.

The sky was mostly charcoal coloured by now, with a few smears of scarlet still visible above the distant hills. Lachie led me around to the front of the house, but then suddenly changed direction, heading away from the parked cars and towards the fence line of Jack's property.

"See how the sun is like a ball of fire when it's that low?" Lachie said as we reached the fence. "Its colour is actually made up of all the colours of the rainbow. The combination usually makes it look white but as it sets, some of the colours become harder to see. First the purple and blue hues become invisible, then green, and finally yellow and orange. The red hues are all that's left. That's why sunsets look red to us. Cool, huh?"

I watched the last wisp of pink disappear, leaving just a small patch of lighter sky in its wake. A sudden and chilly breeze caused me to shiver. I was still only wearing shorts and a t-shirt. Lachie looked at me in the near dark and then reached behind his neck and pulled off his hoodie. He moved closer until he was standing right in front of me and gently tugged the jumper down over my head. I stuck my hands into the floppy, fleecy arms and inhaled the mingling scents of massage oil and smoke that clung to the body-warm fabric. Lachie's hands rested gently against my thighs where he still held onto the bottom of his jumper. I raised my head and met his gaze. His eyes were almost black in the near darkness. After a few seconds, Lachie dropped his hands and stepped backwards.

"I don't kiss other people's girlfriends," he said in a hoarse voice.

"Neither do I!" I said, my own voice thick with indignation.

"Glad we're on the same page," Lachie replied abruptly and then walked off in the direction of the cars.

What the hell just happened?

When I reached Lachie's car, he was pulling a puffer jacket and a long, black carry case from his boot. He set the case down on the gravel path and zipped the jacket up around himself.

"It's dark along here," Lachie said, picking up the case again. "I hope you have your creeper torch."

"I do, actually."

I opened the front passenger door and pulled the little metal cylinder from my handbag. The notification light on my phone caught my eye. It was a message from Dan, saying:

mi66s yod5u

It was either a very sweet but drunken "miss you" or he'd accidentally pocket messaged me and I was reading too much into it. Either way I assumed he was enjoying the Buck's Weekend. I clicked the rubber button on the end of my creeper torch.

"Wow, it's so effective!" Lachie said. "I'm thoroughly deterred from assaulting you!"

I got the impression he was trying to make things normal between us again, but the joke lacked his usual relaxed delivery. I didn't say anything, just directed the beam towards the ground ahead of us.

"So, what did you and my sister talk about while we were gone?" Lachie asked as we walked back towards his friends.

I recognised the sound of someone attempting nonchalance but not quite achieving it.

"Uh…"

I searched my memory for something we'd talked about that I could repeat back to him.

Remy. Heartbreak. Asshole Dad. Dancing.

"Just… the weather."

"Oh great," he said, sounding irritated. "She told you about the dancing, didn't she? She bloody tells anyone who'll listen."

"No! What do you mean dancing?!"

I saw the silhouette of Lachie's face turn towards me in the dark and I imagined the disbelief in his eyes.

"OK, yes. The dancing. You've told me a lot of personal things. Why is it such a secret?"

"It's not a secret. It's just something I don't really do anymore. And I don't enjoy talking about it."

I decided not to push it any further. I wasn't sure I wanted to hear the sad love story of Lachie and Remy anyway, as the idea of them together made me feel sick.

"Really though, is there anything you can't do?" I asked teasingly.

"I told you, I'm a terrible singer."

We were silent until we reached the group. When we got there, Lachie knelt down and started pulling bits of telescope from the black case.

"Justine, I saved you a seat!" Fee called out, patting one of the chairs next to her.

I re-joined the group and laughed along at a story that had obviously been told a thousand times, about the childhood incident that had resulted in Sprinkles's nickname. By the time Sprinkles was allowed to defend his seven-year-old self's reputation, stars were visible above our heads and Lachie was bending over a fully constructed telescope. We could already see the moon, spectacular in its size and clarity.

"Come and check this out," Lachie called. Only half his body was illuminated by the fire, which was now crackling away as it devoured log after log.

I hung back as everyone took turns looking. When the others had drifted back to their seats, I bent down and peered into the little eyepiece. There was the moon—a beige, glowing giant with dark, circular scars across its curved surface. It looked like a huge spherical lantern, lit from the inside by some unseen power source.

"What *is* a supermoon?" I wondered out loud.

"It's a full moon that occurs at its perigee. That means its closest point to Earth in its elliptical orbit," Lachie answered, staring up at it. "Amazing, isn't it?"

I murmured my agreement at the last bit, considering it was the only bit I'd understood.

"Can you believe that almost every atom in our body was once part of a star that violently exploded? And that our universe is expanding faster and faster so that one day the distance between us and the stars will be so far that no stars will be visible to the human eye? Not that humans are likely to still be around then."

Lachie seemed to almost be talking to the moon itself. I blew out audibly.

"You know a lot about a lot of stuff."

"I just like cool facts, that's all," he said quietly.

I was about to tease him on his definition of "cool" but instead I found myself saying, "I like that about you", realising too late that it probably sounded like I was hitting on him.

Am I hitting on him?

I suddenly wished Lachie would call me "Mate" again so I'd feel secure in the platonic nature of our friendship.

I wandered back to my seat next to Fee and Lachie sat down in a spare chair on the other side of the circle. The Tims, who turned out to be a couple, had produced thermoses and began passing around enamel mugs of steaming hot Milo. I sipped at mine, feeling its warmth bloom from my stomach outwards. Jack got out a guitar and played quietly while everyone sat staring into the fire and sipping from their mugs.

"Alright. It's time for some audience participation," Jack finally announced, playing the first few chords of a ballad that had been playing regularly on the radio for months.

A few people groaned.

"Don't do it, Jack," Fee said. "Remember last time? Lachie was the only one who was willing to sing and we all suffered for it."

Jack began to hum tunefully, looking hopefully around the circle. Lachie cleared his throat deliberately and received many loud, good-natured objections in response.

I don't know why I did it. If someone had told me I was going to, I would have patted them on the head and said, "That is a very foolish suggestion." But when Jack played the opening chords again, I began to sing.

Everyone turned their heads towards me in surprise. I was terrified. It was lucky I knew the song well, because at the same time as I was automatically singing the lyrics, my brain was spiralling into a serious panic.

OH MY GOD, WHAT AM I DOING?! Everyone will think I'm some kind of lime lighting weirdo who does crazy things like bursting into song in front of people I've just met—and they will be quite correct! I am that weirdo!

Jack began to join in with the harmonies as I continued. I desperately wanted to stop singing but I knew that would seem even stranger than finishing the song. Finally, it was over. My face burned from embarrassment combined with the heat from the fire. After a beat, everyone clapped and cheered appreciatively. I met Lachie's eye across the circle. He was looking at me with such admiration and pride that my chest felt tight. Fee put a hand on my shoulder.

"Thank you so much for saving us from my brother's mangled vocal cords," she said with a big smile on her face. "Now, have you ever had an Aussie S'more?"

An Aussie S'more turned out to be a toasted marshmallow on top of a Tim Tam and it was one of the most amazing things I'd ever put in my mouth. After we'd devoured a packet of Tim Tams between us, the group played a lacklustre game of Never Have I Ever which started to trail off as the questions became more and more ludicrous like "I've never jumped between two moving vehicles while being chased by the Japanese Mafia." Clearly they all knew each other too well already and there were few surprises between them.

After that, people began to drift off to the farmhouse. Fee stood up and stretched, wished me good night and walked over to where Lachie was in deep conversation with Nate and Jack. Jack was shaking his head vehemently about something, but Lachie was nodding and speaking quietly to him. Fee put an arm around Nate and flicked Lachie's ear with her other hand. Nate looked up at her and nodded, then stood up and they headed towards the house hand-in-hand. Lachie looked up to where I was now sitting alone and beckoned me over. I sat down beside him in Nate's still-warm seat. The fire had died down and most of the light came from the supermoon.

"We were just discussing Covert Cinema," Lachie said. "It's Jack's baby."

"Oh!" I said. "I'm really looking forward to it."

"I'm glad you're coming," Jack said warmly. "And thanks for singing tonight. It was a massive improvement on our usual entertainment at these things, which is Sprinkles's impressions of guys he works with who none of us know. Anyway, I'm going to hit the sack too. Want to come and grab that extra sleeping bag, Lach?"

I used the creeper torch to light our path to the farmhouse. The door creaked loudly as we entered and before I quickly turned off my torch, I saw that the Tims, Pete, Jacqui and Gaz were positioned around the living room in swags and sleeping bags. We tiptoed between them to a hall cupboard where Jack found a sleeping bag and handed it to me. Then he whispered a good night to us and disappeared into a bedroom. Lachie put his hand on my back, directing me to a sunroom where Sprinkles was already snoring on a daybed.

We were silent as we unrolled our sleeping bags next to each other. I went to take off Lachie's hoodie but he put his hand on my arm and whispered, "Don't. It will get cold." We wriggled into our sleeping bags with the occasional bump into each other. Then I lay still on my back, not moving for the paralysis-inducing feeling of Lachie's warm body lying so close to mine.

Well, what is this? Do I have feelings for Lachie?

"I can hear you thinking," Lachie whispered.

AH! Can you?!

"No you can't," I whispered back. "I'm doing it very quietly."

Sssshhh brain! He can hear you!

Lachie turned towards me so that I could actually feel the soft wind of his whisper against my ear.

"I can still hear it."

"I can't believe you can dance," I said, my voice breaking into a quiet talk.

"I don't think that's what you were thinking about," Lachie whispered back. "Good night."

"I—Good night… Do you still do lessons?"

"Good night," Lachie repeated.

"Will you dance for me one day?"

"If you're lucky. Good night, mate."

"Good night."

I drifted off hoping that he couldn't also hear the forceful beating of my heart.

CHAPTER TWENTY-THREE

In the morning, the vibe between Lachie and I was easy and relaxed, and I found myself questioning whether the tension I'd felt the night before had been a complete figment of my imagination.

After a smoky, cooked breakfast and tight hugs from everyone in the group, we packed the telescope and Lachie's bag into the car and left. This time we both sung along to the radio, and Lachie—true to his word and everyone else's—was terrible, but it didn't matter for how much we were enjoying ourselves. The sound of my ringtone interrupted a particularly high note that we were both wavering between hitting and missing. I looked at my phone and saw Dan's name on the screen. I kept singing. Lachie turned the radio off.

"Answer it. I don't mind."

"Ah, OK."

I swiped the answer button.

"Hey, Dan."

"Hey, gorgeous. How was camping?"

I breathed out, not detecting any anger or jealousy in his voice.

"Great, thanks. How was the Buck's?"

"Ah, a bit messy and painful," he admitted croakily. "I'm going to have to detox the shit out of myself and I might be missing some chest hair, but, yeah, all good fun... Anyway, when do I get to see you?"

My heart lifted and I couldn't suppress my smile. He sounded genuinely keen.

"We're on our way back now. I should be home in about halfa."

"Great, I'll be waiting. See ya."

He hung up. Lachie was staring straight ahead at the road. I wanted to turn the radio back on but that seemed a little inappropriate in someone else's car.

"So... Your sister is engaged to your mate. Is that weird?" I asked.

"It was at first," Lachie admitted. "Obviously I had to have the you-break-her-heart-and-I-break-your-legs talk with him. Except it was more like a you-break-her-heart-and-I-break-one-of-your-computer-games-and-then-put-it-back-and-never-tell-you-it-was-me talk. He's into martial arts, so he could crush me."

I was surprised. Nate was small, placid and his hair was always meticulously gelled. He didn't look like the crushing type.

"But it's actually really good," Lachie went on. "Who could you trust more with your sister than your best mate?"

I thought about the mysterious Corey, who'd apparently been Lachie's best mate once too until Corey had hooked up with his girlfriend.

"And who could you trust more with your best mate than your sister?" Lachie continued. "I know it seems like we hate each other, but she's great. Even though she thinks she's my protector sometimes. She liked you, you know. She's not usually so... at ease with people. Anyway, the best bit is that my best mate gets to come to all our family events. So yeah, it was weird at first but it's worked out well. Anyway, what are you up to tonight?"

"Ah… seeing Dan, I guess. You?"

"I'm making a pie," he said.

"Of course you cook too," I said, shaking my head.

"I don't actually, but I'm trying to learn. So far the results have been discouraging. Living by yourself has its downsides and canned meals every night is one of them. But I've got high hopes for this pie. The recipe is called, 'Easy Pie for Idiots'."

"Really?"

"No. But something like it."

"Save me some? You can give it to me on the tram tomorrow morning."

"Actually, I won't be on it this week," Lachie said. "I'm on really early shifts, but don't worry, I'll leave you some at your stop."

I laughed as we merged onto the Monash Freeway. I felt a rising excitement at seeing Dan again, but at the same time I was disappointed that the camping adventure was over.

Do I have feelings for Lachie? My brain asked again, without my permission.

Stop it, he'll hear my thoughts again!

When we pulled into my street, I could see Dan out the front in running shorts. He was shirtless and shiny with sweat as he stretched against the bank of mailboxes. Lachie rolled to a stop across the road.

"I'll keep going," Lachie said quickly, offering me back the bikkie container. "Thank you, I had a great time."

314

I shook the container.

"There's still a few left," I said. "They're yours… I did actually make them for this trip. I'll get the container off you another time. Bye!"

I gave Lachie a quick hug which he barely had time to respond to and then jumped out of the car with my bag. I only realised after the little red car had disappeared down the street that I was still wearing Lachie's hoodie. Dan was already waving to me from across the road, so I couldn't quickly take it off and throw it over someone's fence.

It's just a hoodie. Dan won't care, I thought to myself as I crossed the road.

Oh really? My brain mocked me. *And if he was wearing some other woman's hoodie, you wouldn't have a problem with it?*

His biceps would never fit in a woman's hoodie but that wasn't the point.

I looked up. Dan was smiling at me and I felt the usual weakening of all my important bits. We met on the footpath and he put both hands on my neck and kissed me—a long, deep kiss that took me off to Kissing World where I might have resided for three hours for all I knew. When Dan finally broke away, he looked down at me.

"Nice hoodie," he said and took my hand.

It wasn't a question so I decided that no explanation was required as Dan led me into his apartment. He started making a smoothie.

Oh, crap.

"Want some juice?" Dan asked me, going to the fridge and opening the door. He pulled out an unopened bottle of orange juice. I was pretty sure he didn't drink juice.

"Yes, I'd love some. Thanks."

"Well, I've done all the exercise my hungover body is going to manage today," he said.

"What happened to 'The body is a temple and all that?'" I teased him.

Dan brought me my juice and put his arm around my waist, pulling me close to him.

"It was completely desecrated last night." He smiled deviously. "But, we will rebuild. In the meantime, I'm feeling lazy. Want to go and see a movie or something?"

"Will you eat popcorn with me?"

"No, but I'll pay for yours."

"Good enough," I said, putting down my juice and stretching my arms around his neck.

I felt weird about touching him while I was still wearing Lachie's hoodie.

"Just let me shower and change first. I'll meet you here in twenty," I said.

"You mean thirty, right?"

"Yep."

"Wait, I'm confused. We're back onto Skateboard Guy?" Billy was saying after another shocking round of trivia.

I was pretty sure he and Zoe were holding hands under the table. They were like incestuous Siamese twins, always joined by some body part or another.

"We call him Hardware Ginger," Steph advised unhelpfully.

"It's Lachie," I cut in.

"Whatever the hell his name is, I told you this guy is a genius!" Li exclaimed. "Now he's seen you half-naked two weeks after you locked it down with Dan? How does he do it?"

He forked a sizeable chunk of parma into his open mouth.

"Oh, shut it," I said. "He has not seen me half-naked. It was only side boob."

Rhys nearly spat his drink out laughing. Steph was shaking her head.

"Only you, Justine," she said, writing something on our trivia answer sheet that appeared to be several swear words followed by a smiley face.

"Where is your new man tonight, anyway?" Rhys asked me.

"He's hungover from a Buck's. Also, he's not really a parma kind of guy."

Rhys raised his eyebrows at Steph and she shrugged back at him.

"I can actually see you both," I said.

"Do you at least have a photo of him yet?" Rhys continued unapologetically. "You said he's a dreamboat."

"I don't think I used the word 'dreamboat'," I replied, "And no, not yet."

"Let's just look him up on social media," Steph said.

"Ah, we're still not friends."

I was starting to feel like a politician who was being grilled on the kind of radio station that I didn't listen to.

317

"You're not friends on social media with your boyfriend? Isn't that a bit weird?" Zoe piped up.

"Yes, it is weird," I snapped.

I'd take the third degree from my friends but Zoe had only met me a handful of times.

"But it's actually great," I continued, trying to affect a more neutral tone. "The photo wall in his room is bad enough. I don't actually want the chance to stalk his brains out. I know I wouldn't like it. So really, it's better this—"

"Found him!" Steph said triumphantly, passing her phone to Rhys.

"Woah," Rhys said. "Wouldn't kick him out of bed. Or a car. Or a public toilet. Or anywhere, really."

He passed the phone to Billy, who nodded approvingly and then passed it to Zoe, whose eyes widened before she passed it to Li, who said, "Holy shit, Justine, talk about batting above your average!"

I grabbed the phone off him and stared at the grid of thumbnails, all photos of Dan. *My* Dan. And yes, there were all the photos I never wanted to see.

So many attractive women.

There were other photos too. Dan playing footy. Dan skydiving. Dan surfing. Dan shirtless.

I wonder who's commented on these photos, I thought.

I didn't really know anyone in his life, other than Rosco. I quickly gave the phone back to Steph. It was a Pandora's box that I did not want to delve into.

"His profile says 'single,'" Steph said before putting her phone away.

"Well, so does mine probably. We've only been together for a couple of weeks, geez. Can we just concentrate on the trivia?"

They all laughed. The flashing notification light on my phone caught my eye. I checked it while the others joked about Li's claims that he had recently hooked up with seven girls in seven days. The message was from Dan.

My bed is boring. Buzz me when you get in, gorgeous.

I felt like showing it around the table while yelling, "SEE, HE REALLY DOES LIKE ME!" but just managed to stop myself. I joined in the banter half-heartedly, already looking forward to cuddles in Dan's warm bed.

Dan opened his door completely naked and even though I'd seen his body countless times, I was still taken aback by its flawlessness. He grabbed me by the hand, pulled me inside and playfully bit my neck before leading me to his room. He undressed me in his unsettlingly efficient way and within seconds I was on my back with my hands in his hair as he kissed down my body.

"You seem to have regained some energy," I said appreciatively.

"I always have reserves for this kind of thing. It's my superpower," he mumbled into my stomach.

"That's good. Mine's sleeping."

He snorted and then laughed. The vibrations tickled me and I giggled too. Then I shut my eyes and tried not to think about anything except Dan's hot mouth on my skin.

Later, as I lay in Dan's arms and we hadn't said anything for a few minutes, I remembered Pops's lunch invitation.

"Hey, are you around next Sunday afternoon at around 1pm?" I asked.

"I think so," Dan said, yawning. "Why? Want to do brunch again? Because at 1pm most people call it lunch."

"No, um, my grandfather and I have *lunch* sometimes on Sundays and he said to invite you along this time."

Dan said nothing but I felt his muscles tense around me. The silence stretched for so long that if his body wasn't so rigid, I might have thought he'd fallen asleep. Finally, he spoke.

"Uh... yeah... I don't... I don't think we're there yet."

It struck me like Remy's hip and shoulder; I felt completely winded. I wanted to wriggle out of Dan's arms but I knew that would make it too obvious that I was upset, so I just lay there, wide-eyed and frozen. After a while I felt Dan's muscles relax and he began to breathe deeply. I moved away from him and lay on my side. When my alarm went off in the morning, I wasn't sure if I had slept at all.

CHAPTER TWENTY-FOUR

Everything was annoying as I crossed the park. The sun was too bright, the dew on the grass was too wet and the singing magpies were too warbly. I was trying not to think about what Dan had said, but his words continued to scroll through my mind over and over.

I don't think we're there yet.

THEN WHERE ARE WE?! I wanted to scream at the warbly magpies.

A new wave of grump hit me when I remembered that Lachie wasn't even going to be on the tram. I crossed to my stop in the middle of the road and noticed there was something protruding from the side of the tram post. The few people already standing at the stop seemed to be glancing sideways at it.

I walked towards the pole and as I got closer, I could see it was a box with sticky tape wound around it. I wondered suddenly if it was a bomb and considered calling 000. But everyone else at the stop seemed to have already deemed the strange package unthreatening. I reached the post and, as I looked down at it, recognised the bright green lid of my plastic container. There was a handwritten sign taped to the top that said:

Justine's Lunch. Please do not touch unless you are Justine.

For a moment I just stood there, in a weird alternate reality where magic lunches appear on tram poles. Then I remembered Lachie joking (or apparently not joking) that he'd leave some of his Easy Pie for Idiots at my stop. I unzipped my laptop bag and found a small pair of child's scissors at the bottom.

While the people waiting at the stop pretended not to watch, I chopped through the tape and looked inside the container. It held a piece of meat pie and one of my ANZAC bikkies, with another note.

Hopefully you found this container wrapped in sticky tape attached to a tram pole. If not, don't trust the pie. It may have been compromised. Lachie X

I felt a thick ball of something start to roll upwards from my chest to the back of my throat, gaining momentum and girth as it rose. I swallowed hard and quickly put the container in my bag. Then I messaged Lachie.

Just picked up my lunch. Thank you. It made me so happy. X

My phone chimed almost straight away.

No worries. Don't worry, the tape is biodegradable.

It was close to the end of term so I spent my nights writing reports about my students. I wrote things like "Aimee has a relaxed and calm demeanour", thinking about when she'd fallen asleep during reading time, and "Kai occasionally makes good decisions", meaning the times when he hadn't come to school. I saw Dan on Wednesday night. He made me dinner peppered with small talk and we watched TV, then I made an excuse to go back to my own apartment.

I was still confused and angry but couldn't stand the thought of bringing it up and sounding too needy. He sent me a text on Friday morning to say that he had a mate's birthday that night so wouldn't see me unless I wanted him to come over afterwards, probably very late. I wrote back that I'd see him Saturday night instead. It occurred to me that the mate's birthday was unlikely to be a men-only function and that he probably could have chosen to invite me.

I don't think we're there yet.

On Saturday morning, Steph picked me up and drove us to the massive retail paradise known as Chadstone Shopping Centre. As we strolled through the automatic doors, we were greeted by a burst of cool, perfumed air, glittering Christmas decorations and the buzz of people everywhere. We had an early lunch and then hit the shops. The pretence was Christmas shopping, but really it was just a chance to catch up and gossip.

"So, neither of them will admit anything, but I'm convinced he's been texting her. I can just feel it," Steph was saying, referring to Li and her sister.

I was rifling through a rack of discounted jeans but my heart wasn't really in it.

"Well, Li's a good mate. Would it be the worst thing?" I said, not needing to see her laser-eyed look to know that it was burning two holes in the side of my head.

"OK," I admitted. "It *would* be the worst thing. We love him, but we wouldn't want anyone we love to date him."

Is that what Dan's female friends would say about him?

"Speaking of dating, you've been pretty quiet about Dan," Steph said, tapping into her BFF ESP. "What's up?"

I moved on to a rack of half-price coats. It was definitely the right time to buy them, but I found it hard to think about coats when it was 27 degrees outside. I filled Steph in on the conversation with Dan about Sunday lunch and then for some reason finished with the story about the tram pole lunch.

"Hmmm. Justine, can we just cut through your A-grade denial skills for a minute? Do you have a thing for Hardware… Lachie?"

Steph looked at me seriously.

"What?! That's not what this is about, I just told you that to demonstrate…"

She was still looking at me, unblinking. I blinked three times just thinking about the fact that she hadn't.

Damn it woman, why won't you blink?!

"Yes, I think so," I finally said.

"But you still want to be with Dan?"

"Yes, I think so," I repeated.

"Oh, no."

She finally blinked.

Wanting to do anything to change the subject, I frantically glanced around and spotted the baby section just across the aisle from where we were standing.

"Come on," I said. "Let's go and look at some of this stuff. Get you in the mood."

Steph had barely mentioned the pregnancy since she'd announced it to me.

"Oh, I don't think so," she said, looking panicked.

"Talk about A-grade denial skills."

I raised my eyebrows at her and then took her hand, leading her over. We perused the shelves for a while. Steph kept picking things up, turning them around in her hands and then putting them back again.

"I don't know what eighty percent of these things are," she said, her voice becoming louder and higher as she spoke. "I mean, what the hell is this for?!"

She held up a packet of nipple shields. Hayley had been an unprovoked over sharer during her pregnancies so I had some idea about most of the things we were looking at.

"Not everyone needs those," I said. "And they're not that different from the nipple tassels you bought to surprise Charlie on his birthday so don't freak out. Look, from what I hear, no one knows what they're doing the first time around."

"You don't understand, Jus. I'm facing my life—the life I know, the life I love—disappearing and being replaced by nipple shields and... and..." She picked up a random item. "Fucking bunny blankets!"

Steph shook the blanket so violently that its little fluffy bunny head whipped back and forth. An elderly couple in the next aisle turned to stare at us.

"OK, this was too soon, I see that now," I said as I gently prised the blanket from her hands. "You'll get there. I know I haven't experienced anything like it, but I do know that I've never heard anyone say they wanted to give their baby back after it was out. It's going to be really different, but it's going to be really great. *You're* going to be really great."

I gave her a big hug.

"Now, let's go and get an iced chocolate to cheer us both up."

I was putting away the presents I'd bought for Chase and Isla when there was a knock at the door. Dan had said he'd come round after dinner. I didn't bother with the creephole, just opened the door. There he was. Smiling. Handsome. *Mine.*

Then why doesn't he feel like mine?

"Hey," Dan said.

"Hey."

I couldn't help but smile back. I was sick of feeling angry at him. I just wanted it to be fun and comfortable between us again.

"I have something for you," Dan said as he came in.

I looked at him suspiciously. He wasn't carrying anything.

Is it his body? If so, then yes, I accept his gift.

"What is it?" I asked.

Dan reached into his back pocket and pulled out a key.

"It's Anastasia's key. The one I gave her. I want you to be my contingency instead, if you want. And I can be yours, if you give me a spare to your place."

I was shocked. This seemed incredibly significant.

"But then I would have an unnecessary ladder," I said, starting to smile and reaching my hand out.

"OK, if you don't want it, Anastasia will be happy—"

He pulled the key away and went to return it to his pocket.

"Hey, give that back!" I protested.

Dan suddenly turned all dark and sexy as he looked right into my eyes.

"Come and get it," he said.

So I did.

CHAPTER TWENTY-FIVE

As I turned the handle on Pops's screen door, I could hear the piano notes of "One Last Glimpse of You" wafting from his open lounge room window. Pops came to meet me in the small hallway.

"No fella today?" he asked.

"Just me," I said.

"All I could ever need," Pops answered, putting his arms around me and hugging me close. Imperial Leather and wool enveloped me.

"Come on, love, the roast is nearly done and I'm in need of a dance partner!"

Pops broke away from me and offered me his hand. I smiled at him and took it. He swept me into a waltz and we sang the lines together as we danced around his lounge room.

Well I suppose I've composed
So many lines, so many rows
And none were ever perfect, it's true.
But now we're dancing along
To the tune that we chose,
To the tune of me and you.

The oven began to beep and Pops stopped to bow grandly to me. Then we headed to the kitchen to serve up together.

After lunch and a chat, I was saying goodbye at the door when Pops's eyes widened like he'd just remembered something.

"Just a minute, love."

He shuffled to his bedroom and then returned with a long string of pearls.

"These were your grandmother's. I've been going through some things I couldn't bear to part with when she... passed and I found these. I'm so glad I've only got one granddaughter so no one can give me any grief for giving them to you."

He passed them over like they were the most precious thing he'd ever touched, so I accepted them in kind. I looped them carefully around my neck. Tears gathered in the corners of Pops's eyes.

"Just beautiful, love. They could have been made for you."

"I love you, Pops," I said and reached up to hug him goodbye.

On Monday night I was proofreading my reports when Ellie burst out of her room. As soon as she locked eyes with me, she looked worried, as if she were battling with something. Then she beckoned to me.

Curious, I followed her into her room. She just stood there.

What is going on?

"Ellie, wha—"

"Just listen," she said in an odd voice.

I waited. And then, I heard it: muffled moans. I felt all my limbs sag as my heart rate sped up. A man's grunts reverberated through the floor, followed by a woman's repeated "Ahhh"s. I dropped onto Ellie's bed, remembering the sound of Dan with Really Stupid Pants. All I could hear was their noises and the pulsing of my own blood in my ears.

I remembered the key Dan had given me and for a minute I had the crazy urge to run downstairs, burst into his apartment and catch him in the act. But I knew I wouldn't do that. I just wanted to curl up and disintegrate. I felt myself stand up and walk mechanically out of the room as Ellie watched me go. I went back to the couch, barely aware of the buzzing of my phone or the fact that I'd automatically answered it.

It was Dan.

Dan?! Is he multitasking again?

"Hey, gorgeous. Where are you?"

He sounded like he was outside. Maybe it was windy in his bedroom.

"What... I'm... What? Where are *you*?!"

"Just at Sydney airport. I got an earlier flight so I'll be back tonight after all. Can I come over? It'll be late."

I felt like everything was going really fast around me and my brain was stumbling along, metres behind.

"But... You're not in your apartment?"

"No. Why? Are you lying naked on my bed? Because if so, hold that thought for about... uh... four hours?"

"I'm not... but someone is."

There was a pause.

"What do you mean?"

"I was just in Ellie's room and I heard... noises."

A longer pause.

"*Fuck.*"

I waited until Dan composed himself.

"It's my brother. I forgot I said he could stay in my room because I hadn't made up the spare bed. He's obviously taken full advantage of the situation."

"Oh, thank God. I mean, that's outrageous! How inappropriate of him."

"You thought it was me."

"Yes. I mean, a little bit. It was pretty hard not to. I didn't know you were in Sydney. I didn't know your brother was staying. I didn't actually know you had a brother."

"Well, sorry that you found out this way. See you tonight?" he asked hopefully.

I breathed out, suddenly feeling silly and giddy with relief. My boyfriend hadn't cheated on me.

Hurrah!

"Yes, please."

I woke up with Dan wrapped around me, realising that at some point in the night I must have got up to let him in, although I could barely remember it. He stirred and then opened his eyes.

How can anyone look that good first thing in the morning? I'm pretty sure I have pillow marks across my cheek and my hair is matted with drool.

"Hello, gorgeous," he said, kissing my head. "Sorry about last night. My brother's a pest. He's here for the whole week though, so I might not get to see a lot of you."

"Oh. OK."

"Also, I'm going away for a few weeks over Christmas, to hang with my family in Sydney. I leave next Saturday."

"Your family live in Sydney?"

"Yeah. In the house I grew up in."

"You're not from Melbourne?"

Who ARE you?

"No. I moved here when work transferred me."

I was almost glad I didn't have to extend my mother's invitation to our family Christmas, given how well received the last invitation had been, although I felt disappointed about Dan leaving so soon.

"Well, I'm busy with work too, I guess. Just let me know when I can see you."

"Sure," he said and then threw the sheet off and bounced out of bed.

I admired Dan's body as he dressed in last night's clothes. He kissed me again and then left to shower at his place. I heard him greet Ellie outside my door. She must have looked surprised to see Dan, because I also heard him say, "It was my brother. Sorry for the noise... from both of us. See ya!"

I was dressed for work and rushing down the stairs to get to the tram stop when I ran into Dan and his brother. Even if I didn't know it was his brother, I would have guessed it in a second, regardless of the blonde hair and softer features.

"Hi there," said Brother of Dan, smiling at me.

Apparently *that smile* was a family trait. I wondered if their dad had it too.

Stop hitting on Dan's dad in your mind!

"Hi," I said.

I looked at Dan. He was fidgeting with his keys.

"I'm Justine."

I stuck my hand out. Brother of Dan shook my hand, looking a little confused as to why Dan's neighbour was introducing herself to him. He clearly knew nothing about me.

"Ryan," he said, letting go of my hand.

"Well, I'd better get to work," I said with a last glance at Dan.

He finally met my eye.

"See you, Justine," he said.

"And nice to meet you," said Ryan, still looking puzzled.

I fumed for the rest of the day and all of the evening. I fumed until I had a headache and then I went to bed at 8pm. An hour later there was a knock at the door. Ellie was at work so I ignored it. My phone buzzed with a message from Dan.

At your door. Let me in?

I threw my phone away and clenched my teeth, pulling the sheet up over my head. Twenty minutes later, when I was fuming into my pillow, there was a dragging sound outside and then a metallic thunk against my window frame. I panicked. As if things couldn't get any worse, some opportunist criminal had arrived to exacerbate the situation.

Thanks a lot for that. You really know how to burgle a girl when she's down.

I grabbed the creeper torch, retrieved my phone and crawled out of bed and over towards the noise. As quietly as I could, I pushed up the bottom slats of my blinds and peeked up over the window sill with my torch angled right at the glass. Just as I did, a face popped up, causing me to scream and fall backwards. At some point before I whacked my head on the carpet, I realised that the half-blinded, completely startled face was Dan's.

I stood up, rubbing the back of my head, and pulled up the blinds. There he was, with a guilty look on his face. Dan ducked out of the way as I pulled off the flyscreen and pushed out the window. I stood with my arms folded as he pulled himself through the window frame and then jumped down from the sill. I shut the window as Dan recovered himself. When I turned around, I could make out his grin, illuminated by the street light outside. I did not grin back.

I shall remain grinless.

"Well, you wouldn't answer your door and you haven't given me a key yet," he said, with the good sense to sound serious rather than jovial.

"So you thought you'd break several laws and also scare the shit out of me? Is that *my* ladder? You tried to break into my room with my own ladder?!"

"Yes. Something like that. I thought chicks liked romance."

I wouldn't have been surprised if, in the darkness, he was shrugging like a mischievous child.

"*Women* don't like stalkers."

"Hmmm, fair enough. Anyway, hi."

Dan stepped closer to me. I stepped backward, retaining what little dignity I could in the pyjamas I'd bought at Oktoberfest in Germany, which had lederhosen printed on the front. I hoped it was too dark for him to see them.

"Listen, I don't usually do this stuff. It's not... my kind of thing. But I... care about you, Justine."

I could hear the sincerity, the breaking honesty in his voice.

Wait, what did he do wrong again?

I sighed and flicked on my bedside lamp, revealing the lederhosen PJs in all their glory. I flopped against my pillow on the bed and patted the doona beside me. Dan came and sat down awkwardly, as though he had acupuncture needles sticking out of him.

"I'm just not ready for you to meet my family," he started.

"Is there something wrong with them?" I asked.

"No, they're great."

I felt sick and sad. I tried to take some deep breaths to calm myself. I didn't want to cry. It was so hard to be rational through loud, heaving sobs.

"...Is there something wrong with me?" I asked, my voice teetering on the precipice of a whimper.

"Of course not. Don't think that. I've just… been single for a long time."

"So have I," I pointed out, so that he didn't think it was an excuse for the way he'd treated me in front of his brother.

"I'm a private person. I like to keep the different parts of my life separate. It's just easier that way. But I'm sorry for the… thing with Ryan. I froze. It was gutless. You didn't deserve that."

I was silent. I waited for him to say, "I'd love to introduce you to my brother," but it didn't come.

"Justine? I don't want to lose you."

The tears began to flow. I wiped them on my lederhosen.

"I don't want to lose you either."

I nearly fell into his arms. But then I remembered the mistakes I'd made with Ben, never telling him when he'd really hurt me, never facing it when there were serious issues between us.

"But I don't want to feel like a glorified booty call either. I want you to meet my friends and family and I want to meet yours. If that's not where this is going, then…"

Oh crap, that sounds like an ultimatum. Take it back!

"I might want that too. Just… give me some time? I'm still getting used to this."

I looked over at him. I just wanted to trace the lines of his jaw, his forehead, his nose. I couldn't bear the thought of not being able to touch him again.

"OK. I can do that."

I shuffled closer to him and he put his arm around me, letting out a big sigh as he did that echoed my own relief.

"Justine?"

"Yes?"

I held my breath, not really ready for what might come next.

"Are you going to start yodelling?"

CHAPTER TWENTY-SIX

Dan and I said goodbye in his apartment three hours before he was due to fly out. I gave him a bag of bee pollen for Christmas and he gave me a pair of superhero pyjamas. Then he kissed me, tangling his hands in my unruly morning hair. I ran my hands over his chest and down his stomach, trying to commit everything to memory for the next two weeks. Then the door opened and Ryan, who had been out all night, said, "Ready to go, bro?"

He looked unsurprised to see me there in Dan's arms which meant either Dan had told him about me or he was just used to seeing women in Dan's arms.

"Oh hey, it's Janine, right?"

"Justine," Dan corrected him. "We're... together."

"OK, cool. We'd better head, Danny, our ride's waiting."

Dan gave me a last, quick kiss and then they rolled their suitcases out, leaving me alone in Dan's empty apartment. I trudged up the stairs and flopped onto my couch, contemplating going out for a walk.

It's Saturday. Why don't I have plans?

I looked at my phone accusingly, as if it was entirely to blame for my disappointing social life. It began to ring.

Oh my God, I made that happen with my powers.

I swiped.

"Hey, Lachie!"

I nearly said, "I've missed you" but settled for "Long time, no see" instead.

"I know, it has felt weird. How are you?"

Don't be pathetic. Just lie!

"Sad and lonely."

"Oh no. How come?"

"Nothing. I'm just being dramatic because I have nothing to do. Want to hang out?"

I felt immediately cheered by the thought of seeing Lachie, even though my brain went into alarm mode.

WARNING! WARNING! You've admitted to having feelings for him, now you have to keep your distance. DANGER!

I flicked a little mind switch and the alarm ceased.

"Sorry, I can't," Lachie said. "I'm just on my break from work and then I have to catch up on sleep. Then I'm volunteering tonight. I actually just got my roster for the next few weeks and I got Carols By Candlelight."

"Wow! That's so cool!"

My family had watched Carols by Candlelight every Christmas Eve for as long as I could remember.

"Yeah, it is. It's a pretty easy gig and we mostly just get to enjoy the show. The only thing is that Fee is on a cruise with Nate's family for Christmas and my other sister, Casey, is with her husband's family, so my mum's organised to visit her sister in New South Wales. She wanted me to come, she offered to pay for the flight and

339

everything, but because I'm volunteering on Christmas Eve, it's not going to work."

"Oh no, that's really sad! You'll be alone on Christmas? No! No, you can't be. You can come to my family Christmas, not that you'd want to, but if you do…" I trailed off.

WARNING!   *DANGER!*
ALAARRRRMMMM!

"OK!" Lachie answered quickly. "I do remember your parents saying on the phone that they're always welcoming of new people. Oh. Now it looks like I just called to get myself invited to your family Christmas."

For someone who was constantly making self-deprecating jokes, he sounded unusually embarrassed.

"Yes, because you did, eavesdropper!" I teased.

"No. I called because we hadn't caught up in a bit and I wanted to see how you were."

"Yes, but also a little bit because of Christmas."

"No…"

"I think, at least on a subconscious level…"

"I'm hanging up now," Lachie said, but I could hear the smile in his voice.

I put my phone back down and decided that I might as well go out for a walk, if just to take my mind off the fact that I'd just invited Lachie to my family Christmas.

A week later I was walking through the door into the familiarity of my family home, where Mum waited with her arms open.

"Happy Christmas!" she beamed at me and I hugged her tightly.

My Dad stood up from where he'd been watching cricket beside Pops, who my parents had picked up and brought to Geelong a few days ago.

"Hi, darl," Dad said, stepping forward to embrace me as well.

Then Pops smiled up at me from his recliner and said, "Here's trouble." He didn't stand so I gave him a kiss on his head.

"Now, I got your message, love," Mum was saying, as she went to the kitchen and started piling baked goods onto a plate that was shaped like Santa's sack. "But it was a bit confusing. Dan can't make it to Christmas, but Lachie can? Is that right?"

"Yes, that's the gist," I said, accepting the plate and selecting a chocolate ball and caramel slice before passing it on to Dad.

"And Lachie is…"

I imagined her mentally taking out her spy notebook.

"A mate. Where's Riley?"

"They won't be down until Christmas Day this year. Now, Lachie is the same mate who you went on your Spa Day with?"

"Oh, give her a break, Clare," Pops said and turned to me. "She's just like her mother. Wouldn't let go of something once she had a hold of it."

"No comment," Dad said quietly.

"Now, Juzzy," Pops said. "I was listening to the computer wireless the other day and I heard about one of those telephone applications."

I sat down on the couch with my mouth full, ready to embrace the change of subject.

"Apparently it helps you to make friends who live near you," Pops went on. "You just drag your finger to the right-hand side if you like the look of someone and then you can meet up for a cuppa. That'd be great for someone like me; a lot of my friends are still in the country. I wouldn't mind meeting some new people. Juzzy, do you know anything about it?"

All three of them looked at me. I imagined installing a dating app on Pops's phone and it almost made me spit out my caramel slice.

Ninety, single and ready to mingle, until 3pm when I'll need three different pills and a half-hour nap.

"Uh, yes. I don't know that it's quite right for you, Pops. Maybe we could look into things specifically for seniors in your area though."

"Oh," Pops said, sounding disappointed. "It sounded very convenient."

"A little too convenient," I muttered to myself.

Twenty-three of my family members showed up to the Geelong foreshore on Christmas Day. Pops was our only family on Mum's side, but Dad had four brothers, all of whom had offspring. Some of the offspring had offspring and the whole noisy lot of us were in attendance.

We spread ourselves across a lawn that lay behind a wall of tall palm trees. Beyond the trees was a man-made beach where a giant purple Ferris wheel turned leisurely and five bored-looking camels, roped together and burdened with tourists, were trudging up and down the sand. At least they weren't forced to wear head doilies.

I shook pre-chopped onions across one of the public barbies while Dad plopped about a million sausages onto the hot plate next to mine. Then he headed back to the car to retrieve more meat.

"Uh oh. Who trusted you with the onions?"

I hadn't even noticed Lachie approaching through the crowd of my relatives, which was surprising because he was usually so conspicuous with his hair. He was even more conspicuous now because he was wearing reindeer antlers.

"Hey, Dancer. Don't worry, someone else chopped them."

Lachie watched as I turned the thin slices with my tongs. Dad returned with steaks and put them down beside the hot grill, then wiped his hands on the paper towel he'd also brought with him.

"G'day!" he said, holding out his hand. "You must be Lachie. Great to meet you."

Lachie shook Dad's hand and I felt something jump inside me.

"Likewise," Lachie said, smiling. "Your daughter says wonderful things about you."

"All lies," Dad replied, turning the sausages according to the Hertz Family Method.

"Do all of these people belong to you?" Lachie asked us, gesturing to my aunts, uncles, cousins and second-cousins.

"Yep, all ours." I responded, stepping closer to him to avoid the billowing smoke from the barbies. "Want me to introduce you around? I haven't even said hello to everyone yet."

"Sure! I'm very excited to meet your family and to find out why you're... you."

I wasn't sure if he meant it in a good way. I spotted Dad's brothers chatting together and figured that was as good a place as any to start.

"Warning," I said, as we approached them. "They'll attempt to make jokes."

"I'll be on high alert," Lachie answered, laughing and not looking nervous in the slightest. Maybe his antlers were giving him confidence. I guessed there was no pressure really, he was only there as my friend.

I'd forgotten that, a tiny voice in my head whispered.

"Hey Uncle Paddy, Uncle Tom, Uncle Chris, Uncle Matt!"

"Justine!" Uncle Tom said, his jolly smile widening at seeing me. "Shouldn't you be resting after your big night of delivering presents?"

He was looking at my elf apron, which had come into its own today.

"Oh. Ha ha, yes, good one. Don't worry, I had an energy drink. Um... everyone... this is my friend, Lachie."

"Which one are you?" asked my Uncle Paddy. "She brings home so many."

This was a blatant lie and I was about to say so until Lachie said, "Oh, I'm the one with eight tattoos, seventeen body piercings and a really big motorbike."

All four uncles stared at him for a moment and then Uncle Paddy roared with laughter, clapping him on the shoulder. The others laughed as well.

"This one must keep you on your toes, Justine!" said Uncle Matt.

After that we drifted between groups, meeting all my cousins. We were about to head back to the barbies so Lachie could meet Mum, when my cousin Sarah came up and put her arm around me.

"Hey J-Dog," she said. "Aren't you going to introduce your favourite cousin?"

She was my least favourite cousin.

"This is Lachie," I said quickly. "Lachie, Sarah."

He went to shake her hand but she held out her arms and said, "In this family, we hug."

Gross, get off him.

Lachie hugged her and she said, "Mmm, you're a good hugger."

Have you no shame?! I thought in her general direction.

I guessed that Sarah was attractive, in a bucket-load of makeup kind of way. The hug went on far longer than I felt was decent.

"You know Lachie, if we're lucky today, Justine might repeat her famous nudie run performance." Sarah laughed loudly at her own joke as she finally released him.

"Ah, the great nudie run of '94," Lachie said. "That's mostly why I'm here, actually."

They both laughed together, clearly expecting me to join in.

"It was '96 actually," I said, glaring at him.

"There you are!" Mum cried, joining us.

She was wearing an apron that looked like a gingerbread man. I saw Lachie look at it and nod slightly, as if he'd figured out where I got my impeccable taste from.

"Sarah, would you mind grabbing the salad you brought and popping it on one of the tables? Thanks, love."

You're the best, Mum.

Sarah's face fell and she stalked off. My mother offered her hand to Lachie.

"Hello, I'm Clare, Justine's mother."

Lachie shook her hand and then gave her a kiss on the cheek, nearly poking her in the eye with his antlers.

"Lovely to meet you, Clare. Can I do anything to help?"

"Actually, yes, thank you. I do have a job for you. Follow me."

They headed towards the food tables together.

Oh no, I realised. *She's taken him off for questioning.*

"Meow, meow! Here I am!"

The crowd seemed to part magically until I saw Chase's unmistakable mop of hair flying along behind him as he ran. He banged straight into my legs and then threw his arms around them.

"Meow, meow! I'm a cat, Teeny, and cats like pats."

I stroked his head and then picked him up.

"Hello, Chaser. Did Santa come?"

"Yes, but I only heard three reindeer talking on the roof so I'm worried he lost the others."

"They're magic, they'll find their way home," I said, distracted by my mother's laughter as Lachie helped her move a table.

I frowned.

"Ooh, I think that's a llama! Is that the face you're doing?" Chaser said, staring up at me. He pushed his lips out and furrowed his brow. "Is that right? Or is that more like an alpaca?"

When Lachie returned, Chase and I were rolling around on the grass, pretending to be platypuses. I had no idea how a platypus moved. I suspected I looked more like an electrocuted worm.

"Hi Lachie!" Chase said, flopping the upper half of his body from side to side. "Did you know boy platypuses have poison in their legs?! Even though they're cute?"

"Wow! That's really cool!" said Lachie, lying down on his stomach beside us. "Did *you* know platypuses don't have stomachs?"

"Yes!" Chase said even though I was pretty sure he didn't. I definitely didn't.

Chase leaned over and sniffed Lachie's shoulder in greeting. Lachie responded by sniffing Chase's forehead.

"Lunch is ready, by the way," Lachie said, turning to me and paddling his hands like little flippers.

Chase stopped flopping and turned to me.

"Can we still eat sausages if we're platypuses? Where will they go, if we don't have stomachs?"

"Good point," I answered, "I think we have to be dinosaurs to eat sausages."

The three of us stomped over to the lunch tables.

Sometime during lunch, I lost Lachie. I searched around for the tell-tale flare of orange. There he was, sitting next to Pops. They were both laughing and Pops was wiping his eyes.

"I love Lachie," Chase said.

He was sitting on a picnic blanket beside me and his face was smeared with sauce and green frosting. I realised he'd snuck a cupcake away from the dessert table. I was so proud of him.

"That's really nice, Chase." I said, unable to take my eyes off Lachie and Pops as they continued to share a joke.

"Do you love Lachie too?" Chase asked, I think, as it was a little difficult to decipher with his mouthful of sausage, bread and cupcake.

"I do a bit," I said, telling myself I was just playing along.

"Not as much as I do though," Chase consoled himself.

"No, not that much."

After lunch, everyone sat or lay around on the grass, talking while they digested. Chase begged me to take him to see the Ferris wheel, so Lachie and I walked along the sand as Chase darted around us, stopping to pick up bits of "nature" every three seconds. Christmas music jingled from mounted speakers along the foreshore and suddenly Chase stopped and yelled, "Dance break!"

He stood with his legs wide, his eyes shut and his head thrown back, then waved his hands in the air while bobbing up and down. Lachie and I watched him, both of us covering our mouths.

"Hey Chase!" I yelled. "Did you know Lachie loves to dance too?"

Lachie looked at me with his eyebrows narrowed.

"Dance with me, Lachie!" Chase yelled back without opening his eyes or losing a beat in his enthusiastic bobbing.

Lachie sighed and walked over to Chase. He shook out his arms and then slowly raised one arm above his head and the other out to the side, like a ballet dancer. His limbs were so gracefully poised and his back was so perfectly straight that I couldn't help but stare. I held my breath. Then Lachie shut his eyes, threw back his head and waved his hands in the air, bobbing up and down in a perfect imitation of Chase.

With the dance break over, the three of us stood and watched the Ferris wheel complete several lazy rotations. Then we headed back towards the group, with Chase running ahead to give his precious nature collection to his mother.

Lachie went to step through the palm trees, back to where my family were lounging, but I motioned for him to continue to walk with me.

We followed the path onto the semi-circle boardwalk, where teenagers were screaming as they jumped off diving boards into the ocean. Gentle waves, their underbellies sparkling with the sun's reflection, made soft *plat plat* noises beneath us. About halfway around, I followed some wooden steps down to a tiny dock that sat below the wooden boards of the boardwalk.

"When I was in high school, my friends and I used to come down here and paint our nails," I called up to Lachie as I sat down and dangled my legs over the side, feeling a cool spray on my skin from the waves that splashed against the boardwalk supports. I looked out towards the horizon and breathed in the warm, salty vapour. A short distance away, several tethered sailboats bobbed in the hot wind.

Lachie climbed down the ladder and sat beside me with his arm and knee just touching mine. The dock was small, so I didn't know if he'd done it on purpose, but my whole body flushed from the touch of his bare skin. We sat in silence for a minute, watching a seagull tear through the sunlit fabric of the ocean as it dove for something just below the surface.

"I'd be a seagull," I said suddenly.

"Sorry?" Lachie said, leaning even closer to me as though he might have misheard.

Now his whole arm was warm against mine.

"The reincarnation question. You'd be a mantis shrimp, I'd be a seagull."

"Oh, right! Why?"

"So I could be by the sea all day, gliding around, letting the wind lift and carry me. And also because I love hot chips."

Lachie laughed.

"We'd make a good pair then: a seagull and a mantis shrimp."

"Don't power punch me with your nippers."

"Well, don't try to eat me then."

"Deal."

I watched entranced as the sailboats' naked masts rocked from side to side like silent metronomes.

"I suspect you already know this…" Lachie said, staring out at the horizon.

I waited for one of his "cool" facts that I definitely didn't already know.

"But I want you to hear it from me, instead of No Filter Fee. I was with my last girlfriend for a long time. We met when I was still in high school. She was a dancer too. It was Remy, who you met at footy. We'd been together for five years when I found out from Nate that our other best mate, Corey, was seeing her too. Not just sex; they were actually having a relationship behind my back."

His voice was raw, as though the memory was clawing its way out of his throat.

"So I broke up with her, obviously, and I stopped dancing because it just reminded me of her. All the time. I couldn't do it without feeling her there."

Like my couch, I thought.

"But I knew her when she was sixteen. She had an upbringing you couldn't even imagine, it was so rough. So when she wanted me back, I said I'd be her friend instead. Because she had no one and I couldn't bear the thought of that, even though I couldn't bear the thought of her anywhere near me either."

"I get that," was all I could think of to say.

"I knew you would," he said and the corners of his mouth lifted, not quite in a smile.

Most of my extended family had left by the time Mum and I were loading the leftovers into eskies. I was also half-listening to the conversation Lachie was having with Riley.

"...The problem with this generation is that they're wasting all their money on smashed avocado instead of saving housing deposits. It's disgraceful."

Riley was doing his usual bit.

"I don't know," Lachie argued. "Sounds like you haven't had a good one or you wouldn't be saying that."

I looked over to see Riley break into a smile.

"It's true," he conceded. "I've only had it once. The toast was dry and it was light on the avocado."

"Now that's disgraceful," Lachie said.

"Lachie seems lovely," Mum said quietly, watching me watching him.

"He is," I agreed before I could catch myself.

"How did you two meet exactly?" she asked, feigning a casual tone.

Uh oh, sneaky spy alert!

"It's a funny story actually," I said, glancing around. "Oh, it looks like Pops needs some help!"

I raced away from her. Pops was trying to raise himself from his fold-out chair next to Dad. Dad hadn't noticed because he was playing with Isla on his lap. I took Pops's arm and hoisted him up.

"Thanks, Clare, love," he said.

"It's Justine, Pops," I said gently, feeling scared. He'd never confused me with anyone else before.

"Yes, that's right, I know that," Pops said, looking as though he were trying to convince himself. "I'm feeling tired, love, could you please tell Clare I'm ready to go home?"

"Sure, Pops. I'll tell her."

After we said our goodbyes to my parents and Pops, I got into Lachie's car. He'd offered to drive me home so I wouldn't have to take the train and I'd gladly accepted. As I settled in, I expected him to turn the radio on but he didn't. He also didn't say anything beyond polite conversation until we'd reached the freeway.

"Your cousin Sarah asked me for my number," Lachie announced bluntly as we joined the three lanes heading to Melbourne.

I felt my heart seized by a cold, invisible fist.

"Ha ha! Good on her. Did you give it to her?"

I hoped I sounded normal.

"No."

I didn't know what to say. I kept thinking of things and none of them seemed appropriate.

Good. You're too good for her. You should be with someone who gets you. You should be with me.

I kept quiet.

"Your family is amazing. I didn't once feel like an outsider today," Lachie said quietly.

"I think you fit in better than me," I agreed, looking over at him and smiling.

He turned to meet my eye, then looked back at the road.

"I don't think I can hang out with you anymore, Justine."

What?

"Why?"

"It's just... not right. I can't say anymore without becoming the kind of person that we both hate."

What he couldn't say hung between us, prickling at my skin.

"We're not doing anything wrong. Just hanging out. Friendship hangs!" I said, a little desperately.

"Friendship hangs?" Lachie said, breaking the tension for a minute.

"People say that," I responded.

"People don't say that."

We were both quiet again.

Don't say anything else.

I was terrified of breaking something I desperately wanted to keep.

"But you always call me 'Mate'," I said.

"Yeah, because I've been desperate to tell myself that that's all you are," his voice rose. "Because I could not justify hanging out with you if I had feelings for you. I don't want to be that kind of person. But apparently, I am. And I do, Justine. I do have feelings for you."

I have feelings for you, too.

I realised I couldn't tell him the truth without feeling like I was cheating on Dan. Unfortunately we had forty minutes left of our car trip. After a drawn-out silence, Lachie finally put on the radio, but I felt too sad to sing.

We were only five minutes away from my building when I said, "I won't come to Covert Cinema next week then."

"No, please do come," Lachie said immediately, as though he'd expected this conversation. "Everyone is looking forward to seeing you again. It's not like we'll be there alone. And it might be our last... Friendship hang."

He turned into my street, did a U-turn and pulled up right in front of my apartment.

"Well, see you," I said and opened my door.

Lachie stopped the car, took off his antlers and got out. He came around to face me as I stepped onto the footpath. Then he put his arms around me and pulled me into a hug. I hugged him back carefully, trying not to press my lady bits into his gentleman bits.

"Put some effort in. This might be our last hug," Lachie said, sounding broken.

Without thinking twice, I pulled him tightly against me. The line of my body sealed with his and my heart thumped into his chest. Everything sung inside me.

"I'm having a bit of trouble letting go," Lachie said in my ear.

"Why?" I asked, my feelings mirroring his.

"Because I feel like this will be the best thing I do for a long time and I don't want it to end."

Finally, I broke off the hug, stepping back and dropping my arms limply as though I'd been disconnected from my power source. Lachie looked at me one more time with a pained expression on his face, then got back into his car and rolled silently away.

When I got inside, I tried to call Dan but he didn't answer. Since he'd left, I'd only had one text from him, wishing me a Merry Christmas. It was only when I was unpacking my overnight bag that I realised I'd forgotten to give Lachie his hoodie back again. I sniffed it. It smelled like vanilla and orange massage oil, smoke and Lachie. I folded it carefully and put it away in my wardrobe.

CHAPTER TWENTY-SEVEN

"Being pregnant is like someone slapping you with a wet dog and then dragging you through hot sand," Steph complained through the monster mask she was wearing.

"Wow. OK. A big dog or a small one?"

I struck a pose in the gladiator's breastplate. We were supposed to be looking for costumes for Covert Cinema but had gotten a little side-tracked. Charlie was in a change room trying on a pinstripe suit.

"One of those little, yappy, annoying things," Steph answered, pulling off the mask.

"You feel like someone slapped you with their freshly-bathed Chihuahua?"

"IT'S A FUCKING SIMILE!" she suddenly raged at me. "You're not supposed to question it, you're just supposed to pat my hair and say 'Aww'!"

I reached over and patted her hair gently, a little scared that she might try to bite me.

"Aw... But I do also have some questions about the hot sand—"

"Oh, get off me."

She batted my hand away.

"What'd'ya think, ladies?" Charlie called as he pushed back the change-room curtain and tugged down the pinstripe collar on his suit jacket.

"Very dapper," I said as we walked over to him.

Charlie looked in the mirror.

"I think I need a machine gun," he said.

"The theme is Roaring Twenties, dumbass. *Scarface* was set in the eighties," Steph snapped. Then she stalked off to the hat section.

"So… she's nuts," I said to Charlie.

"Completely insane," he agreed. "But from what the internet says about pregnancy, it's fair enough."

"How are *you* feeling?" I asked him.

He buttoned up the jacket and looked in the mirror again.

"Honestly?" he asked, his eyes meeting mine in our reflections. "I'm so excited. I can't wait."

"Oh, that's beautiful! Stop it, I'm emotional!" I cried, aware that my voice had reached drunk-girl levels of high pitched.

"That sounds kind of funny coming from someone who looks ready to lead the Greeks against Sparta," Charlie said, knocking on my breastplate.

"Great warriors have feelings too," I said defensively.

"Over here!" Steph called.

She was standing at a rack of dresses. I went to lift the breastplate over my head but Charlie stopped me.

"You might need it," he said wisely.

I didn't know I was going to break up with Dan until I saw him again, although the fact that I'd been sniffing another guy's hoodie probably should have been my first clue.

There he was, fresh off the plane and standing in my doorway, smiling. His skin was tanned a golden brown, making his eyes seem an even brighter blue than usual. He was the most beautiful thing I'd ever seen and I didn't want him. Well, of course I did, because I was human, but I wanted Lachie more.

Dan stepped forward to kiss me and I turned my head to the side and gave him a tight hug. I felt his hard chest against my cheek and it hurt to think that this would probably be the last time. After a second, Dan put his arms around me and returned the hug.

"Hey, gorgeous," he said.

I couldn't read his voice so I looked up to see him staring down at me.

Don't look at him! It's like trying to say "No" to cake.

I broke away and went to the couch. Dan followed me. We sat, not touching. I realised he was waiting for me to speak.

"How was your Christmas?" I finally said, stalling.

I hadn't planned to break up with him, so I had no idea what I was going to say. I just knew I had to say something.

"Really good. Relaxing. Yours?"

"Uh, great… Speaking of Christmas, I need to talk to you about… us."

"OK. Interesting segue," Dan said, rubbing his holiday stubble.

I laughed. I couldn't help myself.

I had been in Paris, sightseeing, when I'd ended up stuck behind a Segway tour as I

359

approached a set of traffic lights. One of the men on the tour, who was kitted out in a black helmet and elbow pads, was zooming towards the traffic light button with his arm outstretched to press it. In his urgency, Segway Man accidentally tilted backwards and then tried to compensate by leaning forwards again. This had powered him towards the traffic light so quickly that he'd hit the pole and the whole Segway had rolled out from underneath him. The best bit was that a woman in the group had started hysterically screaming, "SEGWAY DOWN! SEGWAY DOWN!"

Dan was staring at me like I was having a psychotic episode, which I probably was. I took a few deep breaths. This was not a good start; I needed some inspiration. What had the TV bachelor said? "She has an amazing spirit and I've loved the time we've spent together, but my heart is taking me in another direction and I just couldn't forgive myself if I didn't follow it."

That's good. Just say that.

"Dan," I began. "You have an amazing... I mean... It's..."

I couldn't think of one thing to say that wouldn't sound horribly clichéd and cringe worthy.

"I don't want to wait for you to be... whatever you need to be for us to be a normal couple," I blurted out.

"Does this have something to do with the egg-freezing pamphlet I saw on your bedside table?" he asked.

"No, it's about us," I answered quickly. "Although it doesn't help that egg-freezing really isn't an option for me. I couldn't bear to keep my babies in the freezer. They'd be so cold."

"Yeah, maybe get Ellie to explain the science on that one." Dan rubbed his face again. "Does it have something to do with your friend Lachie?"

He said "your friend" through his teeth and I realised he was starting to get angry. I thought about Ben's words to me: "I still love you, but we both know it's over." I wasn't a coward like Ben and I wasn't going to spout meaningless words instead of the truth just to make it easier on myself. People-pleaser or not, I owed Dan my honesty.

"Dan, I feel lonely when I'm with you."

He stared at me but I couldn't bear to look in his eyes.

"I don't feel like you want to be in a proper relationship," I continued, picking at a pull in the couch. "What do you tell people I am? Have you even told anyone about me, other than your brother?"

"I warned you that I don't like labels," Dan said, looking away.

There had been so many warning signs, I realised, but I had ignored them all. I had so desperately wanted my nice, impossibly attractive neighbour to be The One that I'd dived headfirst into a relationship with a man I barely knew.

My phone began to ring. It was my mother; her spy senses were probably tingling. I swiped to reject the call and sighed.

"I guess if it wasn't for Lachie, I might have put up with your lack of commitment and stuck around hoping that you'd eventually accept me fully into your life outside this building. I don't know. I like to think that I wouldn't have. I'm not in my twenties anymore, Dan. I don't have time to wait. I want to get married and have kids."

The look on his face when I said the last bit was enough for me to know that I was making the right decision. We both sat in silence, facing my blank TV screen.

"I should have predicted this one, I guess," Dan said, just sounding tired now as he stood up. "I really did like you, Justine."

I felt the stab of his use of the past tense.

"I know that," I said, standing as well. "I really liked you too."

He looked at me for a minute. Then he turned around and walked to my door. With his hand on the doorknob, he faced me again.

"You can just give my key back to Anastasia."

As the door clicked shut, tears brimmed along my lower lids and began to drip down my cheeks. Desperate to distract myself, I messaged Lachie:

Dan and I just broke up.

A minute later, he responded:

I hope you're OK.

No kisses, no hugs. I was about to write something else but my phone rang. I was excited to think it might be Lachie so we could talk properly, but it was Mum again.

"Hi Mum," I rushed. "It's not a great time but I'll—"

"It's Pops," she said and I could hear the tears in her words.

"What? What's Pops? Does he want to do a roast this Sunday?"

A-Grade denial skills.

"He's sick, love. They think it's a tumour. We're with him now in the hospital. They're saying... he doesn't have long."

I heard her begin to cry and then her voice was replaced by Dad's.

"Riley's on his way here, Justine. He's going to pick you up. We'll see you very soon."

I didn't say anything. I couldn't say anything.

"I love you, darl."

"Dad, no..."

"Oh, Justine," he said, his voice breaking. "We'll see you soon."

I hung up and dropped my phone. I sat on my floor, frozen in fear and shock, until the intercom buzzed and I was forced to stand.

CHAPTER TWENTY-EIGHT

The last time I'd been in a hospital was when Isla was born. That had been exciting. I remembered hurrying to the room, bursting in with flowers and eagerly anticipating tiny playdough mush baby cuddles.

I walked to Pops's room like I was resisting being dragged. Every step felt like a physical fight against an unseen, unstoppable force. But no matter how much I struggled against the tide of it, I was suddenly standing in front of the closed door, marked by its cold, silver numbers.

Dad was there. He embraced Riley and I together and when he pulled away, tears shone in his eyes. He knocked gently on the door and then opened it, revealing a room full of steel furniture and sterile equipment. Mum sat in a chair beside the bed. In both of her hands she clutched a pale, withered hand. Pops's iPod lay mute on a bedside table.

Unwillingly, I looked at the bed. There he was, shrunken against an overstuffed pillow, his eyes shut. Mum looked up and tried to smile at us. Then she patted Pops's hand, stood up and motioned to the seat.

"He's been in and out of consciousness," she said. "Perhaps you'd like to take turns sitting with him for a bit?"

"You go first, Juzzy," Riley said gently. "I'll keep trying to let Hayley know what's going on. I left the kids with her mum."

I sat down on the chair as the door closed behind them, shutting out the comforting hum of the hospital. I felt like I was in a room with a ghost. With his eyes shut and his teeth taken out, Pops could have been gone already. I took his dry hand, feeling the thickness of his lifelong calluses amongst the leathery folds of skin. He breathed heavily at the touch and his eyelids fluttered, but he didn't wake. I wondered if he could hear me.

"Don't go, Pops," I said in a whisper, meaning it to be louder.

After what felt like hours, but may have been minutes, there was a quiet tap on the door and Riley's face appeared.

"Swap?" he asked.

Riley had been a serious, mature child who had always acted as though he was much older than me, despite the fact that there were only two years between us. But now he *looked* old too; deep creases ran along his forehead and from his nose to his upper lip. I nodded and let go of Pops's hand. Pops stirred again but his eyelids remained sealed. As I passed my brother, Riley put his hand on my shoulder briefly.

The next forty-eight hours passed in a strange haze of suspended grief. I sat with Pops, drank water from a cooler that bubbled three times when I flicked its tap, went home to sleep, returned and repeated. I'd seen Pops open his eyes twice and I thought maybe there had been some recognition there, but he hadn't said anything. Voices seemed to echo strangely in the sterile room and synthetic words crackled around me like hospital sheets.

"Another hot day outside," one nurse commented as she changed the bag on Pops's IV.

I hadn't noticed the temperature on my way in that morning. It was like all my sensory receptors were turned off.

What day is it? I thought, vaguely.

"Love."

I hadn't even noticed Mum coming to sit beside me.

"Hi, Mum," I said, sounding hoarse and unfamiliar.

"Love, I think you should still go out tonight."

"What do you mean?" I blinked at her.

"Steph called me. She was worried that you hadn't responded to any of her calls or texts. She said you're supposed to be going to an event tonight? A New Year's celebration?"

New Year's. Covert Cinema. Lachie.

"I'm not going anywhere," I said, turning back to Pops.

"Love, it'll just be for a few hours. You need a break from here."

"I can't leave him, Mum."

I felt fresh tears drip into my lap.

"Justine, he would want you to go," Mum said firmly.

I looked at her again. Her own eyes were red-rimmed and wet.

Go for it, Juzzy! Give 'em hell! I heard Pops's voice so clearly that I had to check if he'd spoken. His eyes were still shut and his laboured breathing continued in a slow rhythm.

I nodded and let go of his hand.

You look lovely, I heard Pops again as I checked my appearance in the bathroom mirror. I was wearing the 1920s Art Deco-style dress I'd hired from the costume shop. The inbuilt corset and plunging V-neck pushed my cleavage up so high that I'd probably be able to rest my chin in it later and have a power nap. The whole dress was sequined in black, with silver beading that ran down the bodice in a geometric design and a hem fringed in black tassels that tickled my knees. The lady at the shop had kindly thrown in elbow-length satin gloves and a sequined headband boasting a plume of black feathers on one side.

I'd rushed through my makeup on autopilot, doing my best to cover up the startling effect that days of crying, little sleep and barely any sunlight had had on my face. My Gran's pearls, knotted once at my chest, swung from side to side as I twisted around to make sure my dress wasn't caught in my underwear at the back.

Here goes.

Steph, Charlie and I waited in a growing line of over a hundred people on the footpath along Little Bourke Street. The GPS on my phone had shown the address on our tickets as a cocktail lounge in the middle of Chinatown. We were somewhere in the middle of the line, waiting for something to happen, although we didn't know what. Motorists stared out of rolled-down windows at the spectacle, taking in the abundance of pinstripe, feathers and sequins. I stood on tiptoe in my heels and looked up and down the line. I couldn't see a curly, ginger head anywhere, although most of the guys were in hats, so Lachie could easily be incognito.

"How are you going?" Steph asked as I lowered myself down again.

"I have no idea," I answered. "Between Dan and... Pops... I should feel something. But I don't. I feel nothing."

She put her gloved arm around me and I lay my head on her shoulder. A guy in a beige waistcoat and bowtie entered my sideways view as he strolled along beside the line, whistling "The Charleston" and swinging a red, vintage megaphone by its metal handle. He looked at us as he passed and then, when he recognised me, touched his fingers to his flat cap with his free hand. It was Jack. He continued to the front of the line, which we could only just see if we craned our necks.

"How's tricks, flappers and fellas?!" Jack yelled through the megaphone in a convincing American accent.

The crowd whooped and whistled, and a few feather boas were waved in the air.

"Welcome to a time when 'kale' wasn't somethin' you got on top of your grain salad, it was money and money talked. And, if you spent your kale right, you might just get yourself into a swanky juice joint like this one. That's right, I'm talkin' about a speakeasy!"

The crowd cheered again and excitement flared in my belly. I thought of Pops and the excitement was immediately doused with guilt.

"So thanks for puttin' on your glad rags and comin' out tonight! Who's ready to get pie-eyed?" Jack called.

There were confused murmurs along the line and the couple in front of us shrugged. Jack put his hand to the side of his mouth as though he was going to whisper, but shouted loudly into the megaphone.

"It means get zozzled, bent, ossified, jazzed, lubricated, lit up like the Commonwealth!"

Having gotten the gist this time, the crowd erupted, causing pedestrians to stop and watch from the other side of the street.

"You'd better behave yourselves now, or you'll be streeted by our friendly security," Jack continued. "So have a real nifty time, but we draw the line at makin' whoopee on the poker tables! This ain't no creep joint!"

The cheer this time was littered with wolf whistles.

"Alright, alright," Jack put his hands up as if to steady the crowd. "We've got some swell entertainment lined up for you tonight, so let's ankle!"

Suddenly, we were moving in the direction of the cocktail lounge. Except, as we entered single-file through the narrow doorway, I realised that it didn't look like a lounge anymore. Cabinets with large mirrors lined the walls and actors with towels draped around their necks lay back in padded barber shop chairs to have their hair fake-razored by other actors in white coats. Jazzy music played from an old-time radio which sat on the bar next to a vintage cash register.

Steph, Charlie and I followed the flow of people through the lounge-cum-barber shop through another narrow doorway that led to a low-ceilinged downstairs room, where loud, brassy notes were pumping from the speakers. More actors were clinking glasses at the bar, rolling dice at casino tables and dancing the Charleston on the spacious dancefloor. A large screen had been set up in a corner of the room and was surrounded by velvet chairs, couches and clumps of gold-tasselled cushions.

"I guess they don't do a Blow Job here," Steph said to me as we stepped off the staircase. I looked over at the bar where bartenders were pouring whiskey and gin into crystal glasses.

"I don't think the Blow Job has been invented yet," I replied, looking around again for Lachie.

Maybe he's not coming.

"Anyway, your Blow Job days are over for a little while," I added.

"Oh, I'm aware. And I could really use a drink. Damn the little life-sucker," Steph said, but as she did, she placed her hand tenderly on the gold fringe that swung over her small bump and looked down with a smile. Something had clearly changed. I put my arm around her and squeezed.

"I'm happy for you," I said.

"Well, let's see if you're saying that when I'm calling you to come over at 2am and hold my baby so I can sleep for more than three minutes at a time."

"I'll be there," I said.

Tears glistened in Steph's eyes as I squeezed her again.

"Come on, cheer up you two!" Charlie said, putting his arms around both of us. "It's New Year's Eve. Let's party like it's 1929! Who wants a virgin moonshine?"

He started to guide us towards the bar, but something caught my eye. I turned my head and there was Lachie talking and laughing amongst the crowd. My heart began to thunder as I took in his three-piece pinstripe suit, which fit him as though he'd had it tailored, and the black fedora that covered most of his hair. His suit jacket was open and a silver pocket watch chain dangled from his waistcoat. Very suddenly, the numbness thawed and I *felt* again.

I broke away from Charlie and began to walk towards Lachie, my fingers tingling with anticipation. But before I reached him, the lights went out. I stopped and waited for my eyes to adjust to the darkness. A red spotlight clicked on and Lachie's frozen silhouette was the only thing visible as the people surrounding him stepped backwards into the shadows.

Am I imagining this?

Lachie started tapping his toe. The black-and-white spats he was wearing made a distinct clicking sound on the concrete floor. He slowly

371

began to shuffle his feet in a series of combinations that made my brain hurt. A drum beat started up and Lachie tapped to it in perfect time, clapping his hands and shouting "Hey!" every now and then. Then he stopped abruptly, clicked his fingers and held out his hand. Someone threw him a cane which he caught. He started dancing again, spinning the cane between his hands as a trumpet joined the drums. The beat increased in tempo and Lachie matched it, his feet moving with inconceivable speed. The music stopped again and so did Lachie, posing with the cane on the ground and his head down.

I raised my hands to clap when another spotlight appeared on the dancefloor where a female silhouette was clad in a figure-hugging flapper dress. She began to tap. Her bare legs were mesmerising as her heeled shoes echoed loudly on the wooden boards and her silver hair flung wildly around her as though it were alive. It was Remy.

Suddenly, Lachie came to life again, tapping out a complicated rhythm which Remy copied easily. He tried another combination and once again, she executed it perfectly. They continued back and forth like this until they were tapping together, their bodies perfectly in sync, despite the fact that she was on the dancefloor and he was amongst the enthralled crowd. He began to dance towards her and she matched his every move until he took her in his arms. The room was silent as Lachie dipped Remy and then lifted her up slowly as she ran her black-gloved fingers down the side of his face.

The house lights flashed on and music played from the speakers again as about twenty more tap dancers emerged from the crowd to join the routine. It was a tap flash mob. I realised Steph and Charlie had somehow made their way back to me.

"That's him, isn't it?" Steph whispered.

I nodded.

"And the twenty hot points go to... Tap Dancing Ginger," Steph said approvingly.

"And that's his ex." I felt sick as I said it out loud.

"Oh," she said.

Remy held Lachie's hand and they smiled at each other as the other dancers crowded around them, every toe and heel still landing perfectly to the beat. As the song drew to a close, the males spun their partners around themselves and then finished with a dip. As Lachie returned Remy to a standing position, she threw her arms around his neck and kissed him. Lachie pulled away as the whole group joined hands and bowed to rapturous applause.

"I think I want to go," I said, more to myself than the others.

"Justine!"

I heard my name called as the applause died down and looked up to see a red-gloved hand waving at me from the dense crowd. The hand was attached to Fee, who was making her way towards us with Nate in tow. I introduced everyone, feeling like I wasn't really present.

"What did you think?!" Fee exclaimed. "Apart from the finale…"

She cupped her hand around her mouth and said, "Vicious bitch", not exactly quietly.

"He was amazing," I admitted.

So was she.

"Let's hear it for my boy, Lachie, he's a real Oliver Twist! And give it up for his fellow hoofers. They were hitting on all sixes tonight!" Jack crowed into the microphone. The audience whistled and clapped again.

"Well, hopefully all you guys and dolls have had the chance to purchase your giggle water at the bar, because now it's time to turn this frolic pad into a petting pantry. We've got a great talkie lined up for you tonight—The Great Gatsby!"

There was an enthusiastic cheer and people began to drift towards the seats. Slow-dance music played as couches and cushions were quickly claimed. Steph and Charlie both looked at me. I shrugged and motioned for them to go ahead as Fee put her hand on my arm.

"I know that didn't look good, Justine, but she's trying to get back in his good books," Fee said. "Lachie kicked her off our footy team last night. For that time she ploughed you down."

I looked at her, shocked.

"You told him?"

I shouldn't really have been surprised; I knew Lachie called her No Filter Fee.

"Not me," she said. "Dan. That's his name, right? We played his team last night in footy. They killed us, partly because most of the girls were just

374

watching him instead of the ball. Hello! Is he a model? He's a model, right?"

"Uh, I don't think so. How did you know he told Lachie?"

"Well, they had a little after-game chat that looked tense as. Lachie came back and took Remy aside. She was all excited about it, but then she went off in a big huff. And Lachie just said, 'Remy's off the team. She hurt another player on purpose and that is unacceptable.'" Her imitation of Lachie's voice was impressive in its accuracy. "It was all really dramatic, which is unlike Lachie. He only told me later that the model was your ex."

It *was* really dramatic. The exhaustion and pain of the last few days hit me in a big wave, nearly knocking me over.

"You can stop talking about me, I'm here now."

I felt Lachie's voice in every muscle, every nerve of my body. Fee looked guiltily at him.

"Right, well, I was joking, but that's awkward," Lachie said, sounding deflated.

He stood beside me, his face glowing with sweat. I just wanted to bury my head in his chest and for the speakeasy to dissolve around us.

"I told you if you were lucky I'd dance for you one day," Lachie said, smiling at me.

He looked so happy and proud of himself.

"It wasn't really for *me*, though, was it?" I said curtly.

What am I doing? I should tell him I felt shivers the whole time he was dancing. I should tell him I found myself picking up rubbish on my walk the other day. I should tell him I'm terrified about losing Pops. I should tell him that it never felt right with Dan, not the way it does with him. I should tell him... everything.

Lachie stared at me as though I'd slapped him. Fee and Nate exchanged glances.

"We'll go and save some seats," Nate said quickly, putting his arm around Fee. "Bye guys."

As they headed in the direction of the big screen, Lachie continued to stare at me.

"I'm going to go," I said, trying to swallow everything that was threatening to surge out of me.

I turned away from Lachie but he put his hand firmly on the small of my back and led me away from the loud music and voices, over to a side-room where the toilets were. There was an actor stationed there who was stirring a bathtub full of ice and what was supposed to be bootleg gin with a wooden pole.

"What d'ya know?" he greeted us as we entered and then continued to tend to his concoction.

Lachie nodded at him but turned to me.

"What is going on with you?" he asked quietly.

"What is going on with *you*?" I said, feeling irrationally furious with him. "Wasn't that your ex who *cheated on you*? Why are you dancing with her? Why is she kissing you?"

"I did it for Jack. After putting together all this," he gestured back towards the main room. "He didn't have much of a budget left for entertainment so I talked some friends into doing it for cheap.

376

Remy offered to do it for free. I couldn't refuse her; she's a national champion and I was helping out a mate. The kiss wasn't planned, she just sprung it on me. Do you really think I enjoyed it?"

"It certainly looked like you did."

Oh no, don't be THAT girl!

Lachie's teeth were clenched tightly together and a muscle twitched under his left eye. I'd never seen him look so angry. He grabbed my shoulders and looked into my eyes.

"What is this *really* about?"

"Are you two gonna start barneymuggin' in here or what?" asked the bathtub guy, leaning against his wooden pole.

"I'm a mate of Jack's," Lachie said in his direction without unclenching his teeth. "Give us a minute, mate."

"Sure thing! I'll just mind my beeswax." The stirring resumed.

"Justine, I will ask you again. What is really going on with you?"

His palms were hot on my bare shoulders.

"You kicked Remy off your football team, so why are you still dancing with her?" I couldn't get the vision of Lachie and the green-eyed, silver-haired beauty performing those close, intimate movements out of my head, not to mention the kiss.

"It was already rehearsed. I couldn't swap her out at the last minute. But I'm actually glad you brought that up. Why didn't *you* tell me that she deliberately hurt you? I had to hear it from *your* ex."

"I didn't tell him either, he saw it. I didn't tell you because I didn't want to start any trouble amongst your team. And I was worried you'd just defend her."

"Well, you don't think much of me then."

"I think everything of you!" I suddenly exploded. "That's the only reason I'm here tonight, because I thought…"

As quickly as I'd erupted, I felt all my energy drain away. I didn't know if I had the strength to tell him what I so desperately wanted to.

I should have eaten more than two party pies for dinner.

"You thought that we'd just get together so you wouldn't have to worry about being single and lonely again?" Lachie said, glaring at me through eyes that were wild and unfamiliar.

"That's not what I—"

"Justine, that message you sent me after our date at the park, did it say anything good about me? Anything at all?"

I had memorised it out of shame. I knew it didn't. We clearly both knew it didn't so I said nothing.

"I was leaving your building when I got it, you know. I was excited. For the first time in years, I felt like I'd met someone I really liked. Dan was coming in as I was going out, so I was bloody holding the door open for him as I read it. How messed up is that?" He shook his head bitterly. "Do you think I'm happy to play second fiddle to a guy like that? Do you think that makes me feel good about myself? I'm not interested in being your convenient rebound just because you got dumped!"

Gentle, familiar piano notes wafted in from the main room. It was the introduction to "One Last Glimpse of You". I knew I was going to cry. I had already cried too many times in front of Lachie during our relationship but I felt like I no longer had any control over my emotions.

"As hard as it may be to believe, *I* broke up with Dan, not the other way around! Because I wanted to be with you!" I yelled, hoping my anger would help me to restrain the tears. "But forget it, it's all been a mistake!"

I wrenched my shoulders away from Lachie's hands and stumbled backwards. As I turned and broke into the fastest jog my heels would allow, I heard the bathtub bootlegger say to Lachie, "You've got ya'self a real bearcat there, but boy, has she given you the icy mitt!"

I was fumbling with my keys on the way to my apartment building when movement through the glass door stopped me. It was a couple and they were kissing against Dan's door. I watched as he entwined his hands through her blonde hair.

I sighed internally.

Of course this is happening.

At this point my options were to risk being caught standing outside, staring at them—massive creeper alert—or to go in and face them.

If I'm a stealthy ninja and sneak past, they won't even notice me.

I tried to tiptoe closer to put my key in the lock but my heels got stuck on the corner of the doormat. Caught off balance, I channelled the unfortunate Segway driver in Paris and attempted to steady myself by leaning forward. Unsurprisingly, I fell and ended up with my face and hands pressed against the door.

Dan broke away from his companion and looked straight at me. His mouth dropped open. The blonde turned around to see what he was looking at and they both just stared.

If I had a squeegee, I could pretend to be washing the windows. I have a makeup remover pad and a tampon, would that work?

I pushed away from the glass, leaving behind a cloudy forehead smudge and a bright red lipstick kiss. Then I unlocked the door and walked in, trying to look casual.

"Oh, hey, Dan," I said, barely looking up and continuing towards the stairs. I noticed that he had at least closed his mouth.

"Hey, Justine… Had a good night?"

"I've had better. Happy New Year," I said.

"Happy New Year," he responded.

"A friend of yours?" I heard the girl say suspiciously as I unlocked my door.

"Just a neighbour," Dan replied, shutting his door.

Too tired to get undressed, I pulled Lachie's hoodie on over my dress, even though it was too hot, and laid down on my bed. There was music pumping from a party somewhere and I heard people counting down to the new year. All I wanted was to be consumed by silence. I opened my bedside table drawer to retrieve my ear plugs and the crowd of condoms in there mocked me silently.

I plugged my ears, shut my eyes and tried not to think.

January

CHAPTER TWENTY-NINE

"Juzzy," Pops smiled at me as though I was walking through the door for Sunday Roast. "You look lovely."

It was 4am on New Year's Day and I had rushed to the hospital after the flashing light on my phone screen finally woke me after four missed calls. It was Mum, calling to say that Pops was awake.

I reached Pops's bedside and saw his eyes brighten when he noticed Gran's pearls around my neck. He looked like he might be trying to raise his hand to touch them, though he didn't manage it.

"We'll leave you for a few minutes," Dad said, helping my mother out of her seat and putting his arm around her to lead her out.

When they were gone, Pops coughed and said, "It's a funny thing to realise your time is nearly up. I feel like I could still be twenty, dancing around that hall with her…"

He coughed again and blinked hard.

"Juzzy, your fella, he seems like a good bloke. He cares for you."

I went to tell him that we'd broken up, and then remembered that Pops had met Lachie, not Dan. My lower lip trembled and my teeth began to chatter together. I was glad I was in Lachie's hoodie. The room seemed so cold.

"Pops, I love you so much. I can't imagine…"

There was nothing I could say that would be enough.

Don't go, don't go, don't go.

"Juzzy, I know, love. But you'll have your own children and your own grandchildren one day. Your life will feel full again, I promise. If only your grandmother could have seen you…"

He blinked as tears pooled in the corners of his eyes.

"Remember, love: I met her, I learnt her, I loved her," he said. "That's all there is to it."

He seemed to lose focus and looked away from me, up at the ceiling.

"…To the tune that we chose," he whispered through cracked lips. "To the tune of me and you."

"Pops, please, stay. Just for…"

His eyes shut and the room was filled with the sound of his strained breaths. Mum, Dad and Riley came in and surrounded the bed. An hour later, Pops was gone.

We all stood around outside the hospital room. It felt like the part I hated in weddings, the bit where everyone remained at the reception after the bride and groom had left. Except that weddings were mostly happy and right now I felt as though my heart was tearing in half. Riley put his arms around me and hugged me tightly. When he pulled away, Lachie's hoodie was damp with his tears.

"Pops wanted you to sing at his funeral," Mum said to me. "I'm sure you can guess the song."

She tried to smile. Her cheeks glistened with tears in the fluorescent hospital light.

"You don't have to do it," Dad said. "We'd all understand."

Mum and Riley both nodded.

I had a flash of holding Pops's hand at Gran's funeral, of looking up and seeing the tears streaming down his face as their song played.

He loves this song. Why is he so sad? I remembered thinking in my child's mind.

"I'll do it," I said.

We all met outside the church in the country town where Pops had spent most of his life. As I watched the mostly elderly crowd assemble in the sun, I felt the hard rock of grief inside my ribcage, its sharp edges pressed against my heart. Riley and Hayley arrived late and looked hassled as they juggled the two children and a nappy bag between them.

"Where's Lachie?" Chase asked as soon as he saw me.

"He couldn't come today," I replied.

"Let's go in," Dad said, putting his hand on Mum's shoulder.

"We're not all here," said Chase, struggling against Riley's arms. "Pops isn't here yet. I want to wait for him."

Riley shushed him gently but he began to cry raw, unapologetic sobs that I felt were torn from my own heart. I nearly broke down myself with the thought that one day Chase might not even remember Pops, the way I didn't remember Gran.

As we walked in together, Dad fell back to speak to me.

"There's a young man from the church choir who's going to be there… As, well, as a sort of back up for you… In case it's too hard… to sing."

We took our seats in the front row as Riley and Dad carried the coffin into the church with some of Pops's more spritely friends.

"Is that a rocket ship?" Chase whispered to me loudly.

"Sort of," I said, patting his hair.

"Oooh, I want to go in it!" Chase yelled.

A few people turned to look at us. Hayley looked down at Chase and put a finger to her lips. Her other hand rhythmically rocked Isla's pram back and forth in the aisle.

"Let's see what we can find in my handbag," I whispered to Chase.

"Some playdough would be nice," he replied.

I unzipped my bag, mentally crossing my fingers that there'd be something in there to entertain him.

"Yes! A torch!" Chase yelled excitedly.

The creeper torch kept him busy for most of the service until the priest was giving the final blessing. That was my cue to go over to the organ.

It had been years since I'd stood in front of a microphone. I watched Dad and Riley hoist the coffin onto their shoulders again as I took a deep breath into my diaphragm. The organist nodded to me, one of her hands finding the beginning notes of the song. I opened my mouth and nothing came out. The organist caught my eye and then played the intro again. Out of the corner of my eye, I saw my understudy—a gangly teenager—stand up and approach the other microphone.

Stand down, back up! I thought. *You didn't even know him.*

I opened my mouth again.

The last dance on your card
And we're finding it hard
To step away, to say goodbye

We ignore the fading stars
And those few, final bars
It was early, but how time does fly

I took another deep breath as the building crescendo swelled from the organ. I raised my chin and projected the chorus to the open-bottomed pyramid of stained glass in the middle of the ceiling.

Well I suppose I've composed
So many lines, so many rows
And none were ever perfect, it's true
But now we're dancing along
To the tune that we chose
To the tune of me and you

Suddenly, I was seven again and riding behind Pops on his quad bike, clinging to him as we flew past bemused cows along a dirt road. The memory was so vivid I could feel the dusty oilskin of his coat under my fingers and the whipping of my hair against my shoulders.

Then I was back in the church, still singing, wondering if I had just imagined the smell of wool and Imperial Leather soap. The music paused before returning to the same slow, single-handed notes of the introduction.

And if it all goes wrong
If we never finish this song
At least I had
One last glimpse of you

I breathed out slowly with the last note and noticed Mum was standing silently beside me with her arms open. I fell into them and I cried until I was empty.

CHAPTER THIRTY

I was on my way back to Melbourne, squished between the carseats of a sleepy Isla and a wriggly Chase. I watched out the front windscreen as the dusty clouds, stretched thin across the sky, turned from white to grey. The descending sun glowed red and I considered trying to explain Lachie's sunset fact to Chase, but decided against it.

"The farmland is all so dry," Riley remarked from the front passenger seat.

"Excuse me, Daddy," Chase interrupted. "Did you say fartland?"

"No, Chase, *farmland*. I meant that the paddocks aren't getting much water."

"Oh," Chase said. Then he turned to me and whispered, "I'm pretty sure he said fartland."

I nodded my agreement, then checked my phone. I had several messages. The first was from Steph, saying:

Thinking of you today. I love you, friend wife and other mother of my bubba. X

The others were messages of love and support from The Boys, who must have been informed by Steph about Pops. I felt like a gaping, aching hole had been dug inside me, but the messages lifted my spirits slightly. They fell again when I remembered I was going home to my lonely bed.

At some point I drifted off and only woke again when Hayley was parking on my street. I

389

kissed the kids goodbye and headed into my apartment building. I was starting up the stairs when I ran into Ellie on her way down.

"Oh, hey," she said. "Was today OK?"

I'd told her about the funeral that morning.

"As OK as it could have been," I answered.

"Yeah, of course. Um, I meant to tell you that I know your friend, Lachie. From the hospital."

What? Why?

"We worked together briefly when he was doing his rounds a month ago. Anyway, he came out for work drinks once and offered to drive me home because we both live in Hawthorn. He's a good guy. When he dropped me off here, he asked if I knew you."

"Small world," I said, wondering why she'd chosen to tell me this now.

"Just wanted to explain that, so it's not weird," she said, and then continued down the stairs and out the door.

That was really weird. What the hell was she talking about?

I found my apartment key and tried for a Dan-style swift, efficient door unlock. I banged the key into the side of the lock, causing a deep scratch, and then dropped the whole bunch onto the floor.

Just open, you stupid door!

I kicked the door and was fumbling with my keys on the floor when it magically opened.

Oh my God, I really do have powers!

Then I noticed the skate shoes at my eye level. I looked up. Lachie was looking down at me.

"Can I help you?" he asked.

I scooped up my keys and stood up. He was wearing a fitted white shirt and black jeans. His hair was unusually restrained, as though he'd put gel in it.

You can hold me.

"You can let me in," I said.

Lachie moved aside and I walked into my apartment. All my scented candles were lit and there was a fancy silver bucket of ice sitting on the table, except instead of champagne it had six orange fruit boxes carefully arranged in it. Next to the ice bucket was a wooden board with a wheel of brie cheese on it, surrounded by an assortment of biscuits. Another person in the room caught my eye and I turned my head to see a cardboard cutout of Benedict Cumberbatch standing by the lounge room window.

"You got my rider," I said in awe, recalling our first online conversation.

"I did," Lachie said, looking like he didn't know what to do with his hands. He settled on putting them in his pockets.

"But, how did you…"

"Luckily Elles was here to let me in," he said.

Elles?!

"Because my plan was to use your ladder and I doubt Mr. Cumberbatch would have appreciated being manhandled in through the bathroom window. Would you, mate?"

Benedict smiled at him mysteriously.

"I'm so sorry about the other night," Lachie said. "I was so pumped after dancing in front of a crowd again, dancing in front of *you,* and then when you had a go at me… I didn't want to kiss her, I really hope that was obvious, but I got defensive because I still felt guilty. Also, we'd just been thrashed the night before by Dan's team and afterwards he'd had words with me for not standing up for you… Justine, I was furious when I found out Remy hurt you on purpose. I couldn't stand the thought of anyone hurting you… but then I hurt you with the things I said and the way I spoke to you. I am so ashamed and sorry for that."

He shook his head and several curls sprung free from the gel's hold.

"It's OK," I said, trying to take in everything he'd just said.

"And then your friend Steph told me about your Pops after you left," Lachie went on. "I felt even worse. I wanted to come to the funeral but I didn't know if you'd want me there… I'm just so, so sorry, Justine."

He looked like he wanted to step towards me, but wasn't sure how it would be received. Neither was I, for that matter.

"Thank you," I said, feeling hot and a bit sick. I took a shaky breath. "I forgot about everything when I watched you dance. You were brilliant."

And…

"And I picked up rubbish the last time I walked the Yarra Trail."

And…

"And I've been wearing your hoodie to bed."

Lachie smiled and then laughed, suddenly looking more like his relaxed self again.

"Well, you're a massive weirdo then, aren't you? I might need my own creeper torch around you."

"You might need more than a torch," I said, walking towards him.

Lachie held his arms out. I stepped into them and looked up at him. He was smiling down at me, his eyes dark in the dim light. A flame flickered in my belly, burning hot and desperate for oxygen. I struggled to take another breath as the fire reached up into my chest. Lachie lowered his head until I could feel his breath against my lips.

"I—" Lachie said as I kissed him.

His mouth was warm and I felt completely cocooned as he drew his arms around my shoulders. It was like wearing his hoodie but ten times better. I'd wafted off to Kissing World and set up camp there when Lachie broke off the kiss.

"I need to tell you..." Lachie began.

I looked into his eyes and waited.

"I... I'm worried that Benedict Cumberbatch is standing too close to that candle," he finished.

After we'd relocated Benedict, we ate perfect room temperature brie and drank fruit boxes.

"These are terrible," Lachie said, slurping his.

"Shut up, they're delicious and taste like my childhood."

Lachie smiled at me and then stood up. He looked at his phone for a minute and then pressed a button. Slow, jazzy notes began to warble from the speaker.

"This is what I actually wanted to do with you on New Year's."

Lachie held out his hand and I took it. He swept me up in one easy manoeuvre. He skillfully spun me around and then pulled me close again. As we moved together, I felt the warmth of his chest against mine. After days of feeling numb, my nerve endings were crackling and my skin felt ultra sensitive. Lachie made expert use of the tiny amount of space in my living room, holding me, turning me, lifting me into the air and then finally dipping me as the brassy tune faded.

I lifted my chin, waiting for Lachie to kiss me, but he just said, "I have one more thing to show you," as he set me back on my fcct.

Lachie led me into my own room, where the light was already on.

What can he possibly have to show me in here?

"The last, and I think best, part of your rider," Lachie announced.

"What was it?"

I tried to think back to the conversation we'd had three months ago, before I knew him. Lachie raised his eyebrows and then turned the light off. The ceiling lit up with tiny, glowing stars. I stared up at them, feeling like I couldn't speak.

"Don't worry, they're removable," Lachie's voice emerged from the dark, sounding worried in response to my silence. "I know you're only renting."

"They're… just amazing. I love it so much."

I thought I'd used up my tear quota for the year already, but more formed and fell.

"Knowing you, this is accurate to the actual night sky," I said, trying to mop up the tears with my shirt in the dark.

"As close as I could possibly make it," Lachie admitted. "I've been here a while."

He found me by touch and then embraced me from behind, trying to point out the Southern Cross and some other constellations he'd meticulously stuck on. I turned around and put my hands up to his face. Lachie kissed me gently and popping candy descended down my body. His fingertips touched my neck and I wanted to grab his hair and pull him closer but managed to restrain myself as his feather-light touch continued down my back. He reached my waist and held me as close as when we'd danced.

I felt Lachie inhale deeply. Impatient, I grabbed the bottom of his shirt and pulled it over his head. He helped to remove the cuffs from his hands and I heard the shirt drop to the floor. Then he cupped my neck and kissed me again. It was even better than our first kiss.

I love you, I heard in my head, so loudly that I nearly voiced it.

I ran my hands down Lachie's body, remembering the time I'd sunscreened him. He kissed my earlobe and then just behind my ear as his curls tickled my cheek. He unbuttoned my shirt slowly and tiny shivers danced across my skin where he'd touched me through the light fabric.

"Do you... ah... have something? Protection?" Lachie asked.

Do I have protection?! Ha!

I pulled away and crawled across my bed, flicking the bedside lamp on and pulling open the top drawer.

"Wow, OK," Lachie said. "Were you a scout or something?"

There was a silence.

"Um... that sounded weird..." he continued awkwardly. "I'm not implying that scouts stock up on condoms or anything... It was just a joke about how their motto is 'Be prepared'. Ah, I was actually a scout."

"Of course you were!" I laughed, deciding not to show him the other two drawers yet.

Lachie took off his shoes and belt and pulled his wallet out of his pocket and tossed it away. Then he crawled over me, his curls bouncing around his face as he looked down at me with his muddy eyes.

"Before we continue, you have to promise me something,"

"Anything," I said, distracted by the amount of clothing that still existed between us.

"That you won't ever fake it with me."

Oh, that. This is the problem with falling for your friend who you've told all your dating stories to.

"OK, I won't."

I bit my bottom lip and looked up at him with my fingers inside his jeans waistband.

"Don't look at me like that, with those big, beautiful eyes. I'm serious. Please don't fake

396

anything at all. I want you to be honest with me, always. Good or bad."

He lowered his face so that his lips were just above mine.

"All I want to do is make you happy. I feel like I can't do that if I don't really know what you like."

"OK. I'll always be honest. Good or bad," I repeated.

"Promise me."

"I promise."

But he needn't have worried; I was gasping and moaning in his arms with complete sincerity before the stars had faded to black.

I woke up sometime later, when the ceiling was dark again. Lachie's arms and legs were wound tightly around me and, in the heat, I felt as though my skin had melted and melded with his like wax. He was stroking my hair.

"The camping crew are going for brunch tomorrow... Today, actually," Lachie said, checking his watch. "They'd all love to see you, if you want to come along?"

"What time?" I asked suspiciously.

"11."

"OK, I'm there. Anything you'd recommend on the menu?" I tested.

"Whatever you want," Lachie said, twirling a piece of my hair around his finger. "I'm having the smashed avocado. Don't tell your brother."

"Cool. I'm having pancakes," I said, snuggling into him.

"Yum. I'll have some of yours," he replied, nestling his chin on top of my head.

"I don't think so."

"Couples share everything," he protested.

"That's right, except for pancakes. Why don't you get your own?"

"Why would I when I can have yours?"

"Why are you awake?" I asked.

He shifted slightly, causing our wax seal to break and then slowly melt together again.

"I was just thinking about what your Pops said to me on Christmas," he said in a half-whisper.

"What did he say?" I asked, feeling my skin flush.

"Well, first he told me that he once knew a lady with the same coloured hair as me. I wasn't sure if he was complimenting me or having a go."

"Complimenting you," I assured him, remembering Pops's words: *I've never seen hair like it on anyone else.*

"And then…" Lachie hesitated. "He asked me if I loved you."

"And what did you say?"

I tried to steady my breathing, which seemed thunderous in the quiet that surrounded us.

Shut up, breath!

"I said I did."

"And what did he say?" I asked, my heart singing with grief and joy at the same time.

Lachie held me tighter as if he sensed it.

"He said, 'Good, so you should.'"

Thank you, Pops, I thought.

We both fell silent, but I knew Lachie was still awake, because he continued to gently pat my hair.

"I love you, too," I said.

THE END

Acknowledgements

The best part of a bad date is sharing the story afterwards. I never intended to write a novel, but some stories are too good not to be shared. An impossibly big thank you to Neeny for being the most amazing storyteller and for making me laugh uncontrollably with your stories. Also, for being the best friend I could ask for and my favourite person to eat pancakes with.

Thank you to Grim for believing I was capable of writing a novel when I wasn't so sure, for being desperate to read each new paragraph as I wrote them, for the constructive criticism and for the glow in the dark stars on the ceiling. I met you, I learnt you, I loved you in a time long before Tinder. You will always be my Lachie and my love.

Thank you to Rafe, Archer and the little one we have yet to meet for "helping" Mummy with my writing. You all inspire me every day to continue to do the things I love.

Thank you to Mum and Dad for supporting my writing in every way possible from the very first stapled pages when I was five. You both taught me to love stories and to follow my heart. I couldn't have done this without you.

Thank you to Em for texting me when the book made you laugh and also when it made you sneaky cry in your car. I know you love Justine as much as I do.

Thank you to Poppa, Pop, Nan and Gran— you're all in these pages and you're always with me.

Thank you to Jess for reading the book in just two days while Joshie was doing special drawings all over your mortgage papers and to Kate for our discussions at the beach. Thank you to Leigh for your notes and enthusiasm for my writing.

Thank you to Adam, Luka and Jase for answering my personal, probably inappropriate research questions and for being my male perspectives.

Thank you to Matt, Leigh, Grim and Geoff for liking cool facts and sharing them with me and thank you to John for your medical knowledge.

Thank you to all the people who let me grab your stories like a seagull with a hot chip, even if they didn't make it into the book, and to everyone who test read the book. I am so fortunate to be surrounded by so many funny, creative, intelligent and supportive people.

9 780648 978602